HE HAD BOUND AND GAGGED HER, SHOVING HER INTO THE COFFIN IN THE DIRT

She knew she was going to die, just like Gretchen, the daughter she had never known.

It was too late to save herself, but perhaps she could save Annette. She still had the nail.

She would leave a message. She might only have the strength to write one word. It would be faint, the letters formed by scratches made in the dark by a dying woman who was going to be remembered as half-crazy.

Her murderer was miles away now. But he was just a man, and would be undone. He had given her the knowledge she needed to turn his deeds against him, and he was not even aware of that. All she needed to do was to let the secret survive her.

She had seen his face. She knew who he was.

"Like a deathly shriek on a lonely night, *Banshee* will linger to haunt you long after you've escaped its page-turning clutches."
—Pam Lansden of *People*

"The most chilling villain since *Red Dragon*."
—Andy Klein of *Los Angeles*

"As intense as it is disturbing . . . *Banshee* is one of those dripping-with-dementia horror novels that dares you to put it down. Barton's portrait of a modern-day monster on the loose makes for one hell of an extended nightmare."
—Kyle Counts of *Cinefantastique*

"Real, vivid and riveting."—Kathy Talley-Jones of *Terra*

BANSHEE

DAN BARTON

WORLDWIDE®

TORONTO · NEW YORK · LONDON · PARIS
AMSTERDAM · STOCKHOLM · HAMBURG
ATHENS · MILAN · TOKYO · SYDNEY

To Mom.
Proof that writers are born not made.

BANSHEE

A Worldwide Library Book/June 1988

ISBN 0-373-97075-7

AUTHOR'S NOTE

BANSHEE is a work of fiction. Although certain settings have been completely fabricated—Jicarita Canyon, for example, does not exist—I have included the names of other real-life locations and institutions for the sake of dramatic verisimilitude. Most notably, I have used the Los Angeles County Coroner's Office as a backdrop for certain aspects of this story, but the characters and incidents portrayed in connection with that office are solely figments of my imagination and are not meant to be regarded as representative of that honorable establishment or its dedicated staff.

Forensic science is a fascinating field, especially for the layperson, and the Los Angeles County Coroner's Office has always been at the forefront of its development. For those who wish to read further about forensic pathology at work I can recommend two nonfiction accounts: *Coroner* and *Coroner at Large*, both coauthored by Thomas Noguchi, M.D., former chief medical examiner for the county of Los Angeles, and Joseph Di-Mona, an outstanding novelist in his own right.

I would like to take this opportunity to thank a few of the people who helped in the successful publication of this novel: Ellen Levine, for her tireless energies in helping me break into print; Paul Dinas, who first developed interest in *Banshee* at Worldwide, and Dianne Moggy, who saw this book through to publication; my family— Mom, Dad, Jean and Ted—who supported me (in more ways than one) through several long, hard years; and Lisa Bradley, whose ideas, criticism, tenderness and love will always be indispensable.

Dan Barton
St. Patrick's Day, 1988

PART ONE

*

Clan Larkin

PROLOGUE

SHE KNEW SHE WAS DYING.

All hope of help had ebbed long ago, sometime after most of the fresh air had been used up and just before she had beaten the heels of her hands bloody on the boards nailed in place over her face and body. She had screamed and screamed, stopping only when she realized that it was quite possible there was no one within a few miles to hear her, and that she was using up what precious air she had left at an alarming rate.

She had been underground for at least four hours.

Why this particular stretch of bad luck had wrapped itself around her neck and slowly pulled together she had no idea. She was a simple person, not one to ever think herself headed for special or undeserving fates. She did not think she asked a great deal out of life, and had received far more from it than she had put in.

She calculated her sins. There was no crime she had committed that would merit this punishment.

She began to weep, silently, then sobbing louder and louder, the sound feeding on itself as her misery compounded into one long moan of pain.

She stopped suddenly, her heart freezing in her chest. The sound she was making echoed in her ears.

She had heard warnings, not from the woman she thought of *as* mother, but the one who claimed to *be* her mother—her real mother, the woman who had abandoned her so long ago—that something like this might happen. For the past few years she had searched, trying to track down the woman who gave her birth, only to be disappointed when her only living birth parent turned out to be a rambling lunatic. Her phone calls and correspondence were filled with ominous prophecies about an impending doom.

There would be signs, the woman had said. A creature of the night, who roamed the earth, wailing a song of impending death.

The spirit of a young woman taken before her time.

Although it was pitch-black, her hands closed over her face in horror. She fit the description perfectly. What would happen to her soul when it was all over? Would she go to that vague conception of heaven that she had carried around in her subconscious since Sunday school? Or would she be unable to rest, murdered and cursed?

Would she become the thing she was warned to fear the most?

Now the screaming was louder, and it lasted for a very, very long time.

CHAPTER ONE

THE DIGGING TEAM from Jicarita Canyon Power and Light had been out in the hot canyon sun since eight, and now it was almost noon.

They had been sent that morning to the top of a ridge, a dry and dusty place, especially during the month of August. It was fire season; smoking was limited to their lunch break, and lunch was taken around the water truck. The cigarette butts from the previous day were ground into the loose dirt. It was hot, boring work, and all breaks were religiously observed.

The twelve-man crew, not including the field supervisor, was divided equally between whites, blacks, Hispanics and Orientals. There were regular fights: at least one a week.

The crew had been assigned to dig the trench for a new power line, to run the length of the canyon, above and below ground, from the shores of the Pacific Ocean at Truces Beach, winding through the Santa Monica Mountains, to the suburbs of the San Fernando Valley. After Jicarita's decades of existence as unincorporated county land, its 8,500 residents had voted themselves cityhood in 1978, thereby ensuring the longevity of strict building codes that had kept the by-products of civilization at bay for a hundred years. Jicarita Canyon had been, at various points in history, a hippie refuge, a wilderness preserve, a pioneer settlement and, depending on the movie, had passed as the forests and hills of England, Ireland, Spain and Colorado. There had been a detective series on network television back in the seventies with a main character—a psychologist who somehow found himself solving murder mysteries—who lived in

Jicarita and took each week's potential love interest for a walk by Jicarita Creek, whether it was wet or dry.

Four hundred years ago, Spaniards had arrived in the canyon and found Indians living there, two tribes they named the Gabrielenos and the Fernandenos, after Spanish missions. The Fernandenos had lived in Jicarita for eight thousand years before being disturbed. In recent years, arrowheads and pottery had been found and sacred burial grounds discovered, although their locations remained secret from the public.

In its current incarnation, Jicarita was Southern California's most worthwhile commute. Just off of the Pacific Coast Highway, ten miles north of Santa Monica and only an hour's drive from downtown L.A., it was home to show biz people and stockbrokers—all looking for a place to leave the big city behind at the end of a day, a weekend nesting place they ventured from only when necessary. Some of the long-term residents still tended small patches of homegrown marijuana. Others were rumored to practice witchcraft. It was a very special place.

It was at 11:30 a.m. that Argus Doyle, one of the men assigned to the backbreaking shovel-and-pick detail—the ridge was too high to bring up any heavy machinery—felt his spade strike something in the dirt.

The trench was knee-deep in some places, almost waist-deep in others, each section a testament to the strength and efficiency of the man who worked it. Doyle's part of the trench was dug down to midthigh level. He looked over at Lamont James, who was working six feet away from him. Lamont was considerably stronger and had already dug several inches deeper, and showed no signs of slowing. His shovel hit nothing except dry brown earth.

Argus wiped the sweat from his forehead and went back to digging. In three strokes, his spade hit something again. It sounded like wood. Rock or metal, he could understand, but wood...

He straightened and let his shovel drop down half a dozen times, feeling out the dimensions of whatever lay buried beneath him. When he discovered that it was more than two feet in either direction, he jammed his shovel upright in the dirt, jumped out of the trench and walked over to Greg Needham, the supervisor on the dig.

"Greg, I found something."

Needham looked up from the surveyor's map he was studying and regarded Argus with interest. The supervisor wore a wide-brimmed hat, sunglasses and a bandanna around his neck. He didn't take the sun well. "What exactly?" he asked.

"I don't know."

"You mean like a rock or something?"

"Something big. May take more than one man to dig it out." This was Argus's way of saying that he would like to ask one of the other men to help him; only Greg had the authority to pull another man off his detail.

"Let me see."

Argus guided Needham over to where he had been digging. Needham picked up Argus's shovel and took a few swipes at the ground. He stepped back, breathing hard, the pack of Camels in his shirt pocket heaving. "Let's get James to help you," he said.

Argus turned toward Lamont, who had already stopped digging to watch what was going on. The other man walked over, shovel in hand. He was shirtless, and sweat shone on his dark, powerful physique. "What's the problem?"

"Don't know that there is one," Argus said.

Lamont bent and fingered through the dirt until he reached the hard surface. "Feels like wood," he said, and stood. "You take one end, and I'll take the other."

They began digging.

Greg Needham turned his back and adjusted the bandanna around his neck. He decided he'd check on Doyle and James in about fifteen minutes. If the object turned out to be something important, he'd have to make a call back to the office. He hoped it wasn't another cable, buried and forgotten. The delays and overtime could mount up rapidly. It wouldn't be his fault, but it would be his responsibility.

These and other thoughts ran through the foreman's head as he walked back to the shade of his truck. He was halfway there when he heard Lamont James scream.

JOHN STRATTON'S BEEPER went off just as he began his fifth and final mile. He slowed down to click it off, accidentally knocking the small black box from the elastic band of his running shorts and into the dirt. He swore gently and stopped to pick it up. One of these days he was going to leave the damn thing behind. He didn't know why he took it with him anymore, except perhaps out of guilt. Or boredom.

Six months ago, he had become the fourth physician on staff at the Jicarita Family Medical Center. "Don't let the name fool you," Stan Rhodes, the senior obstetrician, had said when he interviewed John last February. Rhodes was a friendly, avuncular man. "We're not a big operation. Just me, Bob McCandless, our pediatrician, and Richard Nobles, the resident G.P. The building's not much bigger than your average Burger King." Rhodes and McCandless had started out as partners in the venture when freestanding medical centers—or medicenters or emergicenters or whatever the hell *Medical Economics* was calling them this month—were rumored to be financial salvation for the private physician and the best way for an M.D. to reap bigger profits than most solo practices while spreading the work load around.

The deal had sounded great; John would start off as the center's pathologist—at the only medical facility in the canyon—and fill in here and there on the schedule. He only had to work forty to forty-five hours a week, swabbing skinned knees and looking down sore throats. In return, he got close to double his old salary when he was working for the county. After two years, he'd be up for becoming a partner, pending approval from the other three.

It hadn't worked out quite that well over time. Rhodes turned out to be as sloppy an administrator as he was convivial a colleague. Supplies went unordered, the office staff muddled through without guidance or support, and the DRG reports were backed up for weeks. McCandless hadn't taken up the slack, and Nobles, only one month away from his investiture at the center when John was hired and now a full partner, had greeted the new arrival with the vaguest of professional threats that had blossomed into full-flowering disdain.

Medical politics. The new game from Milton-Bradley.

So it had been for the past six months, and John sensed his ennui and frustration creeping up on him at the same time he became aware of his partners' dissatisfaction with his presence. He'd done well enough—no complaints, no misdiagnoses and, most important, no lawsuits or raised insurance premiums—but all four of them were well aware that John wasn't "fitting in" as well as hoped.

He didn't drink. He didn't play golf. He did not go to luncheons or give talks. He didn't share the other doctors' broker or accountant. He drove a sports car instead of the standard medical-issue Mercedes. He listened to rock and roll. He ran five miles a day during his lunch hour. He was not married. And he was still young: at thirty-three, a good twenty years younger than either Rhodes or McCandless, and supposedly eleven years younger than Nobles, who only admitted to being forty-four.

He didn't look like them, either. His hair, instead of assuming a combed and dignified gray, was solid black and curled around his head a tad more than regulation length. His clean-shaven face was square, bottoming out in a strong jaw. His nose had been broken in a zealous game of soccer when he was nineteen. He had blue eyes that had cleared considerably over the past nine months. He stood six feet and two inches in his bare feet, making him taller than any of his associates. He wasn't in bad shape. He had lost most of his beer fat. He could have had a better tan but didn't think it was worth the risk of melanoma.

But that wasn't all of it. He knew what it was that made them so uncomfortable working with him, even being in the same room with him.

It was because they didn't like what he had done for a living before practicing family medicine, back when he worked for the county. They couldn't even say it out loud.

He jammed the beeper back into his shorts. He had never gotten a call when he was out on a run before. Nobles was there to handle any emergencies.

Something must have gone wrong.

JOHN RAN the remaining mile back to the office in five minutes and forty-five seconds, his best time since high school.

Nobles was waiting in the empty patient lobby to greet him.

"Where the hell have you been?" Nobles demanded.

"Running," John said, fighting to regain his breath.

"I called you ten minutes ago."

John shook his head. "Six. I timed it." He took several deep breaths, letting them out slowly. Nobles was looking at him as if he was imitating some type of surfacing sea mammal. "Besides, you know my route. Why didn't you just chase me down in the company car?" The company car, a 450SL leased as a business expense, rarely sat idle in the parking lot and Nobles knew it.

Nobles pressed his lips together until they were thin and bloodless. When he was talking to someone, he had the habit of avoiding their eyes. Right now he was staring at a spot somewhere on John's chin. "Things were hectic enough with one doctor away. Maybe I'm mistaken, but I thought it was company policy that there were to be two staff physicians on duty at all times—"

"With breaks for meals and personal business, as long as they are arranged in advance." John's wind had returned, and he was making use of it. He knew that what mattered most to Nobles was being right. He had to parry quickly or he would soon be bested. "And in case you haven't noticed, there are no patients out there. There aren't any patients in the office. There weren't any when I left. Maybe if we advertised a little more, like at least in the yellow pages, we'd get someone to meander in here once in a while."

"Nevertheless, I'm a partner now. And I feel that I have the right to address these matters with you as a member of the partnership...."

"Do you want me to say it, Richard? Okay, I'll say it. You're right. You are correct. And I'm wrong." John's temper rose along with his voice. "Now we can keep up this petty bitching over fine points of company policy from a handbook that may I point out I have yet to see a finished copy of, or you can tell me why you had me paged."

Nobles shifted his gaze to John's left temple. Anger had no effect on him. Sometimes John wondered if it was the effect Nobles strove for in other people, because hatred and rejection was what he felt most comfortable with. "We got a call from the power department—a Greg Needham. They've had some kind of problem out in the field and they asked for you." He handed John the message slip. There, it wasn't his problem anymore.

John remembered Needham. His crew had had a few accidents laying in some cable and John had patched them up in the office and in the field.

"What was it?"

"An accident. I phoned for an ambulance, but they won't be here for several minutes."

"You phoned for an ambulance and..." John was momentarily speechless. "You did nothing else?"

"Of course I did. I paged you."

"But it could be a life-and-death matter! That's an industrial accident we're talking about! Time is of the essence!"

"Then don't yell at me!" Flecks of foam speckled Nobles's lips. "You were the one who took so goddamn long!" He turned and walked away.

Flushed with anger, John snatched the piece of paper from the floor and stalked to his office. I quit, he thought to himself. If this is what I have to put up with, then forget it.

He picked up his office phone and dialed the number Needham had left. There were several clicks and a heavy dose of hiss before the phone in the foreman's truck began to ring.

"Hello."

John didn't recognize the voice. "Greg Needham, please."

"Speaking."

"Greg, it's John Stratton."

"Dr. Stratton! We've got an injury up here."

"What is it, Greg?"

"One of my men just about cut his foot in half with a shovel."

"What's your location?"

"At the top of Wilkins Road. Up on the ridge." He began to reiterate instructions, and John fumbled for a pen and scribbled notes on a slip of paper.

"How's your man look?"

"Pale. He cut his foot pretty bad. He lost a lot of blood before his partner could get a compress on it."

"Get him to lie down. Elevate the foot. Keep him warm. Tell him I'm on my way. An ambulance will be there shortly."

He hung up. He didn't have time to shower or change. He grabbed his black bag out of the closet and took off.

JOHN GUIDED HIS CAR up to the ridge at the top of Wilkins Road, following Needham's telephone instructions: down the central winding state highway that cut all the way through the canyon. The route was usually referred to as the

Jicarita Highway or Jicarita Canyon Boulevard or, more commonly, just "the main road," to differentiate it from the old road, which wound farther into the hills and dead-ended in Jicarita State Park without providing any access to the San Fernando Valley. Left on Wilkins Road, and then up, up, up. Past the homes and lots for sale, around hairpin curves one after the other—the kind that made John sick unless he was driving—and up to the very top, where civilization hadn't quite made it and the asphalt of Wilkins Road turned to brown and rutted soil.

John shifted his Camaro into low gear and dug in. The Z-28 chewed up the loose gravel and dirt, spitting it out behind. Needham had offered to meet him where the road turned from a solid line to dashes on the Thomas Guide, but John had declined. It would probably cost him a wheel alignment. The price of Chevy macho.

He bounced and bucked for another five minutes—quite convinced that he wouldn't attempt the drive again unless he was in a vehicle with a four-wheel drive—until he saw the digging crew's three yellow service trucks with departmental emblems on the sides. The men on the crew stood close by in a semicircle, all work postponed until John's arrival, profiles cast in dust.

John stopped his car and got out. He still had his running shoes and shorts on. Needham met him first. He had lost his bandanna in the excitement. John remembered the man was sensitive to the sun—had once instructed him in how to protect himself.

"Where's the patient?"

Needham gestured. "Over there."

John began walking quickly, his black bag swinging at his side, an eighties' version of the country doctor. Needham trotted alongside.

"What happened?"

"Man's name is Lamont James. He was helping another man dig out an obstruction in the ground when his shovel slipped and cut open his shoe. Almost took off a chunk of his foot.''

They were heading toward the top of the rise. John saw a few anxious faces set a little too low on the horizon. He adjusted his perspective when he realized the men were standing in a ditch.

Three men stood upright. The fourth was lying down, his foot dark with blood, caked with dust. He had a cloth over his face. Lamont James.

John hopped down into the ditch, the other workers parting for him. John had long ago realized why the medical community hadn't bothered to update the traditional black bag as the physician's most visible accessory; it was a beacon to others at the scene. The doctor is here. Everything will be all right.

He bent over Lamont's head and lifted the cloth. The man's face was pale and clammy, sweat beading across his brow and upper lip.

''Lamont, can you hear me?''

Lamont's eyes opened, squinting in the sunlight. ''Yeah,'' he said, his voice cracking.

''Lamont, my name's John Stratton. I'm the doctor they sent for. I'm going to take a look at your foot.''

Lamont nodded. ''Okay.''

John patted the man's shoulder and turned his attention toward the foot. It was then that he noticed Lamont James was lying on something.

HALF AN HOUR LATER, the ambulance had come and taken Lamont James to a hospital in the city. John, however, lingered on the scene, listening to Greg Needham describe the events leading up to the accident.

John nodded and listened, his foot nudging the edge of the wooden container that was still imbedded in the dirt. Lamont James had been lying on it, and it was in an effort to pry it out of the ground that the injury had occurred.

"What's your interest?" Needham finally asked as John continued his examination of the box.

"I'm curious. How long would it take two men to dig this thing out?"

"About an hour."

John nodded. He didn't have an hour. He needed to get back to the office. "How long just to uncover the top?"

"Couple of minutes." Needham looked at John again. "You got some reason for wanting to take a look at this thing?"

John looked off down the ridge at the trees and dry brush. He remembered times when he didn't have such a pleasant view.

"I want to know what's been buried here."

JOHN WATCHED as Argus Doyle scraped the dirt away from the wood surface with the blade of his shovel. The box was made of long boards, held together by slats on top. Nails were driven in around the edges of the top. The sides sunk into the earth, how far John couldn't tell.

When the top was cleared, Doyle stopped, breathing heavily and sweating. "Take the rest of the day to get that out of there by myself," he said, obviously not relishing the prospect.

John nodded. "Do you have a hammer and screwdriver I can use to pry those boards up?"

"Ask Greg about that."

"I will." John turned, but Needham was already on his way over. The rest of the crew were working at about half speed. The accident had put a pall on all vigorous activity. No one wanted another injury.

"What's the deal?" Needham looked down at the wooden box still partially buried in the dirt.

"I'd like to try to open this with a hammer and screwdriver, if you have them."

"You think there may be something inside there?"

"Yes."

"Like what?"

John paused. "Maybe a human body."

Needham immediately got his hammer and screwdriver. All work stopped on the site as the men watched the doctor hunch over the box in the ditch. John squatted down in the dirt, feeling the sweat quickly bead on his forehead and neck. He picked up the screwdriver and the hammer, working the tip of the screwdriver under the top of the box and then striking the handle with the head of the hammer. This drove the screwdriver underneath the lid and into the box. John worked it around, prying the lid up a few centimeters.

He caught a whiff of gas seeping out of the opening he had made. He turned to Needham, raising his head to indicate that he needed to speak to him in confidence. The foreman lowered his head close to John's.

"Greg," John said, "I think I smell something."

Needham's nose wrinkled. "Me, too."

John lowered his voice to a whisper. "You want your men hanging around when I open this thing up?"

Needham turned to look at the semicircle of bruisers surrounding the two of them. "You want to try to tell them that they can't?"

John thought. "All right," he said. "Let's just hope they're not too attached to their breakfast."

"You know," Needham said as they looked at the box, "I've heard that there's an old pioneer cemetery hidden up here in the hills somewhere. People just lost track of it over the years and aren't sure where it is anymore. I was thinking maybe we happened across a piece of it."

John nodded, pretending he was listening. He felt his pulse rise slightly, standing there where the ground fell away, looking down at an opening in the surface of the earth, a window to the world beneath the topsoil, where animals burrowed, treasures lay hidden, lava flowed red and molten and nightmares came to life.

Needham stepped away, and John went back to work. He loosened the lid in a few other places, then stood up and reached down, bracing his feet against the sides of the ditch. He could have asked for help from someone, but he had always had a problem doing that.

With a grunt and heave, he felt the lid of the box move in his hands. He smelled more gas. It was a smell he had once thought he would never get used to, never forget. He had been right.

The lid separated from the lip of the box with a sticky, peeling sound, and John nearly lost his balance as it lifted free from the ground. He carefully set the lid on its end in the dirt, leaning it against the side of the ditch. He could tell from the sounds the men around him were making that his guess had been right. He collected himself for the briefest of moments, then turned to look again.

IT WAS A WOMAN.

She was Caucasian, between twenty-six and twenty-eight years of age. She had strawberry-blond hair, cut short around her neck. She was fully clothed, wearing jeans and a UCLA T-shirt. A lace on one of her sneakers was undone. So much for Needham's theory about pioneer graveyards. This woman was from the twentieth century.

Although John had his black bag with him, he took no samples and made no incisions. He merely probed and observed, making a few mental notes. There'd be a full autopsy done later, by the book. He'd request a copy of the report, and see what else they had found out. For now, he just wanted to have first look, to satisfy his curiosity.

The woman had been dead about a month. As her body had decomposed, it had developed hydrogen sulfites that had combined with the red hemoglobin in her blood. The result was that her skin, once pink and healthy, had bloated and assumed a greenish tinge.

In the meantime, bacteria in her digestive tract had broken down the surrounding proteins into amino acids. Hydrogen sulfites again reacted with the amine products and produced gas that had distended her abdomen.

Her eyes had fallen in, and parts of her face and arms were covered with a mossy growth. What he could see of her features was discolored and slightly swollen. Identification would not prove too difficult, however, as it could be easily accomplished through items found in her clothing, medical records or matching descriptions of missing persons. If need be, her jaws would be severed and sent to the staff forensic odontologist at the Los Angeles County Coroner's Office, who would x-ray and document her teeth, sending the information to the Missing Persons Unit of the Department of Justice in Sacramento. Thirty days after she had been reported missing, the police were legally bound to obtain her dental records from her family dentist or orthodontist and forward them to the MPU. If any matching dental information was found in Sacramento, it would be sent back and identification made at the coroner's office in L.A.

John heard a faint scratching, like a pin on paper, and looked around to see what was making the noise. He caught a movement out of the corner of his eye and looked to see a ground beetle scramble out from underneath the body, crawling across the swollen and discolored tissues of the neck.

He wrinkled his nose in disgust. He had forgotten about those pesky little critters. He flicked the insect aside, but did not kill it. Egg deposits made in bodily tissues could provide clues as to how long this woman had been buried. Most outdoor burials endured some sort of beetle infestation, especially at lower altitudes. It was fortunate that she had been buried high in the hills. If she had been found at sea level the casket would have been crawling with them.

There was no apparent cause of death. No trauma to the face or neck. No broken bones. No undertaker, however, had set her limbs in peaceful repose; rigor had frozen them into contorted positions, hands made into claws, fingers bent like talons, legs angled, feet straining against the smooth wooden surface.

John felt himself hovering over the open casket, in the presence of the only clues left behind to a very unusual occurrence. He had been taught that a medical examiner's best guess, unless proved otherwise, was to assume foul play. Homicide.

But he knew that wasn't all there was to this one. This woman had been murdered in a manner so subtle and yet so horrifying that the realization rose in him as slowly and as clearly as a full pale moon.

She had been buried alive.

AFTER JOHN HAD finished looking at the corpse, he slowly lowered the lid back on the makeshift coffin. He looked up and realized that he didn't have quite the capacity crowd he'd had a few minutes ago. Well guys, he thought to himself, I tried to warn you. He carefully picked up the nails and hammered them back into their grooves in the wood. Then he stood, feeling a twinge in his right knee.

He turned to Needham. "Can you get this thing down to my office in one of your trucks?"

"Yes," Needham said. "I can."

"Okay. Then let's do it."

After unearthing the whole coffin, Doyle, a guy called Wilson and two others loaded it onto two-by-fours, and carried it to a truck, grunting and sweating like bearers of a sultan's cab.

"You remember where the medical center is?" John asked.

"Just down the highway," Needham replied.

"I'll see you there."

Needham stopped him. "Dr. Stratton?"

"Yes?"

"Why do you think someone did this? Buried this poor young woman out here in the middle of nowhere where no one would find her?"

"I don't know, Greg. I really don't."

JOHN REVVED THE CAMARO up to ramming speed, taking the turns down Wilkins Road at twice the velocity he had driven on the way up.

When he hit the main road he drove even faster, tires screeching, pulling into the parking lot of the medical office minutes ahead of Needham and his crew. His first stop was the front desk, home post of Linda, the receptionist.

"Linda, there are going to be some workmen here from the power department. They're going to bring in something big and heavy."

"Through the back?"

"No. The front. It's too cumbersome."

Linda nodded. They had a special understanding: she wouldn't mind their going to bed together, but he would. Anticipating his next question, she answered, "Nobles is in his office." She lowered her voice. "He's on the phone with Rhodes."

John nodded. He would explain the rest to her later.

He trotted down the hall to Nobles's office, stopping outside the door to listen to snatches of what Nobles was saying into the phone before knocking.

"Well, I know..." Nobles was saying. He probably had to shout over the noise of Rhodes's athletic club. John had the number of the phone that rang in the locker room hidden in his Rolodex, marked in Rhodes's own hand: For Emergencies Only. "But he doesn't seem to be working out even on a temporary basis. I say we not wait the extra year, and look for somebody else now."

John decided he'd heard enough and knocked loudly on Nobles's door, opening it on the third knock.

Nobles looked up, one hand flying over the receiver. "What?" he snapped irritably.

"Greg Needham and some men from his crew are coming in here. I'm going to be needing the OR." The OR he was referring to was a stripped-down model of an operating room, used only for the occasional ambulatory surgery. They had a surgical laser on indefinite order because Mc-

Candless wanted to expand to cataract removal and draw more trade from Malibu.

"Fine." Nobles waved him away. He obviously had something more important to do.

John closed the door, making sure it slammed extra loud.

He didn't have time to worry about what Nobles and Rhodes were deciding regarding his future with Jicarita Family Medical Center, and he didn't care. He was used to trouble. One bothersome sentence stuck in his mind, though: *I say we not wait the extra year, and look for somebody else now....* What the hell did that mean? Probably nothing good. He'd puzzle it out later, sound out Linda for what she knew.

He headed straight for the back room. He'd been inside it only once or twice, never taking the time to inspect it carefully. It was used infrequently by the other physicians, more of a promise of future medical profits than a realization of present potential. A waste. Typical.

He needed a surface strong enough to support the weight of the wooden coffin and the body inside: something that could withstand the strain of a couple of hundred pounds. He found a gurney shoved to the side that seemed sturdy enough. He climbed on top of it and tested it with his own weight. It would serve.

Linda buzzed him on the intercom. "They're here," she said, "with the delivery."

"I'll be right out."

NOBLES WAS OUT OF HIS OFFICE, feet planted firmly in the middle of the lobby, glaring at Greg Needham's left ear while the foreman patiently tried to explain to him that he was here on instructions from Dr. John Stratton. Was Dr. Stratton here? Needham was certain that he would be able to explain everything.

Behind Needham stood Wilson, Doyle, and the other two men he'd brought from the work site to haul the coffin inside. Now its weight on their shoulders was causing them to grunt and shift as they stood still, waiting for their boss to clear this asshole out of the way. John could see that they had to unload their burden quickly, or their precarious hold on it would slip and they would drop their load. The impact could jar the lid open and spill the contents onto the plush carpet of the waiting room and . . .

John stepped between Nobles and Needham, turning his back to Nobles. "Back there," he said to the men, making a broad and definite gesture, directing traffic. "Through the white double doors and onto the steel table." He touched Needham on the shoulder and leaned in close. "Make sure they find it. I'll handle this."

Needham nodded and left. John turned to Nobles. "Don't ever do that again," he said evenly. "This is my case, Richard, and you have no right to interfere with it."

Nobles looked wildly from side to side, so flustered he couldn't focus his vision within a range of thirty degrees. The biggest problem with being a doctor, John thought, was other doctors. They were such . . . geeks.

"This is an outrage," Nobles spluttered. "I'll have you know that I've already informed Dr. Rhodes of your insubordination, and when he hears of this . . ." He gestured clumsily, uncomfortable with the strength of his own emotion.

John held up a calming hand, the eye of the gathering storm. "I understand that this is probably out of the realm of your experience, Richard."

"If you mean that I've never conducted an autopsy, then you are correct." Nobles seemed proud of it.

"I know what I'm doing, Richard." With that, John moved past him.

Nobles caught John by the arm. "This isn't for you to do," he said urgently, and this time he was looking John right in the eyes. "This doesn't belong here. This is a job for a coroner." He said it as if it was a dirty word.

John carefully removed Nobles's hand from his arm. "Yes," he said, "I suppose it is."

He walked away.

JOHN SEQUESTERED HIMSELF in his office, telling Linda to hold his calls but buzz him if they had any walk-ins.

After he had dictated his field notes into a microcassette recorder, he picked up the phone receiver, holding it halfway between his ear and its cradle. He could look up the number in the phone book, or get it from directory assistance, but he wanted to see if it was still in his active memory bank. He dialed once and got a laundromat. He got it right on the second try.

"County Coroner's Office."

Stratton felt a slight tingle. He knew the receptionist's name: Cindy. She was an aging California blonde with too many tanning wrinkles. He used to flirt with her every time he went out to lunch—before he started taking lunch in his office. He could have said, *Hi Cindy, it's John.* And she would have cheerfully replied, *Hi, John!* And then the two of them would have had to chat. It would have been a chore on both ends of the line. She had known he was on the way out before he did.

"Dr. Hardinger's office, please."

"Just a moment."

Hold . . . hold . . . hold. . . .

"Dr. Hardinger's office."

"May I speak to Dr. Hardinger, please?"

"May I tell him who's calling?"

John gritted his teeth. He didn't recognize the voice. Hardinger's secretary had been a young woman named Jennie. He would have trusted her.

"Tell him it's John Stratton."

"Just a moment."

John held some more.

The line was picked up, and he was talking to Charles Hardinger, chief of the Forensic Medicine Division of the Los Angeles County Coroner's Office, and his former boss.

"John?"

"Dr. Hardinger. Hello."

"Hello, John. How's the new practice?"

"Oh, seems just fine. May be too soon to tell."

"True. What can I do for you?"

"I'm afraid it's the other way around. I have a bit of business here for you." Those were Hardinger's code words that he used at parties and dinners, when trying to skirt tastefully around the subject of forensic medicine while still relating an amusing professional anecdote. *Oh, we had a bit of business in Beverly Hills . . . young fellow with a handgun. . . .*

"Oh?"

"A digging crew found a body buried inside a coffin."

"When?"

"Around noon."

"Where?"

"Here in Jicarita."

"Where's the body and coffin now?"

"My office. The Jicarita Family Medical Center."

"I see. I'll dispatch an investigator at once. Let me buzz Jennifer and tell her to put it on the schedule. One question, John."

"Yes, sir."

"How did you know there was a body inside the coffin?"

John fixed his eyes on a spot on his desk. The old man wasn't going to cut him any slack. "I opened it, sir."

There was a disapproving silence on the other end of the line. "John, you're no longer authorized by this office to act on its behalf."

"I'm still deputized, sir."

"You are?" More silence. Hardinger could have John's status revoked if he wanted to. That it hadn't been already was a surprise even to John: one of the unexpected side effects of being put on permanent leave of absence instead of being fired. John was beginning to think his gamble might have been too great.

"I only looked around, sir. I didn't take any samples or make any incisions."

"All right. I'm going to dispatch someone immediately. Don't proceed any further."

"I won't."

"I'm going to order a complete audit of this situation, John."

"I maintained good procedure, Dr. Hardinger."

"Nice to hear, but John?"

"Yes, sir."

"Never do it again."

John was taken aback. Perhaps there was a bigger rift between the two of them than he had imagined. "I won't."

"I'm sending Fuchs out now. I'll be talking to you later." Then Hardinger hung up.

It had to be Fuchs, John thought as he placed the receiver back in its cradle.

Of the fifteen forensic pathologists on staff that Hardinger could have sent out to retrieve the body, it had to be Fuchs. Fuchs the worm, the constant smirker, the petty gossip or, as John had taken to referring to him in front of others—once even getting a laugh out of Hardinger himself—Fuchs the Hall Monitor.

Fuchs was the type of man who always seemed small to John, although there was not that much difference in their height. Perhaps it was because Fuchs blended in with his surroundings, appearing only when necessary. He was the youngest pathologist on staff, now that John was gone. He was unnaturally thin for someone so close to forty, and he had receding, washed-out brown hair. His thick glasses were encased in red Day-Glo frames, which he adjusted when he talked. He dressed in a style John mentally referred to as "Melrose Hip Nerd." The first time they met, John had thought Fuchs was some sort of sexual deviant. He wasn't. He was just a weasel.

John's reaction was more than dismay at having to deal with a former professional colleague that he personally dis-

liked. It was the anguish at having to be cordial and professional to someone who was a sworn earthly enemy. When he
was still working at the coroner's office, John had been
possessed of the charming cockiness that capable, handsome professional men were supposed to wear like an in-
triguing cologne. He had made the mistake of assuming that
Fuchs was harmless and couldn't, or wouldn't, do any real
damage. After all, John was Hardinger's pet, the one who
had started being groomed for a steady rise through the
ranks when he first arrived at the Forensic Science Building
for his last year of residency. He had been given a good office—a point that Fuchs got considerable mileage out of
during the regular gripe sessions he held with the investigators—and had been one of the few invited to Hardinger's
twenty-fifth anniversary party. There had even been a few
luncheons during which John had shared a table with Hardinger and Dr. Lloyd Ehrenberger, the chief medical examiner. On those occasions when John was invited to speak
up, Dr. Ehrenberger put down his fork and listened, and
John knew that a favorable impression was being made.

Professional jealousies were bound to develop in situations like that. Fuchs, John assumed, was merely an annoying pest. He had been wrong.

It was Fuchs who had first detected the signs of John's
addiction, had made little smarmy remarks in the staff room
over coffee about John's lunchtime activities and had even
started dropping hints to whoever was making out the
schedules that *he* wouldn't want to work the table next to
Stratton in the autopsy room. And John knew—*knew*—it
had been Fuchs who had made the suggestion to Hardinger
that since so many of the other city departments were under fire for alleged drug abuse, and since it was the coroner's office itself that had been instrumental in passing laws
that required mandatory testing of deceased drivers for the
presence of alcohol and drugs in their blood, shouldn't they
squelch any rumors that were already floating around and

have some surprise testing done right here in their own department? Of course, Hardinger had wanted to know what rumors, and about whom, but Fuchs said he didn't want to name any names. There were, however, those who said that one of the pathologists had more drugs in his system than some of the decedents he was working on, and . . . well . . .

Hardinger demanded to know more, but Fuchs refused to turn state's evidence. He had no real proof, he confessed. Not a shred. He didn't want to get anyone in trouble. It was only a rumor.

It was enough for Hardinger.

When John found the cup and cap on his desk the next week, he had briefly considered substituting someone else's urine, or a decedent's urine or even dog piss and turning it in. The more outrageous the better he thought, because then he could simply get out of being called on the carpet by claiming it was a joke. *Don't you guys have any sense of humor?* And immediately afterward—having used the precious three-day delay to try to clean out his system—he'd plunk down his own genuine cap of spankin' clean whiz. But he had decided against that. It would probably be seen as the desperate dodge that it was. So he said to hell with it and he turned in his sample to Hardinger's office and prayed. He hoped that Hardinger would come to him and lay a fatherly hand on his shoulder and tell John that he was going to have to take some time off and clean up, and then he could come back as long as he promised to never touch the stuff again, which John would solemnly vow to do. Or at least, at the very most use it only to celebrate special occasions, like champagne or the Rémy VSOP that Hardinger served at home, the way he had in the beginning when it was all under control.

But that wasn't quite what happened.

Hardinger had paid a surprise visit to John's office to inform John that he had the test results back and wanted John to be the first to know, although it was a matter that didn't have to go any farther than his office, that evidence of cocaine, marijuana and alcohol had been found in John's urine. John had sweated and nodded, knowing that this was coming.

He got the fatherly hand on the shoulder, and he got the advice to clean up as soon as possible, and he got the name of a good man, a really good psychiatrist that Hardinger knew had cleaned out the chief of surgery at a Santa Monica hospital who had been spending a thousand dollars a week on the stuff. What John also got were his walking papers. He was through. He could take his time cleaning out his desk, but Hardinger wanted him gone by the end of the day. And if he made no fuss, then Hardinger would put him on permanent leave of absence instead of firing him, because he didn't want John to get in any more trouble than he already was. He would never confirm or deny anything, would never mention any names, no matter how bad the news hounds from the *Times* came baying at his door, because he never wanted it to be known that he'd had an addict in his department. If John chose not to clean up immediately, Hardinger would go before the review panel of the American Board of Pathology and personally make sure that John would never practice again. Deal?

There was nothing John could have said at the moment but yes. Hardinger got up to leave, but stopped. "This wouldn't have anything to do with that bit of business out at LAX, would it?" he had asked.

John had considered telling him the truth for a moment, but thought better of it. He shook his head no.

After Hardinger had left, John began to slowly take stock of what he could actually walk out with in the next fifteen minutes and what he would have to send for later, because within an hour it would be all over the place. It was still early enough in the afternoon that he could pass his disappearance off as a lunch break and then he wouldn't have to face anyone on the way out. The first thing he pocketed was the half a gram he still had left, because he sure didn't want anyone finding that. He started to look around for some place to throw it away, and then realized it was the last of his stash, and as this was shaping up as unquestionably the worst day of his life he might need a little lift later on.

He was fingering his framed medical diploma when the phone buzzed on his desk. *Probably my last call on the job,* he thought, and picked up the receiver.

It was Fuchs. "I was just wondering," he said, "if you would be out of there by noon."

John said nothing. It all fell into place for him—the who, what, when, where and why of his unceremonious ousting from the L.A. County Coroner's Office. And this little shit on the other line was definitely the who, counting the minutes until he could move into John's vacant slot, enjoying the leftover privileges, position and power that John had so carefully built up and had so carelessly thrown away.

"Go to hell," he whispered, and hung up.

He regretted it later, wincing at the memory of what a shaky mess he must have come across as at the crucial moment, but he had been so full of fear and pain and anger that there was nothing else he could think of to do or say.

It was the last time they had spoken, nine months ago.

Standing in the lobby of the Jicarita Family Medical Center, John looked at his watch. Fuchs should be arriving any minute now.

IF JOHN HAD BEEN a better person and Fuchs not an obnoxious asshole, he would not have taken such a dark glee in the fact that Fuchs's two-year-old Honda Civic looked a little pale parked next to John's Z-28. The private sector did have its rewards.

Fuchs got out of his car, adjusting his glasses as he walked toward John, his hands free of paper or pen. Fuchs never wrote anything down. He claimed to have a photographic memory.

"Hello, Fuchs," John said.

"Stratton."

They did not shake hands.

John gestured toward the building. They walked inside.

"What did Hardinger tell you?" John asked.

"Not much, except that I was to perform an autopsy on a body that had already been examined."

"You'll find I followed proper procedure."

"You've been known to have your off days. Did you make a tape?"

John produced it with little flourish. "It might be a little slow in the middle," he said, "but it's got a good beat you can dance to."

Fuchs plucked it from his fingers quickly, as if he was afraid he might catch something. John was not going to let this man get to him again. He was not.

"Is a meat wagon on its way?"

"No, I was going to rent a U-Haul."

They passed through the doors of the back room. The smell hit both of them anew. Fuchs blinked several times rapidly. "That's some after-shave."

"The Broadway was having a sale."

Fuchs looked at the coffin lying on top of the gurney, the top fitted back into place. "Is that it?"

"Yes."

Fuchs looked the coffin over. "Uhh-huhh." He straightened. "Well, looks like I've got a lot of work ahead of me." There was the sound outside of a large vehicle pulling into the lot. "Ah, the movers are here."

"Fuchs?"

"Hmm?"

"I found no apparent cause of death."

"It's usually a long and painful process."

"I meant there's no apparent trauma. No injuries. I'd say she's been buried at least a month. I think for at least the first twelve hours of that she was still alive."

"I wouldn't rush to conclusions just yet, Stratton."

"I'm curious as to whether I'm right or not, Fuchs. I'd like to see your report."

Fuchs shrugged. "There was this nasty thing called the Freedom of Information Act a while back, so anytime you're in the neighborhood . . ."

"Thanks, Fuchs."

The other man smiled cruelly. "Oh, don't thank me. You can do anything you want but don't thank me."

Then he left.

FUCHS AND THE BODY were gone. Nobles had come back, saying nothing to either John or Linda, and retired to his office, emerging only to treat his patients. Before he left for the day, Nobles had placed a message in John's box that there was to be a meeting tomorrow of all staff physicians and that Stratton's presence was required. Something was in the air, and John could guess that it boded no good for him.

John handled a few walk-ins, forcing himself to concentrate on something other than the events of that afternoon. He got a call from Needham, and John told him that the matter was now being handled by the coroner's office. Needham said he was already getting calls from the media, and that they might try to track John down. Within the hour, John got messages from the *Los Angeles Times* and two local television network affiliates, but he ignored them.

Linda hovered outside his office after closing at eight that evening, dropping hints that she'd love for the two of them to get together later. John politely declined, telling her he had a lot of paperwork to do and he'd lock up.

So he sat alone in his darkening office. He'd called the cleaning service the center used and told them to come first thing in the morning and to bring a lot of sterilizing agent to scrub down the back room.

He had heard nothing from Hardinger or Fuchs. He hadn't expected to. He had been *persona non grata* over there for the past nine months, and he had probably assumed an even lower rank after what he'd done today.

He pondered the recent course of events. Why had he done it? Why had he taken it upon himself to go ahead and open the casket when he should have just called Hardinger, had the department pick up the body and then called back later and asked to see the report? What had possessed him?

He had been in Jicarita for the first half of the year. In that time he had treated little more than chest colds and the occasional muscle or menstrual cramp. He had experienced no real excitement—nothing that got his blood going. This was the most interesting thing that had happened to him since he began recovery from his addictions. He had been engaged, involved, his mind and body working a mile a minute. He had gotten that old feeling back, the one he had had when he first started in forensic medicine: that he was the court of last appeal in matters of life and death, and if he didn't see what there was to see, then no one would.

That was before all the trouble started, but . . .

Maybe he wanted back in.

He sat and stared at nothing, remembering what had happened that had made him turn to drugs and booze in the first place, the one thing that had changed it all for him. Afterward, he had been less like the promising young doctor he had always hoped to be and more like the dead who looked up at him from cold steel tables.

CHAPTER TWO

IT BEGAN a little over a year ago. A Sunday.

John was sitting in the apartment he had then in Ocean Park, watching the Dodgers lose yet another game. He had set out beer for some old friends from medical school who hadn't shown. That was the part of medical social mores that was hard to get used to: the sudden no-show. A day or two would go by before John would get a call, and Tyler or Jack would explain that he was really sorry and would like to apologize, but just as he was driving over his beeper went off, and it turned out that Mrs. Pedavoy had started hemorrhaging again, and . . .

Of course he had to understand. He'd done it to them often enough.

It had become increasingly harder to make and maintain friendships with his demanding schedule. He wished one of these days he could have a weekend like normal people did.

Oh, well, he thought as he cracked open another cold one. Nothing to do but get drunk by yourself. He had never been much for crowds and parties, anyway. He had, however, always been one for drinking, ever since he turned fifteen.

Suddenly, the sound and picture of the baseball game disappeared, and the television station's news logo appeared next to the words *News Bulletin*. John sat up a little straighter in his chair.

An announcer appeared, wearing the grave look announcers have only when they have some very, very bad news. An electric thrill went through John as the man on the television began speaking. He heard that a small passenger plane and a 747 had collided over Los Angeles International Airport, better known as LAX, and some five hundred people were dead.

John reached for the phone and began dialing. It was time to go to work.

OCEAN PARK WASN'T FAR from the airport, so after John had called Hardinger at home and arranged to meet him at the scene he hopped in his car and headed down Lincoln Boulevard. Five miles later, traffic began to stack up just after Airport Boulevard. John pulled his car over, stuck his free-parking card on the dashboard—the one that read Official Business: Chief Medical Examiner/Coroner—set the alarm to go off if anyone so much as breathed on it and began walking. He was glad he had worn running shoes.

He was at the bottom of a hill, the last big rise before LAX came into view. It was one of the few areas of open field surrounding the city. Black smoke was billowing over the horizon.

John ran ahead, passing the other cars caught in the bumper-to-bumper traffic jam, toward the crowd of spectators who had gathered at the top of the ridge. John approached the top, slowing down when he saw the first piece of wreckage.

The planes had landed in an open, fenced field. There were police and fire trucks already on the scene, hosing down the flaming debris. The two aircraft had hit the earth only a hundred yards apart, the twin-engine Cessna with its nose half-buried in the soft ground. The 747 was bent almost completely in half, its shattered stabilizer dangling in the air. John instantly knew that this was destined to be one of the worst disasters in the history of aviation.

There would be bodies, and he would have to see them. He climbed over the fence and headed toward the fires.

John crossed the field over to where Hardinger was using his car and cellular phone as a temporary command post. He motioned for John to join him in the car. John got into the passenger seat and waited patiently, listening to his superior's half of the conversation.

"Lloyd, I'll need them all." John had never heard Hardinger refer to the chief medical examiner as anything but Dr. Ehrenberger, even in private conversation. "Every available M.E. and deputy investigator in the state," Hardinger continued, speaking into his car phone. "This is the worst yet. It'll take several days even if I get twice the help I need. The Go Team's already here and they're overwhelmed."

He finished his conversation and hung up. He turned to look at John. "Have you seen any of the remains yet?"

John shook his head.

Hardinger said nothing. "It's...they're..." Words failed him. "I guess I thought I'd seen it all."

John had an urge to reach out and touch the older man. He refrained. It was a hard enough moment as it was.

"I'm trying to round up at least fifty extra men from around the state. Our department alone would take a month to sort through the wreckage and we've only got a week." He sighed. "It's going to be a long, ugly nightmare, John, and I'm going to need your help getting through it."

He opened the door. "Let's go to it."

THERE WERE NO SURVIVORS of the collision of Golden State Air Flight 738 and Donald Wilson, private pilot. One plane had been taking off, the other one coming in for a landing. A thorough investigation by the FAA concluded that the accident was due to pilot error on the part of William H. Jameson, captain of the Golden State aircraft, who, unbeknownst to his employers, had been taking black market tranquilizers regularly for the past two years. It was Dr. Hardinger who performed the autopsy and made the official report, after having spoken with the pilot's family and physician and doing a little digging around on his own.

John later learned that Hardinger had had some experience working with disasters—or, at least, more than John himself had, which was none at all. Hardinger had worked on two train collisions and three airline crashes, but later that first night, when the older man brought him fresh coffee and every line in his face looked as though it had been freshly drawn that day, he confessed to John that he had never faced anything like this and he doubted that anyone in the profession ever had.

There was no comparison for what John waded through during the next few days.

Ten medical examiners and thirty-five deputy investigators showed up from Riverside, Orange, Ventura, and San Diego counties by sunset of the first day, and after the fires were put out the police set up portable lights and generators and passed out cartons of flashlights. They all started sorting through the mess.

The remarkable finds were the bodies that were still whole, the ones that had survived the crash and didn't really look any worse than the victim of a three-car pileup on Interstate 5. They had that look—not of surprise, but of confusion—as if they had been caught in the middle of a sentence or a thought, and only had time to formulate a startled "What the—?" before the impact. Then heads slammed into ceilings and hearts skewered on broken ribs and life fled their beings.

Fate had not been that kind to many of the victims. Maybe six. There were far more of the other variety.

The front cabin of the Golden State flight was where John's team started. He led five investigators, each outfitted in hard hats, boots and khaki coveralls with CORONER in gold letters on the back. John watched as a fireman forced open the side door that most of the passengers had had to pass through in order to board the plane only a few hours before in Seattle. He heard it being wrenched back on its hinges, offering an entrance into the downed aircraft, which was stretched out on the open field like a dying pterodactyl.

Two flight attendants had been seated in the area just behind the cockpit when the planes had collided. Their seat belts had been fastened. The impact had sent them flying forward against their restraints, and then snapping back. One-two: a quick whiplashing motion that dashed their brains out on the partition in front of them, then smashed the rest of their skulls into mush on the wall behind.

Stratton saw red seeping out from under the bathroom door next to what was left of the two women. The lock on the door read OCCUPIED. He would have one of the firemen cut it open with a welding torch. He didn't want to go in there just yet.

The cockpit, however, was already open. The lock had been shattered in the crash, and the door swung easily on its hinges. Stratton eased it back and shone his flashlight inside. Then he motioned for the man behind him to hand over his light as well. He stepped through the doorway, a flashlight in each hand, using the combined beams to light up the cramped space. He wasn't exactly sure that what he was seeing was real.

In his years as a doctor, John had seen death worked upon a body in a variety of ways—by machine, by nature, by one's fellow man, by suicide's own grim hand—but never with such utter fury. Here, in this place, unnatural forces had taken the human body and remade it into something horrible.

The captain and the copilot and the navigator were not sitting in their seats. They were hardly there at all. Their skeletons sat in their places, the white of their skulls and fingers glistening in the glare of Stratton's light. Their uniforms were dark and sodden, stretched tightly out of shape instead of hanging loose on their frames, filled with something lumpy that shifted as Stratton watched. Then he looked at the shattered windshield of the airplane and saw that when the plane had hit, the force of the impact had been so great that the jolt had literally sent the flesh flying off the bones of the three men; muscle, tissue and tendons were yanked away whole and spattered against the shattered glass.

He backed out of the cockpit and turned to face the men who had followed him into the plane. Their faces were shadowy and pale in the spotty light. "What was in there?" one of them asked.

John tried to think of a way to tell them, but he couldn't. "Let's take a look at the passengers," he said, and stepped through the small crowd of men and into the cabin.

He had hoped he had seen the worst already.

It had not even been a beginning.

THAT NIGHT WENT ON into the following day and and became night again.

The bodies were pieced together, then packed and shipped. John went by the passenger log for both flights, identifying those he could and sending along those he could not. It was hard to measure progress. There always seemed to be more names on the list than bodies on the ground.

Hardinger went home the second morning, exhausted, and John stepped in for him, giving out orders, working the men in shifts, coordinating efforts, dealing with the fire and police departments and appearing before the local media to issue statements.

The whole bodies went out first. Toward the middle of the second day they began to assemble the partials. The surviving relatives wanted something to cry over and bury in the ground and the insurance companies wanted proof before they paid up, so the head and torso of their favorite aunt or uncle often ended up with an arm or leg of someone else—man or woman, black, brown or white...it didn't matter. They just wanted to get it over with.

In the middle of the third night, when John began falling asleep for short periods of time without realizing he had done so—sometimes in the middle of talking to someone—he called a breather and huddled his team in the orange tent that had been pitched as a windbreak. It was meant to be somewhere to sit and smoke and drink coffee and take meals. Now it had become a place merely to share silence. No one felt like eating anymore, the diesel fuel required to run the portable generators prohibited smoking, and the coffee was stale. The men simply stood and shuffled in place, grateful that—if only for a few minutes—they weren't doing what they were there to do.

John looked at their pale and haggard faces, knowing he probably looked worse. He didn't know how much longer they could keep working like this. He didn't know how much longer *he* could keep going. He wanted to go home and just sleep, for hours and days and weeks, without interruptions or dreams.

He had tried lying down in the back of an ambulance and taking a nap, but the pilots in the cockpit and the children in row 12 and all the other horrible victims he had seen kept floating before his eyes. So he had gotten up and kept working, and the dead bodies kept coming his way, as if they were being manufactured someplace within the bowels of the earth and thrown out onto the surface through an opening in the ground that the wreckage had made. He had finally opened that bathroom door next to the cockpit in the Golden State carrier and found the remains of a mother and her six-year-old daughter. He had looked at what they had become in the making of the accident and started trembling.

He needed something. He didn't know what. He just wished he could distance himself from it all a little more, put it on hold for a while, make himself a little stronger. Then he could go back into that bathroom and do what had to be done.

One of the men—Dave Something—to this day, John could remember his face but not his last name—broke the silence. He was an investigator from San Diego, about John's age, but he had a haunted look that had been there long before he had shown up for this toe dance. John couldn't remember him saying much before this but now he was more than eloquent. "I don't know about the rest of you," Dave said to the men who stood around in the close confines of the orange tent, "but I'm going to need more than just another cup of coffee to get me through the night." He turned his empty mug over in his hands, looking at the ground. John barely noticed that he had spoken. A few of the other men murmured something, and then John saw Dave bring out a small amber vial and a thin red straw, the kind you might get with a cocktail in a hotel bar. He unscrewed the top of the vial and dipped the straw inside. He held the end of the straw up to his nose and sniffed. He repeated the action in the other nostril. He capped the bottle and held it out along with the straw, offering it to the man next to him. The other man took it, and began to do what Dave had done.

There were things John could have thought about—all the drug cases he had treated as inpatients when he was a resident, all the other doctors he had seen throw away promising careers because they thought they were immune to the effects of any such substance—but it had not been the time or the place for such thinking. His mind was clouded over with a haze of death and anguish, and when the bottle and straw came his way he dipped in deep.

THE COCAINE GOT HIM through the third and final day, and when the last piece of the last person was on its way to the Forensic Science Center downtown, John ended up carrying some of the fine white powder home, courtesy of his colleague from San Diego. When he found he couldn't get the sleep he long deserved, he drove to the local market and bought a bottle of Scotch and worked halfway through it before he finally passed out.

It would have been nice if that had been the end of it, if he had gotten up the next day and managed to leave the whole experience behind him like a bad dream. As it was, he woke up from nightmares about the mother and her daughter processed in the bathroom like Spam in a can and drove to work thinking about the navigator with his head-phones still on but his nose plastered on the console in front of him. He dictated his last reports and delivered them to Hardinger, and when he opened his office door he half expected that what would be waiting for him would be row 22, seats D, E and F of the Golden State flight from Seat-tle, where the three occupants had been sent up through the oxygen mask mechanism that was equipped to automati-cally drop down in case the cabin lost pressure and into the empty luggage bin overhead.

He waited for the sounds and smells and images of the past three days to go away, to take their place among the rank and file of cumulative memory, but they didn't. In-stead, they hung on, haunting John like vengeful wraiths.

And the only thing that would make them go away was more alcohol and more cocaine.

WHEN JOHN'S REVERIE LIFTED he realized it was night out-side and he was alone in the building. He had been sitting there for close to an hour, lost in recollection. It was time to go home.

He put on his jacket, locked up and warmed the engine of the Camaro. As he took the main road home to his rented house up in the hills on Arrowhead Drive, he realized that the reason he had jumped the gun today was simply to get back on the horse after a fall, to show that there was still a good coroner in him. He had been tested before and he had failed. He had reached the limits of his ability. The experi-ence had drained him, sapped his will and his strength, and he had ended up nearly killing himself in the process. As it was, he had lost his job and the respect of his professional colleagues. But he had recovered; he had survived. His job at the Center was proof of that, if little else.

It wasn't enough. He wanted to do more than just make a comeback; he wanted to surpass what he had achieved before. Today he had had his chance to show Fuchs and Hardinger—to show himself—that he'd left it all behind him. When he had watched Fuchs drive off with the body, he had burned with envy, knowing that he wouldn't be there to read the results, to talk to the lab techs and glean from them impressions that couldn't be transcribed into print. He wanted to make out the official report and spearhead the investigation into this unknown woman's mysterious death.

To find out who she was. To find out why she had died.

To find out who had buried her in such a secret place and why.

THE MEETING OF THE STAFF physicians of the Jicarita Family Medical Center, Inc., was held promptly at 8:30 a.m., just half an hour before opening. Rhodes, McCandless, Nobles and John all took their respective seats in Rhodes's office: Rhodes behind his desk, McCandless immediately across from him, and John and Nobles at opposite ends of the couch. It felt a little like being called into the principal's office.

"Now then," Rhodes began. "For anyone who doesn't know, we're here as per company policy, to settle a grievance that one staff member has leveled against another."

John had felt better vibes inside a morgue.

Rhodes motioned. "Dr. Nobles, why don't you brief us on your complaint."

Nobles fixed his vision on one of Rhodes's earlobes. "Well. My charge against Dr. Stratton is that of insubordination."

"I wasn't aware you were my supervisor or that I was your employee, Richard," John said.

"Hold it, hold it," Rhodes said. "Let Dr. Nobles speak his piece."

Nobles seemed satisfied. He started talking again. He recounted the events of yesterday afternoon, shading his words with disapproval and interjecting his personal reactions and decided opinions as if they held weight equal to factual events. He finished with his own melodramatic leaving in order to find McCandless at the golf course and bend his ear on the ninth hole fairway, a revelation that caused McCandless to shift in his chair as if his butt was itching.

When Nobles was through, Rhodes turned to John. "Dr. Stratton, what do you have to say for yourself?"

John sat and thought, collating his thoughts for several seconds. When he spoke, it was slowly and deliberately. "I have a question for the rest of you as well as for Dr. Nobles."

Rhodes said nothing.

"What did he mean when he said over the phone, 'I don't think we should wait the extra year; I think we should get someone else now'?"

It was as if he had dropped a live grenade into the room. McCandless and Rhodes exchanged furtive glances. Nobles did a slow burn in his chair. John instantly knew that he had stumbled onto something secret.

It was McCandless who spoke first. "John, you've known all along that we—the stockholders—reserve the right to terminate your position here before the two-year probationary period is up."

"No," John said hollowly, "I don't remember anyone saying anything to that effect."

"Well..." McCandless feigned anger as he turned to Rhodes. "Isn't that in his contract?"

"I didn't sign a contract," John said. "It was a handshake deal. It was on your collective word."

"Nevertheless," Nobles said, "it is our right, whether you were aware of it or not. And we want you to know in no uncertain terms where behavior like this will lead."

John looked from one of them to the other. Their faces were set, silently agreeing on their mutual skulduggery.

"You bastards," John said. "You never planned to make me a partner, did you? Any more than you plan to make the next fellow a partner. You're just keeping a permanent revolving door at the front of my office."

Rhodes's face assumed the expression of a KGB interrogator. McCandless looked like his evil assistant.

"How many have there been before me?" he asked.

It was Nobles who finally spoke. "You're the third. And the worst, I might add."

John stood. "Then I'm out."

"If that's what you want, John," Rhodes said.

"No," John said, "what I really want is for you all to go fuck yourselves."

He walked out, and didn't look back.

HE HAD TWO MESSAGES on his answering machine when he walked in through the door of his house, his accumulated office supplies in a box in his arms. One was from Linda, back at the office. The other, surprisingly enough, was from Fuchs.

He called Fuchs back immediately.

"The Jicarita Police Department wants to talk to you, Stratton. I've already spoken to a Captain Rogers and I gave him your home phone number."

"Okay. If I don't hear from him, I'll give him a call."

"Now you said you wanted a copy of this autopsy report," Fuchs said.

"That's right. I'd really appre—"

"I'll make you a deal," Fuchs interrupted. "I send you a copy of the report, and you don't talk to the press."

"You mean, just let you handle it from a news angle."

"Yes."

"Sure. Why not?" Let him be the glory hound.

"Hardinger doesn't want any questions about who you are or why you no longer work for the county."

"It sounds best to me."

"Good. I'll drop this in the mail this afternoon. You should get it tomorrow. What's the address there?"

"Send it to my home."

"What is that?"

"1374 Arrowhead Drive, Jicarita, 90290."

"All right."

"Thanks, Fuchs."

"I warned you about doing that, Stratton," Fuchs said, and hung up on him.

John slammed the phone receiver down into the cradle, walking quickly to his back door and jerking it open. He stalked outside to the edge of his property, where his back-yard dropped off down toward the dry creekbed. This past spring, during rainy season, the creek had flowed high and mighty, spilling over stones in melodious water music. He stood with his arms crossed, listening to the wind rustle the chaparral. He lifted his head and gazed around at the trees. It was a perfect temperature: not too hot, not too cool. One of these days he planned to build a deck out here and perhaps even add on a hot tub.

He laughed at himself. For that you need a job, pal.

In a better humor, he headed back inside. He stopped, however, and walked back to his view of the creek. He looked around him. He could see no neighboring houses from here. There were no hikers down by the dry stream. It was the middle of the day. He could do it.

He took in a lungful of air and screamed at the top of his lungs: "Fuchs, you *shit*!"

He felt infinitely better.

JOHN HAD NEVER BEEN to the Jicarita police station before. It was less than a quarter mile up Blue Jay Way, a street name that had been proposed during the heydays of the late sixties, and had stuck on through the eighties. The town of Jicarita was not much more than a convenient break in the trees, nestling together a post office, a city hall and chamber of commerce, the police station and a cluster of mini-malls and restaurants that catered to the summer weekend crowds.

The police station was the size of a large house, the front desk and waiting area not much bigger than the one Linda used at the Family Medical Center. A uniformed officer said he would tell Captain Rogers that John Stratton was here to see him.

John waited, studying the posters for neighborhood watch programs and safety tips for the home. Carl Rogers appeared, a black man at the far cusp of forty with a thick mustache and droopy brown eyes.

They introduced themselves and Rogers thanked John for coming down to the station without waiting for a formal invitation. Rogers also noticed John's interest in his immediate surroundings. "Care for the grand tour? There isn't that much to see," the captain said.

"Sure. Haven't ever been here before."

Rogers showed him the station's four lockups—including an impressive maximum security cell—three interrogation rooms, offices, dispatch desk and observation room, where television monitors electronically surveyed the entire station. John even peeked out back at the four idle cars in the department's fleet of a dozen. The whole building was as clean and efficient as a small-town high school. The captain's office, where they finally settled down to talk, felt as if it should house a vice principal rather than a police officer.

"Not exactly an environment where Dirty Harry would feel at home," Rogers said, after providing a cup of coffee for himself and a glass of water for John, "but I like it."

"How long have you been here?"

"Five years. Spent ten with the LAPD."

"How was that?"

Rogers grimaced, either at the memory or the taste of the coffee, John wasn't sure. "L.A's a nice place to be from. I venture into the city about once a month. The whole time I'm fighting the traffic and the smog, I can't wait to get back here."

"So you live in the canyon."

Rogers nodded. "Not too terribly far from where that woman's body was found," he said, bringing them back to the subject at hand. "I'd like to hear your story, from top to bottom."

"Sure." John ran through the chain of events, starting with his beeper sounding off and ending with his arrival here at the station.

Rogers listened, making notes and asking a few pointed questions in order to clarify details. The only editing John did to the story was when he got around to the subject of Fuchs and dealing with the coroner's office. Unfortunately, those turned out to be the points Rogers wanted to press.

"Now you saw the body itself—opened up the box it was buried in."

John swallowed. "Yes."

"May I ask why?"

"I was curious. Could have just been some junk someone wanted to get rid of, or even buried treasure." A bad joke.

"But did you suspect there might actually be a body inside?"

"Yes. That was my best guess."

"Is that the type of thing a family physician would normally do?"

"I don't know."

"When I spoke to Dr. Fuchs, he told me that you had once been with the coroner's office."

"Yes. That's true."

"When did you leave?"

"Almost a year ago."

"Why don't you work there anymore?"

"It...I..." John felt flustered. He looked forward to a time in his life when he didn't have to keep telling this to people. "I took a leave of absence."

"How long?"

"Permanent."

"Oh?"

"Yes."

"What reasons did you give?"

"I'd prefer to keep that confidential."

"I need to know the validity of each person's involvement with this case, and until we get an ID on the body, you're most involved."

"I had some problems with alcohol. And drugs."

Rogers nodded. This was nothing new to him. "You're sober now?"

"Yes."

"How long?"

"Almost a year."

"So your dismissal set you on the straight and narrow, eh?"

"That'll do it."

"Dr. Fuchs said something about a violation of departmental policy."

"That's what it was. I wouldn't rely on Dr. Fuchs as a character witness, though."

"Why not?"

"We...had a personality conflict. He benefited greatly from my departure. If you want a more accurate source, I'd call Dr. Charles Hardinger, Chief of Forensic Medicine. He was my direct superior."

"How long have you worked at the Jicarita Family Medical Center?"

"About six months. I...don't work there anymore, either."

"Oh?"

"I quit. Yesterday. They didn't like me doing what I did—bringing the body into the office."

Rogers nodded again. He leaned back in his chair, tossing his pencil on his desk. End of show-and-tell time.

"Now," John said, "I'd like to ask you a few questions."

"Go ahead."

"Any developments lately?"

"You're it."

"No suspects?"

"No. The biggest break I'm counting on is the autopsy and the ID."

"So what angle are you taking with the investigation?"

"I've got uniforms out questioning people who live in the area, see if they've seen anything unusual lately."

"She's been dead at least a month."

"We're being quite thorough. We're also reviewing all previous similar cases, solved or unsolved, to see if there's any connection."

"Previous cases?"

"Jicarita was a favored dumping ground for various unsavory types back in the thirties and forties. There've been something like twenty-three bodies found out here since the turn of the century. A few right in the creek. One of the reasons we get our water from the city."

"Hmm. Interesting."

Rogers stood. "Look, I won't take up any more of your time. Thanks for coming down."

"Can I call you just to see how things develop? I'm still very curious."

"Understandable. Of course." Rogers handed John one of his cards. "And if you think of anything else, any detail that you may have left out, don't hesitate to call me. Can never tell what might be important."

"All right. I will."

"THOSE ASSHOLES," Linda said, not even bothering to open her menu. "I've got a good mind to quit myself."

"Don't," John said, studying the specials on the blackboard by the front door.

"Why not?"

"Because you have a great salary and an excellent benefits package."

"Oh."

He had called her back after he returned from the police station, and she had invited him out to dinner "to celebrate and/or commiserate," and he had lamely agreed. She had picked him up shortly after seven.

"What looks good to you?" she asked, returning her thoughts to the meal ahead.

"Gee, I don't know." It was his first date in more than a year. Was this a date? Did they have anything in common outside the office? His shirt was beginning to feel heavily starched.

"Want to start off with some wine?"

"No, you go ahead."

"Oh, come on. Let's get drunk."

"I'm not in the mood."

"Champagne. Champagne will get you in the mood."

"Linda, I don't drink."

"Ever?"

"No."

Silence.

He decided to answer a question she wasn't going to ask. "I'm a recovering alcoholic."

"Oh. Well . . . that's good."

More silence.

He couldn't wait to see Fuchs's report tomorrow. Damn, he'd forgotten to ask Fuchs if he had gotten a positive ID. If it wasn't on the report, he'd call him about it tomorrow.

They ate dinner, filling in the gaps with general questions about each other's lives that required the other person to reply at length. John gave Linda the abridged version of his career, saying only that before he started at the center he worked for the county.

When it was over, she automatically asked him if he'd like to go somewhere for a drink, then immediately corrected herself. "Oh, I'm sorry. I didn't mean to be rude."

"That's okay. I should be getting home, though. Got to get up and start job hunting." Actually, he didn't know what he was going to do now. He had plenty saved, so paying the rent was no problem. Working at another medicenter held no appeal for him. Maybe he should just take some time off, figure out his next move.

Linda drove him home, parking her car behind his and shutting off the engine. "You know," she said to the dashboard, "I've never seen your house, but you've told me so much about it."

They didn't work together anymore. She was a more than reasonably attractive woman. He had always liked her, and they did have a good, if mild, friendship. Casual sex was a rare animal these days. It would probably do him good.

"Would you like to come inside?" he asked.

JOHN OFTEN UNFOLDED a futon he kept in the closet and set it on the living room floor in front of the fireplace. Canyon nights were cool, and he liked the smell of burning piñon wood. Tonight, he lay in his king-size bed in the master bedroom. Linda's head lay still on his chest. It was two hours since he'd invited her into his home.

He knew he wouldn't see her again after tonight. Her presence in bed next to him made him uncomfortable, so much that he was finding it difficult to fall asleep. God, what was it about him? Any time he got close to someone new he froze up. Was he afraid of intimacy? Of showing weakness? Of being loved?

He didn't know. He had been a lone wolf most of his life, aloof and offhand with most people, able to sustain only the loosest of friendships with other men. He had belonged to a fraternity in college, and he had enjoyed that experience, but those reminiscences were clouded with memories of heavy drinking. Beer busts. Keg parties. Mixers. Smokers. Passing out on dates. Throwing up out of car windows.

Hangovers. Depression. Bloody Marys the next day at breakfast.

He had been too busy during medical school to socialize much outside of class or the library. Then came his residency, and finally his job with the coroner's office.

There had been a few encounters, a handful of women that he had met and dated, some for a period of months. Those had been special times for him. He didn't drink so much. He enjoyed his work more. He was nice to people. There were nights he had spent with certain women that he would never forget, when childhood secrets were revealed, hidden tears were cried, and private jokes made them both laugh until they hurt.

But things never worked out for very long, and after a while the woman went back to her old boyfriend, or she grew more and more distant, or she just realized that John was not the type of man she wanted to share her life with. One by one they left, and he was alone again.

His family ties were not that strong, either. He had realized in therapy during his recovery that his father was an alcoholic, his mother a co-alcoholic. His brother Bill was ten years older than he was. John remembered Thanksgiving last year. The three Stratton men had begun drinking, Dad holding forth on all subjects ranging from the football game on television to world politics, roaring like a lion over anything that caught his rage. His mom had mixed and poured and made runs to the liquor store. Intermittently, Bill had run upstairs to the bathroom, the same bathroom they had shared when they'd all lived at home. He'd come back down, eyes sparkling, a wink at John—a signal that it was his turn. John would stumble up the stairs and into the bathroom to find two runners of coke gleaming on the bathroom countertop, a straw beside them.

When he was done, he ran water from the tap, wet his fingers and sniffed a few drops to clear his nasal passages. Then, feeling more than a little sparkly himself, he'd go back downstairs to slug back more booze and try to generate some real family feeling. It was all so sick. It was what he knew as love.

No wonder he hadn't been successful. He had been programmed to fail. At everything. All his life.

He had become an addict, been fired from his job at the county, entered recovery, got another job and lost that one, too. He was going to be thirty-four in a few months. He had to get something going for himself, find some direction or, before he knew it, ten years would go by and he'd still be lonely and unfulfilled.

A tear of self-pity burned out of one eye and trickled down his cheek. What am I doing? he thought. Where am I going?

HE WOKE UP ALONE. Linda had left quietly, leaving a note behind: *Had a great time. See you later. Call me.* She had drawn a little happy face beside her name, and below that her home phone number. John threw it away.

He ran his miles, made himself breakfast and read the paper. There was a brief story in the Metro section of the *Times* about the discovery of a female body in Jicarita Canyon the day before: a "Jane Doe." John's heart beat faster as he read it. The reporter quoted Fuchs as saying that the body had been identified and cause of death determined, but they were not releasing the name to the press pending notification of the next of kin. Nowhere was John's name mentioned, or any attribution given to his efforts.

He put the paper down. Fuchs had identified her. He knew who she was and how she had died. He could call Fuchs at his office, but he wanted to avoid that if possible.

He looked at his digital wristwatch. It was nine-thirty. The mail didn't arrive until noon.

Damn.

He forced himself to wait until twelve-fifteen, and when he couldn't stand it any longer, John ran down his drive-way to where it met Arrowhead Drive. No cars were in sight. He opened the mailbox, and inside were two bills, a flier from a local market and a business-size envelope bearing the logo of the county coroner's office.

He opened it right there, not even bothering to remove the other pieces of mail, unfolding the photocopy of Fuchs's report, reading it carefully as he walked slowly back up toward his house.

He had been right. She had died slowly, of asphyxiation. Fuchs's conclusion was that she appeared to have been buried alive. With growing excitement, John read the rest.

She was a twenty-eight-year-old woman in otherwise good health. She had never had children. Her height was determined to be five foot seven, her weight 110 pounds. Identification had been made through a crumpled telephone bill she had in her pocket. Her name was Gretchen Seale, and she lived at 2257 15th Street, in Santa Monica. She had been missing since July 16, when her boyfriend claimed she had left to go to the store and had never returned.

The words hit John like an electric shock. He almost dropped the report, his legs buckling underneath him. The world closed in on him for a moment, and blood rushed in his head, fueled by a sudden dose of adrenaline. When he could focus again he reread the name and address, and turned to the final page.

Attached was a photocopy of a photograph a relative had provided of Gretchen Seale a year before her death, smiling prettily, her long red hair not yet cut short, looking exactly the way she had when John last saw her, almost two years ago.

He held the letter away from him, gaping at the surrounding trees, hearing the rustle of the breeze overhead.

He had known her. The knowledge echoed like screams inside his head. He had known who she was.

HE SAT IN HIS KITCHEN, drinking glass after glass of bottled Silver Springs water, waiting until he felt he could do something else besides sit in his kitchen and drink water.

Tree branches scraped against the window over his sink, moving in the breeze. *Even in the midst of life we are in death* . . . or was it the other way around?

In a few more minutes he would get up and go in the next room and call Hardinger. Just a few more minutes.

"COUNTY CORONER'S OFFICE."

"Dr. Hardinger, please."

"Just a moment."

Hold...hold...hold...

"Dr. Hardinger's office."

"May I speak to Dr. Hardinger, please?"

"May I tell him who's calling?"

"John Stratton."

"Just a moment."

Hold...hold...hold...

"John."

"Hello, Dr. Hardinger."

"I'm late for a meeting, John." Hardinger's tone was still a few degrees cooler than the temperature required to keep milk from spoiling.

"I just got the report from Fuchs."

"The report from—oh! About the girl you found yesterday."

"Yes, sir."

"Fuchs said something about you guessing right on the cause of death."

"Live burial."

"Haven't seen one of those in a while."

"Fairly awful way to die, I'd say."

"Can't think of a worse one. Anyway, like I said, I'm late for—"

"I wanted to ask your permission on something, sir."

"Let me hear what it is first."

"I'd like to investigate this case personally, outside of the department."

Hardinger paused. "I believe you're familiar with the phrase 'Over my dead body.'"

"I knew the decedent, sir."

"You *did*? Well. Were you close?"

"At one time."

"I see. It changes nothing, though. John, there's no law saying I can stop you, as long as you don't interfere with police or department business. But I will do everything I can to see that one gets passed.''

John swallowed. ''The reason I asked, sir, was I thought you might hear about it and wonder what was going on.''

''That would probably be the case....''

''And I wanted to let you know what I was planning to do.''

''John, at least you've gotten to the point where you are letting me know your mistakes in advance.''

''Again, sir, I'd like to try to make a case for myself....''

''You can try all you want, John, but you ran out of your share of goodwill around here a while back.''

''I understand, sir,'' John said, and hung up.

Another phone call and John discovered that the body had been taken to Forest Crest Mortuary. A call there told him the funeral was Saturday. Tomorrow.

He had never met Gretchen's family, but he remembered a little bit about them. She had talked about her parents, who had been married for almost thirty years. Her father was a lawyer who had done extremely well for himself and for his family. Her mother was ''active in the community''—whatever that meant. She described them as vibrant, loving people, sacrificing professional concerns for family whenever the need arose. She had a younger brother, who had called her at home once when John was staying over.

He would go to the service tomorrow. He had never been a religious man, but he wanted to pay his respects. For Gretchen, and for what they once had together.

HE WENT ALONE, dressed in his best suit, wearing his darkest sunglasses, hoping that he would blend in as an anonymous mourner, and that no one would ask him how he knew the deceased or her family. What would he say? Well, if you want to know the truth, I was in love with her for about two months once. No, that wasn't right. He had carried a torch for her for a long time. There hadn't been anyone else until, well, Linda, the night before.

Two years. Time flew, whether you were having any fun or not.

He self-consciously parked his bright red Camaro behind the row of dark Cadillacs and limousines, and walked up the hill. The funeral party had already gathered at the top. The family was seated in folding chairs, next to the open grave and the burnished wooden coffin. An older man whom John presumed to be Gretchen's father sat silently, staring at the second casket to contain the body of his daughter. He looked like someone who had been slowly hollowed out over the past six weeks, eroded from inside by sheer despair.

John tried to imagine what it must be like to learn one evening that your oldest child is missing, and by the next morning realize that she hadn't just slipped out for a bite to eat or run into an old girlfriend, but was just plain gone. John had dealt with the parents of missing children before. It didn't matter if the child was two months old or had just turned thirty—the feelings were just as strong. For the first week, every thinking moment of every living day was consumed with the desire that any minute word would come that the child had been found. After the first week, the possibility that the child was most likely never coming back made its unwelcome presence felt, but in order to breathe and eat and sleep next to each other at night, the parents had to continue to hope. They had to hope that maybe he or she was still out there somewhere, banged up in a hospital in another city, stricken with amnesia, and that some good doctor or detective was going to trace their child's identity and bring him home safe and sound.

That's what it was to be the parent of a missing child, to pray those prayers that said you didn't care how long it took or how many nights you went to bed wondering, just please God let your child still be alive. And when you turned to your spouse for comfort you saw that they were being hollowed out, too.

Next to Mr. Seale sat Gretchen's mother. Whatever it was for fathers, it was always worse for mothers. A father mourns for the loss of a child, but the mother grieves for the rending of the family soul. It is the mother who forges a link between the father and the children, between the children and the world, in the bonding becoming the center of love's exchange and, when tragedy strikes, the bearer of sorrow's greatest burden. When a mother loses a child, she loses all love for the world. Life is drained of all color except in memory and dreams, where the dead are alive again.

John saw two young men sitting together on the front row. He assumed the younger one was Gretchen's brother, the other one her...lover.

He knew none of this for sure. He was merely guessing. He might have seen pictures of them but that was a long time ago. He studied each face for telltale signs of family resemblance, but there were none. Gretchen had been redheaded and fair. These people were dark and tan.

The priest began to speak, and John deliberately tuned out the stentorian tones as the eulogy was spoken. John was glad that he didn't have to think of words of comfort and couch them in poetic phrases of religious sentiment. His heart would not have been in it. He had seen death coming and going, and the only constant he had ever been able to determine was that there was not a hell of a lot you could do once the man in the gray suit decided to drink at your table.

When the time came to pray, John bowed his head with the rest of them, blanked out his mind and found within himself a small glimmer of hope for the eternal peace of all human souls.

THE SEALE FAMILY LIVED in the Pacific Palisades, one of the better addresses in Southern California. John waited until Monday afternoon before calling Mr. Seale. A younger voice answered the phone: Gretchen's little brother. John couldn't remember his name—Carl or Chris—but merely identified himself and asked to speak with Mr. Seale. He was told to wait a moment. Carl or Chris was apparently acting as a screening device between his parents and the suddenly intrusive outside world.

"Hello."

"Mr. Seale, my name is John Stratton. I'm a doctor. I was one of the first on the scene when your daughter...was found."

"I see." The man's voice was flat and toneless. John could read no reaction from it.

"I'm investigating the case independently, and I'd like to meet with you sometime and ask some questions."

A long pause. "Of course." John realized that Mr. Seale was most likely on tranquilizers. "When did you have in mind?"

"Tonight, if that's possible."

"Dr. Stratton, I think by now I've learned that anything is possible."

John grimaced. This was going to be tougher than he'd thought. "I'll see you tonight around seven o'clock."

They hung up.

JOHN PARKED HIS CAR curbside on the Seales' block and walked the distance to their home. The street in front of their house was crowded with the same Cadillacs and Lincolns he had seen at the funeral. Subdued light and the sound of voices emanated from within.

He rang the doorbell, and waited until a stranger opened the door, someone who looked like he'd be a friend of Mr. Seale's. "Yes?"

"I have an appointment with Mr. Seale. My name's John Stratton. I'm a doctor."

The man nodded and let John into the hallway. He motioned for John to stay put while he searched the recesses of the house itself.

John passed the time by studying his surroundings. On one wall was a picture taken about ten years ago: Carl or

Chris was a gawky thirteen-year-old with braces, Mr. Seale a robust forty-five, with more black in his hair than silver, and his wife not yet out of her thirties. Gretchen sat beside her mother, while her father and brother stood behind them, a photographer's background draped behind.

John remembered the first time he had seen that picture. It was almost two years before, in October, a month of the year John liked a great deal. Gretchen had invited him over for dinner for the second time. Their first dinner date in her home was awkward and formal; John had overdressed for the occasion. In the three weeks after that, they had had six lunch dates, all within a block of where she worked as an art director for a publisher of trade magazines, and gone out to dinner half a dozen more. He knew because he marked them all on his calendar at home, events as significant as paid days off or trips up to the mountains.

After dinner, she had opened another bottle of wine and brought out her photo album, because she had been talking about her family and he had asked her if she had any pictures. Later, when the album was laid aside, and they were debating whether or not to open a third bottle of sauvignon blanc, he had moved his face to hers and she had not turned away.

He awoke the next morning in her bed and heard birds. She was asleep, her head on his chest....

"Dr. Stratton?"

He turned. It was the same man as before. "If you will follow me..."

John followed through the house. He smelled cooking odors as he weaved his way through the unknown people in dark clothes who were crowding the hallway, living room and kitchen. They looked at him with only vague interest.

He was brought to a back room with a heavy closed door. The man who had led him there knocked softly, and John heard a murmur of assent. The man opened the door, and showed John into Mr. Seale's darkened study.

It was a large, wood-paneled study, with shelves upon shelves of books, a hardwood desk in the center and a fireplace that was now roaring away—the type of room a man goes to when he wants to be alone in his own house.

Mr. Seale sat next to the fire, his tie still in place, looking at John with eyes that were glazed with medication. John wondered if the man had been drinking as well. At the funeral, John had guessed Mr. Seale's age to be around the midfifties. Up close, he looked about ten years older than that.

The door was shut behind John, and the two of them were left alone.

John immediately noticed that none of the commotion outside made it into this room. It must have been constructed to be soundproof.

Mr. Seale rose to greet him. John walked over quickly so the man wouldn't have to move far. He motioned for John to have a seat.

"Thank you for seeing me on such short notice, Mr. Seale."

"No problem, Dr. Stratton."

"Please. John."

"All right then. John."

"How is Mrs. Seale doing?"

"Not too well. She's upstairs, sleeping. The doctor gave her a shot."

John nodded. "Did he give you anything?"

"A prescription. I haven't used it."

John pretended to believe him.

"I forget why you're here, Doctor. John."

"I found your daughter."

"Yes."

"I'm investigating her case. Unofficially."

"Why unofficially?"

"I knew Gretchen, Mr. Seale."

"Oh. How?"

"Well enough to call her Grey."

Mr. Seale nodded slightly, pleased. "And how can I help you?"

"I have a few questions."

"Ask away."

"All right." John cleared his throat. "The day you reported seeing Gretchen last was July 10th."

"That's correct."

"And she was reported missing on July 16th."

"By Robert, yes."

"Robert?"

"Her boyfriend."

"Ah. Did they live together?"

"Yes."

"Did they plan to get married?"

"They had talked about it a lot. They were sort of unofficially engaged."

"I see. What was the occasion of your last meeting with Gretchen?"

"It was Sunday. We always had her out to the house for brunch on Sunday."

"Both Gretchen and Robert?"

"He came sometimes."

"Would you describe them as happy together?"

"He didn't do it, Doctor."

"I'm just trying to get a picture of what Gretchen's lifestyle and state of mind were at the time she disappeared."

"I thought you said you knew her."

"Two years ago. I hadn't seen or spoken to her since."

Mr. Seale looked into the colors of the fire for a while. "Yes, I'd say they were. Happy, that is."

"How would you describe your relationship with Gretchen?"

"Excellent."

"The same with all the other members of the family?"

"Yes. Why are you asking me this?"

"I want to make sure that her disappearance and her death are the same event. Some people disappear of their own free will and then die of someone else's. These are questions any police detective would ask you."

"Okay. Just wanted to know."

"Did Gretchen have any lengthy history of anything like sudden dizziness, heart trouble, fainting spells, sleeplessness or any neurological disorder of any kind?"

"No. Sorry."

"Any family history?"

"My wife gets rather severe migraines. My sister used to—" He broke off suddenly, smiling and shaking his head. "God, I can't believe this. She's dead and I'm still doing it."

"Doing what?"

"Well, every now and then I have to remember to remember."

"Remember what?"

"She never told you? It wasn't something she told many people."

"I'm not sure what you're talking about."

Still smiling, Mr. Seale said, "Gretchen wasn't ours. Chris was ours, but we didn't know he was coming. We'd given up by the time we got Gretchen."

John felt a tingling along his scalp as he began to understand. "Gretchen was not your natural daughter?"

"No. We adopted her when she was just a baby. I guess our family medical history wouldn't apply to her." He shook his head again. "Ever since you found her, I swear to God, this is the first time I remembered that."

CHAPTER THREE

SHE WAS ADOPTED.

No wonder she didn't look like the other members of her family, John thought as he drove home along the coast highway. Her red hair, green eyes and fair skin came from other parents, a set of strangers that Gretchen might have barely known, if at all. Her personal and medical history made a quick dead end.

Intrigued, John had continued questioning Mr. Seale, wanting to know all the details. After consistently trying to conceive during the first three years of their marriage without results, Andrew Seale and his wife had been told they couldn't have children. Their doctor discussed the possibility of adoption with them, but the Seales wanted to stay away from agencies. Dr. Kaufman promised to keep an eye out for a prospective child, as he regularly delivered illegitimate babies who were almost immediately put up for foster care.

It didn't take him long to find a mother. The year was 1960, and the baby boom was in full swing. A woman came into Kaufman's care—Catholic, pregnant, wanting to give her child away. Kaufman contacted the Seales, and when they saw the baby girl who would become their Gretchen they were delighted.

They took her into their home under foster care and applied for adoption, a process that took—even in those days—almost a year. The birth mother requested complete anonymity during the entire proceedings.

A few years later, the Seales *did* manage to conceive, and their son Chris was the result. They had been "supremely happy," Mr. Seale said, for many years. Until this.

As far as Mr. Seale knew, no one had ever heard from the birth mother. It was as if she had never existed, only floating in and out of their lives like a figure in a dream.

Gretchen had never said a word to John about her adoption. It shouldn't have surprised him; they had not been together that long. Still, they had spent some nights together. She had cried in his arms once. He had told her things about his childhood that he had never told anyone before. There had been times when he thought they had something good and lasting. He had been wrong.

Their dissolution had started when she began to be unavailable on certain nights, and refused to explain where she was going or what she was doing. Then she suggested that it might be a good idea for them to start seeing other people. Soon after, she wasn't home a lot when he called, and she had to get off the phone whenever he reached her at work. Finally, she told him the truth; she was becoming involved with someone else.

"It has nothing to do with you," she repeated over and over. He didn't believe her. He knew somehow that this was his fault, some failure on his part. He wasn't good-looking enough. He wasn't the right kid of guy. He wasn't... somebody else.

Looking back, he could see how demanding he had been of her time, how he had sulked and got angry when she wasn't willing to spend enough days or nights with him. She had a whole other constellation of family and close friends. He just had her, and he let it show.

He had mooned over her for months afterward, looking for her in familiar places, writing letters he didn't dare mail, calling her answering machine during the day just to hear her voice and then hanging up. He'd started drinking a lot again. He'd buried himself in his work. It was almost two years since then. What he had learned today was just a glum reminder of what he had always known; she had meant far more to him than he had ever meant to her.

He pulled into the private driveway that led to his house, opening the garage door by remote control. After driving inside, he shut the overhead door behind him and turned off the engine. He sat, listening to his car tick as the motor cooled, wondering what it must be like to have someone waiting for you when you walked through the door at night, because he didn't know.

THE NEXT MORNING, John called Captain Rogers at the Jicarita Police Department. He knew the statistics; if a murderer wasn't caught within forty-eight hours after the crime was committed, the chances of his ever being caught dropped off dramatically.

"Have any motives for the killing been established?" John asked.

No.

"Any clues turn up at the scene? Anything that looks like a signature?"

No.

"Any leads the department is following?"

No.

"Any suspects?"

No.

Any hope?

John hung up the phone. He remembered that once when he was investigating a homicide—a young woman found strangled three blocks from her home—he had been similarly stumped. He had gone to Hardinger and outlined the details for him, and Hardinger had asked a very pointed question: "Is the boyfriend a suspect?"

John shook his head. There was no boyfriend, he said, and if there was he wasn't so sure he would be considered a suspect.

Hardinger held up a finger, indicating an important point was about to be made. Class never let out with him. "There is always a boyfriend," he said, slowly and clearly. "And he is always a suspect."

The old man had been right then. John wasn't so sure about now.

JOHN KNOCKED SOFTLY on the door of 2257 15th Street in Santa Monica, not sure if he wanted anyone to be home or not.

Robert opened the door. He looked as if he hadn't gotten a lot of sleep since the funeral. His expression clearly showed that he had no idea who John was.

"Can I help you with something?"

"Are you Robert Loff?"

"Yes."

"I'm John Stratton. I called earlier."

"Yes. Oh yes." He opened the door a little bit. "Come in."

John entered the duplex apartment that Gretchen and Loff had shared for the past year and a half. She had lived there when John knew her. He had spent the night here a few times, making coffee for the two of them in the morning. Robert had received an invitation to stay permanently.

There were pictures of Gretchen and Robert on the wall, the most recent ones together, the earlier ones separate; some of them seemed to have been taken before Grey had met John, some of them after. Loff's photos displayed varying lengths of hair, going from a frizzy bearded look left over from the seventies to the clean-cut yuppie appearance of the man John was talking to now. He looked to be about the same age as John, Loff a little shorter, a little more soft-spoken. He didn't look as if he'd been kicked around a hell of a lot during his lifetime.

John sat in a chair. Robert took the couch.

"You said you had some questions. Something about an investigation..."

"Right. I'm sure the police have asked you—"

"Over and over. You ever been suspected of murdering your girlfriend?"

"No. But they have to check out all possibilities."

Loff didn't seem to agree.

"Did you have anything to tell the police?"

"No. Nothing that useful."

"I hate to go over what is probably well-worn territory...."

"Go right ahead."

"Gretchen had no enemies, no one that was out to get her, nothing like that, did she?"

Loff emphatically shook his head. "Nope. The sweetest girl in the world. Couldn't think of one person that would want to do her harm."

"Did anything unusual happen before her disappearance? Something that might have some bearing...?"

He looked at John. "Is that what you came over for—to ask the same questions the police did?"

"I'm more curious about Gretchen's background than your involvement with her."

"Okay."

"Mr. Seale told me that she was adopted as an infant, raised as one of their own."

"That's one way of putting it."

John had the indistinct feeling that he had said something indelicate, but he continued. "Can you tell me some more about that?"

"Like what?"

"I don't know...did she ever talk about it?"

"Do you think this might shed some light on her murder?"

"It might. Can never tell what might be important."

Loff leaned forward, his expressions serious. "It was only about two years ago that Grey became interested enough in the circumstances of her birth to begin her search. She joined Samaritan Search, an adoptees' organization, and entered her name in their registry of names." He paused. "That's how we met—at one of the workshops."

Gretchen's sudden need to have certain nights free, never saying where she was going, becoming angry when John pressed the point. "So you're an adoptee, too?"

"Yes. I've been searching now for three years."

"Any luck?"

"I'm getting closer." He sounded unconvincing.

"How about Gretchen?"

"She was fortunate. Her birth mother was also searching for her, and they began to correspond through a post office box here in Santa Monica."

"How about her birth father?"

"Dead. Five years after she was born."

"How did the Seales take this search of hers?"

"They were very supportive. Again, she was fortunate. Some adoptive parents are very threatened by an adoptee's search for his or her birth family."

"How did the correspondence between Gretchen and her mother go?"

"It...there she wasn't so lucky. They exchanged pictures, personal histories, did some catching up over the phone, talked about Gretchen's father some—apparently he wasn't such a great guy—and then things got a little strained. Which is not normally the case in reunions," he was quick to add.

"Strained?"

"Gretchen suspected Mary—that's her birth mother—of being mentally unstable. She said Mary's conversation at times became very strange, almost...threatening."

"Threatening?"

"Mary said her goal in trying to find Gretchen was to warn her."

"About what?"

"Some sort of family curse."

John felt his eyes widen. "Did you say 'curse'?"

"Yeah. Gretchen said it was really weird—Mary got into all this stuff that happened more than a hundred years ago in their family, but Grey didn't really want to hear any more.

She changed her phone number and quit using the post office box."

"How long ago was this?"

"About six months ago."

"Do you remember her ever recounting conversations with her mother about what exactly was said?"

"No. She didn't like to talk about it. Said it made little sense—a bunch of rambling on about their genealogy. You don't think this has anything to do with—?"

"I don't know. Do you?"

"No. I don't believe in any of that stuff."

"What stuff?"

"Occult stuff. You know, astrology, channeling, the tarot…and I'd appreciate it if you didn't say anything about this to reporters. The last thing searching adoptees need right now is some sensational story about the one in a million that doesn't go well. Most reunions are happy occasions. This was an exception."

"I understand. Do you have any idea how I could get in touch with Mary, though?"

"No."

"You don't have her number?"

"No."

"What's her last name?"

"I don't know."

"You don't know?"

"No. An adoptee usually guards that information very carefully. There was never any real need for me to know. I never wanted to call her."

"Do you know where Gretchen kept any information like that?"

"If she didn't throw it away, it's probably among her personal possessions."

"The same with the letters?"

"Yes."

"May I see them?"

"No."

"Did the police ask for them?"

"Yes."

"And you told them—?"

"The same. No."

"How come?"

"Those letters, those phone calls . . . probably constitute the most personal aspects of Grey's life. The search and re-union process is a very precious thing to any adoptee. I think I should protect them the way she would want me to."

"They can get a subpoena."

"Let 'em. I didn't like the questions they were asking."

John wondered if there was a side to Carl Rogers he hadn't seen yet. "I could try to get a subpoena too, but I'd rather not."

"Can I ask what your interest in this matter is? You say you're a doctor, but you ask questions like a cop."

John smiled humorlessly. Time to tell the truth. "I used to work for the county coroner's office. I was in private practice in Jicarita Canyon when Gretchen's body was found. First on the scene, you might say."

"So this is all just extended professional curiosity?"

"No. I knew her. Before."

Loff was taken aback. "Really? When?"

"About two years ago."

"How did you meet her?"

"In a bar. She was out with some friends and so was I."

It was Robert's turn to ask questions. "And after that?"

"We saw each other socially for a couple of months. August to about the beginning of November." John deliberately kept his face devoid of expression.

Loff cocked his head. "What did you say your name was again?"

"John Stratton."

Loff uncocked his head with a slow smile. "You're the *doctor*," he said triumphantly.

John immediately felt his face heat.

Loff extended his hand. "Nice to meet you. Heard a lot about you."

John shook. "Nice to meet you."

"I remember you. When I first asked Gretchen out for a date she told me she was seeing someone, and then..." He looked briefly uncomfortable. "Well, you know."

"Yes."

"But she used to talk about you sometimes. I guess because I kept asking. A little curious about the competition, you might say."

"Well...nice to hear." John wondered how he could manage leaving as soon as possible. "How are you doing?"

"Bearing up, I suppose. I think what I need is just some time to myself."

"Probably be best."

"Get away to the mountains or something."

"Sounds good. Big Bear's nice this time of year."

"I've never been."

"Check it out. Just a few hours away."

"I might do that."

John stood. Small talk made him tense. "Well, thanks for your help." They shook hands again. "Can I call you if I have any more questions?"

"Sure. I'd really like to see...justice done, I suppose."

John nodded and turned for the door.

"Of course, what I'd really like is to have Gretchen back." Loff had walked him to the door and was standing just inside the apartment. "I've had to prepare myself for this. Maybe I didn't do that good of a job."

He was talking very loudly. Perhaps he was leading up to some sweeping emotional statement like what people always seemed to say to each other at the end of television shows, often used as an excuse to cry in front of the other person. It'd be good for him, but John had never been very good at holding another man's hand. "You seem to be fine."

It was as though Loff sensed John's discomfort and closed whatever door he was opening. "Yeah. Right. Well, goodbye." He started to shut the door.

John turned around quickly and put out his hand, stopping Loff before he disappeared inside the apartment. "Look," he said, "I really liked her." His face felt open and hot. "I thought Gretchen was just . . . a wonderful woman. I was lucky to ever meet her at all. And I envy you, and the time you had with her."

Loff's eyes softened. "She was something else."

"If you ever need to talk, or anything...you can call me, if you like." He wrote his name, address and phone number on the back of one of his old business cards from the Center.

"I may do that. Thanks." Loff paused, turning the card over to read the front. "If I run across those letters..."

"Yeah?"

"I'll see if I can make photocopies and send them along."

"Okay. Goodbye."

Loff shut the door, and John walked to his car, feeling sweat cool on his forehead. He couldn't wait to get in his car and rev the engine up to the redline as he zipped down the Pacific Coast Highway. He felt as though he had just crossed a dangerous abyss, breathy and shaking.

Driving took his mind off things. It gave him back his confidence.

"COUNTY HALL OF RECORDS."

"Tom Pozotti, please."

"Just a moment."

Hold . . . hold . . . hold . . .

"Pozotti speaking."

"Tom. It's John Stratton."

"John! Long time no hear from." When John was working for the county, he had used Pozotti's services quite often to determine exact ages when trying to identify John Does.

"Well, I've been taking a little break."

"Oh, yeah? Little time off?"

"Sort of."

"Yeah, we didn't get a chance to say goodbye. You back working downtown?"

So he *had* heard of John's departure. "Not exactly."

"Oh?"

"No, in private practice now."

"How's that going?"

"Good."

"At least Fuchs isn't still giving you a hard time."

"Not nearly so much."

"Good. Hope you coldcock the bastard some day. Save me the trouble. What can I do you for?"

"I've got a decedent here, Tom, woman by the name of Gretchen Seale."

"Yeah."

"Died about a month ago. Suspected homicide. Found out from her parents that she was adopted."

"Yeah."

John thought he detected a sudden flatness of tone in Tom's voice. He continued anyway. "Wondering if you could supply me with a copy of the B.C."

"No can do, John."

"No?"

"No. The original birth certificates of adopted children are sent to Sacramento."

"Sacramento?"

"Right. The office of the State Registrar of Vital Statistics."

"STATE REGISTRAR'S OFFICE."

"Yes. My name is John Stratton. I'm calling from Los Angeles. I want to know how to go about obtaining the birth certificate of an adopted child."

"The original or the adoptive?"

"Beg pardon?"

"There is a new birth certificate made out when a child is adopted, sir. The adoptive parents' names and the child's adopted name are officially entered that way."

"I see. No, I'd need to see the original. I'm trying to find out the name of the birth mother."

"That is a sealed document, sir. You'd need to obtain a court order to open it and get the information you need."

"I see. A court order...?"

"A court order for the contents of a sealed record. After it's signed by a judge of the superior court in L.A., send us a copy certified by the county clerk."

"The copy has to be certified or just the court order?"

"Both, if you wish. But the copy definitely has to be certified."

"Okay." Good God. This was getting complicated. "How about if I get permission from the adoptive parents? Can I get it opened then?"

"No, sir."

"No?"

"No, sir. It is a sealed document."

"Only the adoptee can get it opened?"

"No, sir."

"The adoptee can't even get their own birth certificate opened?"

"No, sir. Not without a court order. It's the law."

Then perhaps it's an unjust one, John thought, but said nothing. He wasn't going to get into a debate. "Okay. What do I do after I get a copy of the court order certified?"

"Send us the certified copy along with a cover letter, explaining why you need a copy of the birth certificate. We need the child's adopted name, date of birth, city of birth—a few vital statistics to help us locate the document. And then there is a fee."

"How much?"

"Eleven dollars."

"I think I can swing that. Can I send this by courier with a prepaid return envelope?"

"Yes, sir."

"And then how long before I get a copy of the B.C.?"

"Pardon?"

"The birth certificate. How long before I can get a copy of it?"

"Well, your request is sent to our legal department for review, and they establish whether there is sufficient reason to open the sealed document or not. We get a lot of requests and not all of them are granted."

"How long does it take to hear from the legal staff?"

"Two to three months."

"Two to three *months*?"

"Yes, sir."

"I haven't got two to three months."

"In your cover letter you can ask that your request be expedited."

"Like in a week?"

"More like six weeks."

"I haven't got that, either."

DR. STEPHEN KAUFMAN had retired to a small private gynecological practice in Malibu where he saw to the needs of a minimal but steady flow of patients, managing to accumulate large business expenses that were all written off against his income from his private investments.

A handsome, genial man close to seventy, with flowing white hair and a full handlebar mustache, he looked as if he should be selling popcorn at a county carnival rather than practicing medicine. He greeted John at the door of his beachfront home and office just a few hours after John had called to explain who he was and what he was after.

"I had the time to call Andrew—Mr. Seale—and he told me to tell you anything you needed to know," Kaufman said. They were sitting in the living room of his home. Outside, waves crashed against the beach, the sand shining gold and orange in the setting sunlight. John imagined Dr.

Kaufman had time to do lots of things, most of them pleasant and relaxing. "So—are you a friend of the family?"

"Not exactly. More like a friend of Gretchen's."

"Ah. Yes. terrible thing, that. I was her doctor, as well as her mother's, you know."

"No, I didn't know that."

"Feel almost like I've lost one of my own. Knew her since . . . well, since she was born."

"About that—her birth, I mean."

"Yes."

"Any details come to mind?" John asked. "Over the phone I asked you about the mother and the adoption. . . ."

"Yes. I had a chance to look over my records before you came over. I was Ellen Seale's doctor for quite a while, and when it became obvious to me that the two of them weren't going to be able to conceive a child, I approached them about adopting." Dr. Kaufman had a tendency to twirl the ends of his mustache as he reminisced. "They said they were interested. I suggested an agency; Andrew didn't know about that, so I kept my eyes open. And then one day a woman came into the hospital, six months along, and said she was here to have her baby and go back home. She was still young: you know, twenty-six, twenty-seven. And this was back when it wasn't as common as it is now. It also wasn't your garden-variety unwanted pregnancy. She confided to me that she was, in fact, married, but her husband didn't want her to have the child. When I examined her, I found evidence of a number of cuts and bruises. She said she got them from accidents around the house. I pretended to take her word for it. Again, this was when we weren't as aware of issues like domestic violence as much as we are today, or I would have referred her to a county agency. Or taken that no-good husband of hers behind the barn myself.

"She had a room in a home in Santa Monica, and a part-time job as well. I tended to her needs, and she followed my advice to the letter. She wanted this child to be healthy. It broke my heart to see her in a situation like this, wanting to be able to have a child again but unable to.''

"Again?" John asked.

"I beg your pardon?"

"You said 'having a child again.' Had she had one before?"

"Yes. A boy."

"Where was he?"

"Dead."

"Ah. Sorry." John paused. "You sound as though you were fond of her."

"Oh," Kaufman said, allowing himself a small smile. "I was rather smitten. I wasn't married yet, you know, and she was a beautiful girl. She had an Irish accent, very pleasant to the ear. Something about red hair, I suppose. Has an effect on me."

John smiled, too. "I know exactly what you mean. So, while you were bringing her along..."

"...I contacted Andrew and Ellen, and they were very interested. After Mary gave birth—"

"Mary?"

"Yes."

"That was her name?"

"She didn't want her married name on the birth certificate. She had it read Mary Larkin Sullivan."

"Sorry to interrupt. Go on."

"Like I was saying, after Mary gave birth, I brought Andrew and Ellen down and they took a look in the nursery, and that's how they chose Gretchen. It's what's known as an independent adoption, as opposed to an agency adoption."

"Did the Seales and Mary Sullivan ever meet?"

"No. This was at Mary's request. I told her all about the Seales, though. Only gave her what's known as nonidentifying information. She wanted the children as far away from her as possible—for their own sakes, she said, not hers."

"Children?"

"Yes."

"Why did you say *children*? Was there more than one?"

"Oh, Andrew didn't tell..." Kaufman shook his head. "I must be getting old. She didn't want them to know, either. I had to choose one to show to Andrew and Ellen, and another to give to an agency."

"One of what?"

"The girls."

"There were two of them?"

"Yes. Twins."

If Kaufman had little to say about Gretchen Seale's adoption, he had next to nothing to say about what had happened to her twin. The doctor had contacted the Good Shepherd Adoption Agency—the only one operating in Santa Monica at the time—and it had placed the child in a foster home. Kaufman's part of the story ended there.

John thanked the doctor and left. It was almost noon by the time he climbed into his car and sped south toward Santa Monica. Music helped him drive, so he turned on the radio. He couldn't pull in a signal from KNAC—the *hardest* rock and roll station on the dial—so he switched back and forth between KLOS and KLSX until he found one of them playing an old Stones cut.

He took the Ocean Avenue on ramp right by the Santa Monica Pier, then turned left up Ocean and then right onto Washington Boulevard; down ten blocks he took a left up to Montana and then a right, and proceeded through three lights to the offices of the Good Shepherd Adoption Agency.

It was an aged gray sandstone building that had been well-kept over the years, steadfastly resisting the yuppie-ization of Montana Avenue that John had read about in the View section of the *Times*. He spotted gourmet delis and pricey clothing stores in a neighboring minimall, the type of things he hoped would never make it to Jicarita. He parked on the other side of the street and entered through glass doors.

"May I help you?" a receptionist asked.

"I'd like to see a caseworker."

The receptionist did not move. "Did you have an appointment, sir? Our caseworkers are extremely busy and work by appointment only."

"No."

"We don't handle clients on a walk-in basis. I'd be glad to give you an application and make an appointment for you and your spouse to attend a group orientation meeting, though." She opened a drawer. John saw paper and an appointment book inside.

"I'm not here to see about adopting a child. I'm investigating a legal matter."

"Could you be more specific?"

"Okay. A murder."

NORA DARBY HAD the stern air of one of the suburban housewives John used to rake leaves and cut grass for when he was growing up in Orange County, although he was probably only ten years younger than Mrs. Darby. Being an adoption agency caseworker was serious business.

"Did you say you were working on a police matter, Dr. Stratton?"

"No, I didn't. I'm investigating this case independently...."

"Independent of what?"

"Well...of the police. I am experienced in these matters, however. I used to work for the coroner's office and on this matter I've got their unofficial blessing."

"Unofficial."

"Yes. I used to work for them."

"Excuse me—you did say the coroner's office?"

"Yes, I did."

"Good grief." She sat behind her desk, not pleased with little Johnny and what he had been doing in her backyard at *all*. "We don't normally handle these sorts of things at the Good Shepherd."

"Surely you must have had children who have been adopted through the agency pass away?"

"Yes, but that's usually handled through other channels. We've never had the police tromping in through here."

"I'm not the police." And I do *not* tromp.

"What exactly are you looking for, Doctor?"

"Information regarding an adoption your agency handled twenty-seven years ago. I'm trying to find the twin sister of a woman who was murdered here in Los Angeles County; she was also adopted. The murdered woman was in contact with her birth mother up until a few months before she disappeared. I'm just following up the lead, wondering if there is anything there. I have the name of the birth mother, and I'd like to look at the adoption case record for the other girl."

"Well, California state laws require that we maintain strict confidentiality of our records. We cannot reveal the names of adopted children or their birth parents."

"So you can't let me look at the case record?"

"That's a sealed document, Dr. Stratton. No one can look at it."

"What can you tell me?"

"Nothing. I can't even confirm that the adoption was handled through this agency. These matters are highly confidential. I've signed a statement to uphold that confidentiality."

"Can I do anything to change your mind?"

"No." Nora Darby stood. "Good day, Dr. Stratton."

Dead end.

THE CAMARO SHOT OUT onto I-10, headed downtown. John was getting KNAC—Pure Rock, 105.5 FM—loud and clear, and they were playing Motörhead album cuts back to back—a style of music appropriately referred to as "speed metal." He easily passed the other cars, watching the exit signs whip by: Centinela, the 405 freeway, La Cienega, Fairfax, the 110 freeway. He took the exit for Grand Avenue and headed up through downtown, passing fashion outlets with clothing displayed on sidewalk racks. A few blocks over on Broadway there were movie theaters advertising films *en español*.

There are several cities called Los Angeles, he thought. This is only one of them.

When he passed First Street, he turned left and into the parking lot underneath the Music Center. He gave the attendant four dollars in advance, and noted the rates: $1.50 for every twenty minutes. Some things about downtown would never change.

He parked on the eighth level, noting his space, and headed for the pedestrian tunnel that would lead to the Central Court House. It was closed and locked.

He took the stairs to the street and jaywalked across Grand. He entered the court building on the fourth floor, walking past the front desk manned by two Oriental security guards, and toward the escalators. Lawyers in suits and ties walked past, one hand holding a briefcase, the other gesticulating as they spoke to a client or a colleague. Other men and women walked by, sporting juror badges.

He passed a bank of wooden telephone booths set against the wall and took the escalators down to the first floor. He looked for room 115—the one that had a sign beside it reading Adoptions/Abandonments—and walked inside.

A few calls from a pay phone in the minimall across the street from the Good Shepherd Adoption Agency had told him what to ask for. He requested two copies of an Application and Order for Approval of the Court to Obtain Information Regarding an Adoption. He left the case number blank. He filled out the parts asking for "other name by which child is known," "name of adopting parents," and "date of adoption." There was a notation to the side: "Civil Code Section 227 prohibits release of any adoption information 'except in exceptional circumstances and for good cause approaching the necessitous.'"

He took a while filling out the section asking for "reason for request." He turned the form over and continued stating his case there.

He printed his name, address and phone number, signed and dated the form and then filled out the other one exactly the same way.

He was told by the clerk behind the counter that the application would be forwarded to a judge of the superior court. He would be notified within a week by a letter from the court whether his application had been approved or denied.

Next door, in room 113, was the office for the *Los Angeles Daily Journal*. For $6.40, he picked up a blue booklet entitled, *Adoption Procedures*. Perhaps it would help him while he waited.

After he got his car out of parking and turned right on Grand, on impulse he turned left on First Street instead of right. He passed the Japanese temple on the left and then crossed the bridge over the Los Angeles River. He turned left at Mission Street, feeling his heart beat just a little faster. He was in Boyle Heights again.

He pulled over to the side of the road, in front of a run-down auto shop that sported a hand-lettered sign reading "Used Mufflers—$10." He stopped to put the T-tops back on the Camaro because it was so hot and smoggy downtown and he wanted to turn on the air-conditioning. The real reason for the stalling was that he needed a few minutes to think this impulsive action over. Did he really want to do this?

He got back in the car, kept the radio off and turned the air-conditioning on low. He put on his sunglasses, and lowered the visors on both sides of the car. He didn't want anyone to see him.

He drove on, idling at a light behind a green pickup truck with a bumper sticker that read "KWKW 1000: La Mexicana." He went under the Santa Ana Freeway overpass, and then he was at the corner of Workman and Mission, at the border of Lincoln Heights, the site of the LAC/USC Medical Center and the County Coroner's office. It was the first time he had seen the building since the day he left.

He pulled over in front of the parking structure by the Women's Hospital and parked at a meter that still had a few minutes left on it. He didn't really know what he was doing here. Maybe he had hoped that it would somehow count in his favor in the great grand cosmic scheme of things if he returned to the site of his greatest personal failure just to see if he could stand the experience.

He looked at the once-familiar surroundings: directly across from the coroner's office was Blanca's Mexican Restaurant, where he used to get *huevos rancheros* to go. Next to it was the Paragon Hotel, where some guy had had a heart attack and wasn't found until three days later. Farther down the street was the Ming Market, which sold beer and wine.

He felt a sudden thirst. He used to go in there regularly after work. Then he remembered the times when he went in there at all hours of the day, just before making little trips to his car. . . .

He lowered his eyes, looking at nothing. The things he used to do.

The meter flag tripped, letting him know that the quarter, which wasn't his in the first place, had run out. He started his car and drove back home.

THREE DAYS LATER, a letter arrived for him, but it was not in response to his application to the superior court. He didn't recognize the handwriting or the return address at first, but when he opened the letter and saw that it held Xerox copies of typed letters written to Gretchen Seale by her long-lost mother, he knew who had sent them even before he read the hastily scrawled note:

John—
Found these while cleaning out Grey's closet.

Hope you find them useful.

Best and all,
—Bob Loff

John brought the mail inside before reading any further.

There were three letters in all, each typed on a typewriter with a cloth ribbon and a sticking lowercase *e*.

He hesitated momentarily before reading them. He knew that he was wading through still and private waters here. He wished he could ask Gretchen for permission.

He would have to assume it was all right with her.

He unfolded the copies. The first letter was dated the middle of last January.

Gretchen—

The watchful folks at Samaritan Search Organization will only tell me your first name, the last probably being too much to give me all at once. Perhaps they have had bad experiences with unwanted parents haunting the children they have given away with midnight phone calls and clumsy detective work. No worry. I have only the pain of family love to offer you.

I am your mother.

I gave birth to you over twenty-six years ago, and handed you over to strangers right after the nurse brought you to my room and let me hold you for a while. I wish I could explain to you all of the reasons why I didn't raise you for my own, but they are too numerous to mention except in passing: bad husband, bad marriage, bad faith, bad timing. Bad family.

I chose to write to you at this time regarding the latter. This is a hard time for those in our clan, whether they bear its rightful name or not. Terrible harm will befall all of us eventually, but at least you should know the reasons why.

Please call or write me back. I do so look forward to hearing from you. Perhaps then I will feel like the mother I was meant to be.

Love,
Your mother,
Mary Larkin Sullivan
2405 South Portland
West Covina
555-2539

An address. A phone number. These were like spun gold to him.

The second letter, dated last June. John realized as he read it that Robert Loff had sent him only a selection of the entire correspondence. Whether he retained the others out of respect for Gretchen's privacy or Gretchen herself had thrown them away, he couldn't tell. Maybe they had been just plain lost. Either way, from the second letter it seemed as though the two of them had communicated in depth and it hadn't gone entirely as planned.

Dear Gretchen:
I can understand your reluctance to meet face-to-face with the mother who deserted you at birth so many years ago. But I don't think you understand the urgency of the situation that I am describing regarding an important family matter.

Your life is in imminent danger. Only if I see you in person can I fully explain.

Please, please let me see you.

Mother

John remembered Loff saying that Mary had said something about a family curse, and that the woman's thoughts sometimes became unfocused. He could see what he was talking about.

The third letter was undated.

> Daughter Gretchen:
> I may be dead by the time you read this—or decide to do anything about it—or you may be, or someone else neither of us have ever heard of before. You obviously don't care enough to find out why. I suppose I shouldn't blame you. I only hope you are spared to the last.
>
> Love,
Mom

There was a fourth page, but it wasn't a letter. Loff had thoughtfully placed the envelopes the letters had been mailed in facedown on the glass top of the copying machine and made a duplicate. John studied the cancellation date on the last letter, the one that sounded the most ominous.

July 7th.

One week before Gretchen disappeared.

John put the letters aside. He was not going to dismiss Mary Larkin Sullivan as a harmless crank. This woman knew something.

HE TRIED THE PHONE NUMBER Mary Sullivan had included in her letter, but got a message saying that the number had been changed, and at the customer's request the new number was not available. He called West Covina information and tried to get the new or the old listing. Neither was forthcoming. Mary Sullivan was in hiding. But from what?

He thought about getting in his car and driving to her home to question her, but held off. There was something else he wanted to know first: had Mary Sullivan's other daughter, Gretchen's twin sister, been contacted by her mother? Was she still living in Southern California? Did she know anything about this family curse?

Was she still alive?

THE FOLLOWING MONDAY John received notice from the superior court that handled adoptions. Inside the envelope was a signed copy of his application and a letter from Her Honor, Monica Raines, saying that his access was granted only to a specific document: the petition for adoption. He would have to contact the Adoption Section once again and ask for a photocopy to be made.

John did just that.

THE NEXT DAY he drove back downtown to pick up his photocopy of the petition for adoption and pay the nominal cost of duplicating. He looked over the petition while still in his car in the Music Center parking lot.

The petitioners were Louise Etta Mandell and Henry Barker Mandell, who were married and lived in Los Angeles. No address, past or present, was included. Good Shepherd was listed as the adoption agency. The child's adoptive name was to be Annette Louise Mandell. Both her adoptive parents had signed the petition, along with their attorney.

A Mr. Wallace Elkind.

BACK HOME, John got Wallace Elkind's number out of the Los Angeles yellow pages—under the firm Elkind, Elkind and Gann—and upon calling, discovered that Wallace Elkind was still in practice. At first he got Wallace Elkind, Jr., but the son quickly transferred John to Elkind senior.

John introduced himself and explained the reason for his call. He wanted the attorney to contact his old clients, the Mandells, and ask them to call him.

"I can't do that, Dr. Stratton."

"Why not?"

"Because the Mandells are dead. Killed accidentally."

"Oh . . . oh, I'm sorry."

"Yes. Tragic."

"How long ago was this?"

"Five years."

"And their daughter, Annette?"

"She's on her own now."

"I see. Is she still in Southern California?"

"Sounds to me like you don't know who you're after, Doctor."

"I am not *after* anybody. I want to contact Annette Mandell because I'm working on a case that she figures in."

"How so?"

John patiently took the time to explain. When he was done, Elkind made a few thoughtful noises. "Sounds like a job for the police."

"It is, but obviously they aren't doing as well as they should be, or you would have heard from them."

"I don't divulge my clients' home addresses or phone numbers as a rule, and that rule especially applies to this case. But I'll tell you what I will do."

"What?"

"I'll see if I can reach Annette. I'll tell her you'd like to get in touch with her. And as her legal counsel I'll advise her on any complications or developments that may arise."

"Thank you, Mr. Elkind. Let me give you my home phone number."

THE PHONE RANG five days after he had spoken to Wallace Elkind.

"Hello?"

"Is this 555-6275?" It was a female voice.

"Yes."

"May I speak to Dr. John Stratton, please."

"This is he." John felt a twinge of excitement in his abdomen.

"Dr. Stratton, I just received a letter from my attorney stating that you wished to contact me."

"Are you Annette Louise Mandell?"

"Yes, I am."

John sat down, holding the receiver with both hands. "I'm glad you called."

"I'd like to know why you wanted to meet with me, Dr. Stratton."

"You can call me John, please."

"All right, John. I want to know why you wanted to meet with me." The voice on the other end of the line was calm and certain. The inflections were different, but the tone and the pitch... *John? Hi, it's Grey. Oh, not much. How about you?*

"I have some news regarding the circumstances of your adoption."

"Such as what?"

"I'd rather tell you in person."

She paused. "Is it serious?"

"Yes, I'm afraid it is."

"And you won't tell me over the phone."

"No, what I'd really like to do is to meet with you in person."

"Then I suppose that's what it will have to be. What part of town do you live in?"

"Jicarita."

"The canyon or the town?"

"The canyon."

"Why don't we meet in Santa Monica, then? Are you familiar with the area?"

"Yes. I used to live in Ocean Park."

"Then why don't we meet at the Rose Café? Do you know where that is?"

"Sure."

"Let's meet there tomorrow at exactly noon, unless you have some other commitment."

"No. That's fine for me."

"How will I recognize you?"

"I'm about six-two, with black hair and blue eyes."

"How old are you?"

"Thirty-three."

"What will you be wearing?"

"A . . . brown jacket. The kind bomber pilots used to wear."

"All right. I'll see you then."

"Goodbye."

JOHN ARRIVED at the Rose Café at precisely 11:45 a.m. the next day. For the hell of it, he had driven past his old apartment on Marine and parked on the street in front. He hadn't been in his old neighborhood for several months. It evoked no nostalgia, just a sensation of time passing, people changing.

The Rose Café was a large, airy structure, serving several types of coffees, salads and desserts. Out on a back patio, lunch and dinner were served. John had taken Gretchen there to brunch. He thought. Maybe.

He got a cup of herb tea and sat at what he hoped was a conspicuous table. He was sweating under the heavy bomber jacket he'd bought at the Banana Republic just over on Main Street. He wished he had chosen a lighter piece of distinctive clothing. It was well over seventy-five degrees outside.

He sat and sipped, until he realized that the heated herb tea was only making him perspire more. He gave up on it and got a glass of water instead. His mouth was dry. He was a little nervous.

"Dr. Stratton?"

John looked up, and for a moment he had a strange sensation of déjà vu. He was looking into one of the most familiar faces he had ever known—Gretchen's face—but it was a Gretchen from a parallel universe. Her hair was longer. Her body a little leaner. A calmer look to the eyes. But it was almost her. He had forgotten how pretty she was.

"Are you Dr. John Stratton?" The woman looked on guard, wary. He didn't want to frighten her.

John half stood up. "Yes. Yes, I am." He gestured to the other chair. "Please, have a seat."

He took off his jacket, draping it over the back of his chair, extremely aware that he was using the time to look away from her, hoping that when he looked back, it wouldn't be so much like seeing Gretchen again, as if he had been granted some fervent wish from the Beyond and was given the chance to start over with her one more time.

She caught his eye. She was watching him carefully. "Is something wrong?"

He forced himself to look into her clear, green eyes. *How come,* he had asked her once in bed, *your hair is red and your eyes are green but they call you Grey?*

"No."

"You seem warm."

"The jacket . . . the hot tea . . ."

"Are you sure there's nothing wrong?"

"You just . . . look a great deal like your sister, that's all."

Annette Louise Mandell frowned a particularly un-Gretchen-like frown, turning her head in the manner of a much more confident and serious woman than Gretchen Seale had ever been.

"I have a sister?" she questioned.

John immediately tried to recover from his fumble. "Please . . . Annette . . . I'm sorry. I thought Elkind had told you."

"No. What's this about me having a sister?"

"Well . . . you're aware of the circumstances surrounding your birth, aren't you?"

"I know I'm adopted. Is there anything else to know?"

"Your mother had another child—a daughter—who was also adopted."

"Older or younger?"

"You were twins."

"I'm a *twin*?"

"Yes."

"Identical?"

"Yes. Very much so."

"Why 'were'?"

"I beg your pardon?"

"You said we 'were' twins. Why 'were'? Are we no longer?"

John paused briefly, trying to think of anything less than the direct approach. "She's dead."

"Dead." She looked at John as though he were a snake behind glass.

"Yes."

"How?"

"I suspect homicide."

"You suspect. Why?"

"It was certainly no accident."

"What happened to her?"

"I'm not sure you want to hear this."

"Try me."

"She was . . . buried alive, in what looked like a home-made coffin. She was found by a digging crew working for the power company up in the canyon."

"Jicarita?"

"Yes."

"Is that how you're involved?" She had both hands on her purse, one thumb on the clasp. He wondered what she kept in there and if it would make it through an airport metal detector. Why was she being so cautious?

"One way. I knew her—your sister."

"How?"

"We were friends."

"And what do you want with me?"

"The police have no suspects, no clues, no leads. No one has any idea why this happened to her. I checked into her family background because it seemed . . . unusual, and I wondered where it would lead."

"To me."

"Seems that way."

"They don't know who did this?"

"No."

"Buried alive, did you say?"

"Yes."

"Just left there for however long it took for her to...die from whatever."

"Asphyxiation. Very little air underground. It takes about twelve hours."

She sat and looked at a point just to the left of John's shoulder.

"I know this all must be a lot for you to take in," John said, "but I thought coming from me might be better than just getting a letter or a phone call from a police detective or from the agency. It's—"

"I think someone is after me," she said.

CHAPTER FOUR

"WHAT MAKES YOU THINK someone is after you?" John had spoken first, after a full minute of silence.

"For the past month I've been receiving a lot of hang-ups," Annette said. "Phone calls where I answer and no one says anything."

"Maybe it's just a malfunction in the phone system."

"I can hear background noises. Someone's there, listening."

"Is that at home or at work?"

"Both. I work out of my home."

"And where is that?"

"Orange County. Laguna Beach."

"Nice neighborhood."

"I like it."

"What do you do down there?"

"I run a crafts gallery. Silver work. Wood carvings. All Laguna artists. I recently got into glass sculpture. It's in my house. The gallery is in the living room and the bedroom and kitchen are in the back."

"Do you own it or do you just manage it?"

She smiled, very slightly, for the first time. "I guess I sort of manage to own it."

"Doing well?"

"Keeping my head above water."

"Any brothers or sisters? I mean, in your adoptive family."

"None that I know of, besides . . . what was her name?"

"Gretchen. Gretchen Seale."

"Ah. Well. None besides her."

"And your parents?"

"Both dead."

"Elkind told me. I forgot. I'm sorry."

"So am I."

"May I ask how?"

"A car accident. Drunk driver."

"Unfortunately, that's a lot more common than you might think."

The statement made no impression. John drained the last of his tea. He was trying to learn too much about her all at once. He had to stick to specifics.

"So you've been getting these hang-up calls?"

"Yes."

"Anything else unusual going on?"

"Well . . . don't you think that's enough? It's rather unnerving. I've been having regular nightmares because of it."

"What sort of nightmares?"

"They're not about ringing phones or anything like that. I dream that I'm home, in my bed, and I hear things outside my window."

"What kinds of things?"

"Noises. It's hard to describe them."

"Please try."

"Well . . ." She gestured futilely. "Sort of like . . . sounds that a man or a woman might make. Sometimes—in my dream—I think it's just the wind blowing across an open pipe or something."

"What does it sound like exactly?"

"A crying of some kind. A wailing."

"Really."

"Yes."

"That's interesting."

"Why?"

"I don't know . . . could mean something."

"Such as?"

"I don't know."

"Can I ask you something else?"

"Sure."

"Was there anything out of the ordinary that happened to—it feels strange to say—my sister?"

"I understand."

"Did anything else happen to her before she disappeared, I mean anything that might have something to do with me?"

"The man she lived with said that during part of last year she had been in touch with her mother—I mean *your* mother, too."

"She was?" Annette was suddenly very interested.

"Yes."

"How did they find each other?"

"Through some search organization. Did you ever try to find her? She ever find you?"

"No. I never tried anything like that."

"So as far as you know—"

"We wouldn't recognize each other if we passed on the street."

"Never been curious?"

"I wouldn't say that, just . . . It's hard to explain."

"So I've been told."

"I lost my real parents—I mean my adoptive parents—and I didn't want to risk coming up against another death or loss."

"I wish I could say I knew how you felt."

"That's all right." She paused briefly. "But what did you learn about her?"

"Your mother?"

"Yes."

"Not much. I found a few letters that she had written to Gretchen."

"What did they say?"

"They alluded to other conversations, other letters—things I have no knowledge of—but from talking to Gretchen's boyfriend and from reading the letters that I did have . . . your mother seemed obsessed with some idea of a family curse, convinced that death was going to befall each and every member of her family, Gretchen included."

Annette said nothing, merely sat and listened.

"I don't know what that means in terms of Gretchen's death or your life. All I have on your mother is a name, an address and a telephone number that doesn't work. It was with her name and information from the doctor that delivered you both that I got your case record opened and discovered how to get in touch with you."

"Now that you have, what's next?"

"I want to try to contact your mother. Her name is Mary Larkin Sullivan, and she lives in West Covina. I'd like you to come with me."

Annette took a long look out the window, toward the patio where people were eating and drinking and laughing in the midday sunshine. When she turned back to face John, there was a directness in her eyes that he found unsettling.

"My God," she said. "You think she may be the murderer."

THE MOONSTONE GALLERY in Laguna Beach was located on a side street off the main drag that faced the ocean. "I only get the adventurous types. It weeds out the surfers and teenyboppers who only want change for a wet dollar bill," Annette explained.

She unlocked the front door after punching a numeric code into the alarm system's keyboard. Her gallery was a converted beach house that she had remodeled into a combination showroom, studio office and living quarters. John wandered around the showroom while Annette went to check her mail and messages. He wondered if he should try to convince her it wasn't a good idea for her to stay alone in her house again. Art galleries were secured against robbery and theft, not murder of the owner by forces unknown. On the way, he had volunteered to spend the night in his car, parked outside, if necessary. She had made demure noises about not being sure he should have to do that.

The showroom was divided into three parts: glass sculptures poised on wooden columns in the middle of the floor, wood pieces on shelves by the windows and silver work in cases by the front desk. A few numbered and signed lithographs hung on the wall. The polished floorboards creaked under John's feet as he moved from item to item, listening to the electronic garble of Annette's answering machine as she ran the message tape back and forth. When it was through, she picked up the phone and made a few quick calls.

She returned, an appointment book in her hand. "Okay, chief," she said, "what's the plan?" She sat down at the desk making notes as she listened to John, confident in her ability to do two things at once.

"I'd like to drive down to West Covina and try knocking on Mary Sullivan's door."

"Uh-huh." She consulted a number on her Rolodex.

"See if she's home and if she'll talk to us."

"Yeah. What if she's not..." Her voice drifted off as she made some notes in the margin of her date book. "What if she's not at home?"

"If she's not, then, perhaps you and I could—are you listening to me?"

"Sure."

"You seem busy."

"I'm just rescheduling all my appointments for the next three days," she said, closing her date book. "Who knows? Maybe we'll have this thing wrapped up by then." She picked up the phone and began dialing.

THEY TOOK JOHN'S CAR, with no protests from Annette. He could feel her wariness evaporating. If someone or something was after her, he sensed that she was fairly certain John Stratton wasn't it.

It was midafternoon by the time they got on the freeway. It would be another hour until they reached West Covina, even with minimal traffic. John raced his Camaro on, feeling as though he were just barely ahead of the four o'clock crunch. A five-minute delay in starting could mean an extra thirty minutes in total travel time.

Annette bore up like a trooper, not flinching as John zipped in and out among the cars at eighty miles per hour as though they were standing still, gunning the engine to an even hundred when he could. The setting sun cast golden reflections in the rear and side mirrors. They didn't speak.

John consulted his Thomas Guide for directions, Annette leaning over to check. "I want to make sure," she said, "that you aren't one of these men who insists they know where they are going, but simply ends up getting more and more lost." But John had made all the right turns and quickly found Mary Sullivan's house and parked the car in front.

"Well," he said, "this is it."

The neighborhood was quite modest. The houses looked as though they had fallen into slight disrepair over the past decade.

"I'm a little nervous," Annette said. She looked at her mother's house as if it might burst into flame at any minute, glass and bricks sent singing through the air like hot shrapnel.

"I can understand why."

"If she gets weird or something, will you get me out of there?"

"Yes."

"And let's not say we just met. Pretend you've known me for a while."

"Okay."

She opened the door, leading the way. John saw that more than one person knew the difference between being nervous and being afraid.

"Let's go."

They knocked and rang at the front door, and it was on the third ring that the door opened. A wisp of graying red hair poked out from behind the door, like part of a childhood image of the weird old lady of the neighborhood.

"Yes?" Her voice had an odd high pitch to it. The chain on the door was still drawn, ready against the world.

"Mary Sullivan?" John asked.

"Yes?" The tone was querulous, the voice cracking with age and uncertainty.

"My name is John Stratton. I'm a doctor—"

The door suddenly slammed shut and the chain scrabbled against the frame as arthritic fingers hurried to unhook it. The door flew open again and Mary Sullivan stood in the frame, fading daylight casting a glow on her face. She was not looking at John; she was looking at her daughter. They had the same green eyes, the same hair, the same set of mouth. She was recognizing a younger version of herself, not much different than she was at that dark and hidden time when she gave this same girl away. Or perhaps, John thought, there is something deep in the womb that senses those that it has carried.

"I'm Mary," she said.

"I'm Annette."

The screen door opened, and Mary stepped forward with arms grown old with longing, and embraced her only living child for the first time.

"You came," Mary Sullivan said, rocking herself and her daughter together as one. "You came back to me."

JOHN AND ANNETTE SAT on a sagging couch in the living room. The walls were dark with wrinkling wallpaper, and a smell of must hung in the air like the memory of a bad meal. What light there was from yellow table lamps illuminated slow-turning motes of dust in the air. The inside of the house had not seen this much company in quite some time. Mary Sullivan sat in a padded bentwood chair, her eyes open and fixed on Annette as John related the events that led them to her door. When he told Mary that Gretchen was dead, she looked at him numbly, without relief or surprise. Then she hung her head, muttering something to herself.

John leaned forward. "Pardon me?"

Mary raised her head, blinking back fresh tears. "When did this happen?" She had a faint trill of a brogue, worn smooth by years on the coast, making her diction almost English.

"Almost two weeks ago."

"No. No, I meant, when did she die?"

"That's not known exactly. Within twelve to twenty-four hours after her disappearance."

"And when was that?"

"She was last seen on July 16th."

Mary Sullivan nodded slowly, leaning back in her chair. She turned to Annette. "I've been calling you."

"You have?"

"I would call and hang up, just to hear your voice, to know you were still alive."

"That was you?" For a moment, Annette looked as though she was going to become angry. "I didn't...I thought..."

"Your sister is dead. It could just as easily have been you. I thought it *was* you."

Annette looked flushed. "I really don't follow what you're saying."

"You've never given me a chance to explain."

"Explain what? Something about the history of a family I've never been a part of?"

"You will always be a part of *this* family."

"The Sullivans?"

"No." A moment of silence, presumably for those long past. "You're not kin to them. But my family, the Larkins, are cursed, doomed to die out within our lifetime. You and I may be the only ones left. All of the others I know of are gone."

"Oh please." Annette pressed her fingertips to her temples, squeezing her eyes shut. "Please stop. I can't listen to this."

"But surely you must have heard it. We all have, at one time or another."

Annette maintained her pose, but opened her eyes. "What? Heard what?"

"Outside your window. At night. Don't tell me you don't know what I'm talking about now. You just don't know its name."

"I've heard...something. Only in my dreams."

"A moaning, perhaps. Like someone crying, but unlike anything you've ever heard before."

"Yes. Like that."

"At least one of us has to hear it, just before another is taken."

"Hear what?"

"In Gaelic it is called the *bain seth.*"

"The what?"

"The banshee."

JOHN LISTENED spellbound as Mary Sullivan began her tale. He sensed Annette at his side, equally enthralled.

The older woman spoke, and for a while it was as if time's essence was slowly stirred round like vapors in an iron caldron, black and burning.

"We come from Ireland: Erin, in the old tongue. For the past century and more, back home, the Larkins were a powerful and loving breed, numbering more than a thousand. As a little girl I heard stories that a Larkin could walk into a strange town without worrying about board and bedding for the night. We owned land, banked wealth, settled grievances.

"Then came the time of the banshee.

"Legend says that a banshee is the lost soul of a woman taken before her time, condemned to roam the earth, warning her kin of impending death. She is mostly heard, rarely ever seen, and her presence is sensed only by family members. Others can't hear her. She is supposedly bound to Ireland, and only those in the homeland can hear her cry. Or so it always had been.

"No one knows who the woman was when she was alive, or how she came to meet her end; if anyone did, they have probably long forgotten, or the knowledge died with them. All I know is that once, generations ago, she was a Larkin, a direct ancestor of you and me. It was years after her passing before her first appearance, but ever since then, the stories have been passed down about how at least one of us had heard her keening, days before another was meant to die. My grandfather claimed he saw her once, sailing into the night, her terrible howling ringing in his ears—which he'd thought had long gone deaf—warning all to be careful, that death was in the air.

"I myself lived in Ireland until I was almost your age, Annette, working the remaining land my family had left. I had a husband, Roy Sullivan, and we had a son, Kelly. The years the three of us were together were the only time in my long and miserable life I was ever truly happy.

"Every once in a while—over months, sometimes years—someone in the family would hear the banshee and tell the others, by phone or by post. Sometimes I'd hear it in my sleep: a long low moaning across the moor at night. I would wake, trembling, my husband wondering what had frightened me so badly. True to the legend, he hadn't heard anything. I would run to my son's bedroom to make sure he was unharmed, and he would already be awake and crying, frightened because he'd heard it, too. The three of us would hold one another until dawn, knowing that another Larkin was going to die.

"Those were hard times in Ireland, and most of what was left of the family was packing up and moving to America to start new lives. Weeks would go by after I'd heard the banshee cry, sometimes months, before we would hear that my Uncle Connor had been struck down by an automobile or Aunt Katherine had succumbed to cancer. Those times I was saddened by the family's loss, but secretly relieved as well. At least the three of us were safe—or so we thought.

"There came a night when the howling was so loud and so long I was certain that anyone within ten miles could hear it. I woke up, thinking that the noise would be rattling the panes and making the animals bolt in terror. I looked down at Roy sleeping soundly beside me, and I knew what it was. The demon had come again, but this time she sounded nearer than ever.

"I wrapped myself in a blanket and ran out into the dark, my bare feet slapping on the cold hard ground. I looked out into the night, and all I saw were trees bending in the wind. The noise rose to a shriek. I couldn't tell if it came from inside my head or was merely the wind playing some cruel trick, but if the sound had a source it seemed to be from within our barn.

"I ran around the house to the back and opened the barn doors, peering inside, hoping that perhaps one of our animals had been frightened by the wind and was making the sound out of sheer terror, the walls of the barn distorting it into the horrible wail that filled my ears.

"And then I saw her.

"She was floating in the air, casting a pale gray light about the loft; I could see the eyes of our horse in his corral, the straw on the dirt floor. If I'd had a printed page in front of me I could have read by it.

"She hung in the air, a good ten feet off the ground, the ends of her shredded gown brushing against the rafters, flapping in slow motion, blown by an invisible breeze. She was an evil wretch, a waking nightmare, with tangled and brittle hair streaming out behind her, eyes black and soulless as open pits. Her cold blue lips stretched across foul and rotten teeth as she turned her head from side to side, screaming out death's knell.

"Then her vacant eyes lighted upon me and I felt the cold of the grave brush my heart. Even mere eye contact provided her with the opportunity to draw more life from the world, slake some unearthly thirst, serve her evil purpose. I thought it was my time, that those were to be my last breathing seconds on earth, and that I was seeing what others of my family, now dead and rotting, had seen when this floating apparition had taken their lives. At that moment she stopped her crying, and a shriveled hand rose from the folds of her filthy clothes and pointed at me.

"And she called me by name.

"Then she cackled and swooped from the air. I fell backward, on the ground, avoiding any contact with that hideous being: I thought she carried the touch of death. She soared above me, out the open barn door and up into the sky, her awful laughter fading into the distance.

"I rushed back into the house where my husband was still sleeping. I roused him and told him what I'd seen, and we both ran to Kelly's room.

"He was gone.

"Roy and I looked in the house, then outside, then in the barn and the chicken house, calling his name. He was nowhere to be found.

"We summoned our neighbors from their beds, and with lights and horses they went searching for him, covering our land in its entirety before dawn.

"They found him, lying still on the ground, underneath a shading tree not far from our house, unmoving. It was as if he had sought refuge from the terrible spirit that had been roaming that night, and one of the branches he thought would hold him safely had snapped and he had fallen.

"They brought him to me. His face was pale, his breath still.

"Roy tried breathing life back into Kelly's corpse, but after a while he stopped, cradling the body in his arms and weeping.

"'It's your fault!' he screamed at me. 'You and your cursed family!' Half-mad with grief, he went into the barn and, laying Kelly's body on a bed of hay, he sawed and hammered together a child-size coffin, tears streaming down his heaving chest.

"I stood out in the cold, and as dawn broke over the sky he emerged from the barn and laid the coffin inside a cart, then went back and got Kelly's body and laid it inside. With our neighbors following, he drove off across our land, to find a place for our son to rest. When he returned, the cart was empty. Our friends waited and offered to fetch a priest and hold a proper funeral, but when they saw they could do nothing for us, they went home.

"Roy slept on the floor of Kelly's bedroom that night, and the night after that. I lay in bed alone, wondering what kind of life we would have left after this.

"The third day I saw him walk into the barn and not come out. When I called him for supper he did not call back.

"I went in, where only three days before I'd seen the horrible wretch that had taken our son away, and saw my husband swinging from the same rafters the banshee had hovered beneath, a rope around his neck, his face purple, his eyes half-open.

"I ran screaming into town and never went back. For all I know he hangs there still.

"I borrowed money for a passage to America aboard a steamer and arrived in New York penniless. Relatives who had fled before me took me in, but they couldn't hide me from the immigration authorities. I married a serviceman I barely knew, a sergeant made cruel by his long years in the Army. He was transferred to California and I came here with him. He drank and beat me as often as he liked. He swore if I left him he would kill me. I never fought back. I had brought death upon the two people in the world I had loved the most. I thought I deserved no better.

"When I found I was pregnant again—with twins, no less—he insisted I see a doctor he knew on the base to get me 'fixed' as he put it. I refused. He thrashed me so badly I thought I would lose my children before I could bring them into the world. I could have the 'bastards' as he called them, but I couldn't keep them. He said if I brought them back to the house he would drown them like kittens.

"So I moved to Santa Monica, took a job to support myself, as my husband would not give me a penny, and arranged for my babies to be put up for adoption. I made sure the two of them would have nothing to do with me or my miserable life—that neither would know the other existed. I tried to put as much distance between us as possible, not because I didn't love them, but because I loved them more than anything else in the world. I so much wanted to be a mother again, even if it meant never seeing my children for the rest of my life."

There were tears brimming in Annette's eyes as she listened to this part of the story. "I thought . . ." she said, and she had to clear her throat before she could continue. "I thought you didn't want me."

"No," her mother said, and smiled for the first time. "I prayed for you both, day and night. I would have given the world for a kiss, a hug or a smile. But I didn't dare try to reach out for you until I felt I had to. No, darling," she said, reaching for her daughter's hand, "I'm your mother. You make me proud."

Annette's composure broke, tears held back too long flooding forth. As sobs racked her daughter's body Mary held her close once again and made soothing sounds to her.

"There, now, sweetheart," she said. "It's all right. Momma's here. She won't leave you. Ever again."

IT WAS JOHN who spoke next, after mother and daughter had broken their embrace.

"What happened to your husband—the serviceman?" he asked.

"Ah." Mary produced a handkerchief and handed it to Annette, who dabbed clumsily at her eyes and nose. "After I gave up my girls he dragged me home to an even worse hell than the one I'd left. He cursed the expense of having had to hire a maid during my absence—he refused to perform any of the basic domestic duties himself—and for days he made me pay with tears and bruises. I'd cook him a meal and he'd fling it about the kitchen, ordering me to clean it up. There were times when I thought about stealing his service revolver, not to use on him but to put myself out of my misery. He kept it locked away, so even that escape was denied me.

"I was left to my own devices. I prayed to God to end my imprisonment, and when that didn't work I prayed to Christ, His Son. I prayed to the Virgin Mary to afford me some salvation, and all my prayers got me was an unflinching silence. For years I waited. Finally, I turned my hopes away from heaven's deaf ear forever.

"In my desperation, I did what no person should ever do, at any time, raging or sane. Better for them to die than to do what I did.

"I prayed to the powers of darkness. I asked the banshee to take my husband's life.

"Days later, I thought I heard something; in dreams or waking, I couldn't tell. It sounded more like the wind, less like a person. I listened for it again, but it didn't return.

"Three weeks later, my husband was killed. He was on a training exercise. Something went wrong with the blanks in his rifle. A metal shard pierced his heart.

"It wasn't until I began to hear the banshee again and again that I realized what an awful thing I had done, consumed by my own selfish need. I took Roy's name as my own again and wrote those aunts, uncles, nieces and nephews that I hadn't seen or heard from in years, even those I'd never met. It took months in itself just to track them down. By their accounts my suspicions were confirmed. Many of them were missing, and their survivors didn't know if they were living or dead. It was as if they had been plucked out of thin air.

"I had brought our family's curse here, out of the homeland and across the ocean, to America.

"My children and I—and all those related to me by blood or marriage—are doomed."

JOHN LISTENED to the continuation of Mary Sullivan's story. She had lived in fear for the remaining years of her life until the present, supported by the meager pension fund supplied by the Army, believing that she had been saved by the banshee to be the last victim. She had devoted herself to trying to warn the other members of her family of the awful fate that awaited them, on the chance that they could fend off the supernatural in the safety of their homes, but either they dismissed her as a kook or her letters were returned undelivered. She said she would finger the envelopes, still sealed, wondering if across the country other mail was gathering in other mailboxes, yellowed newspapers were piling up on porch steps, milk cartons soured in the iceboxes, while what had once been thought to be just the wind howled outside, singing an anthem of dark triumph.

At some point in this narrative—John was unable to determine exactly when—he realized that Mary Sullivan's train of thought had become less coherent, that she had started rambling. Her sentences became more and more disjointed, and she referred to things that had not been mentioned previously, commenting on incidents that Annette had not spoken of. At one point, Mary insisted that she and Annette had met before, that there had been a rendezvous arranged through the mail. Her fingers hung on her daughter's sleeve. Annette's tears had long since dried, and her initial fascination had been replaced by discomfort and anxiety.

As Mary Sullivan's eyes grew wide and her speech became one long run-on sentence, John excused himself to the bathroom. He stopped in the hallway to test the phone set resting in an old-fashioned nook. Dial tone. A phone number, not the one she had included in her letter to Gretchen, was taped to the base, just below the dial. It was written in large numbers, as if Mary was in danger of forgetting it at any given moment. John copied it down on a piece of paper and tucked it into his wallet.

He glanced around at the rest of the house. It was dark and silent. The other rooms seemed to harbor great masses of useless junk, the household equivalent of board game trivia. If it was indicative of its occupant's mental state...

John stepped into the bathroom, closing the door and running the water for some covering noise. He opened the peeling medicine chest and studied the labels on the empty vials of prescription drugs: brand names for psychoactive drugs, dispensed from the pharmacy of a local military PX. The prescriptions had been made years ago, probably when someone concerned had steered poor rambling, disjointed Mary Sullivan toward a base psychiatrist who had to deal with a lot of nervous Army wives. Refills had never been made. John closed the cabinet and flushed the toilet, noticing the accumulation of mold in the bathtub and on the shower curtain.

Annette was trying to disengage herself from her mother, who was in the last stages of lucid thought before another onset of delirium.

"We have to go," John said kindly, intervening between the two of them. "It's getting late."

"But...you don't understand..." Mary looked hurt and lost, following John and Annette as they backed their way out the door.

"We want to stay in touch," John said, "perhaps visit you again sometime."

"Yes...yes..."

John heard Annette fumbling at the door, opening it, anything to get outside and away from this crazy woman who said she was her mother.

"I think it's time for us to go," John said.

"Oh...what time...?"

"I know you don't feel well."

"No...no...I'll be better..."

"I'll call you tomorrow," John said. "I've got your new number."

"Do you know...? I...have to...remember...back...the days...Roy..."

"Goodbye, Mary," John said. "From both of us."

He closed the door on her trembling and frightened face, knowing that eventually she would stumble back into a lucid state, and later, when clear thought returned, she would walk back into the living room and wonder what had happened to her visitors.

John turned around and saw that Annette was waiting for him at the car, one hand on the door handle as if she couldn't wait for it to be unlocked, anxious to be far away from what was already a painful and shaming memory.

IT WAS NEARLY ANOTHER HOUR before the two of them spoke again, John negotiating the freeways and side roads with silent efficiency. It was only when the four-lanes and urban areas had given way to the familiar oceanside surroundings of Annette's neighborhood that she felt comfortable enough to speak again.

"What did you think?" she asked.

"I don't know," John said. "That's what I think."

She turned to face him.

"I found some old prescriptions in her medicine cabinet when I went to the bathroom," John continued, "They weren't for antibiotics either."

"Ah. So she *is* crazy."

"It adds several variables to the equation. I think we can safely assume she didn't have anything to do with your sister's murder." He kept driving. "How about you? What did you think?"

"I think . . ." But she didn't finish the sentence.

"Let me tell you what else I think," John said, to fill in her contemplative silence more than anything else. "No matter what she said or how she said it, nothing changes the peril of your situation. You still could be in a lot of danger, and so could she. Tomorrow, when she's lucid again, I'm going to call her and tell her that she should change locations or seek some type of protection. Your sister's killer is still at large."

Annette snorted. "My sister. My mother." She shook her head. "Those are such strange...ideas." John waited for her to keep talking.

"And I disagree. I don't think I'm in any danger. I think Gretchen's death was a random event, having nothing more to do with me than if she'd been killed in a car accident or contracted terminal cancer."

John parked the car in front of her house. "There could be something to—"

"Oh, there isn't anything to it at all," Annette snapped. "A bunch of superstitious crap—more stuff that doesn't have anything to do with me. All my life I wonder who my mother really is and she turns out to be a nut. Christ, I'll probably inherit Alzheimer's disease or whatever it is she's got."

John shut off the engine. Annette got out and slammed the passenger door.

He followed her inside. She disappeared into the rear of the house, turning on lights as she strode forcefully into her living area. John remained in the darkened gallery, giving her some privacy. She had been through a lot. He wouldn't be surprised if she needed to take it out on something. Or somebody.

He looked at the digital clock on the front desk. It read 11:30 p.m. Late.

Annette came back out, wiping her hands on a bath towel. Her face looked freshly scrubbed.

"It's not necessary for you to stay," she said. "I can take care of myself."

"Please, I insist."

"No, really. It's all right."

"If you have a sleeping bag or something I could just roll out on the floor here, I'd be fine."

"Don't you have to be at a hospital or a medical office tomorrow morning?"

"No."

"I thought you doctors were on call twenty-four hours a day."

"Not this one."

"Suit yourself, then." She headed toward the rear of the house. John could hear her opening closet doors, rummaging around. She returned with a red goose-down sleeping bag, still in its nylon casing, and a pillow. "Here you go," she said, setting them on the floor. She walked back to her bedroom and closed the door.

John looked down at the sleeping bag and pillow, feeling something less than noble.

He unrolled the bag and fluffed the pillow, scrounging for reading material before settling down. That floor was going to be hard. He figured if he slept with his clothes on, using the sleeping bag as a cushion, and if he could ask her for a blanket . . .

He heard the bedroom door open and Annette returned, having changed into a pink nightgown and bathrobe, her red hair pulled back in a long ponytail. With the manner of a bed-and-breakfast innkeeper accommodating a last-minute guest, she showed John how to raise and lower the lights in the gallery, where extra blankets were kept and where the bathroom was. She had a pleasing scent, like lilac soap and rosewater, and John followed in its wake.

"I usually have a glass of wine before I go to bed," she said. "Would you care to join me?"

Upon hearing the word *wine*, John felt his pulse corner a sharp left, leaving his temples tingling. "If you have some herbal tea or fruit juice, that would be better."

"Chamomile tea?"

"Fine."

They retired to the kitchenette, John taking a seat at a table barely big enough for two. She moved around efficiently, boiling water in a brass teakettle and pouring herself a glass of white zinfandel. The squeal of the cork, the sound of the pouring, the slosh of the bottle: those sounds seemed to fill the clean white space. John wondered what was happening to him.

"Sure you wouldn't like a beer or anything like that?"

"No. I . . . it . . . keeps me awake."

Annette sat down with her glass, and the scent of fermented grapes wafted over to John's olfactory nerves, making his mouth practically flood with saliva. He swallowed.

Annette drank meditatively, savoring the taste, swirling it on her tongue. "I'm going to need more than one of these," she said, raising her glass in a solo toast.

John nodded.

"Why are you looking at me that way?"

"I'm sorry, I don't . . ."

"You seem keyed up all of a sudden. Is something wrong?"

"No, it's just . . ."

"Just what?"

"That wine."

"Sure you won't have some?" She was up in a flash, opening the refrigerator door. "I hate to drink alone."

"Really . . ."

He heard her pour. White zinfandel. John had toured the wineries up in the Napa and Sonoma valleys once upon a time, cultivating a fine buzz and bringing home souvenirs by the case.

She set the glass in front of him. "Be my guest. We've had a hard day."

"I shouldn't . . ." he said, but it wasn't he talking. It was some annoying stranger who couldn't see that there was any harm in having a pleasant drink with a pleasant lady. Just one glass. That was all. And it was wine, for crying out loud. It wasn't like Scotch or bourbon or even—as he called his favorite vodka in med school—Holy Stoly, the Russian Wonder.

He watched as his right hand reached out and touched the glass—so cool, like dew on a leaf—feeling the bouquet fill his head like the perfume of a long-lost lover. He had totally forgotten that one out of every four deaths he had investigated at the coroner's office was alcohol-related.

So this is how it happens, he thought.

A picture suddenly came to mind, one of him back in the last days before recovery, after he had lost his job at the county and gone on a three-day binge, doing three grams of blow and two fifths of tequila every twenty-four hours, rolling well-packed joints of the finest Mendocino crop on his bedroom mirror, a one-man party and every hour had been midnight on New Year's Eve.

He remembered lying on the floor, the booze and pot and coke spilled out across the carpet, feeling his heart triphammer wildly, pains shooting across his chest and into his arms, the effort to reach the phone inches from his fingertips made an insurmountable goal....

He set the glass down on the table top unevenly, wine spilling over on his fingers. It stung like spider's venom.

"What's wrong?" Annette asked.

John felt he would crush the glass in his hand, shards tearing into his skin, unless he did the hardest thing there was for him to do, the thing that Dr. Rice had said was at the root of his addictions, and that was to *ask for help*.

"I am a recovering alcoholic," John said slowly, as if trying out a new language. "I cannot drink this." He looked at her, strength in pleading. "Take it away from me and don't let me...touch it."

Annette looked slightly shocked. "Oh. Oh my God." She took the glass from John's whitened fingers and slid it over to her side of the table. She reached for a napkin and wiped up the spilled liquid, handing one to him to dab at his fingers.

John felt fine sweat cooling on his brow. He took several deep breaths, fighting off the feelings.

Just then, the teakettle began to whistle. Annette took it off the stove, her eyes never straying from John for very long, pouring the steaming water over a tea bag nestled in a flowered mug. "There," she said, setting it before him.

John bent over the steaming cup, inhaling the gentle odor, vapors from the waters of Lourdes. He dunked the tea bag slowly, smiling at his simple enjoyment of the act as calm and kindness returned to the center of his being.

"What's so funny?" Annette asked, but she was smiling, too.

"It's at times like these," John said, "that I tell myself one of these nights I'm going to tie on a drunk one last time. I mean get really smashed. Get high, get wired and guzzle champagne by the bucket. Invite over everybody I know, be loud, crank up the stereo, and party for all it's worth. One of these nights . . ." His smile increased. "But *not tonight*."

Annette laughed. "*Never* tonight."

"Never."

"But one of these nights." She laughed again. "That get you through a few hard times?"

John nodded, sipping his tea. "Got me through this one."

"You don't mind if I—" She indicated his glass as well as her own.

"Be my guest. Enjoy."

"It doesn't bother you?"

"No. Just had a weak moment."

"How long have you been . . . not drinking?"

"Nine months and two weeks. But who's counting?"

She laughed some more. She was a very pretty girl.

"But it wasn't just drinking. I had a few other nasty habits. Now, I don't even let white sugar or caffeine into my system."

"Sounds hard-core."

"Just can't stand the idea of being addicted to anything. Except running. I guess I'm hooked on that for now."

Annette smiled. It was time to change the subject. "How's the tea?"

"Good. Great. Is this the kind with drawings of little fuzzy bears going to sleep on it?"

She laughed. "Yes." She giggled. "You know, you're kind of funny."

"I am?"

"I mean, you have a good sense of humor."

"Have to, these days. I remember once I..." He caught himself. He was going to say "I remember once I did an autopsy on a guy"...and then lead into his professional anecdote, but he did some last-minute editing. "I once had a patient who contracted AIDS. And as part of my investigation into his...medical history...I visited a hospice in West Hollywood where he had lived with a number of others, all with the same disease. I found that the way these poor guys dealt with their condition was by telling jokes—about their disease, about themselves, about one another. Even about what they saw as certain death. It helped them somehow. It really did."

"Ah. That's interesting." She finished her first glass of wine and started on John's. Time to change the subject again. "So you're a doctor."

"Yes."

"Is that how you met Gretchen?"

"No. That wasn't through work."

"Then how?"

"Do you really want to know?"

"Yes."

"At a bar. I was with some friends and she was by herself, waiting for somebody that never showed."

"Anything particular about her that drew your attention?"

"She was the prettiest girl there."

"I see. So you two...?"

"We sort of dated for a while."

"And what happened?"

"Things didn't work out."

"After how long?"

"A couple of months."

"Was it ever serious?"

"More for me than for her, I think."

Annette nodded thoughtfully, leaning forward on the table, resting her chin in her hands. "What was she like?"

"Gretchen?"

"Yes."

"She was . . . funny. Sexy. Insecure. The kind of person who thought the world was better than it was. A little different from you, if that's what you're wondering."

"How so?"

"She never would have done this." John gestured to indicate the house, the gallery. "She wouldn't have even considered it."

"I don't understand."

"I think she wanted to be taken care of, and . . . maybe I wasn't the right guy for that."

"What do you mean?"

"I used to think all kinds of things—nothing like love to bring out your insecurities—but now I guess I could trace all of it back to my bad habits."

"Were you in love with her?"

"I guess . . . I thought . . ."

"I don't mean to make you uncomfortable."

"That's okay." John took a hefty swallow of tea, first pulling out the tea bag and winding the string around it in a wringing action. "I cared a lot . . . I was in love. For a long time, even when I wasn't seeing her anymore."

"How does this whole business make you feel?"

"Business?"

"Her death."

"I don't know . . . actually, I do know. A little sad."

"Because she's gone."

"She's gone, and . . . I thought she was a nice person."

He stopped talking and looked at Annette, noticing that her Gretchen-ness had begun peeling off in layers, and that he was seeing a far more direct and capable person than Gretchen had ever hoped of being. Annette looked back at him without reserve, and John felt his face warm from the force of her attention.

"Time for bed," Annette said. She rose gently, gathering up his empty teacup and the two wineglasses, rinsing them out at the sink. John watched the way her robe hung over her body, ending just barely above her knees. He wondered if she wore the nightgown to bed, or took it off and stretched under the sheets naked, the way he liked to.

She turned around, once again gently businesslike. "I'll see you in the morning." She laid a hand on his arm, patting it. "Good night."

"Good night."

He sat at the kitchen table, listening to her walk away and into her bedroom, closing the door but not locking it.

He wanted her.

JOHN TRIED TO MAKE himself comfortable on the unrolled sleeping bag, pulling the soft cotton blanket up under his arms as he looked around at the darkened gallery. The events of the day jumbled around in his head, refusing to lie still. As he had told Annette, there were so many variables to the equation.

He had hoped that Mary Sullivan would be able to give him some solid leads to follow, not this animated Halloween special about a vengeful spirit that roamed the hills of Ireland. It was possible that she had made the whole thing up, distraught over the death of her child and husband, or that the true nature of the events was being masked by delirium. The banshee itself might be a manifestation of crushing Catholic guilt, built up over the years. He had seen it happen before.

Some other doctor obviously felt she was slipping a few gears, or he wouldn't have prescribed the medications John had found in her medicine cabinet. Her reunion with her only living child had been very emotional, and maybe that had triggered some sort of episode.

He sighed, settling his head back onto the pillow. Why were things so complicated? Why did he always feel he had to be the one to sort them out?

He twisted his head to look at the digital clock glowing on top of the front desk. Almost two in the morning. He had been lying there for an hour and forty-five minutes.

Was he ever going to fall to sleep?

ANNETTE'S SCREAM WOKE him up.

John instantly leaped up, throwing the blanket off the sleeping bag and rolling onto the floor in one smooth motion. His socks slipped on the polished wood as he ran down the darkened hall to Annette's bedroom. As he stumbled in the dark, he heard her scream again, high and loud, as if she were being attacked and feared for her life.

His hand reached the doorknob and twisted it to the right. Smooth metal turned, then caught in his hand.

The door was locked.

He put his weight to it, thinking it might just be jammed and in need of a good shove.

It held.

Annette screamed for a third time.

John stepped back, bracing his shoulder for the impact, and threw himself against the door.

The lock snapped, and John stumbled into Annette's bedroom, unable to see anything in the dark except Annette thrashing and tearing her sheets and blankets out from under the corners of the bed.

"Annette!" he yelled. "Annette!"

He ran to the side of her bed. She must not have recognized his shadowy form, for she screamed once more, kicking herself away from him and up against the headboard.

"No, no, no, Annette, it's me, it's John Stratton." He kept his voice low and soothing. He reached for a lamp on the nightstand and turned it on, shading the light low. It cast a small soft glow around the room, warm and comforting.

He could see her face clearly for the first time, her eyes wide with fright, her face pale, her bare shoulders trembling.

"It's all right," John said, keeping his expression calm. "It's all right. Don't worry. I'm here. Everything's all right."

Annette's fright broke, and she started to sob. Instinctively, John reached out to her, and she held on to him as he drew her close, patting her back and giving her the strength of basic human solace. The sheets and blankets between them shifted, threatening to fall away altogether. He could feel her bare breasts pressing through the material and into his shirt. His hands on her back stroked only smooth flesh, not fabric. In spite of the nature of the situation, he could feel himself becoming aroused.

"I saw it," she said, holding her face against his shoulder, trying not to cry. "I saw the banshee. Right outside my window."

John looked. The drapes were parted, the window closed and locked. All he could see outside was blackness.

"It was floating out there, making this terrible moaning sound." She pulled her face back so she could look at him. "She... it... was so old and dead, like a vampire or something, like she'd been buried and dug up a hundred times."

"It was only a bad dream," John said. "That's all. There's nothing out there." He looked across her shoulder at her bedroom window again, just in case there *was* someone there, and for one awful thrilling moment he thought he might see something dead and ancient scratching at the panes: *Let me in. Let me in.*

"It was... so real."

"It's over now. It was just a nightmare." He drew her close once again, and the feel of her body made him want her all the more. "There, there. You'll be all right."

"It... it was calling my name."

"Just a bad dream..."

"I'm not going to die, am I?"

"No. No."

"Don't leave me alone. I'm afraid to go back to sleep."

"I'll be right here. Don't you worry."

"Oh God. Oh God, John. It was awful."

PART TWO

*

Frank B. Lewis

ot private residences. He could follow people he could...

CHAPTER FIVE

ON HIS ID BADGE for Acton Security Services, the man's name read Frank B. Lewis. No one knew what the "B" stood for, not even Frank B. Lewis. The middle initial was fictitious, as were the first and last names. That was one of the things that Lewis liked best about the security business. He could pose a great many questions while he was wearing his uniform and gun, but was asked very few. The most important one had been: Will you start at $6.50 an hour?

Yes.

Other than that, all he had to produce at Acton's Culver City office was a valid California driver's license—also faked—and a signed application. If anyone had ever checked into his background and found that no such person as Frank B. Lewis existed, they never mentioned it to him. To a man standing a little more than six foot six in his bare feet and weighing 280 pounds—stripped, less than ten percent body fat—prying questions were a little slow in coming.

There were other things he liked about the security business. It had a natural turnover rate all across the country. He could move invisibly from state to state, town to town. Everywhere he went, he drove a patrol car that looked very much like a police vehicle. He carried a gun, as well as a can of mace, a billy club and a pair of handcuffs. He could conduct investigations in his spare time, wearing his uniform when it was supposed to be at the cleaners. He could access information, either through computer data or written documents, simply by asking for them. He could stake out private residences. He could follow people. He could, sometimes, gain entry into their homes and walk around inside while the occupants were away.

He also had a great deal of professional mobility. In the past year, he had worked in a variety of locations in the Los Angeles area: a community college campus, a hospital, a mattress warehouse, a supermarket, two shopping malls and several private estates. He was currently working his favorite type of assignment, although the least useful: neighborhood patrol. Patrol meant he didn't have to be anywhere at any particular time, as long as he answered whenever the dispatcher called on the radio.

At eight the previous evening, just when John Stratton and Annette Mandell were arriving in front of Mary Sullivan's home, Frank B. Lewis was checking into the dispatch office of Acton Security on Olympic Boulevard in West Los Angeles. He had arrived on his bicycle, already dressed in his gray and white uniform for the evening's work. His shift stretched from eight in the evening to four the next morning. If he took a lunch break, he got off at five. Tonight, he was going to take a lunch break.

He parked his bicycle next to the chain link fence that encircled the lot, wound his chain through its spokes and into the fence links and snapped the padlock shut, twirling the dial. Then he walked away. He didn't expect to see his bicycle again. Tomorrow's dawn would come and the bike would still be there, and the day after that and the day after that, until someone found a pair of bolt cutters and bit the chain off.

At home he had a change of clothes already laid out, the airplane ticket he'd purchased last week lying beside it. The other materials that he was going to pick up after he checked out a patrol car were neatly arranged against the wall. By the time anyone wondered where he was and why he was late checking back in at the dispatch office, he would be several thousand feet in the air and several hundred miles from Los Angeles. The patrol car would be parked in a lot at LAX.

His uniform would be stashed in a locker, the key flushed down the toilet.

The dispatcher's office itself was in a converted trailer at the far end of the fenced lot. Within the fenced lot were a dozen patrol cars, all painted gray, with clear revolving lights mounted on each. Within each car was a two-way radio, and a partition separated the back and front seats. The back doors had no handles on the insides. The cars were Dodge sedans that had been bought at end-of-the-year clearance sales and repainted, with the Acton Security logo emblazoned on the side.

Frank B. Lewis stepped up to the office and opened the door. The window air-conditioning unit was working on low, but was still producing an inordinate amount of noise. Mike, the dispatcher, was bent over his desk, both hands on a horror paperback, his thick glasses pushed against his pale and bloated face. Lewis looked in disgust at the man's long greasy hair. The dispatcher's radio sat, humming, on the desk, butted up against the wall. Mike and Frank B. Lewis had very little to say to each other, especially on days when Mike had been sweating a lot. The man had not caught on to the true market value of deodorant soap.

"Which one have I got tonight, Mike?"

Mike looked up at the distraction, then reached into the drawer of the scuffed steel desk and pulled out a key attached to a frayed paper tag with a metal rim. "Eighteen," he said, and went back to his reading.

Lewis picked up the clipboard that hung next to Mike's desk, checked his watch and signed in. He had deliberately arrived a few minutes early. He didn't want to have to deal with the other guards who would be checking in soon— overweight men with crude power fantasies or discharged cops who had never been able to cut it on the force. They socialized heavily with one another off the job. Many of them drank or slept on duty, covering their tracks with Mike by giving him hefty samples of marijuana from any drug hauls. Mike liked to eat after getting stoned.

Lewis walked out of the trailer without saying goodbye. After tonight, he would never again have to look at Mike and the other trash like him. They were the things he liked least about the job. By this time tomorrow he would be a mystery to them; after a week, a legend.

He walked to car number eighteen and unlocked it. He checked the water, gas, oil and tire pressure. It was Mike's duty to make sure the cars were serviced regularly and Mike was an incorrigible slob. Tonight, there would be no room for error. Lewis warmed up the engine for three minutes and pulled out, just when Jackson was trying to edge his tired Torino into the lot. The other man waved at him as if there were some secret code of honor that existed between all security guards, whether Lewis cared to respect it or not. Jackson had once showed him a handbook for revenge that he had sent for in the mail, which outlined such techniques as mailing change of address cards to the post office filled out in your enemy's name and pouring epoxy glue into his gas tank.

Lewis took the car out on Olympic. His assignment tonight, as it had been for the past three weeks, was a neighborhood to the east of La Cienega, just north of Pico. There had been some break-ins and Peeping Toms there recently, and the tenants in several apartment buildings had protested to their landlords. To placate them, the landlords had formed a loose association and hired Acton Security for a one-month stint to scare off the would-be burglars and rapists. They had chosen Acton for one simple reason: Acton was cheap.

He was due there in less than half an hour, but would most likely be a few minutes late—as if anyone would notice. His first stop was going to be his apartment. He had a few things to pick up there.

Some boards, sawed and lathed to his specifications, sanded by hand in his bathroom shower where he washed the sawdust down the drain. Several nails. A hammer.

A pick.
A shovel.

HALF AN HOUR LATER, Lewis was cruising the side streets bordered by La Cienega on the west and Crescent Heights on the east, with Olympic to the north and Pico to the south. He could not help but relish the tingle of excitement growing in his abdomen. Tonight would be his last night on the job, his last night in Los Angeles, perhaps his last night in the United States. Tonight would be the last night for many things.

He studied the houses that lined the streets, two-story buildings made of Spanish clay. There had been very little action here in the past few weeks. The neighborhood was barren of pedestrians as well as cars. Everyone was in for the night, reading or watching television. Perhaps his presence alone had been a deterrent to further crime, and that was a satisfaction in itself. He enjoyed being larger and stronger than other people. It gave him confidence, a purpose.

After two hours Frank began to feel restless. He would not have minded just a bit of action, a small matter that needed tending to, just something to warm the muscles and clear the eyes. An appetizer before the main course.

He did not dare to try anything in his own jurisdiction; the resulting attention would not work well in his favor. He drove north and east, toward a Fairfax neighborhood. He cruised the residential streets, searching.

He spotted a figure walking a few blocks ahead: dirty jeans, ragged sweatshirt, a pullover cap. Too hot for such clothes during the day. At night, maybe...

He turned off and parked before the pedestrian could spot him. He got out of the car, locked it and slid his nightstick out of the ring on his belt. This just might be the kind of thing he was looking for, he thought.

He walked quickly and quietly up around the block, just in time to see the pedestrian turn the corner and disappear.

Lewis had caught a glimpse of the man's face. He was black.

Good. He knew that blacks in ragged sweatshirts didn't have expensive lawyers and connections with the police. Their complaints could be routinely dismissed.

Lewis rounded the corner, careful as he walked under a streetlight. He took his hat off and tucked it under his arm. Keeping his head low to the ground, he edged around a bush.

The black man was about three houses down the block, on the other side of the street. He was standing outside the large curved window of a house. He was looking in.

Lewis knew what the possibilities were. The man could be a Peeping Tom. He could be a rapist, or a potential one on a dry run. A number of factors were at play. What decisions would the man make based on what he was seeing in the window? There were a lot of pretty women in Los Angeles. What if a young woman lived inside that apartment? What if she was pretty? What if she wore a nightgown around the house on hot summer nights just before going to bed? What if she was all by herself; what if her boyfriend was out of town?

Then perhaps—nothing was for certain—the black man standing outside her window would break inside, hold a knife to her throat and make her do all the things he had always dreamed of having a woman do to him—fantasies that had become so haunting and heated that the only way to abate them was to act them out like that. All he would leave behind was the residue of his semen and a shattered life. If the woman was lucky, she would still be alive. Never mind the fact that she had just been defiled, humiliated, invaded, her life ruined by the forced lust of a sick human being. The policemen would ask her rude questions that they didn't believe the answers to, the social worker would gently explain the percentages to her on the number of rapists who are caught—and the number of those who face trial and the number of *those* who wind up seeing the inside of a jail cell—and her family and friends, especially her clumsily understanding boyfriend who would eventually leave her, would all try to comfort her. They would all tell her the same thing: that she was lucky.

The injustice made Frank B. Lewis's heart clench like a thick-knuckled fist. All of that would happen unless he interfered. He realized now what he was doing there, scrunched down on the ground, lurking in the shadows. He had been led there, to that juncture, to observe and make a decision. There were other forces at work—dispassionate overseers who did not have his form and strength or his passion and purpose. Whatever he felt whirling about him in the universal ether could only whisper and suggest; it could not judge and act. He was meant to do that. It was why he had been given life—life after death.

The black man had not moved away from the window. As Lewis watched, he changed position to obtain a better view. Lewis could see his eyes in the light from the window now. They were wide and shining.

Lewis watched as the man stepped away from the window and around the side of the house closest to his vantage point. Lewis strained to see. The man stopped under a side window near the back of the house. He waited.

The light in the front window went out.

The light in the window where the black man was standing went on.

He knows, Lewis thought. He knows where her bedroom is.

He could only know if he had been there before, and he would only have been there before if he was planning something, if he was casing her out.

Lewis could visualize the recent past, seeing it trail behind this moment in a fresh glowing path. The man had been here many times before. During the day. At dusk, when she came home. At dawn when she left for work in the morning. He had sat outside and waited and watched for any boyfriends. He had seen them come and go. He knew if she had a steady or not. When he was there. When he was gone.

He was gone tonight.

The bedroom light went out.

Lewis watched the man hunch down, waiting. His victim had to fall asleep first.

Lewis took several steps backward. He could not approach from that side; the terrain was too open. If he walked across the street, he would most certainly be seen. He had to go completely around the block and back up, sticking to the shadows, and then edge around the corner and surprise the man.

It would take a few minutes. Just as well, Lewis thought. The rapist was only going to wait there for his beloved to fall asleep.

Lewis walked quickly away, standing up straight. He deliberately slowed his pace when he got to the street. He didn't want anyone to think anything was wrong, so he wouldn't have to explain anything to them. Concerned neighbors had a habit of calling the police. The last thing he needed here were the cops. This one was all his.

He passed his parked patrol car. He walked in and out of streetlight glare. He kept an eye out for the car that might belong to the rapist. He wanted to make sure the man was alone. He passed a dirty and dented sedan. Perhaps that was it. It was empty of waiting friends.

Lewis turned at the end of the block, crossing the street to the other side quickly. He kept the nightstick aligned along his arm, so it could not be seen in silhouette.

He crept up the block, advancing house by house, making sure that no one had seen him. He saw no one else. Something was keeping them inside, shades drawn, minds closed. The area had been sealed off. The only functioning consciousnesses were his and the rapist's. He could sense the other man's mind ahead of him, followed it like the trail of a slug.

When he got to the curved window where he had first seen the rapist watching, he stopped. He concentrated, trying to slow his breathing from the effort, at the same time bringing all of his abilities to a sharp focus. Although the other man was smaller and certainly not as strong as he was, he had to be ready for the possibility of guns, knives or hidden accomplices waiting their turn.

He tucked the nightstick into his belt and drew his gun. He heard a roaring in his head. Sounds and shrieks replaced words and sentences. Impulse and action was substituted for reason and thought.

He wheeled around the corner, landing in a crouched and ready position. The man was not there. In his place was a window screen, leaning against the outside wall.

Lewis looked up.

He saw two legs wriggling through the window. The rapist's torso, head and shoulders were already inside the house. He was sniffing for his prey.

Lewis holstered his gun. He reached up with both hands, grasping the back of the rapist's pants, and lifted him out of the window, careful not to make any noise. The action was so slow and deliberate that the other man did not have a chance to be alarmed. Lewis threw him to the ground.

The rapist yelled his surprise, but Lewis stopped it with a knee to the chest. Lewis heard ribs crack under his full dropped weight. The yell turned to gasps for air as Lewis rolled off the man. His nightstick slid out of his belt and moved swiftly in his hand, cracking against the side of one knee, and then the other. The black man could barely breathe now, much less scream. All he managed were high-pitched agonized wheezes. He looked up at his attacker, eyes bulging with terror.

Lewis finished him up by driving a foot between the man's legs, and sudden convulsive retching let Lewis know that he had hit home. He ground his shoe into the man's testicles.

The punishment had taken less than ten seconds. Lewis stopped himself, blood and noise rushing in his brain. If he had continued unchecked, he would have killed the man.

Sudden illumination fell across his shoulder. The woman inside was awake. If she came to the window, she would see both of them, and then call the police. He couldn't afford that.

He turned quickly away, retracing his steps back down the block. By the time the police arrived, he would be in his car and gone.

He could feel the sense of power glowing in his muscles and skin. He felt the weight of destiny upon his shoulders. He saw the past leading up to the present, the future forged best by his decisions. He saw himself as immortal, a communer with spirits, one who moved among men and left fear and awe in his passing. He had served those who guided him and they had rewarded him with priceless victory. He knew what this meant.

It was time for lunch.

He turned south on La Cienega, to where it intersected Interstate 10, and took the eastbound route to San Bernardino. He kept an even speed of sixty miles per hour. He checked the time: 11:55 p.m.

He reached down to his two-way radio and keyed the mike.

"Mobile eighteen to base. Do you copy?"

A crackle of static. Then: "Base to Mobile eighteen. I copy."

Mike's voice sounded sluggish. He had probably gotten stoned earlier, eaten half a dozen doughnuts and fallen asleep.

"I'm taking my lunch break. Going to be out of the car for thirty, forty minutes."

"Okay, Barnes will cover for you. Call him when you're back on duty. I'm going to be busy here."

Lewis was right. Mike had been sleeping. "Ten-four." They sounded their respective clear signals, and then Lewis turned off the radio. It was the last time he would use that radio. He would never talk to Mike again.

Mike. The radio. The life he had known was peeling off in layers. A new one was emerging.

He checked his watch again, noting his speed and making mental calculations. He would be arriving in West Covina within the hour.

THE FRONT of Mary Sullivan's house was dark, as were the houses on either side. Lewis cruised by twice. She was home. He could hear her breathing.

He rounded the block and turned up the alley, switching off his headlights. He counted backward by the rooftops, shutting off his engine and rolling to a stop just behind Mary Sullivan's backyard fence. He reached into his back pocket and drew out a pair of thin white cotton gloves, the kind photographers use to keep from getting fingerprints on fresh negatives. He put them on, easing silently out of the car, leaving the door unlocked. He unhooked the round key that unlocked the car doors and trunk, leaving only the square ignition key on the ring. He inserted the round key into the trunk lock and opened it, catching the lid before it swung all the way up. He had unscrewed the trunk light bulb when he stopped off at home, so the interior remained dark. He peered in, straining his eyes to see. The boards could stay, but with the shovel and pick there wouldn't be enough room. He took the tools out and eased them into the back seat. The hammer and nails, too. At last thought, he moved the boards to there as well. She might try to use those to injure him in an attempt to escape, and he couldn't risk a struggle. She needed to be kept alive.

He eased the trunk lid back down until he heard it click, leaving the key in the lock. Then, he carefully stepped over to the gate that led from Mary Sullivan's yard to the alley. The gate was held shut with a latch. He lifted it, and felt it catch. It was locked. He unhooked his two-foot-long flashlight, with its lead base, from his belt and turned it on, shielding the beam with his fingers, letting only a sliver of light escape. Through the slits in the boards, he could see the glint of silver. A padlock.

Jammed locks, rusty door hinges, broken keys and frozen padlocks were all part of a day's work for someone who worked business security. He retreated to the car and reached under the front seat for the pair of bolt cutters he kept there, wrapped in black cloth. He dropped them over the fence, still wrapped in their cloth in order to muffle the sound.

Lewis walked down to where Mary Sullivan's fence joined her neighbor's, a meeting marked by a fence post. He reached up and grasped the top of the post, bracing his feet against the fence, hoping that it had been built to withstand the weight of someone his size.

It had been. He pulled himself up to the top, fitting feet and hands in between the spires of the fence, and dropped to the ground. He froze, listening for any sign that someone had heard him—a dog barking or a door opening.

After a full minute had passed, he began to breathe easily again. He waddled along at the base of the fence, hidden in shadow, one hand out to feel for the bolt cutters. His fingers closed around the fabric wrapping, and he slowly unwound the cloth, dropping it on the ground next to his feet.

He stood up, stooping to stay hidden in the shadows. He fingered the padlock. One good bite and it would go. He fit a section of the hasp into the slot in the lower blade of the cutters, carefully closing the top blade over it.

He grunted. Metal twisted and snapped.

He wrapped the tool back in the cloth and heaved it over the side. He removed the lock from the latch, lifted the latch and opened the gate a few inches, then replaced the lock in the latch housing. He closed the gate. The latch did not close completely, blocked by the hasp of the broken lock. The gate would open inside with one easy motion.

He crawled back down to the corner post. There were supporting boards nailed to the inside of the fence, making it much easier to heave himself back into the alley.

He checked the trunk lock. The key was still in it. He checked the front door. Open.

He put the bolt cutters back under the seat and gently closed the front door. He put his keys in his pocket, and began walking down the alley toward the street. At the end of the block he turned the corner that led down Mary Sullivan's street.

He felt his pulse begin to pick up speed, his synapses sparking like polished crystals. Of all of them, she had been the hardest one to find. She had left Ireland, remarried, had another child, lost her husband and moved a few times. It had taken time and patience and perseverance, but he had finally found her.

She had been saved for last. He'd tracked down the daughter and taken care of her almost two months before the mother. Her suffering would be more complete that way, an equal match to that which she had caused.

There had been other times, other opportunities, when he could have taken her before, but he had had to wait. His granted mission was only to seek and find, not to select. He took orders, he did not give them.

Now, as he saw her house edge into view, he felt a faint breeze pick up, sending leaves scraping down the pavement, rustling stems of grass and lowering the temperature by a few imperceptible degrees. He felt the faint presence of the only power greater than himself, the one who would not be denied, whose will would be obeyed no matter what the cost.

The *bain seth* was near. He could feel it.

Lewis walked up the path and knocked on the front door, then rang the bell. He saw a light turn on inside, and then the peephole open, and heard her muffled voice through the door. "Who is it?"

"Security patrol, ma'am. Following up on a call."

The porch light went on overhead. He kept his hat on, keeping his face in shadow. If she saw him, there was the slight chance that she might recognize him.

The door opened a few inches, held back by a small gold chain. He could have snapped it with one blow of the flat of his hand. "Who?" she asked.

"Security patrol, ma'am. Acton Security Services. We got a report of a prowler in the neighborhood and were wondering if you had seen or heard of any trouble."

"No."

This wasn't going to work on its own. He had to beef it up.

"Someone was reported to be lurking around your house, ma'am, looking in windows and such."

"Who reported this?"

"A neighbor of yours."

"Which one?"

"Call just came in, ma'am. I could radio the dispatcher and ask them if you like."

"No, that won't be necessary."

"If it's all right with you, I'd like to come in and have a look around, just to make sure that you're properly safeguarded against any intruders."

There was a long pause. She might not go for it. If she had just shut the door in his face, he would have had to think of something far more risky.

"All right," she said. "You can come in."

She slid the chain off and unlocked the screen door, holding it open for him. He stepped inside, removing his hat, keeping his face hidden from view until she had closed the door behind them and had switched off the porch light. "Now what is it you wanted to look at?" she asked as she turned around.

She never got an answer. He had the can of mace out and hit her with a good shot of it as soon as she looked at him. Blinded, in pain, Mary Sullivan cried out. He clamped a gloved hand over her mouth to keep her from making any further noise. He left her nose uncovered so she could breathe.

He quickly unsnapped the handcuffs from his belt and clamped them around her thin, bony wrists. It was over before she knew what had happened.

With one hand on the handcuffs and the other around her mouth, he hustled her to the back of the house, stopping to turn off the one lamp she had switched on. He took his hand off her mouth to switch off the light and she instantly gasped for breath. He dragged her to the back door, unlocking it and letting it swing shut behind him as he moved her outside. He knew it hadn't closed all the way, but he couldn't risk taking his hand off her mouth again. Muffling her screams, he half pushed, half pulled her through the overgrowth of the backyard to the fence gate. He swung the gate open, dragged her into the alley, opened the trunk and heaved her inside. She landed on the boards with a thud, the breath knocked out of her. He slammed the trunk lid shut.

Lewis looked around him, the blood thudding in his ears. He knew he had to get out of there. Now.

He jumped into the car and started the engine, slamming the door shut and then heading for the street. When his wheels hit pavement, he turned on his headlights, forcing himself to maintain the speed limit. In a few quick turns he was headed for the freeway.

At a stoplight, he could hear Mary Sullivan's muted cries, her clenched and shackled hands pounding on the lid of the trunk. At sixty miles an hour, no one would be able to hear her except him.

So far, so good.

Lewis headed west on I-10, past downtown Los Angeles, past West Los Angeles, past the San Diego Freeway, past Santa Monica, and onto the Pacific Coast Highway, which was shrouded in thin fog.

At the stoplight just before the Getty Museum, a California Highway Patrol car eased into the lane beside him. They were the only two cars at the light. As far as Lewis could see, they were the only two cars on the road.

The CHP officer nodded at Lewis.

Lewis nodded back.

The light stayed red.

Behind him, accompanied by vibrations carried through the body of the car, Lewis could hear Mary Sullivan move. It sounded as though she was shifting her weight, perhaps pressing her face against a crack in the trunk's seal, prying the rubber insulation apart with her hands, possibly spying the emblem on the side of the patrol car. Her chance. Her only chance.

Maybe she was dazed, Lewis thought, barely conscious of where she was.

"Help," Lewis heard from the back of the car. She was speaking in a normal tone, her voice weak and unsteady. "Somebody help me."

The CHP officer picked up his radio microphone and said something into it.

"Is anyone there?" Mary Sullivan's voice was rising in pitch and volume. "Can anyone hear me?"

Lewis slid one hand off the wheel and felt the butt of his gun. He could. He could shoot the officer if he had to.

"I've been kidnapped." To Lewis's ear, she seemed to be screaming. "Help! Somebody help me! Please..."

Looking straight ahead, Lewis focused his attention on his peripheral vision, trying to see what the CHP officer was doing. He seemed to be looking straight at Lewis, still talking into the microphone.

The light stayed red.

"Heeeeelllllllppppp! Won't someone please help me!" Her voice was torn with sobs.

The CHP car's overhead lights went on, bathing the inside of Lewis's car in swaths of red and blue. Lewis jerked convulsively, as if the colored lights had physical properties he was sensitive to.

The officer revved the engine of his car and sped through the red light, accelerating in pursuit of a speeder or following up on some other call for assistance.

He could hear Mary Sullivan sobbing in the back, her one last chance gone forever. "Why?" she said through tears. "Why are you doing this to me?"

The light turned green.

As if he hadn't heard, Lewis gunned the engine and sped on. Soon, the sound of the road drowned out her voice.

She knew why he was doing this to her. He didn't need to tell her that.

Lewis turned off Highway 1 and onto Jicarita Canyon Boulevard. He had chosen the same area for the daughter, Gretchen Seale, more than two months before. It would serve equally well for the mother. Jicarita was isolated, as yet undeveloped, but still only minutes away from the city. He had been fascinated by it ever since he first came to Los Angeles, spending days and weeks exploring its roads, its life, its history. He had paid special attention to the areas accessed only by the Old Canyon Road, the thoroughfare that led to the state park, where in many places time was preserved and the ground lay undisturbed.

The hills and trees of the canyon could hide anything. It was the fire season now, and the dry and cracking brush would inevitably explode into sweeping fires, traveling at speeds of up to twenty miles per hour, raging out of control for days. All evidence of what he had done would be destroyed forever.

He passed Wilkins Road, where he had taken Gretchen Seale, and the memory of that night came back to him.

HE HAD BEEN WATCHING Gretchen Seale for months, ever since he started monitoring Mary Sullivan's mail and found out that she was writing to a daughter she hadn't seen since birth. He had gotten the mailbox number, and then hung out in the Santa Monica post office for days, waiting until someone showed up to open box 3250. He had followed her home, her red hair making her an easy tail.

He studied her for weeks before making his move, until he received the sign that the time was right. He had watched her leave her apartment that final Sunday night, walking the three blocks to the grocery store on Wilshire as she did most evenings when she had some last-minute need. He had cruised alongside of her, turning on his revolving lights. She had stopped. He had told her that there was a report of a recent robbery in the area, but he couldn't find the address. Would she show it to him on the map?

She had leaned up against the car, flipping through the pages of his Thomas Guide to show him, when he'd placed the cold pressure of the gun muzzle at her back. He had forced her into the back seat, handcuffing her to a bar underneath the front passenger's seat so she could not be seen.

He had driven her out to Jicarita Canyon, feeling his path glow ahead of him with just a shimmer of a light phosphorus gray, as if something unusual had just passed by.

He had followed the given sign all the way up Wilkins Road, to where it was no longer Wilkins Road, but someplace wild and isolated. A coyote had darted in front of his path, surprised to see a pair of headlights lurching over the rocky surface toward the top. Frank B. Lewis had braked. He respected creatures who only roamed at night.

He had stopped the car, sitting at the crest of the hill, at the point of its highest ridge. There had been no trees to obstruct the view. "Kissing the heavens," as his country-folk would say.

He had killed the headlights but left the engine running, pulling his tools and material out of the back seat. He had nailed the box together, used the pick and the shovel to create a trench big enough to accommodate it and then laid the crudely made coffin inside. These actions had been slow and deliberate, performed with an acquired practice familiar to the special conditions of night and wind. He had opened the trunk, gun drawn, and motioned for her to step out. He prodded her over to the open grave and she had lain inside her coffin, apparently preferring a slow and painful death to a quick and violent one. She followed his instructions without protest, as though obedience would earn her some reserve of mercy. He had read of this behavioral phenomenon in his research of the activities practiced by the overseers of Treblinka and the high party officials of the Khmer Rouge.

He remembered Gretchen's eyes, wide and green, as he slid the lid over the top, nailing it into place. He had said little to her, but he thought she still imagined that he was trying some kind of kidnapping scheme, and that when enough money was delivered he would phone the directions to where she could be found to her father, and she would be rescued.

He had wondered when the realization would sink in, that no one would find her, that she was in the hands of fate and nothing could save her, that she was going to die. Perhaps it was when the air inside the box turned foul and her breath came short and fast, when her extremities were numb with cold, and any efforts to free herself had met with unyielding failure.

He had shoveled the dirt on top of the coffin lid, watching it vanish beneath the surface of the earth by the shovelful. When he was done, he had patted the earth down with the flat of the blade. He had stood, breathing gently, letting the keening wind pull and tug at him like a jealous lover probing for reassurances of faithfulness. He had put his face into the wind, eyes tearing at the effort.

There were men—although he did his best to avoid them—who did not know what it was like to experience such moments as this, to know such fear and awe, to realize that there was far, far more to life than civilized preoccupations like a state income tax, the quality of one's drinking water and the plight of those who walked the street homeless. He knew what urge drew people forward in this technological day and land, what it was within that made them seek out institutes and churches as if they held a hidden truth.

They wanted to feel magic rush through them like a surging current, feel the power and love that the presence of the spirit brought, leaving every cell tingling, every sense peaked. It made life among men seem less like reality and more like a stage of purgatory, designed to punish those who lacked any vision of the fantastic.

All mortal thoughts had been scattered as the realization set in that the wind blowing in his ears had begun to rise in pitch.

It was singing to him.

Those who only shook and feared did not know that her shriek was not a cry of woe and pain, but a joyful noise, an annunciation in the night realm that there were places on this earth that could harbor a spirit safely, patches of sparsely populated earth where the air was not disturbed by random signals, where industrial pollutants did not change the sky and make it heavy, and where a beauty lay on the land that could only come from a feasance paid to forces both light and dark.

He had heard her that night before he saw her, soaring out from behind a distant hill, casting gray shadows that lit the trees below, green chlorophyll shining black in her passing. She flew over the distance between them, closing the last leg of her voyage across foreign land and distant ocean, more majestic and terrifying than any living being.

Then she had enfolded him in her embrace and the red dirt beneath his feet sprouted emerald heather, clear night was turned to misty day, and for a moment he was back home again.

In Erin. Dear Erin.

HE SAVORED THE MEMORY, replaying it in vivid detail, the way a sportsman relished a great triumph to psych himself for the next encounter. He wanted it to be like that again. He wanted it to be like that again tonight.

There had been no gray and glowing trail ahead of him yet, and in that past week he had not experienced the premonitions that had led up to that fateful night. He had had to engage in an act of random violence in order to rouse himself to such a state.

But all of that would come. Tonight was his last night, his closing episode. It would be the greatest one of all.

He turned up Miramar Avenue, an even more circuitous route to the top of the hills than Wilkins Road. He eased the car around hairpin turns and switchbacks, and when the asphalt gave way to dirt he slowed to a crawl, feeling the car's suspension bounce wildly over the uneven terrain. His headlights picked out rocks and weeds and fallen branches. He finally hit bare soft dirt, and stopped the car on top of a barren ridge. He had surveyed the area months ago, when he was scouting possible locations. It was unchanged. It was here he would bury Mary Sullivan.

He shut off the car's engine, listening to the gathering wind outside. He opened his door, stepped outside the car and unlocked the back door on the driver's side. He lifted the boards out and set them on the ground, laying the hammer, nails, pick and shovel beside them.

Mary Sullivan was silent. Perhaps she had been dazed by the bumpy driving.

The wind whipping at his hair, he began to assemble the boards. He had had them cut and shaped according to his own specifications. All he needed to do was to nail them together in the dark, a process that had grown easier with practice. First he nailed the side boards together, each one made of two long boards held together by short thick sections of two-by-four. The head and foot panels he had had cut whole. The lid and bottom were last. He nailed the head and end panels to the side boards, leaving the lid off. The coffin's construction took a little more than half an hour. He glanced at his watch. It was now almost three in the morning. Still on duty. Dead of night. Just what he wanted.

He lifted the pick and the shovel together and walked away from the car, toward the nearest rise in the land. He looked up at the sky. Stars. He could hardly see them through the city's smoggy haze, but out here at night... other suns, other worlds.

He chose a smooth spot, one that appeared free of stones and roots. He swung the pick overhead, feeling it sink up to its handle in the soft earth. He was surprised. He had expected it to be harder and stonier. Perhaps the rains from the spring had left it pliable.

He swung the pick half a dozen times, then picked up the shovel and began to clear the loose earth away. After a few minutes, he switched back to the pick. Then the shovel. The exercise kept the wind's chill off his shoulders.

The shovel struck something in the dirt—a root or a rock, he couldn't tell. He leaned his weight on the shovel, twisting the handle. It felt like an underground root. He chopped at it with the blade, trying to cut through it. He made some progress, but it felt quite tough. He took up the pick and swung it, aiming carefully. He made contact only a few times, the impact shivering up his arms.

He picked up the shovel again. He would try to clear away the dirt around the obstruction, then chop at it with the spade. If that didn't work, he might have to try digging somewhere else. Precious time would be lost. He wanted to be finished by dawn.

He dug around the root, exposing a small section of it. It looked black and dull in the dim light, but the lighter shades of its core showed where he had hit home. He reached down to feel its thickness and texture. If it was dead and dry, he would be able to cut through it easily. If it was moist and living the task would be much more difficult.

The shock sent him sprawling backward, every muscle in his body contracting. He hit the ground with a bone-jarring thud. His heart fluttered wildly in his chest. His arms tingled, hanging uselessly at his sides as he struggled to sit back up again. It had been no ordinary root.

When he got his strength back, he stood up and un-clipped the flashlight from his belt, shining the beam into the hole.

The root's sheath was shiny and black, not dull and pitted as it should have been. Its core was not orange with sap, but splayed with multicolored veins, arteries and capillaries, many of them cut open by his efforts, exposing their coppery centers.

It was not a root at all. It was a power cable. He had been sent reeling by a severe electric shock. He was lucky to be still breathing.

He stood, feeling the wind stir about him, realizing what this meant. Power cables were placed by power companies that closely monitored their function and use. Any interruption of service would be immediately sensed or reported, and repair crews dispatched.

People would soon be here. At this very spot. It would only be a matter of minutes.

He had to get out of there.

He gathered up the pick and the shovel, staggering back to the car in the face of what was at best a severe setback. He put the dirty tools in the back, scattering dirt all over the floor. He had never experienced a problem of this magnitude before. His planning and patience had always paid off in the past.

He picked up the hammer and nails and threw them in the back seat. The coffin would be another matter. It wouldn't fit in the car. He would have to disassemble it into its five major sections, and then try to fit those in the car. He had little time to waste.

He reached for the hammer. He pried nails out, bending them out of shape in his haste. He flung them into the brush. He tossed the end boards onto the front seat. He wedged the side boards into the back, and then slid the coffin lid over them, angling it so it stuck over the front seat like a surfboard.

He jumped in the front and started the car, slowly turned the vehicle around and headed back down the hill slightly faster than he had come up, keeping his headlights off.

From the top of the ridge, he could look down and see the black ribbon of the main road. At the farthest end of the valley side, a truck was winding its way through the hills. As he watched, yellow revolving lights switched on, warning all other drivers that the power company was on its way to tend to the latest emergency. Everything would be back to normal in a few short hours.

Why was this happening? he wondered. What had gone wrong?

Less than a few hundred feet down the road, with the help of some frantic consultations of the Thomas Guide, he found an alternate route. If he took Evergreen Drive all the way to the end, it dribbled out into dirt roads and butted up against an annex of the state park that was set aside for campers and hikers. If he worked fast, he could bury his burden in the trees and no one would be the wiser.

He looked at his watch: 4:00 a.m. Sunrise in less than three hours.

He sped down Miramar and off onto Evergreen. It was a quarter of a mile before the road became dirt, and several hundred feet more before that ended in an open meadow, surrounded by trees. He got out, pick in one hand, shovel in the other, and quickly scouted around for a site. He found a place in a clearing on the other side of the trees. He would have to carry the boards a fair distance, not to mention Mary Sullivan, alive and kicking, but it would do. He set to work.

An hour later, he stopped. There were broken and oozing blisters on both of his hands. His back was aching. He was more tired than he ever remembered being. He had had to do too much work in too little time. The hole itself was too shallow, and barely wide enough, but it would have to do. He would pile a lot of dirt over it to cover it up, and all he could hope for was that it remained undisturbed until he was safely away.

He wearily trudged back to the car. He was halfway through the clearing before he saw the vehicle and what he saw made him drop his tools and run.

The trunk lid was up.

He raced around to the back to look inside.

Mary Sullivan was gone.

His breath came short and fast, his thoughts racing too far ahead of his actions. He had to calm himself, he had to slow down.

He was afraid, and he had not been afraid for a very long time.

He reached into the trunk and felt the carpeting that lined the compartment. Parts of it were still warm. She had somehow unlatched the trunk from the inside, guessing accurately that her captor was out of sight, and ventured out into the darkness on her own.

But which way had she gone? he wondered.

He set off in the direction of the paved road. She would most likely try to reach one of the houses. He had to get to her first.

He began at a trot, and then broke into a run, his shoes at first biting into dirt and then asphalt. He knew she was weak and confused. She couldn't have gone much farther.

He stopped, panting for breath, unclipping his flashlight and shining it down the darkened road.

He saw her.

She was staggering along the hillside in her bare feet, barely able to stand, her hands still manacled together in front of her. She turned around, her skin white in the flashlight's beam, and then started to run, a thin wail escaping from her fragile form.

In a matter of seconds he had caught up with her, laying a hand on her shoulder and spinning her around. She struck at him, but he hardly felt the blow.

"Help!" she screamed. "Someone help me!"

Were there houses nearby? he wondered. Could anyone actually hear her? He didn't know. He couldn't take the chance.

He drove his fist into her abdomen, doubling her over with agony even though he severely pulled the punch. Her screams for help were replaced by moans of pain.

He picked her up from behind, carrying her back toward the waiting grave. His sense of destiny was gone. He sensed he had derailed somewhere tonight, and he couldn't figure out where or why. He felt dazed and uncertain. All he could do now was to lurch along and try to finish the job.

The only possibility he could think of was that something had happened that he did not know about. Someone had stepped into his territory and interfered. If fate would just point him toward that person, he would be able to manage the rest.

The woman felt heavy in his arms. He had several hundred yards to go.

In an hour, the sky would lighten to the east. He hoped he would be out of this place and never see it again.

She struggled some more, and when he set her down he ripped off a portion of her nightgown, exposing her pasty and wrinkled legs. He gagged her with one strip of the cloth and bound her hands with the other. He removed the handcuffs and secured them back on his belt.

He lowered the lid over her as she writhed in the box, lashing her head back and forth and champing at the gag. He picked up the hammer and a handful of nails and began nailing it down. She screamed at every blow, as if the sound itself was hurting her.

He picked up the shovel and began scooping the loose dirt on top. As he had feared, the hole he had hastily dug was so shallow that only a thin covering of earth—about a foot— was needed to bring the grave level to the ground. He piled more dirt on top, the resulting mound looking oddly conspicuous. He gazed up through the trees at the starry sky that was in plain view between the trees. Could the mound be spotted from the sky?

He scattered the remaining dirt around and gathered up some loose branches and leaves, tossing them on top of the burial mound, hoping that they would serve as sufficient camouflage. He was running out of time.

When he was done, he trudged back to the car, dragging the shovel in the dirt, the hammer in his other hand. He was bone-weary. Tonight had been full of unforeseen complications, and there could be many more ahead. He could barely wait until he was safely airborne, California receding behind him, savoring the view as he looked down upon the flat farmlands of Kansas and Nebraska.

He looked at his watch: 5:15 a.m. Dawn was only minutes away.

He heaved the shovel and hammer into the trunk, letting them clatter beside the pick and nails, seconds later realizing how much noise he had made. He was tired, and when he got tired he knew that he made mistakes.

He got behind the wheel of the patrol car and started the engine, letting it idle for a few minutes before backing up and turning around. He hit the pavement of Evergreen Drive, and then he saw something that lifted the fatigue from his body with a tingling awareness.

There was a spotlight playing on the road ahead.

He immediately pulled over. He hadn't switched his headlights on yet. He threw the car into park and shut off the engine. From the sky he would appear to be just another empty car.

Slumping down in his seat, he pressed his face against the windshield and watched the helicopter up above, hovering in the night sky that had just barely begun to pale. Its searchlight was darting across houses, trees and roads. Apparently the service truck had been unable to find the break in the line. They had called upon the police to help out.

He lay down across the front seat just as the light flashed over his vehicle, lingering only for an instant like the beam from a curious UFO.

The noise of the chopper abated, heading up and away, the searchlight dancing on. He waited just a few minutes, and then sat up. If there was a police helicopter out looking for the source of the power outage, then there would be police cars as well. If one of them stopped him . . .

He looked up at the sky again. Light was coming.

He looked out his window at the nearest mailbox, using his flashlight to read the name and number printed on the side. The Robinsons. 12573 Evergreen.

He started his car, feeling that unfamiliar sensation of fear creep into his gut for the second time that evening. His higher power had temporarily abandoned him. If he was on his own, he would fare the best he could, and go out fighting.

He switched on his headlights and drove, eventually making the turn off Evergreen onto Miramar successfully, passing only early-morning commuters. They would remember nothing, their minds on bitter convenience store coffee and the chatter of drive-time deejays. He managed Miramar's curves well, and within five minutes he found himself at its base, signaling to turn left on Jicarita's central road.

The tension in his stomach began to lessen. He just might make it out of there after all.

A blue-and-white Jicarita police car passed him going in the opposite direction shortly after he turned onto the main road, and even in the faint blue light he could see the officer looking at him, eyes hard. He watched in his rearview mirror, but the police car disappeared around the turn.

He breathed a sigh of relief. The worst was behind him.

A pair of headlights appeared in his rearview mirror, speeding up to him so fast that he pulled over to the shoulder in order to let the other car pass.

It didn't. Red and blue lights exploded from the roof, illuminating the blue and white colors of the police squad car.

He heard a faint high-pitched whine inside his head as his blood went zinging through his arteries. The fight-or-flight syndrome was taking hold.

He got out of his car and met the officer halfway. He didn't want him looking into the back seat. He'd see dirt. Then he might ask to open the trunk. Then Lewis might have to club him to the ground and shoot him.

"Morning," the police officer said.

"It's certainly an early one."

"You on your way somewhere?"

"Back into town."

"Can I see some identification, please?"

"Certainly," Lewis said, reaching into his back pocket—slowly so as not to alarm the other man. He flipped his wallet open and withdrew his fake driver's license and his photo ID card that he used on the job.

"Acton Security Systems," the cop said, reading the card by flashlight. "Frank B. Lewis."

"That's me."

"Don't think I've seen anyone from Acton out here before."

"I wouldn't know the last time we did a regular patrol."

"What brings you out here tonight?"

"Got a call from an old customer. Said his home alarm had gone dead. We install home security as well as patrol, you know, and we have a year's service agreement we tack on to that. Wanted someone out here right now, so the dispatcher pulled me off my shift and sent me out to check into it, and turns out nothing in his whole house works! There seems to be some kind of power failure or something."

"We just found the break."

"Well, I didn't know for sure, but he said he'd call us when the power was back on and let us know if there was any problem." He fingered his dirty uniform. "Had me crawling out and around in the dirt for an hour, trying to fix the damn thing by flashlight."

"Who did you get the call from?"

"The Robinsons. Up on Evergreen." If he spit out the exact address, that might prove to be too much ready information.

The officer nodded, apparently satisfied. Lewis could sense the other man relaxing his guard. He handed Lewis back his license and ID. "The reason that I stopped you," he said, "is that the power company reported that the break looked like it was deliberate."

"You mean like sabotage?"

"Something like that. Vandalism, maybe. So we're checking out every suspicious vehicle, and..." He smiled humorlessly. "I thought you fit the bill."

"Well, we're both paid to be suspicious."

The cop nodded, and Lewis sensed the faint odor of condescension in the air. Cops regarded security guards as little better than crosswalk guards carrying guns.

"Okay," he said. "You can go."

Lewis grinned broadly. "Okay." The cop was six inches shorter than he was, and had not built up his body as much as he could have. Lewis could have killed him with one hand.

The cop got in his car, switched his lights off, pulled a U-turn in the middle of the road and sped off back up the canyon. Lewis watched him go, edging out onto the highway, heading toward the coast.

He was going back to his apartment. A quick change of clothes there, and he would depart for the airport. His flight out of LAX was not until five o'clock that afternoon. He had chosen the later time to allow for delays.

Still, he did not feel easy. Perhaps it was because he had envisioned this final night so many times, confronting Mary Sullivan again after all these years, revealing to her the horrifying truth so that she would go to her death knowing the horror of what she had done.

He should have done it. As he lowered the casket over her, he should have leaned his face next to hers, close enough so she could see his green eyes, his freckled skin, his red hair.

But he hadn't done it. Maybe the shock of the power cable had addled his senses so much that it was all he could do to accomplish the task at hand, paying no mind to any melodramatic flourishes. What would he have been able to tell her, anyway, that she would have believed?

The truth.

MARY SULLIVAN WAS DYING.

She could feel her breath running short and rapid, her toes so chilled that she wasn't sure she could feel them anymore. Dirt seeped through the cracks in the coffin that imprisoned her and clogged her eyes, nose and mouth, causing her to cough and splutter, using her meager supply of oxygen all the faster.

She was not going to live to see the day, she knew that.

The poor air would leave her with only a few more minutes of clear thought. Then, most likely, the stress on her system would trigger another attack, much like the one she had had when Dr. Stratton and Annette had visited her the day before. She had felt confusion and sorrow descend over her, masking all rationality. Her medication had cleared her mind, leaving her weeping with shame when she realized what kind of display she had put on for her daughter. She had slept fitfully, until the knock on her door.

She had been terrified as she rode, bouncing, in the trunk of the security car. The only time it had stopped she had cried for help, and then pleaded with her captor. When he had shut off the car's engine, she had used the time to explore the inside of the trunk. She had found the latch, felt it and tried to find some way to spring it. Before she succeeded, he had returned, fired the car up and then the car had bounced over rough road again, leaving her bruised and shaken.

When they stopped again, she had tried once more. She searched the interior, feeling around in the dark for something, anything that could be used as a tool.

She had found a nail in the spare tire compartment.

Twisting back around, she had wedged it in the latch mechanism of the trunk, trying to find the spring. She thought she had caught it, pressed and then felt the nail slip out of her hands. She had spent precious minutes groping for it with her hands manacled together, then trying again.

It had worked.

With a click and a hiss, she had watched the trunk lid swing up, expecting her kidnapper to rush over and slam it back down within seconds. That had not happened.

She had eased herself out and onto the cold ground, exhilarating in her freedom, the nail clenched in her fist. She ran ahead, searching for a house, a car or just some lights. Then she had watched the flashlight beam probing the asphalt, and he had caught up with her, overpowering her last vain attempt at a struggle.

He had bound and gagged her, shoving her into the coffin in the dirt. She knew she was going to die, just like Gretchen, the daughter she had never really known. She knew that there was a good possibility that she would be found. Her body and the wooden box that held it would be scrutinized for clues, the slightest one moving the investigation forward by quantum leaps.

It was too late to save herself, but perhaps she could save Annette—make up for all the lost years that lay between.

She opened her right fist. She had kept it tight and closed even while he had opened the handcuffs and tied her wrists with cloth torn from her own nightgown.

She still had the nail.

Shivering, she lifted her hands above her. Even though her fingers were less than an inch from her face, all she saw was darkness. She kept them open and wide anyway, trying to see with her mind's eye.

She would leave a message. She might only have the strength to write one word. It would be faint, the letters formed by scratches made in the dark by a dying woman who was remembered as half-crazy by the last people who talked to her.

Her murderer was miles away by now. He thought he would escape a free man, cloaked in the safety of the Larkin family curse. She had always known she might meet her end this way. The true horror had lain in who the banshee's instrument might be.

But he was just a man, and men could be undone. He had given her the knowledge she needed to turn his deeds against him, and he was not even aware of it. All she needed to do was to let the secret survive her.

She had seen his face. She knew who he was.

CHAPTER SIX

IT WAS ALMOST DAWN.

John had been sitting in a corner chair diagonal to Annette's bed for two hours, ever since she had woken up in a screaming panic. Since then, he had comforted her, assuring her that it was only her imagination. Within just a few minutes, the effects of the nightmare had faded and she was left only mildly spooked. Still, it had taken his promise that he would sit in this chair until it was light to get her to try to go back to sleep.

She had drifted off again, but he hadn't. He'd stayed awake, watching her chest rise and fall, the thin linens brushing against her skin. When she stirred and turned over, seeking a more comfortable position, it made John feel something he thought he had forgotten how to feel.

Something was going on here that had nothing to do with his memories of Gretchen or Mary Sullivan's prophecy of doom.

He was attracted to Annette. He wanted to walk over, pull back the sheets and have her turn her face and body to him, blinking back sleep, unafraid of the boldness of the gesture, welcoming his presence next to her.

But this was real life, not a book or a movie, he told himself. Women who had sheets pulled back from them in the middle of the night by men they didn't really know screamed in absolute terror. Period. Then they called the police.

So John contented himself with sitting and looking around the room. He tried to doze off a few times, but jerked himself awake with a stiff neck. He noticed the first signs of sunrise outside....

"John?"

He started. Her voice was soft, but still the loudest sound he'd heard in hours.

"Yes?"

"Are you awake?"

He nodded. Then, realizing she probably couldn't see him, said, "Yes."

She sat up, holding the covers against her shoulders. "Did I fall asleep?"

"Yes. I think so."

She yawned and blinked.

"Can I get you anything?" he asked.

"No... actually, a glass of water..."

He stood. "I'll be right back."

When he came back from the kitchen she had put her robe on, and was sitting on the side of the bed. He handed her the glass of water. "Thank you."

"Sure." He sat back down in his chair.

She drank slowly, washing the bad taste out of her mouth. "That was some bad dream I had."

"They can seem very real."

She finished her water and set the glass down. "Do you think ... there could be more to it than that?"

"What do you mean?"

"This stuff about a family banshee... I told you that I'd been having regular nightmares for the past month or so."

"Yes."

"Something moaning outside my window. The most haunting sound you can possibly imagine."

"You told me. Do you think there was anything to them?"

"I wasn't sure at the time, because... It's just that whenever I woke up I had the feeling that someone was trying to get to me—a premonition that wouldn't go away, even in daylight. That's why I was so cautious about meeting you."

"Makes sense."

"This nightmare last night had the same feeling to it. It was just so much more explicit. But it was still part of the same set of recurring dreams." She gazed out the window, the predawn glow making her face shine with blue light. "It's just...I was thinking...perhaps it's possible for members of the same family to have the same recurring dream, whether they're in touch with one another or not." She looked at him. "You're a doctor. Did you ever hear of that happening?"

"No. But anything's possible, Annette."

She traced the rim of the water glass with her finger, an action John found distinctly erotic. "Do you think dreams have meaning?"

"Sometimes."

"Have you ever had dreams where you thought you were being...*shown* something?"

"Shown?"

"Like there was no other way for you to know it. Like some dormant method of sensory input came alive during the state of sleep and was open to suggestions from...anything. And that input found its way into your dreams. Have you ever had an experience like that?"

John thought for a moment. Honesty was a powerful tool. "Yes," he said.

"You have?" She was very attentive. "What happened?"

It was John's turn to look out the window. "It's a long story."

"Please. Tell me."

"No, really..."

"It would even the score. I hardly know anything about you, but you know so much about me." She was looking at him. "I'd like to hear."

"My last job..." He stopped, then started again. "The day before I met you, I quit my job. I was a physician at a family medical center in Jicarita. The fuss that the discovery of...Gretchen...caused...was enough for someone to try and get me fired. Except I found out that they were planning to fire me anyway, so they wouldn't have to make me a partner in the medical center. So I quit.''

"Are you going to sue?"

John was startled. "Well, I don't know. I hadn't thought about it.''

"You could sue them for two months wages, I bet. Triple damages. Sounds to me like you've got a case.''

"I've never sued anybody before.''

"I've done it. I sued my last two employers for pulling shit just like that. That's how I got the money to start my gallery.'' She shook her head. "Don't just walk away. They screwed you. Screw 'em back. They need to pay up.''

John laughed.

"What's so funny?''

"You sound so hard-nosed.''

"Hey, I haven't kept this place open for a year and a half by selling Girl Scout cookies. If you don't learn how to wheel and deal in this world, it'll run right over you.''

John wondered what had happened to the woman who had been terrified of a bad dream and had asked him to stay in the room with her until it was light. She was probably still in there, somewhere under the sheets.

"Anyway, please, go on with your story.''

"Well, like I said, I quit this job. I'd worked there for six months. My job before that...I was working for the county.''

"What did you do?''

"I was a forensic pathologist.''

"What's that?''

"A coroner.''

"You mean...one of those guys who does autopsies?''

"Well, there's a lot more to it than that....''

"I always thought that that would be very interesting.''

John was used to a less enthusiastic reaction. He'd seen people take a step back, look at the hand that had just shaken his or wrinkle their noses as though they had just smelled formaldehyde. Rarely did he hear from a layperson that his chosen specialty was *fascinating*. Maybe he wasn't doing too bad here, he thought.

"It was. I liked it. But...I let some things get to me, and...I started to drink and use on the job."

"Use?"

"Cocaine."

She made a face. "Do doctors do that?"

"More than you might think."

"I guess. They're under a lot of pressure, aren't they?"

"Just being human puts you under a lot of pressure. Everyone is highly stressed these days. You start making excuses for yourself like 'I'm a doctor, I can handle it,' and that's just the first part of a very dangerous process."

"I see."

"To make a long story shorter, I got caught. My boss told me I had to go."

"Oh."

"So I went home and I started on a binge that was still going three days later: drinking, snorting coke, smoking dope...the works."

"You did that for *three days*?"

John nodded. "Drugs and alcohol had gotten me fired and I still didn't see the damage they were doing."

"Didn't you pass out?"

"No. I just did more blow."

"I've done cocaine once in my whole life," Annette said. "That was at a party. I threw up and didn't sleep all night long."

"Your body was trying to tell you something."

"I listened."

"So there I was..." John painted the scene for her, knowing it could never be as vivid as the one in his mind.

HE WAS SITTING on the edge of his bed in front of the television set, channel changer in one hand, straw in the other. He had his wall mirror balanced across his lap, the one that had a Jack Daniel's label printed on its reflective surface. He had been there for the past twelve hours, having made his last run to the corner convenience store for a fifth of tequila. The bottle had somehow been knocked over on the floor, its contents soaking into the carpet. He was switching back and forth between MTV and an old horror movie he had seen once before when he was in junior high. He'd begun to favor the movie. It had been a current release when he was in ninth grade. He remembered he went by himself because he didn't have any friends. He didn't even like horror movies. He had gone because he wanted to get out of the house, out of his father's sight, escape from his reality, even for a few lonely hours.

The memory made him sad. He was glad he had something handy that would make him happy again.

He bent down and fit his nose to the straw and the straw to the mirror, inhaling deeply as the finely ground crystals burned up his sinuses. He lifted his head, fingering his nostrils, numb with the effort, and wondered what time it was. The last time he had checked it was two-thirty. Was that a.m. or p.m.? he wondered. He didn't know. There weren't any windows in his bedroom. Shit, he thought, he didn't even know what day it was.

He knew what he'd do. He'd call the operator. The operator would tell him. He set the mirror aside, heart doing double time in his chest, and reached across the bed for the phone, grunting with the effort.

That was when it hit him. The pain blossomed in his chest, fingering out through his arm. He couldn't move; he couldn't breathe. It felt like someone was skewering him through his rib cage with a red-hot branding iron. Sweat broke out instantly across his forehead.

He was having a heart attack.

He slid to the floor, watching the whole scene as if it was being played on closed-circuit TV. He saw the phone fall to the floor on the opposite side of the bed. He saw the carpet swing up and smack him in the face. He saw the mirror with

the last remnants of coke and grass go tumbling, shattering
into pieces.

Oh God, oh God, oh God, he thought.

He was going to die.

He felt himself slip underneath the real world the way a
drowning swimmer goes down for the third time. He saw the
bedroom recede from view as if he were traveling backward
down a long dark tunnel, away from light and life and toward a realm where evil walked in myriad forms and death
reigned as the power supreme.

"HOW LONG DID YOU LIE there?" Annette asked.

"I don't know. Could have been minutes or hours. It
seemed like days."

"And you thought you saw something?"

"I didn't think I saw anything. I actually did see...things.
Whether they were real or hallucinations, I don't know.
Maybe too much reading about life-after-death experi-
ences."

"No, I don't think so."

"Anyway." He was silent for a long time. The sun was
coming up. "I've never told anyone that story before."

"I'm honored. I'm also glad."

"Why?"

"Now you won't think I'm a flake."

"For what?"

"I want to call Mary Sullivan again."

"What for?"

"To see if she's all right." She paused. "You have her
number."

John reached into his wallet. "You don't think—"

"I don't know what I think, John. But there are some
things I'd like to know."

He handed her the piece of paper he had written Mary
Sullivan's phone number on. Annette picked up the phone.
"Isn't it a little early to be calling?" he asked her.

"Why?"

"She might still be asleep."

"God, I hope so," she answered as she dialed.

After three attempts Annette finally hung up.

"How long did you let it ring?" John asked.

"Ten times each."

"What time is it?"

Annette looked at her alarm clock. It was quite light outside by now. "Six-fifteen." She looked back at John. "I can't think of anywhere she'd already be at this time of day, can you?"

"She could have disconnected her phone."

"Why?"

"I . . . don't know."

Annette shook her head. "She's not there."

"We don't know that for sure."

"Or she could be there but unable to come to the phone."

"You mean like injured or something?"

"I don't know."

"Well, there is one way we could find out."

"I'll get dressed."

THEY ARRIVED at Mary Sullivan's house just a little before ten. John parked his car at the curb. Little had changed in the eighteen hours since they had first been there.

"I don't see anything unusual going on," John said.

Annette unbuckled her seat belt and got out of the car. "I don't see anything going on at all." She slammed her door shut and waited for John to get out.

They walked together up to the front door. John knocked. He waited. There was no answer. He knocked again, louder. There was no answer.

Annette was trying to peer in through closed drapes. "There aren't any lights on inside," she said.

John rang the doorbell. Once. Twice. Three times.

"Let's go around to the side," Annette said.

John followed her as she walked quietly around to the side of the old brick house, stopping to look in windows that were covered with shades, checking the screens for any signs of disturbance. There were none. "No lights," she repeated.

They reached the backyard, enclosed by a wooden fence, the gate held shut by a bicycle lock and chain. With a glance in John's direction, Annette noisily clambered over the fence, catching part of her shirt on one of the top spires. "Not used to this sort of thing," she said, as John easily vaulted the barrier.

The backyard was overgrown with weeds and long grass, badly in need of a mowing. An orange tree had long since withered and died, its remaining fruit lying shriveled and black on the ground. All of the back windows were closed, showing no signs of foul play. Annette turned around, scanning the yard, and gasped.

"John," she said. "Look."

John looked.

From the back door to the gate, a faint trail could still be seen. The grass had been trampled down and broken, as if someone had recently walked through. The gate had been held shut with a padlock, but it had been cut open. The lock dangled by its severed hasp. The gate had been forced open, clearing a swath through the overgrowth. It stood agape, an indication of how hasty the departure had been.

John and Annette walked to the back door, blazing their own trail, grass and weeds brushing against the legs of their pants. The screen door was closed, but the door to the house was slightly ajar. Whoever had closed it hadn't thought it was necessary to make sure it was locked. John pressed against the door with his forearm, careful not to use his hands. The door swung open easily, inviting them into the dark interior of the house.

"Hello?" he called. "Mary? Mary Sullivan?"

There was no response. John's voice sounded muffled and flat.

"It's John Stratton," he called, "and your daughter—Annette."

Dust. Stillness. Old black-and-white photographs that hung on the wall.

He took a step inside. "Don't touch anything," John whispered to Annette. "We don't want to ruin any fingerprints."

Annette nodded.

John stepped inside. Annette followed, easing the screen door shut with her elbow.

They entered through the kitchen. Dirty dishes were left in the sink, comprising several days' worth of disorganized cooking and eating. Coffee circles and food crumbs were scattered across the countertop. It explained part of the musty odor John had smelled yesterday. The house had probably not been aired out in weeks.

No appliances were left on. Nothing was broken. The *Marie Celeste*, adrift at sea.

John walked into the living room, where he and Annette had sat and listened to Mary Sullivan tell her stories of prophecy and doom. With the drapes drawn, the furniture was shrouded in heavy shadow. Annette touched him on the shoulder and he involuntarily jumped.

"I'm going to check out the bedroom," she whispered.

John nodded. He watched her go.

He turned his attention to the front door and the inside windows. The front door was closed, not left casually ajar as the back door had been. The chain was unhooked. He squinted through the doorjamb in the slight space by the dead bolt. The dead bolt lock was still turned back. The door had been left unlocked. John hadn't even thought to try it when he was standing on the front porch ringing and knocking.

John thought back to how carefully Mary Sullivan had been about letting him and Annette in the day before. If anyone had entered Mary Sullivan's house last night, they had been let in freely.

"John," Annette called from the rear of the house. She was not whispering now. "John, come here."

John moved quickly toward the sound of Annette's voice. She was standing in the darkened bedroom, pointing to the unmade bed. "She was asleep," she said, "and something got her up."

John nodded. "The front door's unlocked. She apparently just left it open. It's possible she let someone in."

They stood in the midday dark, alone with their thoughts.

"I think we should call the police," John said, picking up Mary Sullivan's phone and dialing.

"Jicarita Police Department," said the voice at the other end after two rings.

"Captain Carl Rogers, please."

"Just a moment."

John held.

"Carl Rogers."

"Carl, it's John Stratton. I've got something here."

"Oh?"

John filled him in on the chain of events, from meeting Annette to Mary Sullivan's disappearance.

"You've been busy," Rogers said, impressed.

"I've had a run of good luck."

"I'll send someone down, but we'll have to call the West Covina PD. We don't have jurisdiction down there."

"I understand. I just wanted you to be the first to know."

"I appreciate it." John heard a noise in the background, someone trying to get Rogers's attention. "I've got to get off the phone now. We've got something happening up here that's got me running."

"What's happened?"

"Someone vandalized a power line, not too far from where Gretchen Seale was discovered."

"Vandalized? How?"

"They cut into it with a blunt instrument of some kind."

"Did it look deliberate or accidental?"

"I'm assuming it happened as a side effect. I think whoever did it was trying to do something else."

"Like what?"

"John, can we talk about this later? I have to go."

"What did it look like he was trying to do?"

Rogers sighed. "It looked like he was trying to bury something."

John pressed Rogers for details, but the police captain had gotten off the phone with a haste that John reserved only for solicitors trying to get him to subscribe to the *Herald-Examiner*. He still had many questions.

"What did he say?" Annette asked, breaking the silence.

"He's sending a car down, and they're putting in a call to the West Covina PD. We're to wait here." John realized he was mumbling. He didn't like being left outside of things. What if the patrolman had orders to take Annette back to the station so Rogers could ask her more questions, learning everything John already knew without having to bother with John himself? He liked Rogers, maybe even trusted the man, was certain that he was more than competent, but . . .

He took Annette's hand. "Let's go."

"Where?"

"Back to Jicarita."

"I thought we were supposed to wait here."

"They can ask their questions later."

She balked. "John, what's going on?"

"The man that killed your sister and may have already killed your mother could have been back in the canyon last night. If someone isn't careful, he's going to slip out of our hands, and you'll have to spend every minute in fear of your life until he's caught. Now do you want to come with me, or should I leave you here alone?"

It was an empty threat. He would never leave her there alone. He was playing on her fears. He wanted her to come with him. She was his ace card in this game of cat-and-mouse.

His shameless manipulation worked. "I'm coming with you," Annette said, and followed him out to the car.

She held on tight as John coaxed the Camaro to life, surging through the midday traffic all the way back to the canyon, taking Jicarita's turns and straightaways as though they were just annoying obstacles on the screen of a video game. They raced past John's house and down to the police station, raising a cloud of dust as John screeched the car into the police parking lot and shut off the engine.

Through the settling haze, John saw Rogers emerge from a side door, flanked by a patrolman, heading for a squad car. John opened his door, stood up and honked loudly. Rogers turned to look. When he recognized John, his face drew tight with anger. He met John halfway across the parking lot.

"I thought I'd told you to wait in West Covina for questioning."

"I'm not just some ordinary witness. I've been investigating this case as much as you have."

"Unofficially. That doesn't give you the right to leave the scene of a crime."

"But it doesn't give me the need to sit around and answer questions from one of your flunkies. As far as I can tell, I've made more progress on this matter than you." John's voice was rising. Annette hung back, watching the scene.

"You're not with the county anymore, Stratton. I did call Hardinger and ask him for a recommendation, and if it had been a wholehearted one I would have had you as a consultant on this case in no time."

Now John was hurt as well as angry: angry that Rogers had felt it necessary to check up on him, and hurt that the results hadn't been as sterling as he had hoped. "What did Hardinger say?" he asked, a trifle less loudly.

"The truth. That at one time you were the most promising doctor he had ever brought into the department. He told me your record was once unsurpassed."

"So what's your problem with that?"

"Your last three months on the job. Your results became spotty, your record-keeping careless and your performance inadequate."

The words stung. "You know the reason for that."

"Yes, I do."

"I'm clean, Rogers. I have been for months."

"I don't need any deadweight hanging around my neck."

"I found Gretchen Seale's sister," John said, finally introducing Annette. "I found her mother. I spoke to her yesterday. She said she thought Annette was already dead. She thought she herself was being saved for last. She had a theory as to the cause of Gretchen's death."

John hadn't told him everything over the phone. He'd kept something in reserve. Rogers was hooked. John knew he only had to reel him in.

"Why?" Rogers asked.

"She spoke of a family curse. A banshee. A spirit that wandered around and warned of the death of a family member."

"That's superstition, Stratton. That's nonsense."

"She says it's been happening. For the past five years, members of the Sullivan clan have been disappearing, one by one. None of them are ever found. You know what I think? I think they're hidden somewhere—just like Gretchen Seale was hidden and Mary Sullivan probably is hidden right now. If she's not dead already she will be soon."

"So what are you saying—that I should believe in this family curse?"

"No, but I think you should give it some credence. It could lead to the solution of this case. I don't think there's some vengeful spirit behind all of this any more than you do. I think there's another living, breathing person who *believes* in the banshee the same way that Mary Sullivan did—maybe strongly enough to kill for it."

Rogers said nothing. He was obviously thinking. John had gotten through to him. "A serial killer?" he said finally.

"Exactly. Except all of his victims are drawn from the same gene pool."

"But why?"

"I don't know."

Rogers was silent again. John waited. The moment was decisive, and he knew it. Rogers was deciding whether or not to let John act officially as a consultant on the case. He forced himself to say nothing, do nothing, let Rogers make up his own mind.

Rogers turned from John to the patrolman at his side. "John, this is Officer David Sacks. David, this is John Stratton."

The two men shook hands, John making sure his grip was the firmest. The officer was young and tall, not yet filled out.

"I began asking around to see if anyone on duty had seen anything peculiar last night, especially just before or just after the trouble with the power line. Turns out only David here had anything to report."

"What'd you see?" John asked.

Sacks cleared his throat, altering his manner. He had kept his hair at academy length and spoke to John as though he were an instructor of one of his classes.

"Around 4:30 a.m. I was headed east on state highway 35—Jicarita Canyon Boulevard—when I noticed a private security vehicle headed in the opposite direction. A few of the neighborhood groups employ private security, but all the ones that I'm aware of are located on the valley side. They're closer and can respond to an emergency faster than one from the city. Acton Security is headquartered in Culver City, with its closest office in West L.A.; I called directory assistance and got the address."

"I see," John said.

"So I turned around, switched on my lights and pulled the car over. The driver was a large fellow, about six foot six, with green eyes and reddish hair. I asked to see some ID and he showed me some. He said he was there following up on a call they got on a home alarm system. He'd been called out to repair it. I thought he checked out so I let him go, but after Captain Rogers mentioned that he was looking for something, I told him my story and we began to check out the details."

Rogers cut in. "The man said he was tending to an alarm at the Robinsons' up on Evergreen Drive. I followed up that lead. The Robinsons don't have a home alarm system, and have never heard of Acton Security Services."

"Did you get the license number of the vehicle?" John asked Sacks.

Sacks cleared his throat. "No."

"How about the car make and model?"

"No."

"Did you write down his name?" John couldn't keep all of the sarcasm out of his voice.

Sacks looked down at the ground. "No, sir. I thought he checked out at the time."

"David told me that he might remember the security guard's name if he heard it again," Rogers interjected. "So I called Acton and told them we were looking for a wayward guard of theirs, and the person there told me that the night dispatcher, a—" he consulted a notebook "—Mike Peterson, had said that one of the men on duty last night had not turned his car in. We got Peterson's address and phone number. I called, but the message on his answering machine says he's asleep. We were going over there now to question him."

"Did you get the name of the security guard?"

"Yes. We wanted to get his file, but that's going to take a warrant." Rogers consulted his notebook again. "His name is Frank B. Lewis."

MIKE HAD LEFT WORK at five that morning, weary and dragging. After midnight, when everyone had checked in to let him know if they were going to take their lunch break or not, he had locked the parking lot gate, set the alarm and unpacked his pocket one-hit bong, a dandy little water pipe that was just the thing to get him in the mood for the mid-night-to-dawn shift. Nestled together in his nylon back-pack was a six-pack of Jolt colas ("all the sugar and twice the caffeine"), a bag of Bar-B-Q potato chips, a microwave corndog—the kind he liked to munch cold—and half a pas-trami sandwich from the neighborhood deli.

Snack time.

He kept his folded bag of dope in the side pocket and within ten minutes he was blissfully wasted. Thirty minutes later, gorged on cheap fast food, his waistline thickened by another few centimeters, his eyesight blurred with sugar, his senses respectfully dulled, Mike dozed off. He dreamed that he was no longer Mike Peterson, the night manager and general geek slob of Acton Security Services, who was thirty-four years old and had yet to make more than ten dollars an hour at any one time in his life, but Mitchell Dane, the mysterious suspense novelist, who lived a se-cluded literary life somewhere in the Canadian woods, shipping his latest bestseller by Yukon pack mule to the nearest post office, where it was sent to New York and re-ceived there with wide-eyed wonder and declarations of ge-nius echoing off the hallowed halls of publishers' row. The news was brought to him by Helen Bradford, a bouncy blonde in tight shorts and T-shirt, who just happened to be the current Playmate of the Month. So impressed was she with her Great Dane—one of her pet names for him, along with Mad Genius and My Mister Stiff—that she immedi-ately undressed his muscular frame and begged him to make love to her right then and there.

Mike was awakened at 4:00 a.m. by Jackson, who pounded on the trailer door until he answered, stumbling from behind his desk, knocking over a half-empty can of Jolt that subsequently knocked over the bong, spilling var-ious rank liquids over the desk. Jackson, Lathrop and Hill-erman were all checking out and going home. Mike recorded their returns, noting that Lewis hadn't yet checked in. When he was finally done, he was so tired that he gathered up his paraphernalia and dumped it in the back seat of his car, weaving home in the early predawn traffic, aware only in some dim corner of his consciousness that Lewis—the huge cold man whose very presence made Mike nervous—had not checked back in.

Mike arrived at his one-room apartment, kicked his way through the scattered debris of empty fast-food cartons and open copies of *Twilight Zone* and *Night Cry* and flopped on the unmade unwashed sheets of his bed. He dozed off, once again back in the Canadian wilderness, bringing Miss August to yet another shattering orgasm that left her shaking and sweating.

This time he was awakened by a pounding on his apartment door. He stumbled out of bed and peered through the peephole. Three men, all strangers: one black, one white, one cop.

"Who is it?" he called through the door.

"Police," the black man replied.

Mike looked wildly around his apartment. Police. Did he have any pot out? Shit.

He opened the door just a crack. The black man raised his badge so Mike could see it plainly as he squinted against the bright morning sunlight. "Captain Carl Rogers, Jicarita Police Department. Are you Mike Peterson?"

"Yeah."

"I'd like to ask you a few questions."

"Uh…yeah…sure. I'll be right out." Mike left the door ajar as he pulled his jeans and T-shirt on, fumbling for a pair of sunglasses. He slipped outside, standing on the cold cement porch of his apartment in his bare feet. "What's up?" he said.

"This is Officer David Sacks and Dr. John Stratton." The other men barely nodded. "We're investigating the disappearance of one Frank B. Lewis, who was on duty last night at Acton Security Services at the same time you were serving as the company's night dispatcher."

"Yeah. So?"

"According to the morning dispatcher at the same office, Lewis did not check in at the end of his shift. Did you notice that?"

"Yeah."

"Did you think it was anything unusual?"

"Not really. I thought he'd been delayed and he'd return his car in the morning."

"I see. When was the last time you spoke to Frank B. Lewis—when he checked in the night before?"

"Yeah. No. I talked to him when he was going to take his lunch break."

"In person?"

"Over the radio."

"And when was that?"

"Around midnight."

"Around midnight or exactly at midnight?"

"I don't know for sure."

"And did you hear anything from him after that?"

"No. I radioed Barnes and told him to cover for him until he got back."

"Ken Barnes?"

"Yeah."

"And did Barnes check in?"

"Yes."

"On time?"

"Yes."

"Did he mention anything about Lewis never checking back in with him?"

"I think so. I had . . . I'd fallen asleep. It was hard to remember what anybody said."

"I see."

Mike's feet were getting cold. "So Lewis hasn't shown up yet?"

"No."

"Do you think something happened to him?"

"We don't know."

"Has he done anything wrong?"

"We don't know that, either. Do you have any idea where he might be, what he might be doing?"

"No."

"How long did you know Mr. Lewis?"

"I don't know. I was working at Acton when he started."

"Which was when?"

"About a year ago."

"Could you describe him for me?"

"Yeah. He's big. I mean really big. Like a pro ball player. About six-six. Red hair, going a little thin. Ruddy face. Green eyes. And he talked kind of weird."

"How do you mean?"

"When he started, he talked a little strange. He over-enunciated his words. Made him sound a little British."

"Did he still talk that way?"

"No. He lost whatever it was. I don't know if he was trying to overcome a speech impediment or an accent or what. I didn't ask him."

"Were you friendly with Mr. Lewis?"

"Nobody was friendly with him. We could all have just up and died for all he cared."

"How would you describe your relationship with him, both personal and professional?"

"They were one and the same. Very...terse. I didn't care for him at all. He acted like he was so much better than everybody else."

"Kept to himself a lot, then."

"Nothing but."

"Did he ever mention anything about his personal life or history—where he lived, where he had come from, anything like that?"

"No."

"Did he ever mention anything about his family?"

"No."

"Did he ever have any special plans that required his taking special nights off or long breaks on the job?"

"Not that I knew of. Maybe he did, but it wasn't anything that I would remember. Look, you can find out a lot of this stuff at the office. They've got his home address, his résumé, even a Polaroid picture of him on file."

"We tried to get that information. The dispatcher said it was company policy not to divulge personnel files without a warrant. We've got to go back and appear before a judge to get one signed."

"That's too bad."

"So we'll get it. It just will take another few hours. Meanwhile, Frank B. Lewis could be on his way to Mexico for all we know."

"Think he's really done something rotten, eh?"

"He might have."

"Is he a suspect in some case?"

"We're not at liberty to say."

Mike Peterson looked at the black cop, reading between the lines. This guy was sending him signals, he knew. He was really saying: *We need your help, son. The lives of innocent citizens depend upon your secret and valuable skills.*

Peterson shifted his weight, a gesture that was almost coy in its execution. "I can get his file for you. I've got access. I've got a key."

"But the morning dispatcher..."

"The morning dispatcher won't be a problem." Mike smiled. Mitchell Dane was taking control. "You guys just stay cool and do what I tell you, and within half an hour you'll have Lewis's file in your hands."

"Look, we don't want you to lose your job."

"Forget my job." He turned away from them, opening his door. "Let me get my shoes."

TRUE TO HIS WORD, Mike Peterson was able to retrieve the file from Acton's trailer office within thirty minutes. He made John, Rogers and Officer Sacks wait in the squad car just around the corner while he got out and walked the half

block remaining to the fenced car yard and entered the office trailer.

John, for one, was relieved to have Mike out of the car.
He had had to share the back seat with the sweaty, smelly
man who talked nonstop.

John had left Annette at the police station, with the keys
to his car and house along with directions. "I think I'll just
stay here," she had said. "I'll probably feel safer." John
said he understood; he just wanted her to have someplace to
feel welcome. She was welcome to stay with him until this
whole mess was over. She had smiled at him gratefully and
told him he was being very kind.

It wasn't just kindness. John knew he was in the unre-
lenting grip of sexual infatuation. Perhaps if he returned
with her tormentor handcuffed, his jacket thrown over his
head as he and Rogers rushed the criminal inside, she would
realize that the kind, gentle Dr. Stratton she had known only
a few days was actually a strong, handsome, charming,
throbbing love machine who wanted nothing more than to
put a smile on her face and a spring in her step.

I have no strength when it comes to women, John
thought. None whatsoever.

Mike reappeared within minutes, manila folder tucked
under one flabby arm. He was walking so fast his stomach
and chest jiggled and bounced under his tight white T-shirt.

He heaved into the back seat, sending a strong whiff that
caused John to turn his head. "Here you are, gentlemen,"
Mike said, handing the file over the seat to Rogers.

John leaned forward to look over Rogers's shoulder as the
captain opened the file and perused its contents.

"What do you think?" Mike said, anxious for some sign
of approval from the outside world. "What do you think,
huh?"

"Very impressive," Rogers said.

Clipped to the inside of the manila folder was an impos-
ing Polaroid shot of Lewis. There was a strong red tinge to

the photograph—someone forgot to remove the Type A filter—making Lewis's hair redder than it actually was.

Rogers read the vital statistics aloud. "Six feet, six-and-a-half inches, 280 pounds. Home address: 1505 South Shenandoah, apartment number 3. That's just off Pico. Go for it, David."

Sacks hit the accelerator, Rogers leaned over the back seat and looked at Mike.

"Would you be willing to identify this man for us?"

"You mean, like in a lineup or something like that?"

"Something like that. If he's out wandering around in public we may need you to help us find him."

Mike hesitated only a second. "Sure. Be glad to. Can my safety be guaranteed?"

"Of course."

"Then let's do it."

Rogers turned back to face the front, picking up the radio microphone, asking for a check on Lewis's driver's license number, to see if the man had a record.

There was a short pause, and then the reply came back, so garbled that John couldn't understand it. "What'd they say?"

"Says he came up with nothing. That license isn't real." He looked at Officer Sacks. "Faster, David. We're cops. We can break the law."

ON THEIR WAY to Lewis's apartment, the call came in that the warrant to search the offices of Acton Security Services had been signed by the judge. Rogers radioed back and asked for the place to be changed to Lewis's residence and for backup officers to meet them there with the warrant.

Sacks turned on the siren and the lights, slowing only at stoplights.

"What is it?" Mike asked. "What's going on?"

"When we get our warrant," Rogers said, "we'll probably pay Mr. Lewis a surprise visit."

"Listen, I feel it's only fair to warn you guys that Acton Security officers are armed. They have to turn their pieces back in at the end of the night, but since Lewis didn't come back..."

"We're well aware of that possibility, Mike. Thank you, though."

By radio Rogers coordinated his efforts with those of the LAPD, who agreed to supply another backup unit.

The Jicarita police car was the first to arrive. Sacks killed the lights and siren for a slow cruise by. The apartment on Shenandoah was on the second story of a run-down four-unit building. Sacks drove the car around back. The LAPD unit radioed and said they were within a block, and Rogers told them to cover the front, they were going to have to wait a little bit for the warrant.

They sat there for twenty minutes. No one went in or out of the building.

The backup from Jicarita arrived, and the officer at the wheel handed Rogers the signed warrant. Rogers switched to walkie-talkie, telling the LAPD officers they would all meet in front, except for one of the other Jicarita cops, who would cover the back. John followed Rogers but brought up the rear, not wanting to be at the front of the action. Mike said he would stay in the car.

Rogers, Sacks, John and a Sergeant Griffin met the LAPD team in front where Rogers outlined a basic plan. He would lead the bust, with Sacks at his side. LAPD was to follow immediately. Griffin was to cover.

Rogers pounded on the door. "Police!" he yelled. "Open up."

There was no response.

Rogers braced himself against the upper balcony railing and kicked the door in, shearing away several inches of wooden frame. He spun to the side, flattening himself against the wall in case someone started shooting.

Nothing happened.

Rogers wheeled around into the three-point stance, gun ready. Nothing moved.

Rogers raised his gun and stepped inside. Sacks and the others followed, John last of all.

The apartment was dark and empty, furnished cheaply and with no regard to comfort. The shades were drawn, the blinds closed. No one was home.

There was a bedroom, a bathroom, a living room and a kitchenette. No television. Lots of books, mostly historical nonfiction.

Rogers walked up to John with a plain white envelope. "Found this on the kitchen table." He shook it out on the floor. A key bounced on the green-brown carpet. Rogers speared it with a pencil and handled it with a handkerchief. "This most likely goes there," he said, nodding at the front door.

John turned the envelope over, finding a note on the back, written in large, coarse script.

Dear Mrs. Norton:
Sorry I can't give you this in person, but an emergency has called me out of town for a while. I can't say when I'll be back.

Sincerely,
Frank Lewis
Apartment No. 3

"He's skipped town," John said.

"Or he wants someone to think he has," Rogers replied.

John handed the envelope back to Rogers. "I wonder where home is."

"Or how he's getting there."

The remark gave John an idea. He almost spoke up, telling Rogers first, but he wanted to see how far he could go on his own. He wandered away from the captain, pretending to be interested in the apparently meaningless surroundings of Lewis's apartment.

Sacks returned from the bedroom. "Closet's been cleaned out. Sheets are still on the bed, though."

John nodded thoughtfully, as if the information was meant for his benefit, too, and kept up his meandering until he found himself in the kitchen, out of sight of the others. Then he ducked his head and opened the door beneath the sink. Stained newspapers were laid down beneath the pipes to catch any stray debris, but all that was there was an empty and scuffed yellow plastic trash can and some leftover white plastic liners.

Lewis had taken the garbage out before he left.

Rogers was calling in on his radio for a fingerprint team to come over, and he wanted a photographer to take some pictures. He also wanted an APB out on the security vehicle. He told Sacks to remind him that they needed to get the car's license number from the security company.

John wandered outside, pretending there was really nothing to see inside and that he was going to go back to the patrol car just to kill time. He walked around the corner of the building, picking up speed as he disappeared from sight of the police.

Mike was still sitting in the patrol car, and he immediately began to pepper John with questions. "What's going on in there? Did they find him? Is he still on the loose?" he asked.

John waved him away. "Just a minute."

He walked over to the garbage cans and began sifting through the leaking paper and plastic bags. He heard the patrol car door slam behind him and smelled Mike before he heard him.

"What are you doing?"

"What does it look like I'm doing?"

"Why are you going through the garbage?"

"I want to see what your friend Lewis threw away just before he left."

"So he left? He's not there?"

"No."

"Where'd he go?"

"I don't know. Mike, I need you to do me a favor."

"Sure."

"Stop talking for a minute, will you?"

Mike took a step back. "Yeah. Sure. Just asking, that's all. You don't have to get mad."

I said shut *up*, John thought viciously as he stuck his hand deep into one of the metal trash cans and came up with a handful of ooze. There was nothing in there but paper bags, plastic bags from the grocery and large green garden waste bags. He was looking for the medium-size white variety that he'd seen under Lewis's sink.

He went on to the next metal can.

He heard the crunch of hard shoes on gravel before he heard Rogers's voice. "Going through the neighbors' garbage?"

John looked up at him, not stopping. "Believe me, I've had my hands in worse."

"Looking for something in particular?"

"Yeah. The last thing Lewis threw away."

"What do you think it was?"

"I don't know. Ah-hah!" He pulled a medium-size white plastic bag out of the metal can and set it on the ground. Tearing it open, he spilled out its contents. Rogers hunched down on the ground with John, and the two of them began to sift through the refuse.

"What exactly are you looking for?" Rogers repeated.

"I don't know," John replied. "First, some proof that this stuff was his."

"Here's a phone bill," Rogers said, holding a piece of paper up to the light. "It's his, all right."

"That could be important."

"Uh-huh." Rogers pocketed the find.

"Well, what have we here?" John found an opened envelope with the name of a travel agency on the outside. "No

postmark. He must have picked it up from them personally." John opened the envelope. Inside there was a com-
puter-printed voucher, showing that Frank B. Lewis had
paid $758.00 two weeks ago for a one-way ticket on an air-
line John had never flown.

"Aer Lingus," Rogers read aloud, mispronouncing the
name. "What kind of name is that?"

"It's Gaelic, I think," John replied.

"Who are they?"

"An airline company."

"Where do they fly?"

"Ireland."

CHAPTER SEVEN

As CARL ROGERS and John Stratton rustled through yesterday's garbage, Frank B. Lewis stood in line at the Edmund G. Brown, Jr. International Air Terminal of Los Angeles International Airport, blissfully ignorant of his pursuers.

After dumping the nails, hammer, pick and shovel in a nearby dumpster, he had left the Acton Security patrol car in the terminal parking lot, tucked in a concrete corner where it was not too conspicuous. The keys were still in his pocket. He had stuffed his uniform and gun in a locker and thrown the locker key into a trash can. He had thought of tossing the car keys in after it, but something made him decide to hang on to them for a little while longer.

His ticket had been purchased in advance through a travel agency and paid for in cash. All he had to do now was show his ticket at gate 11 and he would be able to board his flight within the hour. By the end of this day but before the beginning of the next one, he would be back home in Ireland.

Green hills. Muggy meadows. Brisk ocean breezes. Amber pints in smoky pubs. Peat cut fresh from the bog. Misty valleys at sunrise. Cowbells clanking in the afternoon.

He was carrying all his luggage with him, wanting to risk nothing in the confusion of overseas freight. His garment bag was doubled up, held together by clasps and hung by a strap on one shoulder. In his other hand he had a blue nylon carryon bag stuffed with toiletries.

He was standing in line at the security checkpoint, where X-ray machines and metal detectors scanned all persons passing beyond that point for weapons either in their luggage or on their person. Lewis had all of his change and the car keys in one pocket, where he would be able to reach them easily. He watched as people who set off the metal detector were told to empty their pockets into a small plastic tray and then walk through again while one of the four uniformed security guards carried the tray to the other side of the barrier where the passenger would retrieve his personal belongings.

Lewis watched and waited for his turn, listening to the speaker overhead for any news of his flight. He had already checked its status at the ticket counter. It was on time.

As the person ahead of him stepped through the metal detector, Lewis slung his garment bag onto the conveyor belt that fed luggage through the X-ray machine. He unfastened its clasps, opened it up and laid it out flat on the belt, watching it slide out of sight. He sent the carryon bag after it, then he scooped his change and keys out of his pocket and put them on one of half a dozen white plastic trays.

The security guard who took the change and carried it around the detector was a heavyset black woman. Another female guard—who could have been her sister—sat behind the X-ray monitor, one hand on the speed control for the conveyor belt, stopping and starting it as she examined the contents of bag after bag. Two male security guards, one white, one Hispanic, stood with their arms folded on the other side, chatting with each other, laughing over some light joke. The Hispanic one had stopped the last passenger, who had set off the metal detector, politely asking him to dump his change and step through again.

Lewis walked through the frame of the metal detector, ducking his head slightly. He stepped over to the end of the belt, where luggage was dumped on top of an angled metal surface. He found his garment bag, refastened its two ends together and slung it over one shoulder. After scooping up his change and keys he dropped them in one pocket.

"Would you step away from the conveyor belt, please?"

Lewis wasn't sure where the voice was coming from, or even if it was directed at him. He turned around slowly. It was the Hispanic security guard who had spoken to him. Both he and his white counterpart had stepped forward, hands on their holsters, expressions serious. They were trying to keep the matter quiet for now.

"What's the matter, fellas?" Lewis asked.

"Just step away from the conveyor belt, please." The Hispanic guard motioned with his hand—the one that wasn't resting on the butt of his revolver.

Lewis glanced at the other passengers, who were still waiting in line, walking through the metal detector, dropping their change into plastic trays. If he did not move, there would be a slowdown. He would attract even more attention to himself. The two female security guards were looking back at Lewis. The one who had carried his change over the barrier was speaking into a phone. The one behind the X-ray monitor was opening a door just below the television screen, and Lewis watched as she removed his blue nylon carryon bag. She handed it to the white guard.

The Hispanic guard motioned again. "Over here."

Lewis edged his way around the barrier, toward the far wall and a portable table. The Hispanic guard, whose name tag read H. Gomez, escorted Lewis there. The white guard— M. Anderson—brought the bag over, setting it on the table in front of Lewis. Lewis let his garment bag slip off his shoulder and onto the floor.

"Do you recognize this bag, sir?" Gomez asked.

"Yes," Lewis replied.

"Is it in fact your bag?"

"Yes."

"Would you please open it?"

"Of course." Lewis reached for the zipper, moving slowly and deliberately, so as not to cause these men any alarm. He noticed they still had their hands on their holsters.

"Would you remove the contents and place them on the table?"

"Certainly." He pulled out his toilet items one by one, setting them on the table in neat order: toothbrush, toothpaste, socks, a change of underwear, deodorant, shaving mug and brush, soap, straight razor...

Gomez turned to Anderson. "Get Betty, will you?" Anderson nodded and left. Betty was the woman who operated the conveyor belt that ran underneath the X-ray machine. Anderson filled in for her while she consulted with Gomez.

Lewis finished unloading his bag. He set it to the side and waited patiently. If they asked to see his passport, that could mean trouble, for if they examined it too closely, they might detect signs of forgery. Then arrest and detention. He would have to act before then. He was glad he still had the keys to the patrol car. He might need them. He could take Gomez by force, whip the man's gun out of the holster and hold him hostage while he made his way out of the terminal.

"See anything?" Gomez asked.

Betty looked. "This," she said, and pointed at the straight razor.

Gomez picked up the straight razor and opened it, its long thin blade unfolding from the pearl handle. He tested its sharpness with his thumb.

"I use that to shave with," Lewis volunteered. "Electric razors make my skin break out and the disposable blades nick me badly." He put a hand to his face, rubbing it. "I have a very sensitive complexion."

Gomez looked at him. "This could be classified as a weapon."

"It isn't. I have my shaving mug and cream here—" he pointed to them "—and I use this brush to stir it up. I guess I'm kind of an old-fashioned guy."

Gomez turned the blade over and examined it. He ran a finger along the dull edge to see what he came up with. Little red whiskers. Some crusted remains of foam. Lewis was telling the truth.

Gomez folded up the razor and set it down on the table. "All right. You can pack it up. You're free to go."

"Thank you," Lewis said, immediately throwing his possessions back into the bag.

"Sorry for the delay."

"Oh, it's perfectly understandable."

"Hope you enjoy your flight."

"I will." Lewis zipped up his bag, heaved his garment bag onto his shoulder and walked off with a final nod to Anderson.

He was heading straight for the bar. He felt like a drink.

OFFICER DAVID SACKS HAD the lights and the siren on, as he'd had when he was driving toward Frank Lewis's apartment, but his driving style had been considerably modified. The guy may not be much for remembering details, John thought, lurching against Mike Peterson's pliant frame as the squad car rounded a curve down South La Cienega, but he sure makes up for it in the chase-and-pursuit department.

Rogers had checked by phone: Aer Lingus only flew in and out of LAX. He radioed ahead to alert airport security to anyone fitting Lewis's description. He was on his way with a picture. Mike piped up and said that they should be on the lookout for the car, too, as Lewis might no longer be wearing an Acton Security uniform. He supplied Rogers with a description of the Acton logo and the uniform, his voice pitched higher in his excitement. Rogers relayed the information to the airport.

A portion of La Cienega between the airport and the city was relatively free of lights and cross traffic, and Sacks was making the most of it. John would like to see what the officer would do behind the wheel of a Z-28.

There was a garbled bit of static, and Rogers immediately snatched up the mike. "Repeat that?"

He listened to a long stream of a clipped radio transmission that John could catch only a few words of. "Tell them to hold off any search until I get there." He hung up the mike and turned his head to talk to John.

"They found the car, parked in the lot in front of the international terminal. He's got to be in there somewhere."

Mike gulped.

"David," Rogers said, "can't you make this car move a little faster?"

"Yes, *sir*."

LEWIS WAS SITTING in the bar nearest gate 11. His flight would not be ready for boarding for another forty-five minutes. He had already checked in at the gate and gotten a boarding pass from the young female clerk. All he had to do was wait. He sipped a Bushmill's, his first in many weeks.

He had fantasized about this moment, dreamed of it for years, but now that it was here it seemed surprisingly hollow. He'd thought he would feel vindicated, the great burden of responsibility that he had borne for so long lifted from his shoulders forever, but instead he was experiencing a kind of dread—as if something unforeseen was about to happen.

He was seated at the end of the bar that was the farthest from the door. Light was low, but he was afforded an expansive view of not only the terminal but, through the tavern's windows, of the corridor leading back toward the security checkpoint.

That had been a close one, he thought. If he had been forced to act, he would have had to think very fast and trust his instincts a great deal to get him out of the situation alive and free. It had not even occurred to him that a straight razor in a carryon bag would cause any fuss when X-rayed. He had thought he'd foreseen every possible problem that could develop. The incident left him feeling shaky and less than confident. He only wanted to hide out in there and not let any more trouble find him.

He didn't trust that it was all over for him yet. He knew there was something else lurking out there, waiting for him to make a mistake.

The bar was less than half-full. Only a dozen or so fellow travelers were sitting at small tables positioned around the dimly lit room. He was the only one seated at the bar. The bartender, a portly fellow with a beard and thinning hair, asked Lewis if he wanted a refill.

He saw the trio of security guards walk by the bar briskly, one of them peeling off to duck into the men's rest room just directly across from the bar's entrance. The other two security guards headed for the terminal area, splitting up yet again, one of them heading straight for gate 11.

Lewis felt his stomach sink and burn, the whiskey the only thing keeping the blood in his face.

The guard heading for gate 11 was Gomez, the one who had asked him to step away from the conveyor belt.

Why was he headed for gate 11? What was he looking for?

The other guard emerged from the men's rest room, and Lewis felt his heart lurch again.

Anderson. The only other one who had gotten a good look at him.

Lewis watched him pluck his walkie-talkie off his hip, mutter something into it, listen for a reply and then clip it back onto his belt.

Then he headed straight for the bar.

Lewis felt fear creep up behind him.

There was a distance of perhaps fifty feet between himself and Anderson, and Anderson was closing the gap in a brisk, purposeful stride. There was no way that the guard could see him yet, sitting in the far shadows of the bar. But there was only one way in or out of the bar. He could not leave without being seen.

He looked to his right. The nearest table was empty. Beyond that were locked windows that looked out over the terminal area.

He looked to his left. There was a door at the end of a short corridor. Perhaps a storage room. On one wall of the corridor was a pay phone.

Anderson was perhaps fifteen feet away from entering the bar. The bartender had seen him and was watching him approach.

Now was his only chance.

Lewis slid off his stool, silently picking up his luggage, ducking into the small corridor as if he were about to make a phone call. Instead, he tried the handle on the door.

It was open. It led into a small pantry, barely big enough for him to fit into, lined with bottles of whiskey, jars of cherries and cases of warm bottled beer. The door had no handle on the inside. He bent down and pulled it shut with his fingers. He noticed that as the door shut, the overhead light went out.

He stayed inside for five minutes, sweat trickling down his face in the darkness. He unzipped his carryon bag and brought out the straight razor, feeling it swing open in the darkness. He had never thought of using it as a weapon before—he had been telling the truth about his delicate complexion—but now he could completely understand why it was considered so dangerous. If the bartender came poking his head back here, Lewis would whip one arm around his neck and slit his throat before the man could cry for help.

There was a time, he remembered, when it was as though something had cleared a path before him, as if his life—all of the people he spoke to, the chance encounters he made, the lucky clues he discovered—were all part of some great master plan. His daily tasks had had the feeling of being arranged, the work of a power greater than himself or anyone else. He had felt guided, shaped, formed, protected. That feeling was gone now, as if he had been cut loose and forced to fare among his fellow men like Samson shorn of his empowering hair. Six months ago, he would have felt he was not alone here in the dark. He would have felt the presence of another.

He corrected himself. Six months ago this wouldn't have happened. He would not have been hiding in a dark closet hoping to remain undiscovered.

He hefted the razor again. If he had to rely on his own abilities to make it out of this, then he would make the best of them. If that door opened...

Nothing happened. After another five minutes, he eased the door open and slipped out.

Anderson was gone. The bartender was pouring a new customer a draft beer. No one had noticed Lewis's absence.

He looked out through the windows of the bar toward the terminal area. The clerk he had obtained his boarding pass from was still at the desk in front of gate 11. Had she been questioned? he wondered. Notified? Would she be taking boarding passes, waiting to see if he turned up again? The guards were gone, but he still couldn't risk showing his face.

Anderson had checked out the bar and the men's room. He might check them again, but not for some time.

Lewis had an idea. It would take some time, and it might not work, but it was worth a try. All he had to do was to pick up his bags and walk across the corridor to the men's room.

He glanced down at his old seat at the bar. His drink had been removed, but he hadn't settled his bill yet. He laid a five on the bar and walked out into the bright light, looking straight ahead, waiting for the shout of harsh voices, the scurry of polished shoes, the unsnapping of leather holsters.

Nothing but the hum of fluorescent lights and human drones.

He pushed open the door to the men's room. A bald man was washing his hands and did not look up at Lewis as he searched in vain for fresh paper towels. He walked out, wiping his damp hands on his trousers, muttering to himself. Lewis watched him go. An omen.

He walked straight down the line of toilet stalls, entering the handicapped stall at the end. It had the most room, and he would need the space to work in.

He undid the garment bag and hung it on the hook on the back of the door. He lowered the toilet seat and set his blue nylon bag on top of it. He unzipped the garment bag and searched inside for a change of clothes. He was going to have to present a totally new front, choosing clothing that was inconspicuous but still markedly different from the coat, dress shirt, tie and slacks he was wearing now. He fished out a pair of dungarees and a thin cotton sweater. He pulled out a pair of sandals as well. His feet might get cold on the flight, but it would be worth it.

He set the clothes aside and began to strip to the waist, stuffing his dirty laundry inside the garment bag, making sure to keep the straight razor. He searched for his mug, brush and shaving cream and set them around the rim of the toilet seat. Then he zipped up his bag and hung it on the door hook over the garment bag.

The water in the toilet looked clean, as did the rim and the bowl. He wiped them thoroughly with toilet paper anyway, flushing several times to get clear, fresh water. He had to hurry.

He stared at his rippling reflection in the toilet water as he dipped his brush down into it, whipping it around in the mug to produced a frothy cream. This was a desperate situation, and called for desperate measures.

When he had a mugful of shaving cream, he set it on the floor. Then he knelt before the toilet and immersed his head underwater, the cool temperature giving him a start. He pulled his head out, feeling cold water river down his back and across his chest in steady streams. Blinking his eyes open, he reached for the mug and brush and, with the practiced skill of one who has spent a lifetime shaving, began to apply a halo of foam around his head.

"THAT'S IT."

Rogers pointed straight ahead at the gray patrol car with the Acton Security Services logo painted on the side. Two airport police officers stood to the side, the blue lights on the top of their car flashing.

Sacks braked the squad car to a stop, and the four of them—Sacks, Rogers, Mike Peterson and John—all got out at the same time, doors slamming.

Rogers made quick work of the introductions and immediately proceeded to the car. He tried the front door. It was locked. Without looking up from the handle, Rogers merely said, "David," and Sacks was there with a long, flat, flexible metal blade. He handed it to Rogers the way a nurse hands a scalpel to a surgeon. Rogers slid the metal strip down the side of the driver's window, between the glass and the rubber trim, and felt around in the inner workings of the car door until the tool caught. Rogers jerked upward and the locking mechanism was undone.

Rogers immediately opened all of the doors, searching quickly in the front and back seats, poking into the glove compartment and looking under the cushions. He emerged, a light sweat beading on his forehead.

"Anything?" John asked.

Rogers shook his head. "I'm going to call a lab team and have them come out and—" But then he got another thought and ducked back inside the car. He fumbled around at the side of the driver's seat until he found the lever to release the trunk latch and pulled it.

The trunk lid popped open, easing up all the way with a hydraulic hiss. Rogers got out and looked inside, almost climbing in, carefully examining the trunk's carpeted interior. "Ah." He reached in and pulled out something. To John it looked as though the captain had captured an invisible mote of dust between his fingers. He walked over to John with it. "Take a look," he said.

"At what?"

"This." He made an effort to pass John the invisible mote of dust, and as it turned in the light, John could see it was a strand of human hair.

John took it. "It's light," he said. "Strawberry-blond."

"Was Mary Sullivan's hair that color?"

"Yes. Yes it was."

"But he's got red hair, too," Mike piped up.

"This long?" Rogers asked, showing the strand to Mike.

"Uh. No. I guess not."

Rogers turned back to John. "We can have a lab team vacuum the trunk and compare what hairs they find in there to hairs in combs or brushes back in her house. It'd be enough to book him." Rogers carefully took back the hair from John, placing it in an open blank envelope he produced from a breast pocket. "We've got our proof. C'mon, let's get the man."

FRANK B. LEWIS FLUSHED the toilet and immersed his head in the clear water one last time. When he pulled it out, noticeably less water dripped down his back than before. He dabbed at the half dozen small cuts that he had inflicted upon himself in his haste, waiting for the water in the toilet to settle so he could study his reflection.

He was now completely bald.

It would be an obvious enough change, one that would perhaps attract more attention to himself as a person, but less to him as a suspect. He no longer fit their official description.

He folded his straight razor, sticking it down into his jeans pocket. In case his new bald disguise didn't work, he might have to resort to other measures to escape guards with persistent questions.

He fumbled in his garment bag one last time, pulling out a blue navy watchman's cap. It would cover the cuts, but leave enough skin showing to attest to the fact that he was completely hairless. If someone asked about his baldness, he would drop his eyes and shift uncomfortably and mutter something about chemotherapy. That would shut them up.

He gathered up his things and emerged from the stall, looking at his watch. He had heard the boarding of his flight announced twice already. He had just enough time to walk straight out of the men's room and over to the gate area. He got out his boarding pass. With no interruptions, five minutes from now he would be safely on board, his plane taxi-ing down the runway.

He left the men's room, standing in the open corridor, looking toward the gate. The clerk who had issued him his boarding pass had closed up shop and was gone.

Anderson, the guard, was standing next to the steward, who was collecting boarding passes, riffling the thick pack of orange plastic cards through his hands. The two of them were chatting. The steward broke off to pluck a telephone off the wall and punch a number.

"This is the final boarding call for Aer Lingus flight 112 to Shannon Airport. All passengers please report immedi-ately to gate 11 at this time. Again—"

Lewis didn't wait to hear it again. He walked quickly to angle the empty desk at the gate, with its tall backing and Aer Lingus logo, between himself and the gate door. He set down his luggage and picked up a flight schedule, pretend-ing to study it.

If Anderson would just leave, if he would just need to go to the bathroom or if he'd decide that all passengers were aboard that were coming aboard, then Lewis could pick up his bags and make the flight.

He edged around the barrier, still pretending to study the flight schedule, just barely glimpsing Anderson and the steward out of the corner of his eye. They exchanged final words, and then Anderson nodded and walked away. The steward kicked out the doorstop and let the door swing shut on him. Time to prepare for takeoff.

Lewis retreated. Not until Anderson had passed...

He listened, straining to hear Anderson's footsteps. With all passengers on board, the terminal was almost deserted and the noise wasn't hard to pick out. Lewis glanced over at the waiting area on the other side of the gate desk, trying to gauge Anderson's distance and position by his inner radar.

Anderson's path would lead him right by the desk.

Although Lewis had drastically changed his appearance, the guard might recognize the bags. Lewis thought quickly. It was all or nothing.

He shoved his bags underneath the gate desk, between a box full of flight schedules and a wastebasket. They would remain hidden there, not to be discovered until long after he was gone.

He pulled back, crouching to the side of the desk, pretending to tie his shoelaces. He listened as Anderson walked by on the other side, passing within three feet of the man he was probably looking for. Lewis listened to his footsteps retreat another fifty feet before risking a look behind him.

Anderson was walking away, talking into his radio, perhaps letting Gomez know that he'd come up with nothing there, that the suspect hadn't shown up.

Lewis got up and walked briskly toward the closed door of gate 11. He glanced out the window. The plane was still in position. They had closed the door, but if there was someone on the other side who could hear him . . .

He broke into a trot, his orange boarding pass slippery with sweat in his hands.

He knocked softly on the door, then quickly started pounding rapidly, in three-knock bursts. He knocked five, six, seven times. . . .

He heard the door unlock and saw it swing open just a few feet. It wasn't the steward he had seen standing there before. It was a new face—a stewardess whose last-minute duties had required her to be within hearing range. "Can I help you, sir?" she asked with strained politeness.

"I'm on this flight," Lewis said, presenting her with his boarding pass. "I'm not too late, am I?"

She looked at him, then at the orange card, and back at him before taking the card. "Almost," she said. "I was closing the door of the airplane when I heard you." She stepped back, holding the door open for him. "Come on in."

"Thank you," Lewis said, smiling broadly. "Glad I made it."

He walked inside, hearing the gate door shut and lock behind him.

He was safe.

JOHN STOOD TO THE SIDE of the barrier that marked the security checkpoint at the Edmund G. Brown, Jr. International Air Terminal. Since he was not a police officer but a civilian consultant, he had had to walk through the metal detector just like the travelers walking through a few feet away from him. He stood beside Rogers, listening to Gomez's story.

It sounded as if they had had him, just minutes before word had come in from Rogers that they were looking for a suspect. He had been carrying a straight razor in his bag. It had shown up on the X-ray screen. Gomez and Anderson had taken the man over to the side and asked him to empty out his bag. They found the razor and, upon inspection, saw that it was used for barbering purposes. Gomez had decided to let him go.

"Did you look at his ticket?"

"No."

"Did he say where he was going? What airline or flight number he was on?"

"No."

"Did you notice a name tag on any of the luggage?"

"No."

"Okay," Rogers said, calming himself. "Okay."

John stepped in. "What did the luggage look like?"

"A brown garment bag, the kind that folds in half and fastens together with clasps, and the bag we had him empty out was a blue nylon carryon. Kind of looked like a workout bag, except a little larger."

"What was his manner when you dealt with him?"

"He was fine. Polite. Nothing unusual."

"Did he overenunciate his words?"

"Did he what?"

Rogers cut in. "And you did a complete search of the whole terminal?"

Gomez nodded vigorously. "Absolutely. Every bathroom stall, every seat in every waiting area. We've done this type of thing before."

"Who was in the search party?"

"Myself, Anderson and Pratt." Gomez indicated another guard, one who wore glasses.

"Did Pratt ever see him?"

"No."

"But Anderson did?"

"Yes."

"Where is he?"

"I posted him at gate 11 to scan all boarding passengers on Aer Lingus. I stayed here, and Pratt continued the search."

"Did Anderson see anything?"

"No. He just radioed in before you showed up, saying that—there he is."

Anderson arrived, and proper introductions were made. "Any luck?" Gomez asked.

"No," Anderson said. "I stayed there until the steward closed the door. I saw no one that matched the suspect's description. Not even anyone more than six feet tall."

John could see that Rogers was grinding his teeth. "Maybe he's still hiding somewhere," John ventured, "and is going to try to catch a later flight."

Rogers asked Anderson, "Did all of the passengers who had reservations check in?"

"I...I don't know."

"You don't know."

"No." Anderson was getting a little defensive.

"Where is the flight now?"

"It's departing."

"It's *departing*?"

"Hey, the orders were to hold the flight only if someone matching the suspect's description was on board. No such person got on board. So I didn't hold the flight."

"All right, all right," Rogers said impatiently. He turned to Gomez. "Where can I get a passenger list? I want to see how many people checked in compared to how many people are on board the flight right now. That'll tell us if he's still hiding out in here or not. Meanwhile, get Pratt and this guy—" he jerked his thumb to indicate Anderson "—back out in the terminal on another search."

Gomez nodded. "All right."

"I want you to come with me."

Gomez nodded again.

Rogers turned on his heel and walked away, John keeping stride with him. They had left Officer Sacks and Mike Peterson back in the parking terminal, Sacks waiting for the lab team to show up.

"So what do you think?" John asked Rogers.

"I don't know. He could be in the terminal, he could be on the plane. This is one slippery son of a bitch, I tell you."

"It just lends credence to our theory."

"What theory?"

"That we're dealing with a serial murderer. Someone who is used to eluding detection."

"That's your theory, not mine, so save it until we have someone to try it out on. Right now, I want that guy because Mary Sullivan may still be alive and I want him to take me to her. We have a chance to save a life here, Dr. Stratton. You of all people should appreciate the importance of that."

But I do appreciate it, John almost said before he stopped himself. He knew that something was happening to Rogers; he was entering an obsessive state of mind, caring only for his own objectives.

Gomez led them back to the gate desk, stepping behind it. "There should be a passenger list here somewhere..." he muttered, looking underneath.

John heard Gomez's voice, muffled from his crouched position behind the desk. "Oh! Oh my God!"

He came back up, placing the blue nylon carryon bag on the counter first, and then heaving the brown garment bag up beside it.

John and Rogers stared at the luggage.

"Get on the phone," Rogers quietly told Gomez. "Call the tower, call the airline, whatever you have to do. Get that plane back here. Don't let it get in the air."

"LADIES AND GENTLEMEN, may I have your attention, please."

Lewis looked up from his seat next to an elderly couple, who had taken the middle and window seats. He leaned away from them to compensate for his size, and straightened the watchman's cap on top of his head. He had his wallet in one back pocket and his passport in the other. The only other thing he carried was stiff and sharp and beneath the right front leg of his dungarees.

The airplane had been taxiing out on the tarmac and the stewardess who had let him on board had already given the spiel about safety procedures and oxygen masks. Lewis had pulled out a magazine from the seat pocket in front of him and had begun to read through it when the interruption came from the overhead speaker.

He strained to see where the female voice was coming from. It was one of the stewardesses, perhaps the one who had let him on board. Whoever it was, she was hidden from view.

"We're sorry, but the captain has informed us that due to a mechanical difficulty we are going to have to return to the gate and all passengers will be required to disembark for a short period of time."

There were collective groans and mutterings.

"We regret any inconvenience this may cause you, but the captain has assured us that we should be able to have this problem taken care of and be under way in a short while. Thank you."

With a click, the voice was silenced. Frank B. Lewis sat in his chair, not wanting to fully comprehend what he had just heard.

He had thought that he was on his way, that he was free, that all of the major obstacles had been cleared.

It was obvious that there were still more surprises yet to come.

He felt the plane turn around and head back to the gate, watched the scenery turn and wheel outside the windows.

Due to a mechanical difficulty . . . all passengers will be required to disembark for a short period of time. . . .

What mechanical difficulty?

He did not believe them. Not entirely.

What if he got off the plane and there were security guards with guns drawn, looking for someone of his size, bearing in mind that the suspect might have tried to disguise himself. Would they have a description? His height alone could give him away. Would he run? Would he surrender? Would he force one of them to shoot him before he could be taken? Before, he had always depended on the guidance of a voice that was now curiously silent. He was left alone, drifting about in a sea of uncertain events, left to fend for himself.

He felt the straight razor in his pocket.

He knew exactly what he would do. He would fight.

SACKS ESCORTED Mike Peterson up to gate 11, where John and Rogers were standing, the captain briefing four LAPD officers and four airport security guards—Gomez, Anderson, Pratt and another one, Romero—as to their positions and plan.

"I want him alive," Rogers was stressing in a tone of command. "This man may be able to lead us to his latest victim, and her safety and life depends on his ability to cooperate with us. I want you four," he said, turning to

Gomez and company, "back down at the security check-point as a backup. Everyone's guns will stay in their holsters. We're going to try to detain him with the use of sheer numbers. If we don't succeed here, I want you four down there just in case. Gomez, Anderson—you've seen Lewis, you can identify him. We have a witness here—" he indicated Mike "—who will point him out to us as the passengers get off the plane. If he's on board.

"The captain is fully aware of our plans, and he has been instructed to inform his crew. The other passengers just think they are heading back due to some type of mechanical problem.

"Our first priority will be to identify him, and then isolate him from the other passengers to ensure their safety. Let me warn you: this man has killed, and most likely more than once."

Several times, John thought to himself.

"He is to be considered armed and very dangerous." Rogers paused for effect. "And he is one big mean motherfucker. No one of us could take him. Any questions?"

There were none.

"Places everybody," Rogers said. He put a hand on Mike's cold and quaking shoulder. "It's show time."

THE STEWARD—the one Lewis had seen collecting boarding passes—opened the door of the plane, swinging it outward. The seat belt sign went off with a tone, and everyone got to their feet, grumbling.

"Ladies and gentlemen, we will be handing out boarding passes as you deplane and they will be collected as you reboard the aircraft. Also, please remain in the terminal area, as we expect to be reboarding shortly. May I remind you to take all carryon luggage with you as we cannot be responsible for its safety when you are not on board the aircraft. Thank you again for your understanding and cooperation, and we'll be under way very shortly."

More grumbling.

The elderly couple next to Lewis wanted to stand up. He moved out into the aisle, towering over everyone else in his proximity, and helped the elderly couple get their luggage down from the bin above them, the whole time feeling his heart rate slowly edge up the scale. Pools of sweat collected under his arms and in the small of his back, making him feel clammy and sick. He felt himself being carried along by the crowd as they shuffled toward the door like prodded sheep. He barely heard the voices around him or saw the faces beside him.

He saw the steward look up at him as he handed him a boarding pass. Lewis took it automatically, searching the man's eyes for any sign of fear, panic or betrayal. There was none.

Perhaps, he thought as he walked down the tunnel toward the gate, perhaps this is exactly what they say it is. Some mechanical trouble. Sorry for the delay. We'll get it fixed. Maybe an hour from now he would be winging it home, looking back on the events of the day and smiling.

He inched his fingers into his right front pants pocket and extracted the straight razor, palming it in the thickness of his hand. One quick flick would open it. He had been trained in hand-to-hand defenses against a knife. He wondered if there were any against a straight razor, especially one that had been stropped daily for months, its sharpness a point of honor with its owner.

His feet felt cold. His sandals made a flap-flap noise as he walked. He did not feel strong and mighty as he had the night before when he had beaten the Peeping Tom within an inch of his life. He felt scared and weak, as if rabbits and does had suddenly been appointed his chosen familiars.

Help me, was the message his heart telegraphed into the spirit world. Help me, help me, help me.

He stepped out from the gate and into the waiting area, realizing that there was no crowd of welcomers or well-wishers waiting. They had all gone. And then he saw them—four uniformed LAPD officers, two men in plainclothes—

one white, one black—and they were all flanked around Mike Peterson.

Mike the slob, Mike the geek, Mike the pain in the ass. Mike, whom Lewis had thought he would never have to see or talk to again, was now standing in the Edmund G. Brown, Jr. International Air Terminal at gate 11 not five feet away, surrounded by armed police, pointing a trembling finger right at Lewis, saying, "That's him."

LEWIS REACTED INSTINCTIVELY, raising his hands in a mock surrender, stepping forward, then opening the razor with a quick motion that seemed to be contained entirely in his thick muscled wrist.

The police still had their guns in their holsters, their expressions only now catching up with their thoughts. In a split second, he had taken control of the situation merely by the speed of his actions. These men did not have the instincts he had.

This was not going to be so hard at all, he thought.

Lewis swept out at Mike's mouth with his right hand as he sprinted away, feeling the blade of the razor make hard contact and hearing Mike's cry of pain as the fat bastard staggered backward, blood spurting from his face and neck. The other men had no choice but to tend to the victim whose heft proved to be the best barrier Lewis could have thrown between himself and his pursuers.

The passengers were still fanning out from the gate area, walking in slow motion, just starting to turn around at the sound of the commotion behind them. Lewis needed them out of his way and fast—didn't want any heroes chasing after him—so he kept the blade out as he ran, slashing at sleeves and buttons, nicking hands and bare arms, occasionally opening a vein in a fellow passenger's arm or hand. The confusion would muddle his path behind him.

He was out and open and free, running. He had the razor ready. He might go down in a hail of bullets at any second, or he might make it all the way to the terminal parking lot and have the patrol car started before anyone even wondered where he had gone.

Strength poured into his legs. The scenery rushed by.

He was going to try for it.

JOHN SAW THE MAN come out of the gate door, had noticed him even before Mike pointed him out, but hadn't sorted it out enough to think that this bald giant with the watchman's cap and fisherman's sweater might actually be the Frank B. Lewis they were looking for until Mike had raised his chubby hand and pointed, saying, "That's him."

The giant had seen them and stepped over, as if he were about to give himself up to those present. And then both massive hands came up in surrender, John saw something flash gray and steely, and Mike's head jerked backward as he screamed.

He started to crumple, and Rogers grabbed him first. John reached under Mike's left armpit, dimly aware that the fabric of Mike's T-shirt was wringing wet with perspiration—he had been scared to death, not saying a word to anyone, just staring and sweating. But John was even more vividly aware that Mike had his head turned toward Rogers, and Rogers's white dress shirt, coat and tie were fielding huge bright red spurts of Mike's blood. John could hear the liquid make contact with the fabric, fleeing Mike's body in a panic.

He looked up at Rogers and saw in the police captain's face that Mike was hurt very badly.

John eased Mike to the floor. He made eye contact with Rogers. "Get an ambulance," he said. "Quick." Rogers whipped out his walkie-talkie and began shouting into it. "Mayday, Mayday, we have a man down...."

John bent over Mike so he could view the wound, and when he saw the bubbling slice that had slashed the carotid artery, he knew that Mike Peterson had twenty, maybe thirty seconds to live. He grabbed a handful of Mike's T-shirt and pulled it up, exposing his pink and flabby belly, crushing the cloth down over the gash, compelled to make any gesture at aid no matter how futile.

John angled his body over Mike's, unmindful of the blood that was drenching his clothes as well as the carpet. These were this man's last moments on earth, and John was going to make sure they counted for something.

Mike was looking around wildly, his glasses skewed up over his forehead. John brought them down over his face so Mike could see. Mike was making choking noises, his arms and legs weakly spasming as he tried to understand what had happened to him. He looked up at John, and saw the prognosis in John's eyes.

John reached down and took Mike's hand in his, as Mike held John's gaze. John squeezed it tight, pouring every last bit of fear and hate and love into Mike's dying time. John had seen death before in many forms. But, this was the first time he felt it so near, its leather wings beating at his back, talons outstretched and clicking, waiting for an opening.

Mike's mouth opened and closed, spittle flying off his lips. He was trying to say something.

"What?" John said. He bent closer to hear.

"Puh...Gigg...opp..."

"What?" God, he thought, what a terrible thing: to have last words but be unable to say them.

Mike's attempt at speech stopped and his breath became a whistling gasp, his body violently trying to overcompensate for the loss of blood. He made two final sounds in the back of his throat, and then he was dead.

John felt something dark and greedy pass by, flapping off into the unseen world, sated with another feeding.

He sat up on his knees and looked at Rogers, who looked from Mike to John. "If the reporters ask..." John started to say, and then broke off.

He felt something inside him take shape, rise to the surface as if summoned by the extraordinary circumstances. There was a snap—something stretched so far it had to become undone.

He took the walkie-talkie from Rogers before the man could protest. He found the transmitting button and pressed it. "Gomez," he said, his voice low and urgent. "Gomez."

A crackle of static. "Yes, sir."

The man probably didn't know if it was him or Rogers. Good. "He's headed toward you, trying to escape."

"All right, we'll—oh *God!*" John heard Gomez shouting.

And then John was shouting, too. "Don't shoot him, you hear me! Do everything you can to stop him but *don't shoot!*"

He listened for a response. There was none.

John got to his feet, dropping the walkie-talkie next to Mike's body, feeling the instinct overwhelm him, rage and fury fueling his need.

He was wearing his running shoes. He forced his way through the crowd, people parting for the man in blood-soaked clothes, and when he hit open country he broke into a run.

GOMEZ HAD HEARD the captain tell him to look out for Lewis when he saw the demon heading for them, and suddenly four guards with sticks and guns didn't seem like so much.

The demon was a giant, the same size as the man whom Gomez and Anderson had taken aside and asked to open his bag, but now he had changed clothes and shaved his head so it looked like a pale, washed rock. The watchman's cap had fallen off. His head was exposed, the cuts from the rushed shaving job opened and bleeding from Lewis's adrenaline burst. Blood dripped off the top of his skull in rivulets, streaking his face with gore.

He was running at them full speed, aiming for the exit walkway to the side of the barrier. Gomez had positioned himself and the other three men at equidistant points across the wide corridor, separating them by fifteen feet each.

Now, as Lewis bore down on them, Gomez dropped his walkie-talkie, shouting for all of them to close in, close in.

Anderson was directly in front of the exit, right in Lewis's path. Three months on the job, he fumbled to get his stick out and assume some sort of ready position. Gomez screamed at him to pull his gun, just because they weren't supposed to shoot *him* didn't mean they couldn't fire a warning shot or at least show the enemy some steel, but Anderson was hypnotized by the sight of this human steamroller hurtling itself his way, all motion and force.

Anderson didn't see the razor, either.

Gomez did, and popped the strap off his holster and drew his weapon just as Pratt, who was closest to Anderson, and Romero, who was farthest from him, tried to reach their comrade before Lewis did. Pratt ducked behind Anderson while Romero timed his rush so his path would intersect Lewis just as he reached Anderson.

Lewis barreled right into Anderson, knocking the man to the floor, sending his nightstick skittering across the tile. Anderson, not to be counted out, tried to whip an arm around Lewis's legs but couldn't close his grip before Lewis had flashed out with his right hand and laid Anderson's cheek open, skin flapping back like tread on a blown tire.

Romero tried to tackle the man but Lewis met him with a knee to the face. Gomez heard the crunch of crushed cartilage and Romero slumped to the floor as if someone had pulled the plug on him. Gomez would later learn that an unhealthy amount of Romero's nose had been driven into the man's brain, killing him instantly.

That left only Pratt and Gomez. Gomez had his gun out and fired a warning shot in the air, panic seizing his heart. He felt the shocks as he squeezed off another round and another one and another, while Lewis felled Pratt with a vicious strike of the razor. Blood streamed over Pratt's cheeks and nose. Glass shattered above Gomez's head as his bullets hit home, and shards fell about him in a tinkling rain.

He decided to hell with what they'd been told and lowered his gun sight on Lewis as the man ran through the exit and toward the stairs that led to the upper level. But there were people in the way, people whom he would kill if the bullet didn't hit home.

We did nothing, Gomez thought as he ran to his fallen comrades: Pratt screaming and rolling on the floor, both hands covering his face; Romero deathly still; Anderson deep in shock, fingering the razor cut on his face that exposed cheekbone and muscle, looking around him as if he'd just woken up from the worst nightmare of his life and found it was all real. We did nothing but slow him down.

JOHN WAS RUNNING.

Once he broke free from the crowd, he had picked up speed, passing the two LAPD officers who had taken off after Lewis. They were in street shoes and John wasn't sure if they ran five miles a day, every day, averaging a six-minute mile like he did, but when he passed them within a few seconds he figured it was a good bet that they didn't.

He wasn't in sight of the security checkpoint yet. He was racing past the bar, the rest rooms, the gift shop and newsstand, the snack stand, weaving in and out of people who were still shuddering in the wake of Lewis's passing. The man had knocked over anyone who was in his way, his size and strength sending those of smaller stature spinning to collide with the floor or the wall.

John knew that for most doctors in most situations, tending to the wounded would have been their first priority, but this wasn't most situations and John wasn't most doctors. His head still burned with the sight of Mike dying.

He heard shots being fired up ahead.

He poured on the speed, his thigh muscles stretching out to cover more ground. He thought he noticed a flurry of violent activity through the filter of moving people in front of him, and then he was in the clear. He saw Gomez standing over the three prone bodies of his fellow guards, two of them still moving.

John could have stopped to ask Gomez what happened, listened to Gomez plead with him to help his men, losing his rhythm and resuming the chase trying to catch his wind, but he didn't. Out of the corner of his eye, he saw Gomez look at him, heard him call his name but didn't break stride. He could see where Lewis was heading. Toward the stairs. To the second level, a miniature four-lane one-way freeway that circled above the ground level of the airport, built to reduce the street-level congestion. If Lewis reached it, he could lose himself among the cars and concrete.

John couldn't let that happen.

He sprinted over the sprawled bodies in front of him, sidestepping broken glass and spilled blood, over to the other side of the security barrier, looking straight ahead with good visibility. Fifty feet in front of him on the stairs, he saw Lewis, his head bald and bloody.

John hit the afterburner.

Lewis was nearing the top of the stairs, the ones that led to the ticket counters and almost immediately to doors to the outside. Two escalators, one leading up and one leading down, flanked the wide stairs. A handrail ran down the middle of the stairway. Lewis had to slow down, taking the stairs in long-legged strides of four and five at a time. If he made a false step in his haste he could twist an ankle or lose his balance. John knew he was as vulnerable as he would ever be.

At the last moment before Lewis's feet disappeared from view, John looked down to see whether the man was running in hard shoes or soft ones, and he heard a distinct flapping sound just as he saw what Lewis had on his feet.

Sandals. The most difficult kind of footwear to run in.

John did not slow down, did not hesitate. He saw Lewis's head lowering out of sight as the man bounded down the stairs, and John had to keep his eyes on him if the crazy idea that was forming in his head was going to work.

John was maybe fifty feet away from the top of the stairs. If no one suddenly popped into his flight path, he could hit the top stair at full speed. No one did.

He covered the ground in a few seconds, the rubber-soled cushioned heel of the running shoe on his right foot gripping the lip of the stair, allowing him to thrust himself out and away and into open space.

He sailed through the air, arms outstretched, legs splayed, in what had been called in Boy Scout lifesaving training the "fireman's entrance." The idea was to hit the water splashing so as to keep your head above water, never losing sight of the person you intended to rescue when you went after him.

John estimated his airborne speed at twenty miles per hour, his trajectory figured accurately down to the decimal point. The element of surprise was definitely in his favor.

He hit Frank B. Lewis from behind, his arms wrapping around the big man's neck and shoulders, screaming in his ear, his legs tangling with Lewis's, and the two of them went tumbling down the stairs.

John hung on, forcing Lewis's body to absorb most of the damage. They hit the floor with a brutal impact, and John still did not relax his hold. He felt the blood from the top of the other man's head smear his cheek as Lewis twisted around, his massive arms beating at John even as he lay on the floor. John tucked his head down, felt Lewis grab a handful of his hair and pull.

John jerked his head up, determined to hang on, saw the fleshy lobe of Lewis's ear and bit it.

With a roar, Lewis let go. He brought his arms underneath him and forced himself up, bringing John up with him. If his added weight made any difference to Lewis, John couldn't tell. It was like wrestling a mad bull.

Lewis staggered to his feet, twisting his upper body back and forth in an attempt to shake John off. John's grip slipped, so he tightened it all the more. His head was so close to Lewis's he could hardly see, and only when Lewis stopped trying to shake him off and started running did John look up.

They were headed for the doors.

John's eyes widened and his hold relaxed as he realized he was wrong. They were not heading for the automatic sliding doors that let passersby in and out. Lewis was charging head-on into the plate-glass window next to the doors.

He's playing chicken, John thought wildly. He's hoping I'll let go before we hit.

He buried his head in Lewis's neck, tightened his arms and legs an extra notch and held on for dear life.

Lewis did not stop, did not even slow down but hit the glass window at full speed, his arms splayed out in front of him. John felt a thousand knives cut into him, felt his arm lock on Lewis break as they both hit the pavement, and then all was merciful blackness.

CHAPTER EIGHT

HE HEARD VOICES.

The sensation of being borne upward.

Light, then darkness again.

Hands touching, probing, tending.

The rhythm of his heartbeat. The comfort of his dreams.

JOHN REGAINED CONSCIOUSNESS slowly, coming up like a swimmer trapped under Arctic ice, feeling his way toward air and light.

He opened his eyes, sticky with sleep, and let them rest, half-closed, before looking around him.

He was on a bed. Not a hospital bed, but the kind they used back at the Jicarita Family Medical Center. An examination table. He'd been treated and left to rest.

He didn't feel strong enough to get up just yet. He barely felt like moving. He pressed the rewind button on his memory and played back the last recorded tapes before he blacked out.

He remembered chasing Lewis at the airport. Leaping onto his back like some kind of mad chimpanzee, not letting go. Lewis charging through the plate-glass window...something about playing chicken.

He didn't know who was crazier: Lewis for crashing through the window or he for hanging along for the ride.

Where was Lewis now? For that matter, where was *he* now?

He felt bandages wrinkling stiffly on his skin. He reached up and touched one cheek, feeling the gauze and tape that had been fastened there. How long had he been out?

He brought his arms to his sides, feeling for the steel supports on the table, lifting himself up to a half-sitting position. His clothes were gone, quite possibly hanging in the closet-size cupboard in the corner of the room, next to the basin and scale. He was wearing a disposable hospital gown, yet this was definitely not a hospital room. Well, he couldn't be that badly banged up if he hadn't been treated for anything more than minor injuries.

He felt around at the side of the bed. There was no television in the room, but there might be some kind of paging device to summon a nurse.

He found it: a flexible tube with a black button on the end of it. He mashed it down with his thumb.

He waited, strength and clarity returning with each passing minute. He was thinking about getting out of bed and trying his land legs again when the door opened and the nurse entered—although the last time he had seen Carl Rogers, John had thought he was working as captain of the Jicarita Police Department.

"And how are we today?" Rogers asked. He had changed out of his bloody clothes.

"I don't know about you," John said, his voice sounding fluttery and cracked, "but I've got one hell of a...headache." He was going to say "hangover." Old joke, no longer funny.

John cleared his throat several times. It was sore and dry. Rogers drew him a glass of water and brought it to him.

"Thanks," John said, and drank up. He handed the glass back to Rogers.

"Refill?"

"No, I'm fine."

Rogers set the glass down on a countertop.

"How long have I been out?" John asked.

"Oh..." Rogers looked at his watch. "About two hours."

"You've been here all this time?"

"No. Nice sentiment, but I just got here and they told me you were still sleeping. When the front desk got your page I told them I'd poke my head in and see how you were. How are you?"

"Okay... I guess. Who patched me up?"

"A Dr. Phillips. He's in charge of this operation, the airport infirmary. A medical facility set up to handle cases just like yours. Part of a funding package, I'm told, that came about after that midair collision between a Golden State flight and—"

"I remember."

"Well. Anyway. That's where you are. In the bowels of the LAX machine."

"Where's this Phillips guy now?"

"Someone passed out on an incoming flight. He rode out there on an electric cart with an oxygen tank and his little black bag."

"What did he say about my condition?"

"Said you were fine. A few minor cuts and abrasions. No stitches. Said the best thing for you was rest until you regained consciousness. Willing to release you if you behave yourself and watch out for signs of a possible concussion."

"Great. Let's get out of here." John swung his legs over the side of the table and suddenly felt faint. He put his head down in his hands and saw spots swimming before his eyes.

Rogers paid little attention. "That is the medical prognosis. However, being somewhat of an amateur psychologist myself, I'd have to say that leaping onto the back of a known killer and hanging on as he threw himself through a plate-glass window indicates that you have a slight problem differentiating between fantasy and reality. People do those kinds of things in comic books and TV shows and walk away without a scratch. You could have been very seriously hurt, my friend. You're lucky you're not dead."

"I'm not so sure I'm not."

"Oh, you're fine. You're a sight better than our friend Lewis."

John raised his head, his dizzy spell forgotten. "Where is he?"

"In lockup, back at the station, surrounded by enough men and hardware to guard Moammar Khaddafi. He killed two people today. One of them a witness, the other one an airport cop. That doesn't sit well with people in my profession." Rogers paused. "Another guard has lost sight in one eye, maybe both. A third one is scarred for life. As for Mike Peterson, his body has been picked up by your former colleagues at the coroner's office. Tomorrow it will be flown back home to Michigan."

"Is that where he's from?"

"Yes. I had the pleasant duty of informing his parents of his death."

"Ah. Hang on to their number. I'd like to give them a call and tell them what happened."

"All right."

"Was Lewis hurt?"

"He had more lacerations than you did—cuts about the face and neck from the window glass. Needed a few stitches here and there. Believe it or not he was still conscious when we caught up with you two, trying to get to his feet to take off again."

"Strong fellow."

"One might say almost superhuman."

"Have you questioned him?"

"Tried to. I've yet to hear him utter a sound. He's not talking to anybody. We're running everything we can find on him through the computer, collating it with evidence from Mary Sullivan's house." Rogers's voice grew heavy and dark. "I've got helicopters out searching and ground teams with dogs, but we're losing the light. I don't think we're going to get to her in time unless he starts talking. She may be a goner, John."

"Maybe," John said. Even in his debilitated state he was thinking things over, examining possibilities, devising solutions.

"Anyway, I came up here to take you back to the station. There's someone back there who's very worried about you."

"Really? Who?"

"Oh, take a wild guess."

THE DRIVE BACK from LAX was a pleasant one, Rogers taking Highway 1 up from the airport. The setting sun put on a spectacular show for them, changing colors from yellow to gold to orange to azure, John catching the full spectrum while Rogers drove along the coast and turned into the canyon. Light receded behind them as they traversed the Santa Monica mountain range. When they finally arrived at the Jicarita police station, the sky was a bare dark blue.

John followed Rogers inside, at a slightly slower pace. He had, indeed, found his clothes in the closet in the infirmary examining room and pulled them on, wincing at the pain of strained muscles. He would have to do some stretching and soaking tonight.

They passed through the lobby and into Rogers's office, where Annette was waiting. She saw John and immediately stood. She made a motion as if she were going to come to him and hug him, then perhaps realized that they didn't know each other that well. Or—John immediately rationalized—she was put off by the bandages on his cheek and hand, thinking that perhaps she might come into contact with a cracked rib or some stitches hidden underneath his bloodstained clothes.

Out of the corner of his eye, John saw Rogers grab something off his desk and disappear, leaving them alone for a few minutes.

"How are you?" she asked.

"Fine," he said, aware of the incongruity the statement must have made with his appearance. His cheek, besides being cut, was swelling slightly. It might bruise and purple before the day was over. How sexy, he thought.

"I'd heard about what happened, but I wasn't sure...they said you were unconscious."

"Yeah, I knocked myself out pretty good." He was trying to sound like Bogart. *Yeah, they set me up for a fall, but I was too smart for 'em. Think I'm a sight, you should see the other guy.* They were standing less than a foot apart, speaking softly to each other, like the lovers they were not.

"But you got him," she said, and she couldn't keep the admiration out of her eyes. "Captain Rogers said you ran after him and you stopped him."

"Yeah...well..."

"If he had escaped, he might have come after me."

"I...no one knows for sure...."

Then Annette did a curious thing. She reached for John's hand, the one that wasn't bandaged, and held it in her own. She brought it up to her cheek and nuzzled her face against it, giving his middle knuckle a soft kiss before returning John's hand back to his side.

"My hero," she said, and kind of smiled.

"WHAT'S UP?" Rogers said as John walked into the observation room. The lights were slightly dimmed so as to reduce the glare on the half-dozen video screens that monitored various points in the station, including the cell that held Frank Lewis. To the side was a computer terminal, its cursor bright and blinking. Rogers was seated by himself, several folds of freshly printed paper in his hands. He had been studying them when John walked in.

"I was thinking about heading home for some rest."

"Sounds like a good idea." Rogers kept a straight face. No comments about Annette. He had most likely seen the concern in her face and answered her questions earlier. John was tempted to ask the detective about it—*Did she seem anxious? What did she say? Gosh, do you think she likes me?*—but now was not the time for lovesick guessing games.

John looked at the monitor trained on Lewis. He didn't know if it was the angle of the camera or the wide-angle lens, but the man seemed to dwarf his surroundings, giving John second thoughts about whether one room was enough to hold him.

Lewis's cell was a prison within a prison, made of painted white bars that stretched from floor to ceiling, with a narrow bed to one side and a toilet on the other. The cell was contained within another room with no bars and no way out except for a single door with a narrow window set in it. The camera monitoring Lewis was perched somewhere above the door, its lens shooting through the widely spaced bars, hanging just out of reach. Still, it didn't seem like enough. Lewis was seated on the edge of his bed, his eyes fixed on a spot on the wall, concentrating. John imagined he could stand and watch Lewis in captivity for days and weeks and months and years, examining his every move, poring over every evidence report, even—if he could get him to respond—interview him for hours on end and never know what really went on inside that bare and shaved head.

"How secure is that cell?"

"It's our maximum-security facility," Rogers answered, a slight offense in his tone as he studied the printouts in front of him. "It'd take him a few hours to get out of his cell if he had an acetylene torch with him—providing of course, that the sprinkler system and smoke alarms were already disabled and we just sat here in this room and watched him with our thumbs up each other's asses. Then he'd have to get out of the room itself, which would require nothing short of some serious plastic explosives, and then he'd have to get out of lockup and try to make it out of the station."

"Schwarzenegger did it in *The Terminator*."

"They didn't film that here." Rogers raised his head. "I have two men posted outside his door, trading off in shifts, and there'll be someone in this room watching the entire station when I leave. He so much as gets hold of a Jonny Quest decoder ring they have orders to shoot." He made a notation in a margin. "Personally, I hope he goes for it."

"Why the cell within a cell?"

"For questioning. I always want a barrier between him and somebody else. I doubt his court-appointed attorney will mind very much, once he sees the charges we're pressing."

John looked away from the monitor, eerily aware of its glowing presence in the room. He looked over Rogers's shoulder at the sheaf of papers he was shuffling. "What have you got there?"

"Some information on our friend, there. Or rather, the lack of it. His driver's license was a fake. So is his passport. There's no proof that Frank B. Lewis is his real name, or even that he's in this country legally. The man himself is a cipher."

Rogers turned another page. "Results came back from the lab. The hairs found in his trunk correspond to those found in Mary Sullivan's home. He had her in the car, and sometime within the past twenty-four hours. The lab examined the trunk lock and determined that it had been tampered with from the inside. She may have escaped." He looked up at John. "There's some hope in the world, I guess."

"Some. Any word from the search parties?"

"No."

"Oh."

"When we searched Mary Sullivan's home, we found a few other things as well. Letters from relatives all over the country. A lot of their responses seem to indicate that she was talking the same kind of stuff she was talking to you—something about a family curse."

"A banshee."

"Yeah. A banshee. As opposed to a vampire or a werewolf or something like that."

"There have been murders where the killer mimicked the signs of a werewolf or a vampire, leaving his victims in such a state that it looked as though one had been at work on them."

"Well, as you know, I didn't give it much thought." He folded two sheets together and tore them away from the rest, ripping away the perforated edges. "Until I got this. We ran a check on all of those who wrote back, and a few who didn't. Mary Sullivan kept an address book in an attempt to keep up with all of the members of her family—at least those that would write to her. Most of the letters indicated that they thought she was some kind of kook—the banshee was a story told to them as children to get them to come home before dark—and they didn't want to hear from her anymore."

He handed John the pages. John looked at the names and the dates, followed by code letters and numbers. "What's this say?"

"It's a list of all of Mary Sullivan's blood relatives, or at least the ones she knew of, who were alive when she contacted them. Some of them married, changed their names, moved away... before the age of the computer we would have had a little trouble tracking them down. But here they are." He pointed with his finger. "These dates over here are the days they were reported missing by family or friends."

"Missing?"

"Yeah. They're gone. Every last one of them. I'm getting copies of the reports, but what do you want to bet that they all say he or she went out for a pack of cigarettes and never came back?"

John looked at the names in silence: Donald David Larkin. Gregory Michael Larkin. Anna Larkin McGee. Michael Jonathan Larkin. Timothy Patrick Larkin... He looked at the cluster of code letters and saw that they were abbreviations for cities and states. Atlanta, Georgia. Washington, D.C. Bangor, Maine. Knoxville, Tennessee. Lubbock, Texas.

He counted them up quickly. Twenty-six names in all.

"They're all missing?"

"All gone. How does it feel to be right?"

John handed the pages back to Rogers, walking slowly over to the monitor with the dancing electronic image of the man who was not Frank B. Lewis sitting and thinking.

"We're trying to place him in those cities around those dates," Rogers continued, "but the fact that the man has no recorded identity makes it a little difficult. Even his fingerprints draw a blank. It'll be slow going, but we'll do it."

What was this man thinking? John wondered. Was he wondering why he was here? What had gone wrong for him? Who it was that had caught him?

He turned back to Rogers. "One favor."

"Shoot."

"I want to talk to him."

Rogers didn't look surprised. "Tomorrow?"

"Today. Now."

ROGERS LED HIM AROUND, taking him from the observation room to the lockup, through a guarded solid door and down the row of six doors leading to the individual cells. Rogers stopped outside the only door with a guard posted: Sergeant Griffin. John recognized the man from the search of Lewis's apartment.

"All right," Rogers said. "I'm going to let you in there. Griffin here is going to be right outside. He tries anything—anything—you call out and Griffin will be inside before you can say spit. If you just want him in there with you, tell him. I'm going to be in the observation room, taping your conversation with Lewis."

"You already have microphones inside there?"

"Yes." Rogers did not fool around. "Stay away from the bars. If he tries to talk softly to get you to lean in closer, tell him to speak up. You're going to be locked in there with him. When you want out, just knock and Griffin will open the door. He may have his gun drawn, but don't take it personally." Rogers felt around in John's shirt and pants.

"Hey... what...?"

"No sharp objects," Rogers said, withdrawing a pen from John's shirt pocket. "He could turn this into a weapon. Remember, I'll be watching." He looked at his watch. "I'll come and get you in ten minutes, either way. You've earned your rest for today already."

John nodded, and Rogers stayed to watch as Griffin unlocked the door to the cell. John stepped inside, and felt it close behind him, the key turning once again.

Then he was locked inside the same room as a madman.

There was a small steel bench bolted into the wall, set a healthy distance away from the bars of the cell, presumably for the comfort and convenience of legal counsel who had the habit of balancing open briefcases full of all kinds of sharp objects on their knees as they rifled through documents and depositions.

John felt the metal's cold touch seep through the fabric of his jeans, chilling the backs of his thighs. He looked over at Lewis, sitting in his cell. His eyes had lifted up and focused on John when he walked in. He had shown no surprise, no fear, no anger. Just . . . interest.

John leaned back until his vertebrae met with the unforgiving hardness of white-painted brick. His gaze held Lewis's in return; he concentrated on keeping it steady and unblinking, although he felt—with the bars prodding the image—as if he was studying an example of some new kind of life, alien and dispassionate.

"Hello," John said. "My name's John Stratton. I'm a doctor."

Lewis said nothing. His face was slightly swollen, with small red scratches around his eyes and nose. Angry red gouges ran across his forehead, up into where his hair should have been. They were held together by stitches. There had been bandages covering the wounds, but Lewis had removed them. The man was sitting forward, his elbows on his knees.

"They tell me your name isn't really Frank Lewis. I don't know what to call you."

There was nothing forced about the other man's silence—nothing to suggest the air of performance. He had simply chosen the right to remain silent.

"Maybe you don't recognize me. I'm the wise guy who jumped you at the airport."

A slight flicker of something. Increased interest, perhaps.

"Remember? I leaped on your back, we both went down. You tried to shake me off but I wouldn't let go. Then you decided to make a rather hasty exit." John chuckled, touching his cheek. "Man, you don't know when to quit."

The other man looked as though he would jump through a dozen more plate-glass windows if John were on the other side of the twelfth, and still have the strength left to snap John's neck with one hand. His bare forearms were solid, his biceps bigger than John's thigh muscles.

"Captain Rogers tells me that you haven't said a word to anybody. I asked to see you anyway. I have a theory I want you to help me with."

John looked up at the ceiling, assuming the manner of an obsequious graduate student. "You see, we know you took Mary Sullivan. I knew before the police did. I was at her house this morning. I saw the alley gate left open, the back door ajar.

"The police found strands of her hair in the trunk of the car you were driving. If you will tell us where she is, what you've done with her, then it could count heavily in your favor. Rogers thinks it's possible that she escaped. If she did, I think you tracked her down.

"My theory is that you buried her somewhere, just like you did Gretchen Seale, and that she may still be alive." John dropped his gaze to meet Lewis's. "If you tell us where she is, and if we find her in time, then that could go very well for you. As it is, I think you're facing the electric chair."

Nothing. For all appearances, the man could not speak English and didn't care to learn.

"The electric chair," John repeated. "Snap, crackle and pop. Enough juice flowing through you to light a Dodgers' night game."

No response.

"Will you tell me where she is?"

Lewis looked at him, his eyes tunneling back into his head.

"Please?"

No response.

"You could save her life." He let that one sit for a while, and when it got no reaction, John shifted his position. His muscles were starting to become sore from the chase that afternoon. "There's something else you don't know. I met Mary Sullivan before you kidnapped her. I talked to her a while."

There. Yes. Definitely. A change in expression. Like a pebble dropped in still waters.

"She told me an interesting story: that her side of the family—the Larkins, from Ireland—were cursed by a...*bain seth*. A banshee. She said it followed her over here to the States, taking the lives of all her blood relatives here and abroad, saving her until the last. She had tried to reach Gretchen before the banshee got to her, but she was too late."

A momentary tension, now relaxed. Confidence. Pride in a job well done.

"Do you believe in this legend as well?"

Lewis said nothing. He didn't need to.

"I have another theory. I think you have a banshee too, but this one's inside your head. It tells you what to do, guiding your actions and thoughts. Other members of the family may be able to see it, but you're the only one that it talks to—that it guides and instructs. That it loves."

A smile, more in the eyes than anywhere else.

John went on. "Of course, that would mean that you're a member of the Larkin family, too."

The mask was back on, seated firmly in place.

"Only we're checking into all of the surviving members of the family, even back in Ireland. That's how we plan to find out exactly who you are. I'll bet there aren't any. I'll bet they're all dead, except for you. You were headed back home because you were going to... I don't know: maybe your work is finished here. You've done your job. You've fulfilled your calling."

John stood, feeling Lewis's eyes following him. Ignoring Rogers's advice, he stepped right up to the bars and spoke in a low and menacing voice.

"Well, you missed one. Mary Sullivan had another daughter: Gretchen Seale's twin sister. She's still alive and you're never going to get to her. There is no banshee, Lewis or whatever the hell your name is. There's just you, and you screwed up."

John backed away, watching Lewis's expression break, the man deeply shaken by what John had just said. He had been hit at the center of his belief system and the effect was too great to be hidden. He was looking up at John as John reached behind him and knocked three times on the door.

"You think about it," John said. "Your only chance is to tell us where you put this girl's mother."

The door opened. John was glad. Lewis was standing up, walking slowly toward the bars, as if to say: Don't go. Not yet. Tell me more.

John stepped out. "I hope they fry you anyway," he said, and did not break eye contact until the door swung shut and he could still see Lewis's face through the thick window set in the steel door. Then he walked away.

ROGERS MET HIM in the hallway before John had made it to the observation room. "What the hell did you say to him right at the end?"

"You couldn't hear?"

"No."

"I told him that he missed one—that we had Annette and he was never going to get to her, his whole sick scheme would never achieve its purpose."

"Well, he's now pacing like a caged animal."

"Ah. Good. I'm glad he was able to get in touch with his true self at last."

"And what was all this stuff about us checking into his relatives in Ireland? We're not doing that."

"Well, we'd better," John said. "Because what I said to him is what I think. He's probably a Larkin, too, even though that may not be his name. He was headed back to Ireland; that's probably where he came from. Remember Mike Peterson said something about Lewis overenunciating his words? Sounds like he was trying real hard to overcome his accent. He probably warmed up in his homeland by wiping out his entire clan before crossing over here. I'd make a call to Scotland Yard or whoever over there, but don't tell them what for. They may want to extradite him and I don't think you want to lose him right now, do you?"

"No." Rogers seemed a little confused himself. "Why didn't you tell me any of this before you went in to see him?"

"Because *a*, you wouldn't have thought they were valid theories, and *b*, you would have made me promise not to say anything to him about it. The reason you're not getting information out of him is because you've got none of your own. He's got to think we know more than he thinks we do, or he'll see no reason to play ball."

John could see Rogers was trying to suppress his anger. The man didn't like being shown up, but that was going to keep happening to him until he realized he didn't listen to other people well enough. John decided to soften the situation a bit.

"I'm sorry. I should have said something to you. But if we can hang on another day and convince him that there's a chance Mary Sullivan is still alive even though you and I know that she's probably dead by now, then we can get him to lead us to where he buried her and—'' John snapped his fingers ''—he's confessed.''

Rogers looked off, processing the information through data control.

''There's not much at stake here, Carl,'' John said. ''He just may be the worst serial killer in history. A few dozen open cases could be solved, and you and I will be heroes. Who knows? Maybe the city will give me my old job back and they'll make you mayor.''

Rogers looked back at him angrily. ''I don't look at this as a stepping stone for my career, Stratton.''

''Then look at it another way,'' John said.

''How?''

''Good versus evil. For once the guys in the white hats win.'' John suddenly felt very tired. ''I've got to go home. I'm about to fall asleep on my feet.''

''All right,'' Rogers said, and let him walk away. ''John?''

''Yeah?''

''When you were with the city... working as a coroner...''

''Yeah?''

''Were you good at your job? I mean before the trouble started.''

''Yes. I certainly was.''

HE FOUND ANNETTE, still sitting in Rogers's office. He had told her she could accompany him when he excused himself to go speak with the captain, but she had declined. She had said she didn't want to get any nearer to the man who wanted to kill her than she had to. He found her reading the late edition of the *Times*, including the front-page story about Lewis's capture. All of the information in the story had come from a police press officer. John's name was mentioned several times, and a fuzzy black-and-white photograph from the newspaper's archives taken at the site of the Golden State disaster served to illustrate what he looked like when he didn't get his beauty sleep: eyes haggard, skin drawn. John threw the paper aside.

"I'll probably have a dozen messages on my machine when I get home," he said, "none from people I want to talk to."

She looked up at him and smiled. "Maybe it'll be some producer who wants to get the rights to your story."

"No, they always call the guy who's sitting behind bars. I'd like to see some network executive try to get through to *him*, though." He tilted his head in the direction of the lockup.

Annette nodded, finding the humor in the joke somewhat strained.

"You ready to go?" John asked.

"Anytime."

"You have my keys?"

"I sure do." She stood and dug into the pocket of her jeans, pulling them out and dangling them in front of his face.

"Home, James," she said.

They drove back through the dark, not saying much, John concentrating on driving. He couldn't remember being this tired in a long time. The little aches and pains from all the minor cuts and bruises had formed a lobby and were demanding that their needs be met. He envisioned a hot bath, then maybe a fire...

He was suddenly aware of Annette's presence at his side. What about her?

"Listen," he said, breaking the silence, "what did you have in mind for tonight?"

She looked at him quizzically.

"I meant, did you want to go home, did you want to try to find a hotel..."

"Actually, I'd like to take you up on your earlier offer."

John's turn to look a little quizzical.

"Staying with you."

"Oh! Sure. Of course."

"You forgot."

"No, no . . . I didn't forget. . . ."

"I'd be glad to find something else."

"No, no, I really insist. It's just that I'm so tired I can hardly think straight."

"Do you mind?"

"Mind? No. Not at all. You can have my bed and I'll stay out in the living room."

"Oh, I can't do that. I'll take the living room."

"No, it's all right. I drag a futon out in front of the fireplace and go to sleep to the sound of crackling wood. Often do it, anyway."

She turned to him, her eyes lit up by unexpected pleasure. "You have a fireplace?"

"Yeah."

"A working one or one of those kind that lights up from behind while hot air blows out from underneath?"

John laughed. "No. A real one. I keep firewood out in the garage."

"Sounds wonderful."

"Oh, it's nice. Better than what I used to do at the end of the day."

They drove on in silence, trees bordering the curves, occasionally giving way to darkened valleys and hills.

"Do you like living out here?" she asked.

"I love it. I'll never live in the city again."

She smiled. " 'In the city.' Sounds odd, but I guess you really do live in the country."

"Feels that way. Reminds me of . . . Colorado sometimes. When I'm home, I can put the answering machine on and pretend I'm on vacation. More like a weekend retreat than a regular home."

"I can't wait to see your place."

"Coming up," John said, leaning over to her side and peering through the dark. "There. See that building?"

She looked. "Where?"

"That one there."

"Yeah . . . I see it. . . ."

"I used to work there."

"Jicarita Family Medical Center," she read. "That's where you were . . . ?"

"When this whole thing started." He shook his head. "Seems like months ago."

"You don't miss it?"

"Nope."

"How about your old job? Do you miss that?"

"Sometimes."

"Lately?"

"No. Because . . . it felt like I was doing it again."

"Do you think you ever will?"

"I hope so. But . . . there are some things that can't be undone. It's very hard to change people's minds about you once you show them something really bad."

"Were you that out of control?"

"I was that out of control."

"But you're better now."

"I'm alive," he said, sounding grateful. He flicked on his turn signal, slowing down for the turnoff. "Here we are."

He took the paved road up for half a mile, then turned off on his own private driveway, following it back into the trees for a few hundred feet. He reached up to the sun visor and pressed the remote-control button that operated the garage door opener. They sat, car idling, while the door slowly lifted, and John eased the Camaro inside. He pressed the button again and the door lowered behind him. He shut off the engine and they got out of the car.

He unlocked the door to the house, holding it open for Annette. "Thank you, sir," she said with mock graciousness as she stepped into the darkened kitchen. John closed the door behind them and turned on the lights. "Would you like the grand tour?" he asked.

"Of course."

He took her from room to room, pointing out the bedroom—"where you'll be sleeping," he said. She protested, saying she could take the couch. "I won't hear of it," John insisted.

She especially liked the living room, with its fireplace and sliding glass doors that led out to his backyard. They stepped outside and she folded her arms against the nighttime chill.

She walked to where his yard dropped off into wooded darkness and stood. "What's down there?" she asked.

"A creek."

"Really?"

"Really. You can see it in the daytime."

"I don't hear any water."

"It's dry now. Fire season. Won't fill back up until October or November."

"Can you get down there on foot?"

"Sure. It's a nice place to be at sunset."

She turned away from him and listened some more.

"Are you hungry?" he asked.

"A little." She turned to look at him. "Actually, a lot." She smiled.

"I am, too. Why don't I make us some dinner?"

"You can cook?"

"After a fashion."

THE FIRST THING HE DID was to start a fire in the fireplace. He went out to the garage and brought in an armful of firewood along with a chemical log. He put the log in first, lighting it with an elongated match, then set the real wood on top of it.

He took two swordfish steaks from the freezer and put them in the microwave to thaw while he set up the hibachi outside next to a wall to catch any sparks.

"It seems like you're going to a lot of trouble," Annette said, but John overruled her objections.

"I want to return your hospitality from last night," he said.

"I made you sleep on the floor, and besides, you're not all that healthy."

"I'm fine," he replied, touching match to charcoal.

He built a fire in the fireplace, boiled some corn on the cob and fresh broccoli and whipped up a hollandaise sauce. Annette asked if she could help in any way, but John told her to just sit back and relax in front of the fire.

He turned the swordfish steaks, took the corn and the broccoli off the stove and set place mats and plastic dinnerware in front of the fireplace. "Just like a picnic, except it's indoors," he said, making her laugh.

He opened two bottles of Crystal Geyser to drink, and then took the fish off the hibachi. He came out from the kitchen balancing their two plates on a tray. "Ta-da!" he said.

They ate in front of the crackling fire, squatted on the carpet, he listening to her polite compliments about the food. John had surprised himself with how easy the meal had been to prepare. He had never felt comfortable having women visit him wherever he lived. He wasn't used to entertaining.

When they finished, he cleared the dishes away and made some hot herbal tea, which he served in a set of stone mugs he had bought at a crafts festival in Topanga.

They sat and sipped and watched the flames.

"What kind of wood is that?" Annette asked.

"Piñon."

"Ah. It smells good." She turned to face him. "Thank you again for dinner. It was very good."

"You're more than welcome." He didn't know why it bothered him that she should say something like that. He should be able to take a thank-you without feeling... guilty about it.

"I'll go make up your bed." He rose, feeling her eyes on him as he walked out of the living room and into the bedroom.

He got out fresh sheets and changed the bed, emerging from the room to find her standing in the hallway, arms folded, leaning against the wall.

"Are you quite done?" she said, smiling. There was something flirtatious in her manner that he found unsettling.

"Everything's ready."

She put a hand on his shoulder and said, "Would you mind if I took a quick shower before bedtime?"

"No." The shoulder where she was touching him suddenly felt like dead wood. "Help yourself. I'm going to make up the couch in the living room." Then he turned away from her, feeling her hand slip back to her side.

I could have touched her back, he thought as he unfolded the futon couch and spread sheets and blankets over the mattress, pushing it near the fireplace. Maybe even tried to kiss her.

He heard the bathroom door close. Water ran in the tub, then through the shower head. There was a bathrobe on the back of the bathroom door that she could use. He went into the bedroom to get a spare for himself. He moved quietly, as if he was in someone else's house, not his own.

He walked past the bathroom door. He could hear water spray irregularly against the curtain. He tried to imagine her nude body, wet and soapy, through a haze of steam. The image wouldn't focus.

He stayed dressed, fiddling with the fireplace tools until she emerged, her hair slightly damp, wearing his bathrobe. "I borrowed this from the hook on your bathroom door," she said, fingering the terry cloth. "I hope you don't mind."

"No. Not at all. I've got a spare."

She looked down at the embers of the fire. "It's going out."

"Yeah. Not a good idea to go to sleep with it blazing away. A spark might jump the screen and set the carpet going. You never know."

"I'm going to get into bed," she said, and walked away.

John watched her go. The robe rode high on her legs, exposing a healthy length of her thighs. Her skin wasn't pale and freckly, like Gretchen's, but a kind of golden tan. He clenched his fists at his sides. She hadn't said I'm going to bed or good-night or I'll see you in the morning. It was "I'm going to get into bed." What did that mean? Were there any implications?

He saw the lights in his bedroom go out but the door stayed half-open. He stepped over to a corner where she couldn't see him and got out of his own clothes, slipping on the bathrobe. He supposed that to some men this was a moment of arousal and anticipation, not anxiety. He had been able to turn his feelings around in the past, but only with the help of a lot of unnatural substances. Now he had to stand his own nervous ground.

He pulled back the comforter and sat down on the futon.

"John?" Annette called from the bedroom.

He stayed where he was. Maybe he could pretend he hadn't heard her.

"John?"

"Yes?" His voice sounded oddly loud. Strained.

"Would you come here?"

It could be something else, he thought as he stood and walked toward the bedroom, his feet feeling cold on the warm carpet. It could be a spider she wants me to kill, or maybe she can't find an extra blanket, or there's a window open that she can't close.

He eased open the doorway, his eyes adjusting to the dark. She was sitting up in bed, the sheets and blankets he had fitted on the mattress bunched loosely across her knees. Her breasts were barely covered by the material. He could see their curving sides, the gentle cleavage, the shadows they made against her skin. When he looked at her face he saw that she wasn't playing the part of some scheming seductress or love-starved vamp. She was just a nice woman who thought maybe she'd found a nice man in the middle of some madness in her life.

"You don't have to stay out there," she said softly, twisting a corner of the blanket, "if you don't want to."

John swallowed. He'd been afraid something like this might happen.

"I'm not so sure that would be a good idea."

"Why? Because of... my sister?"

"No. It doesn't have anything to do with her. It doesn't have anything to do with you, either." His stomach felt as if it was about to pull itself apart with tension. "I...it's me. I kind of need... I take time, I guess."

"All right. That's okay." She couldn't completely hide the disappointment in her voice.

"I'll see you tomorrow morning," he said.

She lay down, turning her face away from him. "Good night."

He closed the door.

He went back to the futon in front of the fireplace and lay down on it, staring up at the ceiling. Why did you do that? he asked himself. Why didn't you do what you really wanted to do and walk over to the side of the bed and kiss her? You didn't have to perform. You just could have... responded.

I don't know, he thought back. I don't know why. I guess I'm just too screwed up. I can't let myself be that happy yet.

Now he knew he would never get to sleep. Again.

JOHN DID, EVENTUALLY, fall asleep.

And began to dream.

He was alone, on a green countryside, a place far from where he lived. Hills rose up on either side, swallowed in a dense mist. No buildings were in sight, but the land did not have the feel of the open wild. Mystical, but not savage.

That was the first dream. It came and went.

IN THE SECOND DREAM he was in darkness. Only when he put out his hands did he realize that the darkness had form and shape and substance, and when he used his hands and feet to determine its borders he found that the darkness was in the shape of a box, big enough to hold only one person.

He pressed upward with both hands, then kicked with both feet. Something slipped through a crack above him and touched his face.

Dirt.

The air inside the box was cold and damp, and there did not seem to be much of it. His breathing became labored and rapid. He forced himself to calm down and breathe slowly and deeply, conserving what oxygen there was. He had to try to think his way out of the situation. He had to consider the alternatives. After a while, he gave up. There didn't seem to be any way out of his predicament.

His breathing was coming harder and harder with each passing minute. He had to do something, make some kind of gesture, no matter how futile, before he lost consciousness and then—how did that go?—the worms crawl in, the worms crawl out, the worms play pinochle on your snout....

Whoever came up with that little schoolyard ditty wasn't a coroner. They hadn't presided over court-ordered exhumations. They didn't know what a corpse looked like after it had been buried without even the benefit of embalming. John was surprised that there were some people who thought that embalming a loved one's body meant preserving it against decay for years, even centuries. The undertaker's art lasted only a few days, long enough for the family to hold their service and friends to give their best regards. Shortly after interment, moss began to cover the face, fingernails and hair grew out to abnormal length, the eyes fell in on themselves.

Oh God, oh God, he was going to die.

Panic seized him momentarily, adrenaline shooting into his bloodstream, and in his frenzy he lost his bearings and found himself facedown, pounding and prying on the boards at the bottom of the box, the ones he had been lying on just a few moments ago. He had known something was different when they began to give.

He stopped, rational thought returning even though his head was pounding and his chest was heaving. Seeing with his hands, he felt the irregular edges of the long pieces of wood that formed the bottom of his coffin. They were not nailed in place or fastened with glue. They came up quite easily.

He pried up three of them, bracing himself on his elbows and knees. If the earth was soft enough…but he stifled the thought, knowing the chances were his hand would meet cold stony ground.

It did not. His right hand passed through the opening in the bottom of the coffin and met nothing but open air. He felt around in the space that was underneath the coffin until he touched the edges of the opening, the dirt walls of what seemed to be an underground hole. It felt big enough for a man to pass through. Cold dry air passed up through it; where it came from John had no idea.

He felt a combination of exhilaration and fear. He had a chance to escape, but where did this route lead to?

He pried up the rest of the boards and eased himself through the opening, headfirst, hands pulling, feet pushing. He began to crawl, sensing that the tunnel was angled downward.

Time passed as he moved underground. He had no way of knowing how much.

He saw light at the end of the passage, heard sounds. The light came in blue-white flashes, the sounds in stormy bursts. He pressed on, more curious than frightened.

When he got closer, he stopped and tried to back up, then found that he couldn't.

The tunnel was sealing itself up behind him.

He stopped, holding his position, sweating out his options, until he felt the dirt behind him shift and move over his feet, covering first his shoes, then his ankles, then his calves…and in the recesses of the earth surrounding him he sensed other movements, things shifting around and behind him like moles.

Arms reached out to grab him and propel him forward, limbs attached to beings that moved through the dirt as fish moved through water, bearing him onward, spilling him out into a cavernous space. He scrambled to his feet and looked behind him. A sheet of lightning illuminated his exit from the passage he had just negotiated and he would always wish it had remained dark.

The hole he had been thrown out of was clogged with hands and faces, pale as worms, clambering over one another as if they were nothing more than obstacles, and in their efforts tore away at one another's flesh to reveal the pale and shriveled musculature beneath, a condition that John had only seen in patients who were already dead.

He felt more than fear at the sight. He had a terrifying sense of recognition.

He was in the same place he had envisioned when he had lain on his apartment floor and felt his heart seize in his chest—an underworld, where life was a sacrilege and death a grace attained.

Light flashed down from an unseen source, giving glimpses of an immense cavern, so crowded with detail even a close and studied examination would have strained the eye. Visions of torment and agony seared his brain.

He heard a sound behind him, turned and came face-to-face with Gretchen Seale.

She had decayed even more than when he had found her, the marks of Fuchs's examination leaving openings in her body where organs oozed out and fell to the cavern floor.

"John," she said, her voice choked with maggots. *"John . . ."*

He felt her hands upon him and began to scream.

HE WOKE UP, not screaming, but still in the grip of the night terror. It took him a while to get his bearings, and for several seconds he looked around him fearfully, afraid that he would turn and find that it was not a nightmare after all, that he was trapped with the living dead. Maybe they had that power, to come back and do unto you what had been done to them by those who'd sent them to their graves.

After a few minutes he felt his head clear and lay back down, doubting that he would be able to get to sleep again. He had never been one to place great stock in dreams, but if this one had a meaning, it was not a subtle one.

The events of the past few days were not over yet. This case was not closed. This evil had not been laid to rest.

PART THREE

*

The Bain Seth

CHAPTER NINE

ESCAPE.

The word had not occurred to him until just then, lying awake as others slept. The bed that was bolted to the floor of his cell was too narrow for him, so he had pulled his blankets off the mattress and now huddled on the floor, trying to rest.

He had not known who had attacked him at the airport until the doctor visited him in his cell. When he had heard what the doctor had to say, he felt confusion and doubt such as he had never known before.

He had been conscious the entire time he was treated and brought here, to this prison. He ignored the manner of those around him. They acted as though only the restraints placed on them by legislators kept them from taking their charge out in the hills and shooting him like a mad dog.

The black man, the police captain, had sat on the bench outside his cell and asked him questions for an hour, hoping his prisoner would talk. And then there was the doctor, who tried to do the same. He wasn't talking to either of them. He had nothing to say. They wanted to know the most irrelevant things: Where were you at this date? This time? Did you kill this woman? Will you take us to her? It was obvious they knew nothing, could not harm him in any real way.

Except for the doctor.

The doctor had said something truly surprising, something that almost made him stand up and call after him: wait....

The doctor had said there was another Larkin. A twin sister of Gretchen Seale. One whom he had missed.

The doctor had said something else as well—that he thought his prisoner was also a Larkin, a member of the family he was trying to destroy, even though that had never been his name. Interesting theory, more than a germ of truth in it. The man would never guess the reality. Yes, he had been a member of that family, that cowardly breed he had hunted down and eliminated like sick and muddy animals, but he was no longer. He had been a part of them once, for a brief time, and then everything had changed for him. He was no longer a Larkin; he had been transformed, remade, born again. Instead of Larkin he was anti-Larkin, their opposite in the universe. Collision of the two random particles meant an immediate and radical conversion of matter into energy.

He had thought he was done, finished, ready to pack up and go home, but something had held him back. Obstacles had been placed in his path, one after another, until he had finally tripped over one and injured himself. After he had had time to think about it, he realized it had not been bad luck or a series of unexpected stumbling blocks. It had been planned that way.

He could not return home, should not be allowed to, while there was still a Larkin left living. His job was not complete while this unnamed *she* still lived. He had been intentionally detained by forces who knew the truths that he did not.

It was right that he was here. It was meant that he should know these things. It was ordained that he fulfill his destiny.

He had to get out of here. He had to find the girl—he didn't even know where she was—and do with her exactly as he had done with her sister, her mother, and her many distant relatives.

But how?

Escape...

Lying there, on the cold hard floor, he felt the presence of something else, something familiar yet terrifying, the power that had guided him all these many years, that had lifted him from death and made him into something more than mortal, the creature that harkened back not only to his childhood, but back to a time of stone monuments, bringing with it a racial memory of runes and druids, of deeds done that were done no more, of living spirits that dwelt in rocks and trees, of power untold, of magic, of mystery, of a life beyond death and of a world that lurked alongside this one, seeing but unseen.

THE FIRST TIME HE SAW IT was when he was very young.

His life as a child was difficult to recall clearly at times, but it would surface in the middle of dreams with startling clarity, each sensory detail vividly recreated, from the soft green landscapes to the smiling faces of his mother and father.

He had been born and raised in the countryside of Ireland, in County Wicklow. The nearest town was fifteen miles away, and as his parents were too poor to own a motorcar, they drove a horse and cart. They had no television, and the wireless only received one station that broadcast daily news in Gaelic every night at eight. His mother would listen as she held her only child, her son, in her lap, trying to teach him the words, and the old tongue would light about him like fine down. She could often be heard muttering to herself or singing short songs in the language of her people. She had come from a very old and once-powerful family, or so she said.

Once they had taken a trip after the death of his mother's father, and they traveled by horse and cart all day to get to Branden, where the old man was being buried. Even these many years later, he remembered looking into the open casket and seeing the sunken eyes, the waxen skin, and wondering what could happen that could do this to the same man who had played the piano and sung for him just last Christmas. He sensed that his grandfather was still around somewhere; he had just become invisible.

After the service there had been a wake, which his father attended alone. He had not been allowed to attend. He stayed in a spare room with his mother and the other family women. They talked among themselves in whispers, switching from English to Gaelic and back again. He caught only snatches of what they were saying but two words were repeated with a certain regularity.

His father was slow waking up the next morning, and looked pale and sick as he hitched up the cart. He drove back slowly, not in the mood to talk or eat or sing songs.

It was dark by the time they got back, his mother hurrying him to bed. It was beginning to "weather up" outside, as she said, and she wanted to make sure that they were not caught out in the rain.

That night, as he slept, he dreamed of a shapeless mass of cloth and wind that fluttered outside his window, calling his name, scratching on the glass panes to be let in.

He woke up and called for his mother, who came to him and held him. When he told her the dream, she did not dismiss it as a mere fright as she had his other bad dreams, but instead listened to him the way she listened to his father when he talked of important things.

When he was done she held him closer and told him it was no ordinary bad dream. What he had seen was something that had been in her family for generations, a roving ghost-thing that haunted the land, one that only they could see, a spirit that foretold of family death and grief, forever cursing those who shared the bloodline.

The *bain seth*, it was called in the old tongue, and he recognized the words as the ones he had heard yesterday from the other women. He asked her what it meant in English and she told him.

It means 'banshee,' she said. *And I see it too.*

From then on he dreamed of it frequently, certainly more often than his mother did. He learned that there were nuances and conditions to the banshee's appearance that he could read like signs on a road. If it was far away, hovering out of hearing distance, only a spot of gray on the horizon, then it meant that something unpleasant was about to happen to him. What followed those dreams in real life was some kind of bad luck, like losing a fight in the schoolyard or getting a spanking from his father. If the banshee drew near, close enough so that he could see its face, then harm and misfortune were nearby and would most certainly strike. Someone in the family might have an accident, or a horse might nearly run him down, or a rock might bash him on the side of the head and he would look around, blood trickling down his neck, and see that there was no one there who could have thrown it.

If he heard the banshee but did not see it, then that meant death was very close to someone in the family, even if he did not know them. It was only later that he might hear of a relative's grave illness or trip to the hospital that had proved quite serious, even debilitating.

When he heard it and saw it, up close, so that he could see that its body was transparent like thin clouds, the bedraggled ends of its shredded gown fluttering just out of reach, its eyes glowing green and hollow as they gazed upon him, then he knew someone in the family was going to die. Those dreams were the most terrifying. It would come swooping up—not down from the skies but up from the ground, as if it dwelled down in the recesses of the earth with the other ungodly spirits—making a terrible racket, a keening that he felt as much as heard. It would hover before him for what seemed like hours in dream time, howling and wailing until he realized that the noises were not just sounds but syllables, parts of words. If he could see through his fright enough to listen, then the parts of words became a whole word, and the word became a name, followed by another name and then another. It recited a litany of those already dead before announcing who the next one would be.

He told no one of these visitations, not even his mother. He believed the legend as she had told it to him: that only those in the family could see the banshee. With a child's faith, he had assumed that all other family members had the same dreams as he had. After enough time, he began to wonder if that was true. His mother did not often speak of unusual dreams. When he had received the naming of the next relative to die, she took no particular steps to contact them or any others in the family. He finally realized that she did not see the banshee every time there was an impending family death, only when there was one particularly close to her—such as when her father died—as if her sensitivity to the spirit was in direct correlation with her bloodline. And she never seemed to see the *bain seth*; only hear it.

He, however, seemed to be unusually sensitive. The same way that he had seen dark hair and swarthy skin suddenly pop up in the son or daughter of a long line of fair Irish, he had a genetic trait that had surfaced after generations of recession. Perhaps no one had had this kind of ability to see and hear the spirits the way he did for more than a hundred years. He was a prodigy, a fluke, possessing powers that others might envy or misunderstand.

He was not like other people and never would be. He had to remember that.

The first time it came to him outside of the realm of dreams, it had appeared in the darkness outside his window, floating, its fingers squeaking against the glass, then pulling back, carried away on the wind, beckoning him to follow.

He stayed in bed, afraid, pulling the covers up over his head, waiting until the wind had died down and it was safe to look.

He edged his head out from underneath the blankets of his bed and peered through the window. Nothing but the darkness and the still night air outside. Perhaps it had been a dream, only so real he hadn't realized he was asleep. He pulled the shutters over his window so he wouldn't stare at it all night and turned over to try to get to sleep, and that was when he saw that it was in his room.

He would have cried out to his mother and father, but his fright was so great the breath caught in his throat.

It hovered over his bed, the tips of its gray and dirty nightgown brushing against the ceiling, some of them passing through the wood and pitch as if it wasn't there.

It made no sound, only drew nearer to him, angling itself between him and the door, using his fear of its touch to force him to unlatch the shutters over the window and slide the window up. When the wooden frame of the window creaked, it reached out and touched him, and he looked down at its thin and bony hand. He could see through the fingers and when he looked at his own arm he saw that it was turning gray and cold, that the feeling and warmth were seeping out of it as if it had been cut with a knife.

It let go and he crept through the window, his ten-year-old body scraping along the sides of the frame as he worked his way out into the night.

He dropped to the ground, his feet touching cold and rocky earth. The banshee floated through the window, parts of it passing through the upper glass that wasn't open. It trailed ahead of him, facing him, its eyes changing colors, from green to blue to red to black to green again, mesmerizing him until he no longer felt the cold stones and dirt beneath his feet, didn't hear the wind that whipped at his thin pajamas, didn't know that he was following the apparition far from home, listening only to it recite the litany of the family line, a chant that seemed to fill his head.

It brought him to the base of a tree and reached out again to him, drawing him up into the tree's high branches where he clung, listening to the banshee's song, not looking at the ground below, hearing the last of the names, bracing himself for the shock of the new one.

He clung to the top of the swaying tree, feeling the wind pick up in speed and force as the banshee reared back its hideous head, its features contorting, and with a vengeful scream shouted out the name of who was next to die. The sound was so sudden and painful that he clapped his hands over his ears, holding his position aloft only by the faint strength of his knees. Even through the flesh of his palms the sounds vibrated into his skull, and when he realized who was doomed he felt himself grow weak, his knees slipping off the thin branch, his hands scrabbling for a hold that wasn't there, and he floated in the air for a moment before falling, the wind and noise swirling about him, until the back of his head struck the point of a rock in the ground and he was sent spinning down into unconsciousness, knowing that the last thing he heard was his own name, screamed out into the night as a death knell.

He died, and remembered nothing after that for a very long time.

HE WAS SENT SPINNING, down into the hollows of the world, to a place forbidden. He saw rock that flowed as molten lava, giant lizards frozen in hardened stone, and when he finally stopped at the earth's core and looked around him, he saw the banshee there to meet him.

It was not hell. It was not even purgatory. It was more than that. It was the otherworld.

She enfolded him in her garment and visions filled his head. He saw that the universe was not what he had thought it was; mortal life was all illusion, not a goal but a way station, a gaming board where important conflicts among the ethereal were played to resolution.

He was presented with a choice. He could return with this new knowledge and work the banshee's will upon the world, or he could stay here and cast his lot with those who had refused so far. They were shown to him—gray souls that wandered aimlessly beneath the living for centuries, soldiers in an army of endless nights, casualties of a war they would never win.

He looked upon the banshee's face and saw fear and death, but also a power that could protect and nurture him, making his life so much more than those of other men. He was special, he knew that, and could accomplish special deeds.

He accepted the banshee into his being, and within a heartbeat felt himself whisked upward, through layers of rock and soil and dirt, to just beneath the ground where he had first hit.

HE AWOKE TO DARKNESS, riding consciousness like swelling waves, first awake, then asleep, until finally he felt strong enough to keep his eyes open and try to see.

There was nothing, only the tangy smell of freshly over-turned soil. He reached out with his hands and felt the sides of the coffin he had been buried in, rubbing grains of dirt between his fingers.

He thought back and remembered his fall from the tree, his trip to the otherworld, and what had transpired there. He pieced it together with what must have happened. He had been found and given up for dead. Someone—perhaps his family, perhaps strangers—had taken him up and put him in this box, burying him underground.

He felt no fear, no panic. He had bargained for a new life, and in that bargain he had found protection from sources greater than the confines of this box and the dirt that sur-rounded it.

He pressed upward with his hands. The lid shifted, then stuck. It had not been securely fastened, only placed on top to keep his face from being covered while he was buried.

His fingers, smaller than those that had measured and cut the wood around him, felt for loose nails, weak boards, knots or flaws in the lumber. He found one of the boards near his head had been split open by the force of the ham-mering, dividing neatly around the nail, leaving the nail bare and exposed. He worked the nail completely out of the wood, then snapped the board down, bringing a light driz-zle of dirt on his face, causing him to sputter. He freed the other half of the board, and then the one next to it. When he had three boards free, he was able to reach through the opening, clawing his way through the loose dirt that was cascading down on top of him, finally sticking his head through to the surface. It took him a while longer to work his body out, but he eventually crawled out from under the ground and collapsed on the nearby green grass. It was night. The wind was still, and there were no other humans in sight.

The effort had exhausted him. His head was swollen and throbbing. Dizziness overcame him and once again he slept.

WHEN HE AWOKE, it was daylight, and hunger and cold prompted him to struggle to his feet and set off in search of home. If his parents had thought he was dead, he could imagine their surprise when they saw him walking back from his grave, dirty and pale. They would either faint of shock or be overcome with joy. Perhaps both.

He was on the far reaches of his father's land, a place he had been only once or twice before, so he wandered in circles until he found the landmarks of familiar hills to guide him back to the farmhouse. He saw it in the distance, quiet and still. No one seemed to be home. Perhaps they had gone to the church to do their mourning. There had been a book in school, one that took place in America, about two boys, Tom and Huck, who had shown up at their own funeral. He knew how they must have felt, like weary adventurers, returning home to tell their tales and to have the adults listen to them for a change.

He saw that the cart and horse were gone, but his father had left his woodworking tools out. That wasn't like his father, who had once spanked him for leaving tools out where they could get rained on and ruined.

He called out, first for his mother, then for his father and then for anyone who was there. There was no answer.

The door to the house was open, and he wandered from room to room. He saw the beds made, the floor swept, even food left in the kitchen cooked and warm. What had happened? Where had they gone?

He left the house and searched the yard. Except for the missing cart and horse, there were no signs of departure. Maybe an animal had gotten suddenly ill and had to be taken to town for immediate treatment, he thought.

He decided to look in the barn.

He walked inside, the door creaking back on its rusty hinges. He peered into the darkness, listened to the silence. Chickens clucked as they ran in and out.

He heard a fluttering sound overhead, and watched as a pair of crows flew in through the open door, circled up high in the rafters and then settled on something that hung there.

He stepped closer. There was something strung up, dangling from the rafters. It looked like a large sack or weight, something that he hadn't seen there before.

It was the body of a man.

It was hanging from the rafters by a rope around its neck, twisting slowly in the air, the rope's creaking the only sound in the stillness. With a rising sensation of horror, he watched as the crows perched on the shoulders of the corpse and began to peck at its face.

He stood, gaping, rooted to the spot, thinking that nothing could be more horrible until the twisting action of the rope slowly brought the face of the dead man into view. Even through the damage wreaked by the crows' feeding he could clearly distinguish the features of his father.

He watched as a crow jabbed into his father's cheek, poking around in the slack flesh to try to get at the eyeball.

The boy turned and ran, his breath hot in his throat, his blood burning in his veins. He did not know how long he ran, or where he finally fell over from exhaustion, or how long he lay there in mute shock, seeing nothing, hearing nothing, knowing only that his bargain with the devil had drawn a far greater price than he had figured on paying. His memory, identity and name should just as well be erased, for that life no longer existed for him.

When he finally mustered the reason to get up and move again he was no longer the same.

HE WANDERED in the opposite direction from the nearest village, where there were people who could recognize him, perhaps even his mother, who would still want to claim him as her own. He knew that even if she was there, their reunion was unthinkable. Her son was dead, truly dead, in his mind as well as hers. Nothing of his former self remained, save memories.

He wandered down strange roads, over unknown land, across the property of people he had never met, passing strangers on the way, ignoring their questions as though he hadn't heard them. He avoided towns and villages, foraging for food on his own, stealing from closed shops and vacant farmhouses. When his clothes became too ragged and thin to wear, he would spy on a house where a boy his size lived, waiting for the whole family to leave for mass on Sunday, and then he would enter and take what he needed. He occasionally faced angry watchdogs, snarling and snapping at his heels as he crawled in through an open window.

Sometimes, even for all his precautions and watching and waiting, he was surprised by an errant son, a boy larger than he was who had been playing hooky from the family holiday and had returned to catch whoever it was rustling chickens in the henhouse or stealing corn from the crib. He suffered the first few sound beatings, losing teeth and hair in the process, until he figured to arm himself better.

He learned to steal knives along with food, hiding them in his coat pockets until they were needed. Once, while he was gathering eggs from a chicken coop, a dog leaped at him, its jaws closing in on his throat. He whipped a blade from his inside pocket and drove it up into the dog's breastbone, warm blood letting him know he had hit home. The dog froze, its snarl turning into a whimper, and rolled off him. He stood, leaving the blade buried in the dog's body, and fled. It was his first kill, and he could sense silent, dark approval.

He began to make it a practice to take the dogs out first, enticing them to charge and cutting their throats while he wrestled with them on the ground. If he was surprised by another boy, he turned and ran, making sure he had an escape route planned out in advance. The first time he was caught, it was by two brothers, and he knew they would leave him badly crippled before dragging him in front of the local authorities. He whipped his kitchen knife out and slashed one of them across the arm, causing him to howl with pain. He drove the blade into the other one's leg, twisting it once and leaving it there. He ran off into the countryside, unharmed.

As he lived and traveled alone, he began to grow, his constant adventures building his muscles as well as his reflexes. He was big for his age. When he was fourteen he could pass for sixteen, and there were a few jobs a sixteen-year-old could get without being asked too many questions. He cut peat, delivered coal, hauled stone and grew even stronger. With the money he made, he managed to get a roof over his head and some steady meals. He avoided the social overtures made by his fellow workers—refusing to drink or womanize with them. He was not like them, and never would be. He was waiting: for what, he wasn't sure.

He took different names, never using his own: O'Conner, Macready, O'Reilly. John, Paul, Timothy.

He was eighteen and driving a truck under the name of Jimmy Doyle in a town called Kinfe in County Bray when he met a man not much older than he. Patrick Donald—Pat, for short—had the same red hair and green eyes that he did, drank on his lunch break and told loud stories about his kinfolk, bragged about their faded wealth and position, all of them bearing the same name as dear Pat.

Larkin.

HE INTRODUCED HIMSELF to Patrick Larkin, easing the barrier he usually erected between himself and those he worked with. On payday, he let Patrick take him to his favorite pub, and there they bought each other pints until

closing. He had been content to let Patrick do all of the
talking.

Patrick came from up north, he said, driven south by
"the troubles," as they were called, and had a bit more of
the city in him than most. He was far away from his closest
relatives, but he claimed that they were all planning to go off
to America, life in Ireland being so hard these days, and he
planned to go with them, to live in the kind of places you
saw only on television or in magazines.

His kinsman listened to Patrick's tale with a proper air of
bemusement, never letting on that there was more to his interest than what flowed out of a tap. He let the man drink
up a day of his wages, pound him on the back and call him
Jimmy. When the pub closed, he walked Patrick Larkin
home, feeling the drink far less than the other man did.
Even at his young age, Patrick was already showing the
florid face and ruptured capillaries, or drinker's tattoos,
that marked a lifelong alcoholic.

After dropping Patrick off at his boardinghouse, he
walked home, his thoughts made slightly more fluid by the
pints of ale. If this man was a Larkin, he could lead him to
others. Perhaps he could learn what had happened to the
woman who had been his mother. It seemed as though this
had been his purpose all along, that he had been guided to
this very end by being isolated from the family line, and then
infiltrating it as a virtual stranger. For what reason, he did
not yet know.

But he would find out. Of that he was certain.

HE MADE DRINKING with Patrick Larkin a daily ritual, the
way he capped his shift. It wasn't difficult to insinuate himself into the man's life. Most of the others at the trucking
company found Patrick so loud and obnoxious that they
didn't want to have anything to do with him. It was only the
size and strength of his friend Jimmy Doyle that kept him
from being ousted, beaten up or worse.

He felt the other man out for information. He wanted to know where the other Larkins were, what had been happening to the family. He sensed that too many questions would make the man suspicious, even in his constantly inebriated state, so he satisfied himself with learning only of the man's closest ties in the family tree.

Patrick came from a large family: besides his mother and father, he had three brothers and four sisters. Gradually, he told of their names, their ages, where they lived, what they did and whether they had any children or not.

When Jimmy Doyle learned all of this, he knew the banshee would be pleased. His family was large and sprawling, far beyond his childhood comprehension, but now it seemed as if it was within his grasp to enumerate them all.

SHE CAME TO HIM one night—he had assigned the banshee an identity and personality even though he would never know her living name—floating through the walls of the cheap and leaky one-room apartment that he shared with two other laborers he barely knew. She hovered over their sleeping forms, her bedraggled hair twisting in the air. He lay on his bed beneath her, listening to her sing the names of the dead, ending with one that he knew, one that belonged to the man he drank with: Patrick Larkin.

He would be the next. Out of the entire family, he was meant to die.

In the daylight, he puzzled over the meaning of her appearance. It was Patrick Larkin's time, that much he understood, but was the banshee merely warning him that something was about to happen to the man? Or was she signifying that she wanted something done?

Did that mean he was to murder him? Murder all of the Larkins eventually, one by one? Or was it something more subtle, more complicated than that? He remembered that when the banshee appeared to him as a child, it foretold a death in the family. That hadn't meant murder on anyone's part. The person had been struck down by accident or disease, not by another family member's hand.

He thought back. He remembered when he had been a Larkin, when the banshee had sung his name and he had fallen from the top of the tree on his father's farm. Something had happened to him that he found hard to explain. He had not truly died, for he was alive and breathing. He had died in spirit, giving up his soul, and been reborn in the womb of the *bain seth*. He had been in a state of near-death, one so convincing that whoever had found him had taken him for a corpse and buried him alive. He had woken up in a wooden box, buried under the earth. He had not panicked, had not feared, because he knew that he had been saved for a specific purpose, but...

Was that what had happened to all the others? Had their illness or accident not been true death, but merely a cover, a state of predeath—one that they assumed while their true fate was being decided upon in the spirit world? Hadn't there been times before, even in his own family, when someone had been taken gravely ill only to be nursed back to health?

Perhaps it was not his place to murder, to actually take a human life. Perhaps he was only there to deliver the lives up unto the banshee herself—place them in a state similar to the one he had been in, so that their lives were within her power and she could do with them as she wished.

Perhaps it was her way of feeding.

HE BEGAN TESTING his theory by collecting wood. There was a carpenter in Kinfe, one that cut wood to order for building and other needs. He visited him that weekend and purchased what he needed, roughing out his specifications on a piece of paper. While he waited, he picked up a few things from a general market.

A hammer. Nails. Digging tools.

There wasn't room for him to work in his shared apartment, and he didn't want to have to explain the noise to his landlady or the sawdust to his roommates. He didn't own a motorcar, so he set out on foot to explore the countryside, looking for a secluded spot. He found one, only two miles' walk from town, in a forest next to a running stream. Except for a few cows, there was no one around who could see or hear him.

He brought his boards and tools there in the middle of the night, hiding them under a tarpaulin. He returned during daylight on his Sunday off, hammering them into shape. He left the lid unhinged. This was a live body he would be dealing with, not a dead one.

He dug a hole next to the stream, as deep and as wide as a real grave, leaving plenty of dirt piled to the side to fill it back in. The excess could go in the stream, where it would be washed away.

He lowered the finished and open coffin down into the hole. It fit snugly. He tested the bottom with his weight. It held.

He put the shovel, spade, hammer, nails and lid inside the coffin, covering the hole with the tarpaulin, weighing it down with stones.

The next day was Monday. He would wait until Friday, when he and Patrick got unusually soused, but this time he would be pouring his beer between the floorboards, goading Larkin into outdrinking him. When the man had passed out, he would easily heave his unconscious body onto his shoulders and say he was taking Patrick home, thereby arousing no suspicion.

Instead he would take him here, to this place in the woods. If the man awoke he would knock him out with a single blow. Otherwise, he thought, there should be no trouble.

He would place him in the coffin and bury him as he breathed. If the banshee decided Patrick Larkin was to live, most surely she would find Jimmy Doyle and tell him so. She would give him some kind of a sign to go and dig the man up. If not . . .

Then when the following Monday came around, Patrick Larkin would be nowhere to be found.

And neither would Jimmy Doyle.

THAT MONDAY AT WORK, Patrick Larkin was in a rare mood: sober. He was clean-shaven, dressed in clothes that weren't too badly rumpled, and at lunchtime, instead of heading for the neighborhood pub or ducking into an alley to nip off a bottle, he went into the supervisor's office inside the warehouse for a closed-door meeting. When he came out, he shook the hands of all the workers present, saving Jimmy Doyle's for last.

"Well, this it," he said.

"What?" Doyle asked.

"I've given me notice. Today's me last day."

Doyle set down the crate he had been holding. "What do you mean?" he asked.

"I'm goin' back up north, up to me brother's place. He an' his wife are headin' off for America in a week. They offered to pay half me passage and so I'm goin'."

"To America?"

"Aye."

"When are you heading off north?"

"Today. Now. I've got me bag packed and I'm gonna hitch a ride on the main road."

Doyle stuck out his hand. "Pleasure knowin' ya, Pat."

Larkin shook it vigorously. "Same to you, Jimmy."

And with that he was off. Doyle watched him go, wondering how he could have possibly foreseen such an unexpected turn of events and how in the world he was going to deal with them now.

He had to think quickly. Patrick Larkin was walking away.

He let him get a minute's lead. It was just after lunch, and the other men were still dragging their heels about getting back on the job. They were nursing hangovers from the weekend. The supervisor wouldn't notice he was gone. He could get by with skipping an afternoon's work, but if his roommates came home and saw him healthy and whole, they might wonder what the story was.

He would have to move now.

He walked quickly and quietly away from the work yard, keeping his head down. He passed the supervisor, who was shouting into the telephone, without being noticed. He walked down the narrow alley that led to the loading dock and turned out onto the street. He looked one way and then the other, spying Patrick Larkin, several hundred feet away.

He took off running after him, calling out Larkin's name as he ran.

Patrick stopped and looked to see who it was. When he recognized Doyle's face, he broke into an easy grin.

"I couldn't let you go," Doyle said, "without buying you one last pint."

AS THEY WALKED in through the door to the pub, Patrick Larkin breathed in deep. "I'm gonna miss this place," he said.

"There's probably none like it in America."

"No, probably not." He clapped a hand on Doyle's shoulder. "And no one like you to drink with, either."

"Then we have to make this last time one to remember."

They took their seats, Larkin raising two fingers to the bartender. "Only one for me," he said to Doyle as he unfolded his money. "Then I've got to hit the road."

"We'll get you on your way," Doyle said, thinking of the place by the stream in the middle of the forest. "You'll get to where you're going."

One pint led to another and then to another and within two hours Patrick Larkin was roaring drunk. Doyle managed to discretely nurse his drinks, and when he had a full pint sitting idle while he wasn't halfway through with another, he generously slid it over to Patrick Larkin's part of the bar. "Don't mind if I do," Patrick said as he downed the ale.

Doyle carefully watched the time. He wanted them to be out of there before the other men came in from the shipping yard. Otherwise, there might be questions, witnesses left behind. He had to speed up the action.

He signaled the bartender. "Two more," he said, "but this time make 'em Jameson."

"Jameson!" Patrick Larkin spluttered. "I can' have ya buyin' me whiskeys! I've gotta getton a' road."

"One for the chill," Doyle said as he slid both jiggers Patrick's way. "And another for your health."

Patrick gladly drank both.

"Another round," Doyle said.

Within the hour, Patrick Larkin was out. His head slumped forward until it touched the polished wood of the bar. He breathed loudly, a sound that threatened to rupture into a snore.

"Want me to call a taxi?" the bartender asked.

"No," Doyle said, shouldering his burden. "I'll take him home. A bit too much of traveler's cheer, that's all."

The bartender nodded, not knowing the importance he would play in the legend. *I seen the two of 'em go off, one over the other's shoulder, but couldn't tell ya which was which. If I'd known at the time that no one would ever see hide nor hair of 'em afterward . . .*

Doyle easily carried Patrick out into the daylight. It was still a workday around most of Kinfe, and the main thoroughfare that led out of town was only a block away. If he could get across the road and over the hill without being noticed . . .

He hadn't even thought of what he would do once he got Patrick out of sight. His possessions were still at the boardinghouse. There would be no way he would be free to go back and retrieve them before tomorrow. His roommates usually drank until eight or nine at night, but he couldn't risk being seen.

He moved slowly, keeping up the guise of a man helping a drunken friend home. He moved the two of them down

the street as one, Patrick's feet making no attempt at loco-
motion. He waited until he got them across the main road
before hoisting Patrick across his back like a duffel bag. He
grunted at the strain, but was up and over the hill within a
few minutes. No shouts from the local constable dogging at
his heels, no one asking what he was doing.

Once they were out of sight, he set Patrick down on the
grass, scouting around him. Not a soul in sight. He lifted
Patrick back up onto his shoulders. If he kept a steady pace
he could be there before dark. If he ran into anyone, he
would try to explain with some improvised lie. If that didn't
work and they remained too suspicious, he would kill them.

He arrived at the forest by the stream just as the last of the
light was fading from the sky. He had to work quickly. He
didn't have a lamp with him, and he didn't want to end up
fumbling around in the dark.

For the last half mile, Patrick had begun to mumble un-
intelligibly. As Doyle set him down, he realized he had to
move quickly if he wanted to get Patrick in the ground before he was conscious.

He pulled the tarpaulin back, flinging it to the side. He
reached into the hole and drew out the shovel and pick, setting them on top of the tarpaulin. He brought out the hammer and nails with one hand, the coffin lid with the other.
He set the hammer and nails on top of the coffin lid.

Patrick was making more and more noise with each passing minute, a sign of encroaching sobriety. As Doyle bent
closer to pick the other man up, he saw that Patrick's eyelids were fluttering and that his pupils were rolling wildly.
He lifted him up, cradling Patrick Larkin in his arms, and
stepped down into the hole.

He lowered him into the box, making sure Patrick's hands
and feet were fitted inside. Patrick's right hand had suddenly come alive and was clutching feebly at Doyle's coat.
Doyle took it and stuffed it into Patrick's pants.

He stood up and reached for the coffin lid, pulling it over
to him slowly so the nails wouldn't roll off and into the dirt,

putting them in his pocket when they were within reach. He set the hammer aside and brought the lid up and lowered it inside the hole, bracing his feet against the edge of the coffin, balancing himself.

He lowered the lid over Patrick Larkin, careful not to trap a finger or a shoe between the lid and the coffin. When the lid was in place, he set one knee on top of it to hold it still, and reached for the hammer.

He started nailing the lid down at the top, working his way down the edges from head to foot. The noise of his hammering roused Patrick even further, and Doyle listened as the man attempted whole sentences, his hands and feet feebly bumping against the wooden box that now held him prisoner.

When the lid was securely in place, he climbed out of the hole, put the hammer into his coat pocket and walked over to pick up the shovel. He set the spade in the mound of dirt and began shoveling it back into the hole, a shovelful at a time. He listened to the muffled sounds the soil made: first dirt on wood, then dirt on dirt.

He buried Patrick Larkin with three feet of loam, patting it down with the blade of his shovel every few minutes.

He smoothed out the top of the grave, then began to shovel the leftover soil into the stream, listening to it hiss as it hit the gurgling water.

When he was done, he carefully arranged his tools beside the grave and gathered the tarpaulin around him. He knew that he wasn't going to be able to go home, so he decided to spend the night right there.

He braced himself against the chill and waited. He wanted to see what was going to happen.

HE HEARD PATRICK after a few hours. The cold had sufficiently counteracted the effects of the alcohol to rouse the man to coherent thought. He first heard him knocking against the wooden sides of the box, grunting and straining, trying to find out where he was and what was keeping him from moving.

Then his voice came up, muffled by three feet of dirt, barely audible. Doyle had to press his ear to the ground to hear.

"Jimmy," Patrick called out. "Jimmy, where are you?"

The man who had called himself Jimmy Doyle said nothing.

"Where am I?" More pounding, followed by cursing. "Where the hell am I?"

There was silence. Then more racket, grunting sounds as Patrick tried to force his way out of the box, with no success.

"All right," Patrick called. "Let me out. Enough's enough. Whoever locked me in here, let me out."

Silence.

"A good joke. Come on. It's over. I got to go to the bathroom."

Nothing.

More pounding and shouting. "Help!" There was a panicky edge to the Larkin's voice now. *"Help! Will someone let me out of here?"*

He listened to the sounds that came wafting up through the ground a while longer. Shouting. Pounding. Screaming. Crying. Begging. They faded off as the hours of the night lapsed by, until finally there was only silence.

He sat upright, his attention suddenly shifting to something that he hadn't even noticed was happening before. There had been a change in his immediate environment, one so subtle that it had been hidden under the sound of Patrick Larkin's pleas for help.

The wind was building up.

She must be coming, he thought. She's on her way here.

His body tingled with anticipation.

He stood, casting the tarpaulin aside, pacing around in the darkness, looking for any sign of her. He hoped he had done exactly what she had asked. Her signs had been open to interpretation, and he didn't want to be guilty of making a mistake.

He felt the temperature in the blowing air shift from warm to cool, the texture changing from dry to damp.

He looked around him, ready to receive her company. He heard her cry, far away, echoing across the hills.

The wind picked up, scattering dirt and leaves around him. The tarpaulin snapped like a downed flag.

He saw her first as glimpses of gray ghostly filament between the trees. She passed around them like a fish skirting reeds in a pond. As she drew closer, he felt his being tingle, something within him responding to her visitation that hadn't been there before. As she drew nearer he saw that she was smaller than in his previous visions, her presence muffled, her cry not as piercing, as if she were weakened by time and strain.

She floated over the grave, her eyes on him, hollow and black, as she seemed to extend herself, reach down and extract a vital essence from the box that lay three feet underground. He saw her satisfy her need, strength returning until the blowing wind circled around her in a maelstrom, once again in her control, and he saw her face shift and change into something darker and malevolent, as if the creature of legend was merely a host form, a cover for a greater power, older than his sense of time could encompass.

She turned to him again, enfolding him within her embrace like a great gray bird. Clutched to her bosom, he found the only love he knew.

HE RETURNED to his boardinghouse the next day and collected his meager belongings, hiking over miles of open countryside before venturing back down toward paved roads and hitching a ride. He journeyed north, to find Patrick's brother, Michael. He got a job there, this time calling himself Jack Shaughnessy, but he spent most of his time watching the household of Michael Larkin. He saw Michael and his wife, Susan, wait for Patrick's arrival and, when he didn't show, post letters to Pat's former employer expressing concern. When the letters came back, they apparently did not satisfy Michael. Their content could easily be guessed: *The last we saw of your brother, he was on his way to see you. He came to work and said goodbye. No one has seen him since. Regretfully, we know of no other . . .*

Jack Shaughnessy found another carpenter, only a few blocks from where Michael Larkin lived, and bought what he needed there. This one would be more difficult. Patrick Larkin had been a despicable loner, but Michael Larkin had a wife, friends and a respectable job. He would have to be patient.

After another week had gone by, Shaughnessy watched as Michael Larkin packed his bag, kissed his wife goodbye, walked to the train station and bought a ticket south. Before he had a chance to board his train, Shaughnessy went to the telegraph counter and had him paged. When Larkin showed up, Shaughnessy greeted him with his hat in hand, saying that he was sorry to be the bearer of bad news, but he had some information regarding his brother Patrick. He had a car in town. If Mr. Larkin would walk with him . . .

"Is my brother dead?" Michael had asked, his face strained with concern.

"It's best if we wait until we get into town, sir," Shaughnessy had replied.

They took the walk into town, passing by a wooded glen. Shaughnessy excused himself, saying he had to seek relief from nature. Larkin understood, and stood with his back turned as Shaughnessy ventured a few feet into the trees, then silently crept up on the man and dragged him in.

He let the wife live. He broke into and searched their house while she was out until he found out where the rest of this branch of Larkins were, disguising the action as a normal robbery. But he let the wife live.

FROM THEN ON, that was how it was for him.

He traveled from town to town in Ireland, spending

weeks, sometimes months tracking down the next link in the family chain. There were men and women, young and old, some of them living in prosperity, some in wretchedness. There were those who lived alone, and there were families of twelve, all of whom had to be done in, one by one. It was tricky work, and he had to have his wits about him, but at the end of every conquest, there was his glorious reward.

As he became more proficient at his task, he saw that the banshee was growing stronger and greater, filling the sky with her fearsome cry and shining light. The day finally came when he was done in Ireland, when it was time to move on. To America.

It took him the better part of a year simply to adjust to the change of living in another country and to find a decent job. He worked hard at erasing his brogue, so as not to arouse suspicion. He had ransacked the houses of those he had already taken, looking for the names and addresses of relatives who had already made the journey across the Atlantic. He learned of a family in New Jersey, a bachelor in Florida, and a sister in Kentucky. He would find them, he knew, bring them all to their appointed end, but there was one he would save for last.

The one who had declared him dead, buried him alive in a crude box in a cold patch of earth, who had left his father swinging from the rafters of the family barn.

The woman who had been his mother.

Mary Larkin Sullivan.

HE LAY IN HIS CELL, the memories fading.

He realized he did have a chance at escape, but he had been too confused to see it.

Both the doctor and the police captain were most concerned about the same information. They wanted him to show them the grave he'd given Mary Sullivan. She was certainly dead by now; the banshee had most likely come and been done with her. It would do no harm if he showed them where she was.

And it might give him the opportunity he desperately needed: to break away from them, find the last living Larkin and take her as well.

He felt hopeful, able to close his eyes and finally sleep.

Tomorrow would be a day of surprises. For all of them.

CHAPTER TEN

JOHN LAY AWAKE, staring at the ceiling, his nightmare long over but still unable to relax enough to fall back to sleep. Disjointed thoughts crowded in, making drowsiness impossible.

He had an underlying feeling of...something. A premonition. As if the next day would be some sort of—

"John?"

He turned quickly and saw a figure outlined by a white garment, almost startlingly similar to the form of Gretchen he had seen in his dream. He momentarily panicked, but then realized that the shadow was natural, not supernatural, and belonged to a friend, not a foe.

"John, are you awake?" Annette called. She sounded as though she couldn't see him very well.

"Yes," he said, rising up on one elbow. "I'm right over here."

She followed the sound of his voice and sat on the carpet next to his made-up bed, her face hidden in the darkness. "I can't sleep," she said.

"Neither can I."

"Why can't you?"

"I had...kind of a bad dream."

She nodded understandingly. "I think I did, too."

"What was yours like?"

"Don't remember."

He peered into her shadowed features. He couldn't tell if she was telling the truth or not.

"Wish I could say the same," he said.

"What was yours like?" she asked.

"You don't want to know."

She didn't press the issue, taking his word for it.

"What time is it?" she asked.

"I don't know." He strained to see the clock over the mantel above the fireplace. "Four-thirty," he said finally.

She sighed. "I don't think I'm going to get much sleep tonight."

"Same here."

It was different now with her. He felt relaxed. Natural. The tension from before was gone. Something had changed, but he didn't know what.

"What's going to happen tomorrow?" she asked. "I guess I mean today."

"I don't know," John replied. "We've got a suspect, but if he won't talk . . . we may not be able to make much progress until he does."

"How do you plan to persuade him?"

"No idea. He won't talk to me. He won't talk to Captain Rogers." He looked up at her in the darkness. "He might . . ." He didn't finish the thought.

"What were you going to say?"

"It's not important."

"No, please."

"What I was going to say was . . ." He took a deep breath. "He might talk to you."

The idea visibly unnerved her. "Why do you say that?"

"Because I think the two of you are related."

"You think he's from . . . the family."

"Yes. I think he's a Larkin. Just like you."

"How do you know?"

"I don't—not for sure. Call it a hunch or whatever . . . when I met him I thought: here was what Mary Sullivan—your mother—was talking about. A family curse, an evil force walking around killing off all the members of her family, except it was a real human being. He was headed back to Ireland when we caught him. He may have had an accent at one point, but trained himself to lose it. He showed great surprise when I told him that there was a surviving Larkin left in Southern California—almost shock. And the features... I'm going to ask Rogers to call my old department and see if they'll do computer simulations comparing your face to his to see if there is a resemblance."

She touched her face, as if the procedure might damage her somehow. "Does he know who I am?"

"No. He knows you're alive. That's it. But if he saw you, heard your voice... it might challenge his delusions of grandeur or whatever it is that keeps him killing. It might break his will and cause him to spill his guts. If we could get him to take us to where he disposed of Mary Sullivan, then... we'd have a very solid case against him.

"How solid?"

"Prosecution might be able to get the death penalty."

"Would you like to see that?"

"I don't know. I kind of talk tough about it, but... can't help but feel that it's still murder, only murder sanctioned by the state."

"Do you think you could ever kill somebody?"

"I don't know. I never have. If it was necessary... but then you get into the whole rigmarole of what would make it necessary."

She nodded, as if she felt the same way. "I just wonder what makes him do it."

John smiled, although he wasn't sure she could see him in the dim light. "What makes anyone commit any violent crime? Anger. Fear. Hate. Emotions so complex there probably aren't names for them yet, and never will be. Our society—especially this one, right here in L.A.—is highly pressurized. We're all fighting for what scraps of land are left, the division is so great between the haves and the have-nots. We have the entertainment industry here, the dream factory, that draws misfits and wackos from all over the country, thinking that they can be a part of the fantasy they've seen on the tube or the big screen. L.A.'s always been a haven for serial killers. The smog, the traffic... stress is a major commodity here. It's our biggest import."

"Why do you stay?"

"Never lived anywhere else. Guess I'm too wary of trying it somewhere different."

"Where would that be?"

John thought for a moment. "Oregon, probably. Maybe Washington."

She nodded. "I've been up there. It's beautiful, especially the coastline."

"I used to fantasize about saving enough money to move up there, buy a piece of land and—I don't know—become a fisherman."

She laughed. "Why don't you?"

"Fantasies don't always made the best realities. Besides, I tried to take the easy route and look what I'm doing now. I'm an action junkie. When this is all over I'm sure it won't be long before I'm involved in something like it again."

He realized he had been talking too much about himself. He shut up and let some silence speak for him. He seemed to have a chance to make something of a second impression on Annette here, and he didn't want to blow it.

It was getting a little lighter outside.

"If I agree to see him—what's his real name, anyway?"

"We don't know."

"You don't know his *real name*?"

"No. His prints didn't show up anywhere. He's a cipher. Someone who slipped through the holes."

"Are there people who can still do that?"

"Apparently."

"Well, if I agreed to see him what would the circumstances be?"

"Circumstances?"

"Where would I meet him? What would my protection be?"

"It'd be in his cell at the Jicarita PD." He described the maximum security cell for her. "I went in there when I talked to him. It's a little spooky, but believe me, it's safe. There's a guard posted outside and you're under constant video surveillance."

"You want me to do this, don't you?"

"Would it make you feel better if I went with you?"

"Into the cell?"

"Yes."

"If I could have someone else there . . . I wouldn't know what to say to him."

"Ask him what he did with his latest victim."

"But you'll go with me? You'll sit beside me on that little bench and if something goes wrong . . ."

"I'll be there."

There was a long silence. Birds began to chirp in the predawn. John could already tell that it was going to be a hot day.

"All right," she said. "I'll talk to him."

They got up shortly after that, John boiling water for herbal tea, and then the two of them took turns getting dressed in the privacy of the bedroom. John threw together some eggs, toast, and squeezed some fresh orange juice. They ate at what used to be the bar, watching the sunlight spread over the trees.

"How hot does it get here?" Annette asked.

"Eighty. Ninety. Hot. Dry, too. This time of the year it's illegal to smoke in your car with the window down."

"I like it best at the beach in the spring. Nothing like getting fogged in as an excuse to postpone all your errands and read a good book."

John smiled and munched on a piece of toast. He didn't know whether he should broach the subject of the previous night or not. What would he say? he wondered. Listen, I'm a closet neurotic, and you're just better off without trying to come near me again. Sure, I'll go into the same cell as a dangerous killer, but human relationships, well, that's a little too much for me.

"Is something wrong?"

He looked at Annette. Her voice made his stomach twinge nervously. All of the calm and ease he had felt with her this morning was gone. The old nervousness and fear were back.

"No," he said. "Nothing's wrong."

"You just looked a little serious there for a minute."

"No." He wouldn't say anything. He'd pretend it hadn't happened, that there was nothing to deal with. Maybe it would go away and then he wouldn't have to worry about it anymore. "Everything's fine."

After they ate and John loaded the dishes into the dishwasher, he backed the Camaro out of the garage and the two of them drove down the main road to the police station.

When they arrived at the station, John found that Rogers was already in his office. Except for the change of clothes, he looked as though he had spent the night there. He probably didn't get much sleep last night, either, John thought to himself.

"I tested your idea," Rogers said after he had greeted John and Annette and directed Annette toward the coffee machine. "I made a few overseas calls. Because of the time difference, I had to get here at something like five in the morning to talk to whoever could help me. Turns out you were right again." He held out a printed sheet. "The Larkins are an endangered species in Ireland as well."

John took the report from the detective and began to study it. He ran his eyes down the list of names: Patrick Donald Larkin, Michael William Larkin, Alice Larkin McAnswell...there were more than twenty names.

"What do you think?" Rogers asked.

"I think..." But John wasn't sure what he thought. There was something about this list of names that bothered him. He couldn't put his finger on it specifically, but it seemed somehow...insufficient. "Are there any surviving members of the family?"

Rogers shook his head. "Not over there. In the continental U.S., I think she's the only one," he said, nodding after Annette, who had yet to return from getting her coffee.

"Except for him," John corrected.

"Except for him."

John studied the list again. Something just around the corner, just out of reach... "Can I make a copy of this?" he asked.

"It is a copy. Keep it. Let me know if you have any additional thoughts. I'll play one of your hunches anytime."

John folded the list and put it in his pocket. "Well, I just happen to have one."

"I'm listening."

"I think our suspect—any ID yet?"

"No. I still call him Frank B. Lewis, but sometimes I slip and refer to him as 'he' or 'him' or...'it.'"

John laughed mirthlessly. "Me too. Anyway, I think our suspect may react favorably if we play our trump card. Just lay it on the table and see what he says."

"And our trump card is...?"

"Getting herself some coffee."

Just then Annette returned, a full Styrofoam cup in one hand, a half-empty one in the other. "Mmm... Captain, your Sergeant Griffin makes a great cup of coffee." She drained the rest of the cup and dropped it in the wastebasket, shifting her attention to the full one. "I feel almost human again."

"This is rather odd," Rogers said.

"Why?" John asked.

"What?" Annette said.

"He... early this morning..." Rogers stepped out the door, motioning for them to follow him. John took Annette by the elbow and escorted her, following Rogers to the observation room. Cameras were still trained on the maximum security cell, where the suspect was sitting on his bed. There was something different in his face. Instead of resignation, almost... expectation.

Rogers rifled through fresh videocassettes, each one labeled and numbered. He found the one he was looking for, stuffed it into a machine, quickly rewound it and set the machine on Play.

A monitor flickered to life, switching from silent gray static to another view of the maximum security cell that held their suspect. By the man's posture—different from the one on the live observation screen—John could tell that it had been taken sometime during the past twelve hours.

"This is about an hour ago," Rogers said. "Just after we fed him breakfast."

As they watched the tape, the man with the shaved skull stirred and rose to his feet. He crossed the narrow breadth of his cell and leaped up onto the bars, jamming his feet in the rungs for support, pressing his face close to the camera, the wide-angle lens distorting his head so that his features leered wildly even though his expression was blank. Annette drew back. It was a disturbing sight. Up close, one could see the stitches in the ridged cuts on his scalp.

"I wish to speak to the doctor," he said, his voice sounding unnatural, filtered through the small microphone in his cell. He paused, as if for effect.

"The doctor," he repeated.

He dropped off of the bars like some great gorilla and sat back down on his bed. John looked from the monitor playing the videotape to the one that showed the current scene in the cell. The man's position was exactly the same; since making the pronouncement he had not moved.

Rogers shut the tape off and looked at John. "He wants to see you."

THE DOOR TO THE CELL CLOSED behind him on well-oiled hinges, the metal clang attesting to the absence of rubber weather stripping along the frame. Strength at the expense of comfort.

One of the few surviving Larkins in the world looked up from his sitting position on his bed.

John took his seat on the bench. "You wanted to see me?" he asked.

Lewis nodded.

"What's your real name?"

No reaction.

"Why did you ask to speak with me?"

"The other one," Lewis said.

The sound of his voice startled John. The tiny microphone underneath the surveillance camera did not do justice to the range of the man's voice. It was low, rumbling, resonant.

"The other what?"

"The other one. The other girl. The other daughter."

"What about her?"

"Who is she?"

"She's . . . you know already: the daughter of Mary Sullivan, given up for adoption. Gretchen Seale's twin sister."

"What's her name?"

John hesitated a moment before answering. "Annette."

"Her last name."

"No. You want something from me, I've got to get something from you."

The man looked at him levelly.

"I want to know where Mary Sullivan is—what you've done with her."

"If I tell you?"

"Then you get to see Annette."

He thought about that for a moment. "I don't believe you," he said.

"Don't believe what?"

"That there is such a girl. It's a trick."

"No, she really exists. Do you want to see her? I can show her to you. I can bring her in here and you can talk to her if you wish. She's agreed to do so. Only one condition: we have to know where Mary Sullivan is."

John wondered what the man would have done if the bars were not there? What would he be like if John had just met him, standing in line at the bank or sitting next to him on an airplane? How many people had shared proximity with this man and not known what he really was?

"I see the girl first," he said. "Then I will tell you."

ANNETTE ENTERED the cell cautiously, clinging to John's arm. The man behind bars stood, either out of deference or in order to make himself appear more threatening. John wasn't able to tell. He guided Annette to the bench. She sat up straight, her back pressed against the wall, keeping as much distance as possible between herself and the man she had come to see. She was very frightened, but made a good show of keeping her fear under control. Her hand found John's and did not let go.

John looked from Annette to their prisoner and back to Annette again. Neither of them said a word. John wondered if the man had anything to actually say to Annette, or if Annette could think of anything to say to him. Such details of conversation were unimportant. The man had his proof that Annette was real, and what mattered now was that he keep his end of the bargain.

It was Annette who broke the silence in the room. "Who are you?" she asked, her voice barely above a whisper.

No response.

"Are you what they say you are? Are you the man who's killed all those people in my family?"

No response.

"Why don't you say something?"

No response. The man merely sat and stared, etching her face into his memory in indelible ink.

"What have you done with my mother?" On the last word her voice trembled.

"I've hidden her away."

Annette jerked slightly. John had not expected him to ever speak up.

Annette tried again. "Where did you hide her?"

"Away."

"Where?"

"Out of sight. Underground."

"You buried her alive, didn't you?"

He nodded.

"Why? Why did you do such a terrible thing?"

"You don't need to ask me that question."

Annette didn't reply. She didn't know what to make of his answer.

"You've seen it, too," he continued. "Don't deny it."

"Seen what?" She was a bad liar.

"In the night. At certain times. In your dreams."

"What are you talking about?"

"The banshee."

It was her turn to say nothing.

"You know what it means."

"No. I'd never heard of such a thing until a few days ago."

"It means that you're doomed, too. Even after I'm gone, it will haunt you as well."

Annette turned to John. "I think I want to get out of here."

John nodded and rose, Lewis's voice taunting her. "It's what killed your family, not me. I am only its medium."

Annette hurried out the door, unable to bear it any longer, anxious to have the door closed and locked between the two of them.

"It'll get you, little one." His voice trailed after her, following her outside the cell and into the hall. "It'll get you as sure as it got the others."

John handed Annette off to Rogers, who was standing just outside in the hallway. With a reassuring squeeze, he let Annette's arm go and ducked back inside the cell before the guard could close the door.

He reentered the cell. Lewis was still standing in front of his bed, arms across his massive chest in an air if triumph.

"What the hell did you do that for?" John said angrily. "You scared her half to death."

The man sat down as if he hadn't heard John, lying back on his bed and staring up at the ceiling. "We had a bargain," he said. "You kept your part, now I'll keep mine."

He rolled his head and looked at John. "But I have to take you there. I need to be the one to show you."

ROGERS MET JOHN in the hallway, just after the metal door to the cell had clanged shut behind him. He had left immediately, wanting to intercept the captain before he walked into the cell. Annette was nowhere in sight.

"I heard," Rogers said.

"How much?"

"To the part where he says he'll take us there himself."

"You're not considering doing that, are you?" John asked.

"Of course."

"You want to take him out of there? Outside, where he'll be among people again? You heard what he said to Annette."

"I don't want to, but it looks like I'll have to."

"I wouldn't negotiate with him."

Rogers's eyes narrowed slightly, as if he were studying John through a pane of dusty glass. John wondered if he had said something to the police captain that had offended his ego, but realized that this was just the man's way of listening.

"I don't think it matters to him at all whether we really find Mary Sullivan's body or not. He may not really lead us to it. I think all he wants is to get outside, in the open, away from his cell."

"What for?"

John swallowed. "I think he may try to escape."

Rogers squinted at him some more, then looked off a few degrees at a place on the wall. "I disagree with you," he said.

"You don't think he'd try to make a break for it?"

"I didn't say that. I think if the opportunity were presented to him, he'd definitely take it. What I disagree with you on is the fact that he might be presented with that opportunity."

"But at the airport . . ."

"That wasn't a situation I was in charge of. In this case, I would be."

"But do you think that's enough?" John asked, immediately wishing he could take back the words. So far he had not managed to slight Rogers's ego grievously, but he thought he might have hit a tender spot for the first time.

"Yes, doctor, I think that's enough." John winced at Rogers's tone. "I think my police department can handle any situation you might care to think of, without backup from any other local or national force. We're real cops here."

"I didn't meant to say anything to offend you," John said softly. "I didn't mean to imply that your department was of anything less than the highest caliber."

Rogers had an expression on his face that John had only seen in photographs of Afghanistan rebels, men armed with rifles and hand grenades preparing to do battle with Soviet tanks and jets.

"I, myself, have worked with the LAPD numerous times, and wish that at least once I had encountered there the professionalism and dedication that I've found dealing with the Jicarita police force. Especially yourself."

Rogers's face softened an angstrom, one ten-billionth of a meter.

"You've given me a role in this case as a police adviser, and I greatly appreciate it. I know my credentials probably don't mean a whole lot to you on paper...."

"I didn't say that."

"Well, I know that the coroner's office to you is probably—"

"The coroner's office to me is a valuable resource, an aid to police work." He stressed the word *aid*. "As such, it is indispensable. But it is not the sum of police work, or its central science."

"And that is...?" John lowered his head humbly, waiting to hear the great knowledge.

"Instinct. You should know that by now. All of your best guesses so far have been on instinct."

"Yes."

"And my instinct tells me that I should let this man get out in the field with us and show us exactly where he buried his last victim. If I have to." He took a deep breath and let it out, quieting himself. "Now, maybe your instinct is telling you that there may be a way to get the information I need out of him without having to do that."

"That's probably it."

"Then that's all I need to know." Rogers reached for the door to the cell.

"What are you going to say to him?"

"You'll see."

THEY WALKED IN together. When Lewis saw them, he stood up.

Both men sat on the bench, John closest to the door.

Lewis was the last to sit. He looked from one man to the other, obviously wondering which one was going to speak first.

It was Rogers. "I understand you've agreed to tell us where you buried Mary Sullivan," the captain said.

A nod. "We struck a bargain."

"You and Dr. Stratton did."

Rogers let the statement hang in the air like stale cigarette smoke. John thought he saw a flicker of worry in Lewis's expression.

"Perhaps you are unaware of Dr. Stratton's position in this case. He is a police adviser, an expert whom I consult with on certain matters. His expertise allows me to make the best decisions."

Rogers paused for effect. "He has, however, no real authority. He was not authorized to make any deals with you, just as I am not bound to live up to them."

Lewis's expression shifted between a look of concern and a look of anger. He was obviously having difficulty donning his mask once again.

"So let me tell you what bargain I am offering you." Rogers shifted his position. The man was casual in his manner, almost relaxed. "You tell me where Mary Sullivan is buried, and we go find her."

"But I must come with you."

"I don't negotiate."

"That is part of the deal."

"There is no deal. There is what I will do, and there is nothing else to consider. What I will do, however, is I will think about it. I will not say yes or no at this time."

Lewis hesitated. "But you will think about it?"

"Yes."

"So it's possible that I could come with you."

"Yes, I will say that's possible."

There was a long silence. I definitely underestimated you, Carl, John thought. Definitely.

Lewis spoke, his voice halting, searching for the exact words.

"You know the old road?"

"Yes."

"Down there."

"How far?"

"Three miles."

"Almost to the state park?"

"Yes. Almost."

John didn't know the area, but he knew of it. It was undeveloped, hardly touched. Since the new highway had been built to allow traffic through to the valley, the old road was rarely used, except by those hardy souls who ventured in there to get to the state park hiking trails and campgrounds.

"Up an unmarked road."

"No name?"

"No."

"How will we know it?"

"It has a gate across the entrance—the metal kind used to keep cattle in."

"Up the road?"

"Yes."

"How far?"

"To the top. Where the trees thin out."

"What's at the top?"

"There's an old cemetery."

"A *cemetery*?"

"Yes. It's not used anymore."

"I'd hope not."

John remembered Greg Needham's tale of an old cemetery in Jicarita. He wondered if Rogers had heard a similar
story. John knew that there had been pioneer settlers dat-
ing back before the turn of the century, and he knew that
Indian burial grounds had been found around the post office, but a lost graveyard . . . If this man had found it his research must have been quite thorough.

"What dates are on the gravestones?"

"The last ones date back fifty years. Others a hundred."

"How did you find it?"

"On my own."

"So we go up to the top—is the road paved?"

"No."

"Up to the top and then to the graveyard. Then what?"

"Then you must drive through the graveyard to a rock
levee."

"You mean a wall?"

"Yes."

"How tall is it?"

"Not too tall. Eight feet. You'll have to climb over it."

"So we climb over the rocks and then what?"

"Walk up the hill to where there are three rocks."

"What three rocks?"

"Each rock is twice as tall as a man. Everything else
around is dirt."

"How are the rocks positioned?"

"In a semicircle. They aren't difficult to see. It's the
highest point in the canyon."

"How do you know that?"

"Surveyors' maps."

Rogers continued. He wasn't going to let this man surprise him. "You buried her there?"

Lewis nodded. "Between the three rocks. You will see."

"Could we spot this place from the air?"

"Yes."

"Then that's what we'll do." Rogers stood, brazenly scooting past John, pressing himself up against the bars of the cell as if he was totally unconcerned about the threat the man behind them posed. Lewis could have easily reached through and grabbed him.

Rogers opened the door. "John, you coming?"

John rose. "Yes."

"Good." He held the door open as John passed through. John turned around as soon as he was in the hall to see that Lewis was standing, pressing up against the bars like an anxious child in a crib.

"Oh," Rogers said, in an exaggerated display of carelessness. "And no," he said, turning to Lewis, "you're not coming along."

Rogers closed the door on him, walking away with the assurance of a fighter who has just won the deciding round.

The two men went back to Rogers's office. "I'm going to get our chopper pilot up there and see if he can spot it from the sky," he told John. "It sounds like a hell of a lot of trouble to get to by car."

"Are you going to go up with him?"

"No, I'll be down here, watching."

John didn't understand.

"The helicopter has a television camera that will show us what the pilot sees. That signal is transmitted down here and we communicate by radio. With luck, we should get a good picture."

"How long will that take?"

"About an hour or so. More if the weather is not on our side."

"You need me until then?"

"No."

"I thought I might take Annette home. Get her out of here after her experience with Mr. Hospitality."

"Probably a good idea. But I'd like for you to come along when we exhume Mary Sullivan. I'll need you then."

John smiled in spite of himself. "In my capacity as expert police adviser."

Rogers smiled, too, the humor breaking the tension between them. "The prosecution's star witness."

"Hey, I'll end up on TV."

"I want a cut of the movie rights."

"Oh, I think we're talking five-part miniseries here."

"Well, I want Denzel Washington to play me. He's ten years younger and a lot better looking."

"Don't sell yourself short. Hold out for Cosby." He found Annette in the lounge, fussing with the coffee maker, trying to make a fresh pot of java.

"You drink too much of that stuff," John said.

She whirled and screamed, the glass coffeepot cracking against a tiled counter.

"Oh, good God," John said, immediately rushing to her side. "I'm sorry. I didn't mean to frighten you."

"No...no...it's okay," she said, putting a hand to her breast. "I just...didn't know anyone was there."

"He must have really shaken you up."

"You could say that."

John took the coffeepot from her and put it back on the burner. "Well, the last thing you need is more caffeine. Come on. Have a seat."

"No...that's all right. I've been sitting and sitting. Wondering where you were."

"I'm sorry I took so long. The madman says he'll do what we want. He's going to cooperate."

"Then I guess it was worth scaring the hell out of me."

"Hey. That's not a nice thing to say."

"It's true," she said angrily. "That was the deal you made. 'Show her to me and I'll talk.' All that remained was for you to turn on the charm and get me to buy it." She put a hand on her face, covering her eyes. "What am I saying? I don't know what to think." She dropped her hand and John saw that she was fighting tears. She was not going to get hysterical. She was not. "Do you have to do anything else now?"

"Not for a few hours or so."

"Can you take me home? I mean, back to your place? I don't want to be here any longer."

"Sure."

"I just want to get out of this building. I want to get away from him."

SHE WAS LEAVING the building. He could sense it.

He had seen and felt her thoughts in vivid patterns, spiking through the walls and hallways toward him, passing through layers of concrete and steel as if they weren't there. He could sense her proximity, a sensation he had experienced only a few times before with the others, a phenomenon in direct correlation to how much blood they shared.

They were children from the same mother. He had known it as soon as she entered the room. It was the only way he could have known for sure, and the doctor had done as he had hoped, even though the policeman was not going to live up to the original bargain. Yet.

Now that he knew what she looked like, she would be easier to find again. His inner radar was the most unreliable of measurements, but...it was all he had to rely on for now.

His plan had not worked entirely. True, he had frightened her badly enough to want to seek shelter outside the building, away from the police. *Just get me out of here* had been one of her thoughts. He doubted that that was what she said word for word, but he knew it was close enough. Most likely she had said this to the doctor—the doctor had been the one who introduced her, not the detective. He wondered what their relationship was, man to woman. He had seen them together and he felt the sexual tension run between them, invisible but distinct, like a current of warm air. If they were not lovers yet, they would be soon. He wondered when the doctor had first met her? How exactly was he involved?

He knew that if Annette had expressed anxiety to Stratton, she would also have made it his responsibility to take her away from the police station to a place more comforting. His home? Hers? Where did either of the two of them live?

John Stratton, and what he knew, was still a mystery. The scars on his own head from the incident at the airport were still in place, but if he was not mistaken, he had just witnessed the captain put the doctor in his place. Obviously the doctor had overstepped his boundaries.

This Dr. Stratton was a random factor, the one that could possibly undo his plans, if he did not plan his actions and reactions properly. He suspected it was he who had talked the captain out of letting him be taken outside, to point out the grave himself.

Stratton could either remain with Annette, or return and join the police search party. She certainly would not want to return to the police station under any circumstances. If Stratton came back alone, he would have to leave her somewhere, perhaps unguarded, alone.

He was temporarily satisfied. He had accomplished the first step in the process, the one that had been the basis for all his previous successes: identify, then isolate.

He had told the police he would tell them where he had buried Mary Sullivan, and he had every intention of fulfilling that promise. But not right away. He had to wait until he got what he wanted. Until it was closer to dark. In twilight, his chances of turning the odds entirely in his favor were the greatest. After that, things could become more unpredictable.

He settled back on his bed and waited. Things were not so bad.

They would come back for him. Not immediately, but soon enough.

JOHN DROVE SLOWLY and carefully back to his house. "God," he said, "I think it must be at least eighty-five degrees out today."

It was a lame attempt at conversation and he knew it. Apparently she did, too, because she didn't feel any great need to respond. She sat in her seat with her arms folded and looked out at the countryside.

He took Arrowhead Drive up to his house and pulled into the garage, letting the door close behind him automatically. She didn't say anything until they got inside the house.

"Could I build a fire?"

"Um...yeah. Sure," he said, thinking it was entirely too warm to do so. "Perfect day for it." He went out into the garage, privately wincing at his own stab at humor. He came back with a Duraflame log and an armful of piñon, stopping on the way to edge the air-conditioning up a tad. He arranged the logs in the fireplace and lit the wrapper of the chemical log with a match.

"There we are," he said, stepping back to watch the flames build. "Instant cozy. Only thing you have to be careful of during the day is that the chimney screen stays in place. Don't want any wayward sparks drifting out."

He turned to look into her eyes but found that she was gazing out his sliding glass doors. He walked up behind her and put both hands on her shoulders. "Annette," he said, "I'm sorry I manipulated you the way I did. You were right. I made sure you'd cooperate so he would. But I wouldn't have done it if it hadn't been so damn important that he confess. Literally dozens of open cases could be solved, both here and overseas."

He paused. "He told us where he hid your mother and it's someplace we would never have thought to look: down the old road, up on a hill, next to a forgotten cemetery. There's a rock wall—"

"Shut up," she said, low and urgent, not even looking at him. "I don't want to hear it."

John shut up. He didn't protest her harsh words. He knew he probably deserved them.

She turned to face him, then to look into the fire. "He would kill me, wouldn't he? If the guards weren't there, if the bars were gone, if it was just him and me, he'd kill me, wouldn't he?"

John swallowed. She didn't cut corners on life's harsh realizations. "Yes," was all he could think of to say. "But the walls and guards and bars are there and he can't get to you. Now or ever."

"How do you know that? How do you know there haven't been other cells, other policemen who've tried to detain him while they attempted to figure out who he is. Maybe he escaped, and their reports don't show up on his record. Christ, he doesn't even *have* a record. You guys don't know who he is, either. Maybe he's been arrested three or four times, maybe half a dozen, and nothing's ever come of it because he's just too..."

"Slick?"

"No. I was going to say something like 'dangerous' or 'powerful' but that's not precisely what I mean." A log popped, sending a shower of sparks against the metal fireplace screen. "I feel like he's...different from the rest of us somehow. He feels a special connection with the spirit world. He thinks that this banshee thing is real. It shows itself to him, talks to him the way you talk to me."

"You got all of that just from meeting him once?"

"It wasn't just meeting him: it was like I could sense that about him. Does that sound silly? It was like I felt a parity with him, and I didn't want to."

"It's possible the two of you are related."

"Yes, but how closely?"

"I don't know."

"We could be fourth cousins three times removed for all I know. Or we could be..."

She left the thought unfinished. Or they could be what? John wondered. He concentrated on comforting her. He didn't want to lose her trust in this mess.

"Look," he said. "There are a million what-ifs in any situation—especially this one. I know this must be disturbing for you. I wish I could say I know how you feel, but I can't. I don't know how you feel. But I imagine it's equal parts fear, anxiety and depression. You've had your self-image severely challenged. You thought your family was one set of people, but it's turned out to be another: one of them is—was—mentally unstable, the other is a homicidal freak. You have a right to feel some sense of loss over that."

"You sound like a therapist."

"Well, I've been around enough in my time to do a good fake."

"But it's not just that," she said. "He knows what may be in store for him—life imprisonment at the very least. But I don't think that matters to him. He lives on a different plane. He's got something else in mind. I can just feel it."

"Like what?"

"I don't know."

"It doesn't seem to me like he's got a lot of options."

"True . . ."

"You mean something having to do with showing us where Mary is buried?"

"I don't know."

"Then what?"

"I don't know. But I want to stay here until that's over with. I don't want to go back with you to the police station." She looked around her. "This place is safe, right?"

"Safe? Yeah, sure . . ."

"I mean, he couldn't find it, could he? There's no way he could find out where it was?"

"No."

JOHN LEFT HER an hour later, giving her an extra key in case she left the house for some reason, although she assured him she wasn't budging. He drove back to the police station, arriving a few minutes before one o'clock, slightly troubled. Annette's caution had disturbed him. She saw something inside the man that neither he nor Rogers did. It was as though she suspected the man's belief in the banshee made it more real somehow, and *that* feasibility made him more powerful.

But he did agree with her on one thing: she would feel better when today was over. His mood was buttressed by a growing morbid excitement. He was looking forward to this in spite of himself. He couldn't help it. He walked on the dark side of the road. The most fascinating thing about life is its interruption.... Who had said that? He couldn't remember. Maybe he had, muttering to himself in a drunken stupor one night.

He stopped by the side of the road, leaving the engine running as he took the T-tops off his car. As he drove the rest of the way to the station, the air whipped in and out of the interior of his car, bracing against his face, like the spray of the sea.

He found Rogers inside his office, playing the role of team commander to the hilt: barking orders into the phone, handling the constant stream of requests for approval on details and beckoning John inside so he could close the door. The few minutes of privacy were meant to give their conversation an air of confidence, as if John were second in command on this operation. He wondered if the effect was real or illusory.

"You ready to go?"

"Sure."

"How's Annette?"

"She's fine. I left her at my place. How about things here?"

"You're right on time for the first feed." Rogers took John down the hallway to the observation room with its glowing monitors and fished for another videotape cassette. He slammed it in and the monitor immediately to the left of the tape machine went from static to some sort of moving pattern.

"This is coming in over the canyon from the airport."

John didn't understand what Rogers was saying at first, but then the cloud cover broke to give way to an aerial view of the coastline. The helicopter. Of course.

"Coming in over the ridge," Rogers explained.

John saw the tops of the hills that were on both sides of Jicarita. The camera passed over the first one, and he could see the place where Gretchen's body was found, and the very top of Arrowhead Drive, not far from where he lived. Where Annette was now.

There was no sound as the camera moved over the land, giving an eagle's-eye view of the canyon, one that John had never seen. It was a strange experience, like watching silent films of violent battle.

"Down there," Rogers said, touching the screen where the hillsides met. "The main road. When he turns left is when he follows the old highway—there he goes."

The camera tilted as the helicopter banked and headed north. John could see even from this height that the area was less inhabited than the rest of the canyon. Lewis had done his homework. No one would have found a body buried there for a long, long time.

"Wait," Rogers said, and hit a button on the tape player. The image froze, warping slightly at the top and bottom of the frame. "See that. Right at the edge of where the trees break up on this hill."

John bent down and looked closely at the hilltop. Rogers was pointing at a barely noticeable strip of unimproved road that bled out into a clearing near the top. He wasn't able to tell what exactly was in the clearing, though.

"I see something..."

"It's the old graveyard he was talking about. The rock wall is right past...here."

John could barely see a thin gray smudge at the edge of the screen. "I see it."

Rogers pressed a button and the tape resumed playing.

The helicopter banked again, following the directions Lewis had given them, toward the bald peak. The highest point in the canyon, the man had said.

The helicopter circled, and with no help from Rogers the camera zoomed in slowly and focused on three small pale specks in the surface of the mountain.

"The three boulders," Rogers said. "Just where he said they would be. Mary Sullivan must be buried between them."

Rogers shut off the tape and straightened.

"Let's go," he said.

THERE WERE SIX of them, two uniformed patrolmen each in two squad cars, with Rogers and John leading the way in an unmarked car. They drove out of the parking lot, heading west toward the coast, back toward the old highway. It was five miles to the intersection, but on the turning road it took a good fifteen minutes. Still, Rogers slapped the bubble light on the dashboard and over the radio informed the two units behind him to turn on their lights but not their sirens. What few motorists were out slowed and pulled over to the side until the convoy had passed, a behavior radically different from that exhibited by drivers in the city. John could remember being in thick traffic when the siren of an ambulance or fire truck or even a police car was heard, and most drivers only slowed instead of pulling over, and only then when the emergency vehicle was right upon them. It was a common gripe among workers in city services.

Once they turned off onto the old road there was even less traffic. Rogers handed a map to John and John played navigator, peering at signs and trying to guess where they were exactly. A few unused mailboxes with rusty address plates provided some landmarks, but it was slow going.

They found the road leading to the top, after having driven by it twice. It was unmarked, and nothing indicated a break in the trees except for an aged metal gate that

screeched on its rusty hinges as John forced it back, holding it in place with a convenient rock.

The helicopter video had shown one thing correctly: the
path to the cemetery was not paved, and what at one time
must have been a used thoroughfare was now covered with
grass, sprouting shrubs and sticks, and the remains of several rock and mud slides from years past. Rogers eased the
unmarked Ford into low gear and proceeded gently up the
steeply graded hill.

The road was only wide enough for one car. If they had
met someone coming the other way, they would have had to
either reverse their direction until they came to a spot that
had a shoulder wide enough to accommodate the Ford's
girth while the other car squeezed by or somehow persuade
the other driver to do the same, except of course, he or she
would be driving backward and uphill.

The scenery, however, was unmatched in the canyon, and
John was certain that he would return here when it was
cooler to scout the place out, and maybe do some running
or overnight camping. It struck him that this was one of the
last few wild corners of Los Angeles County, and if he could
enjoy it before it, too, was ruined by development and
planning, he would have found a rare treasure.

After ten minutes of careful driving—sharp turns, slippery gravel, sudden drop-offs—the abandoned cemetery
came into view and they found themselves at the edge of a
large clearing. Here the road widened and smoothed, and
for the first time the tires didn't crunch loudly on gravel and
rocks.

The cemetery grounds were square—fifty feet by fifty
feet—and had long since fallen into disrepair. Headstones
and markers were scattered about among long grass and
bushes. A lone funerary statue of an angel, her eyes black
and sclerotic, stood to one side. Names etched into stone
and wood were faded by time and weather. It was difficult
to attach individual plots to their markers; in most cases the
two seemed to have drifted apart over the years.

There are some places, John thought to himself, where the sun shines less brightly than others.

Rogers had stopped the car automatically, and now eased his foot off the brake, uncertain of the sacrilege involved in driving over old and forgotten graves. There were no headstones directly ahead of them, but Rogers did have to do some careful steering. If there had been a central path through the cemetery, it had long since been overgrown.

The other cars followed reverently, their overhead lights switching off.

John saw a sign dangling off a post, held up by a single nail. He tilted his head to read:

"*Tres Rocas*. What does that mean?"

"I don't know," Rogers said. "Probably the name of this place."

John watched the sign pass by, inches from his window, and turned to look ahead.

About fifty yards beyond the cemetery was the rock dam. As the unmarked Ford eased up next to it and parked, John could see that there was no way around or through the barrier—only over.

He and Rogers got out as the other squad cars pulled over, the officers squinting as they emerged into the heat. John had been introduced to them all, but he was bad with names and wasn't sure he could keep them straight. The oldest one, with short graying hair and a slightly larger paunch than the other men, was Sergeant Griffin. The one who rode with him was Halloway, and the other two, who seemed to have a kind of generic presence, were named Tibbets and Sorrento. Which one was which, John couldn't tell.

John paced the length of the rock wall, studying it carefully. Rogers did the same.

"I have a question," Rogers said.

"Shoot."

"What is this doing here?"

"To divert water from heavy rains away from the cemetery grounds."

"Why?"

"A good downpour could loosen the topsoil and send it sliding. Except it'd take the bodies with it."

"Does that happen?"

John nodded. "It sure does."

The uniformed officers began unloading shovels and picks from the trunks of their squad cars. "Are we going to dig her up and take her back right now?" John asked, slightly incredulous.

"No," Rogers replied. "We'll get our chopper back in here to airlift her out."

"If I'd known we were going to be handling a body, I would have tried to round up a body bag."

"Just let me know what you want and I'll have the pilot put it on board before he takes off."

"All right." John ticked off what he needed, Rogers making a few hasty notes. John stood by while he radioed in and told the pilot what he needed. John could tell from the transmission that radio signals were getting lost, up this high and this deep into the hills. Rogers had to repeat himself several times, and so did the pilot when the transmission broke up too badly.

Griffin gave the word that all the men were ready, and Rogers led the scramble over the barrier, taking off his jacket and slinging his tie over his shoulder to clamber up the shallow rise, raising dust and loosening stones that rattled to the bottom.

He stopped at the top, straddling the apex, breathing slightly. "John," he said, "why don't you come on up and over? I need you to stand on the other side as we pass the tools over."

John nodded and made the climb, carefully negotiating the downward side. He stood on the ground, listening to Rogers position another man below, and then the tools began to come over, one at a time. John laid them in the dirt, side by side. The three boulders where Mary Sullivan was supposed to be buried were nowhere in sight.

After the digging tools came the men, one by one, Rogers giving them a hand up and John giving them a hand down. Griffin was last, and he slipped and skidded, scraping open his shin. John wanted to take a look at the wound but the older man, embarrassed at his sign of weakness, declined.

Rogers came down and they all picked up a tool, except for John. Rogers led the way up the rise, watching where he put his feet in the dirt. John walked abreast, unconsciously passing them.

What a strange and remote place, John thought. How carefully Lewis must have chosen it, the detail that had gone into his planning.... They were not dealing with an ordinary criminal.

John walked on, his hands free, and after a few minutes realized that he had left everyone else behind. He turned around to see Rogers a good fifty feet back, with the other officers straggling behind, Griffin trying to huff his way out of bringing up the rear. True, John wasn't carrying anything, but...these men weren't in shape for this kind of work. John had worked with investigators at the coroner's office, specially trained to work in environments much harsher than this—they were nicknamed the Mountain Goats—who could be dropped into a mountain site by helicopter and survive for days while they searched for remains left over from an airplane crash or a forest fire. If Rogers was proud of something about his department, it sure couldn't be their physical conditioning.

He waited patiently, saying nothing in his face or expression as Rogers passed him, sweat trickling down his face. The captain was not a man who liked his weak spots pointed out.

He kept stride with Rogers, whose city shoes became caked with dust and slipped on rocks and dead tree branches. Once, a shoe caught and almost twisted its way off his foot, exposing a blue nylon dress sock. Rogers immediately bent down to fit the shoe back on, and without looking at John muttered between gasps: "Why don't you take the point and see what's up ahead? If we have the wrong goddamn hill I'm going to take it out on somebody."

John nodded and walked on. He resisted the urge to break out into a light jog just to show them, holding the desire back. He lengthened his stride, however, letting his arms swing freely, looking where to place his feet, keeping his head down for about a minute at a time before looking up to see where he was.

That was how he found the boulders, after negotiating a particularly steep section of the hill, the kind that almost forces a walker to resort to hand-and-knee work in a kind of improvised climbing. He had kept his head down for a few minutes, watching out for rattlers that might be sunning themselves or tarantulas hiding in the stones. When he looked up, the rocks were simply *there*, as if they had risen out of the bare ground against the backdrop of low cloud and sky just moments before he arrived. They were high and narrow, and looked as though they could have been the product of either nature's forces or man's design. As the sky rolled behind the three rocks, a name came to mind for John, one that immediately explained how this formation had attracted the man they held back in their cell, and why he had chosen it as the site for a certain type of sacrifice.

"Stonehenge," a voice said and John was slightly startled.

He turned around to see Rogers standing ten feet behind him, sweating but looking at the rocks with the barest hint of wonder.

"Looks kind of like Stonehenge," Rogers repeated.

"Exactly what I was thinking," said John.

Rogers turned around and called to the other men. "Hurry up, guys! We found it!"

IT WAS TWO HOURS later.

The men, working in teams switching every fifteen minutes, dug at the appointed spot. There was no sign that the ground there had been disturbed recently, but John and the others attributed that to the dry climate. Dust could have covered the upturned soil. But after they had gone three feet down and still hit nothing, Rogers instructed them to widen the hole, expanding its borders until it touched the base of the rocks.

Nothing.

Halloway was tapping Griffin off early, as the older man was rapidly becoming tired. The other men were faring little better. They had either untucked their shirts or unbuttoned them all the way down to the waist, and checked their hands regularly for blisters.

John stood by, watching all of this with a sinking feeling.

Lewis had said he would show them, if he could come along.

Rogers had said no. At John's request.

Lewis had given them a false location.

Rogers was standing by the edge of the hole, looking down into it. He raised a hand. "Stop."

The men stopped. Rogers took a shovel from Sorrento and hopped down inside the grave. He took the blade of the shovel and dropped it down into the bottom of the hole several times, feeling around for something that wasn't there.

"All right," he said, handing off the shovel and getting an arm up out of the hole. "Pack it up. Let's go back."

"Fill it in, sir?" Halloway asked.

"We haven't got the time," Rogers snapped.

He passed by John, looking straight ahead. He was going to walk by without speaking to him. John was aware of the man's ego and temper, but approached him anyway.

"Carl," he said, "I didn't think that he would lead us on a wild-goose chase. I thought we could get him to talk in advance. Now that was a reasonable assump—"

Rogers stopped and turned on his heel, cutting John off, his anger overriding his fatigue. "I was the one who made the mistake, Stratton. I listened to you."

John stared at him blankly, caught off guard by the attack.

"I followed your instinct instead of my own. I shouldn't have done that. As a result, we have been up here for two hours." He looked at his watch. "Three hours since we left the station. And for what? Nothing." He took three steps away, and then turned back. "This," he said loudly, pointing forcefully at the four men who were gathering up their tools, buttoning up their shirts and wiping their brows, "is police time and effort that *I* am responsible for."

Then he walked away.

The patrolmen walked by, each of them staring John down as they trudged back toward the rock dam and their waiting vehicles.

It was John who brought up the rear this time.

BACK AT THE STATION, Rogers got out of the car, slamming the door so hard John's window rattled. The captain walked inside, John tagging a respectful distance behind him, ignoring the people clamoring for his attention. He strode into the detention area and went straight to the maximum security cell. He impatiently motioned to the guard to let him in.

Rogers walked into the cell, stopping just inches away from the cage. The prisoner immediately opened his eyes and sat up, as if he was expecting company and was using the spare time to catch some sleep.

"All right, you son of a bitch," Rogers said with a vehemence that kept John out in the hall. "We're going to take you with us."

CHAPTER ELEVEN

JOHN STOOD WATCHING in the observation room, the monitors tuned not only to the maximum security cell, but to several angles of the detention block itself, including hallways leading out of the police station and even a view of the back parking lot, where a uniformed driver stood beside the idling van. Eight other officers manned various points along the way. If the prisoner tried anything while being led outside, there was no place where at least half a dozen policemen would not have him under observation.

John watched on one monitor as the barred door to the cell was unlocked by Sergeant Griffin. Two officers flanked him, one with a pump-action shotgun cradled in his arms. He stood up against the far end of the cell, beyond where the bench ended. It was a tight squeeze, but it gave the officer the best position to fire if need be.

Lewis rose from his bed. John could hear Griffin fasten handcuffs on each of Lewis's wrists and watched as they led him down the hallway, out of the detention area, through the back hallway of the police station and into the parking lot. They loaded Lewis into the van. Rogers climbed into the passenger seat and the driver took his place behind the wheel. The van was closed and locked by the backup officers, who headed for their patrol cars. The vehicles left the lot, led by the van, lights turning without sound, leaving ghostly trails on the monitor screen.

John let himself out of the room. He hadn't been invited to ride in any of the patrol cars. Rogers had said there was no room, but said John could follow in his own car if he wanted to.

He knew that if he didn't hurry he was going to lose them.

LEWIS SAT IN THE REAR of the van, his back rigid against the metal wall near the rear doors. He looked out the windows, thick safety glass strengthened with crosshatching wire. He had told the driver to head north, toward the valley, but that was not where the body was. He needed time, and he needed to look out the rear window of the van for only a few more minutes. He had not seen John Stratton in the procession, and wondered where the doctor was.

They passed out of the parking lot and down the road, stopping at the intersection with the main road. He heard the driver switch on the turn signal and felt the van slow to a stop. He gazed toward the visitor's parking lot in front of the police station and saw John Stratton hurry out the front door and get into a red T-top Camaro, the engine roaring to life, its sound vibrating even inside the confines of the van.

The doctor was driving himself, following them wherever Lewis told the driver to go. He would remember that.

There was a sound from up front. Rogers was telling the guards to let him come toward the front of the van. The captain wanted to speak with him.

He got up, unable to use his hands to steady himself. The van suddenly lurched forward, turning left onto the main road, and he lost his balance, striking his head against the roof and his elbow against the side.

Immediately, one of the policemen in front had his shotgun level and cocked. The others were looking at him, ready, alert. Waiting.

He righted himself slowly and sat down.

They had put him in chains. He would put paid to that. When the time came, he would even the score.

"AND AFTER YOU TOOK her out of her home?"

"I drove out here."

Rogers was asking his questions through the metal grate between the cab of the van and the rear space. Their faces were only inches apart. The partition made the prisoner Rogers was questioning look shaded, hidden. He felt like a priest hearing a confession from a murderous monk. *And then, my son? In the eyes of the Lord all men are guilty....*

"What made you choose Jicarita Canyon?"

"I had been here before."

"Gretchen Seale?"

"Yes."

"What made you choose Jicarita for her?"

There was a silence. Rogers could barely make out the four policemen in the back of the van. They all sat together, watching one another, averted from the questioning, as if playing a telepathic game of cards.

"It was close to the city," came the reply, "but distant in terrain. Do you understand?"

"Yes."

"The city, but really the country."

Rogers nodded.

"Also, the hills, the high spaces..."

"High spaces?"

"The tops of the mountain range. Out of sight of everything."

"Was there a reason you wanted to be so high up?"

"Yes."

"Why?"

"I...can't tell you."

"Why not?"

"Because I don't know how to explain."

"Try."

"To be close to the sky, to be near the stars."

Rogers was getting nowhere with this line of questioning. He had stepped into the man's metaphysical parameters. Better to step out while he was still speaking English. "So you brought Mary Sullivan here."

"Yes."

"And where exactly did you bring her?"

"I brought her to one place, and then another."

"I don't understand."

"I was going to bury her at the top of a ridge, but when I dug a hole, I hit a cable."

"The power outage."

"Yes. Would you like to see where that was?"

Rogers hesitated. Was this a ploy? "Did you eventually bury her there?"

"Not exactly there, no. But nearby."

Rogers hesitated again. The man could be stalling. He could be, or his story just might be what it seemed to be: an honest attempt to recreate the events of two nights ago.

Rogers didn't have to agree. He could force him to take them to the burial site first.

Or could he? A promise had been made, a bargain struck, but with a murderer.

Why didn't he feel in control?

"All right. Are we headed in that direction?"

"No. We'll have to turn around."

"Then why did you have us drive all this way? We're almost out of the canyon and into the valley." Rogers couldn't keep the irritable tone out of his voice.

If the other man was offended by the remark, he made no sign. His face was deep in shadow.

"I wanted us to talk first," he said. "To know I could trust you."

JOHN WATCHED as the police van and the three squad cars he was following slowed, their taillights glowing dimly in the sunlight. What the hell . . . ? he thought. He pulled the Camaro to the side of the road and watched as the van turned onto a side road, disappeared and came back out, turning back onto the main road but heading in the opposite direction. The squad cars dutifully followed.

John had no choice but to do the same. He wished he had realized before what a handicap not being in radio contact with the others was going to be. He didn't bother to use the side road, but did a doughnut in the middle of the boulevard, tires squealing, and sped on, catching up.

They would turn around only on Rogers's command, and he was following the directions of the man in handcuffs. For some reason, he had told them to drive almost all the way down the highway to the valley side of the Santa Monica Mountains, then go the other way.

Lewis was playing with them. He was buying time for some reason.

John had no choice but to watch and wait and see where they ended up.

THE VAN TWISTED and turned up Miramar Avenue, its suspension sending the passengers rocking back and forth. Rogers turned and peered through the grate to look at the face behind him. "Can you see out through the windshield?" he asked.

"Somewhat."

"Are we anywhere near?"

"No. Keep going."

"How far?"

"All the way to the top."

"But at the top..." He looked at the map. "The road runs out and turns to dirt."

"I know."

"What then?"

"We keep driving."

"This isn't a four-wheel drive—" He started to say more, but shut up. He was nervous, unsure, and he was letting it show. He had no choice but to sit back and watch the driver turn the wheel back and forth. He didn't know where they were going, and his prisoner wasn't telling him any more than he had to.

I'm being led along, he thought. He's in charge now. Not me.

JOHN SAW THE HOUSES thin out as they left civilization behind and climbed higher and higher. It was oddly reminiscent of the route John had taken up Wilkins Road when

Gretchen Seale's coffin had been found, but this road was even more winding. He kept both hands on the wheel. He had not seen the van since it had made the turnoff. All he saw ahead of him was the last patrol car, and he often lost sight of its taillights around the curves and bends.

Eventually, the road straightened and narrowed as the drop-off on the side of the hill became sheerer. The asphalt pavement was barely wide enough to accommodate one car, let alone two. John guessed that anyone else who was driving up here would have to pull over and let police cars going in the opposite direction pass. He doubted that was much of a problem, as he didn't think anyone lived up here.

In a cloud of dust up ahead, he could make out the other vehicles. The pavement ended a few hundred feet ahead and the cars all slowed one by one, bumpers bouncing over the ruts and rises in the road as the paving broke up and eventually disappeared. John groaned inwardly. He didn't want to risk a broken axle again. His car wasn't built for terrain like this.

He saw they were stopping. Good. He hoped they would walk the rest of the way.

He parked and got out, squinting his eyes at the dust. He walked over to where Rogers and the backup officers were gathering. John nodded to Rogers, who didn't nod back.

"We're going to leave the cars here and proceed on foot," Rogers said. "Our man says he's going to take us to where he first tried to bury her. This was where the power break occurred, when he was digging a hole."

The officers nodded silently.

"I want you all to stick together. We're going to have to let him out of the van. That's a hell of a lot less of a controlled situation than back in the station, so everyone be on their toes."

Rogers walked up to the driver's window. "Okay," he said. "We're going to let him out."

John watched the backups gather around. If there was a strategy on Lewis's part, it was working. The tension apparent in the police station had been slightly reduced. The men were an iota or two off their guard. Lewis was going to have them proceed on foot, stripped of their cars and unwieldy shotguns, not nearly as formidable.

The driver opened the back doors, the hinges groaning. The officers inside the van half stood as they prodded Lewis out. He hopped out of the van and down onto the rocky dirt. He looked at John impassively.

With a nod from the captain, Lewis led them on, Rogers at his right side, Griffin at the other, with John and the backups trailing behind. They covered about a hundred yards on rough uphill terrain.

"I brought her here first," Lewis said, stopping at the top of the ridge. John was breathing slightly, the other men more heavily. He wondered if any of them smoked. The officers riding in the van were the same ones that had accompanied John and Rogers up to Tres Rocas and were already worn out. Lewis had not worked up a sweat. "I built a box out of lumber I had in the back of my security patrol car and began to dig a hole. After about three feet, that's when I hit the cable."

"Then what did you do?" Rogers asked. He was breathing deeply, trying to regain his wind.

"I pried the boards apart, stuck them in the back and drove down the hill, looking for another location."

"Where did you go?"

"Come on," Lewis said, walking back toward the van. "I'll show you."

JOHN WAS BACK IN HIS CAR, following the convoy, although he'd managed to be quick enough to snare the number-two spot behind the van. He couldn't shake the nagging suspicion that this was all part of some plan of Lewis's. He didn't buy the possibility that the man had just rolled over for the police and was going to throw himself upon the mercy of the courts. No, John suspected he had something else in mind.

But what? Escape was impossible. The man was too heavily guarded.

Perhaps there was nothing to it at all. He was just showing them, step by step, what had happened that night. Maybe Rogers was right. John watched too much TV.

They plunged back down the hill and wound down Miramar Avenue, turning off on Evergreen Drive, a side street that also ended in unimproved road, impassable except on foot. John parked his car, pocketing the keys. It was slightly cooler than up at the top of the ridge. He didn't have a watch on him, but he guessed it must be around three or four o'clock. Sunset in the hills came around five. They only had about an hour left of good light.

Lewis was let out of the van again. The prisoner stepped down onto the brown long grass, his shoes snapping dry twigs. One of the patrolmen tried to sneak a cigarette, but Rogers called out to him by name before addressing the rest of them. "Gentlemen, this is fire season, and until we get a good rain the brush remains dry and the danger high. No smoking outside of your vehicles."

Lewis led them on into the grass, stopping at the edge of a dense cluster of trees. "Here is where I parked my vehicle. I left her in the trunk to go and dig in there." He pointed beyond, to somewhere in the trees. "When I came back, I found that she had opened the trunk from the inside and escaped."

"She had?" Rogers made no effort to hide his surprise. "How far did she get?"

"A ways. I didn't catch up with her until she was back on the asphalt, where the houses started."

"Where exactly?"

"I'll show you."

Lewis turned and walked back where he had come from. The brush and dirt that slowed the other men didn't seem to faze him. He walked straight ahead, his massive legs covering the stride of two men. Everyone else was so busy trying to wade through without ripping their clothes that they didn't seem to notice that Lewis was walking several feet ahead of the rest of the party, free and clear and unguarded.

When Rogers saw what was happening he immediately snapped to, his fatigue and shortness of breath temporarily forgotten. "Hey," he called out to Lewis. "Hey!"

Lewis kept walking.

"Stop!" Rogers called, drawing his gun from his belt holster. Griffin and the other officers followed suit. The air was suddenly filled with the sound of clicking metal. "Stop or we'll shoot."

Lewis stopped. He didn't turn around to look back, didn't say anything. He merely waited for the other men to catch up. They trotted ahead, tiring themselves out even more. John was among the first to reach him. He stood at Lewis's side, staring at the man's impassive face. What was going on in his mind? Was this part of the confession, or part of the game?

Rogers and Griffin were the last ones to catch up, and it didn't put them in any better a mood.

"Why didn't you stop?" Rogers asked angrily.

"I didn't know you were talking to me." Lewis's voice was calm, even.

"Who the hell did you think I was talking to?"

"I didn't know until you said you would shoot."

"Remember," the captain said, "we made a deal. But you play by our rules or the game gets a lot rougher."

Lewis gave a passive nod. "Let me know when you're ready to proceed."

After a few moments, Rogers motioned ahead, holstering his gun. "Show us."

Lewis's pace was slower, his steps smaller. He wasn't going to risk another scene.

"HERE WAS WHERE I first saw her."

They were back on the pavement, the men grateful for the rest. A few of them took off their hats to wipe their brows.

The one whom Rogers had admonished for smoking was bent over, his hands on his knees as he breathed deeply, like a runner after a marathon.

"Is this the same place that you caught her?" Rogers asked.

"No. That's up ahead."

"Show me exactly what happened from the time that you saw her to the time you caught her."

Lewis did as he was told. He reenacted the scene, colorlessly describing his struggle with the middle-aged woman to the point where he'd managed to pick her up and carry her back toward the burial site. There was no hint of remorse in his tale, no suggestion that what he had done was an antisocial or immoral act. John had heard mechanics talk about malfunctioning automobile engines with more emotion.

"Then you took her back in the woods."

"Yes."

"That's where we're going next?"

"Yes."

"All right." Rogers signaled the other men. "On the way back into the trees, we're going to stop and I want everyone to get the tools out of their cars. Work in teams, one man carries the tools, the other man keeps his hands free."

On the walk back John carefully approached Rogers. It was the first time they had spoken since leaving the police station.

"If we find the coffin, do you want to dig it up right now?"

"Sure. Why not?"

"When do you want me to look at the body?"

"As soon as we open the coffin."

"You want to open it here, in the field?"

"You bet."

"You don't want to wait until we call Dr. Harding—"

"Doctor, if we call the coroner's office without being sure that we have a body, we're going to look pretty stupid to them, to the press and to the taxpayers. For all I know, he's just made this whole thing up and either there's nothing buried among those trees or what is there is a bunch of flour sacks in a crate. That's why I let you come along. You saw Mary Sullivan while she was alive. She couldn't be that far gone if she's just been dead a day or two. I want to make sure that we have an open-and-shut case before we bring in anyone else. You may like making those kinds of mistakes, but I don't.''

John fell back. He immediately began to rationalize Rogers's last statement, saying that the man wasn't feeling well, he was under a lot of pressure. But the comments stung deeply.

You may like making those kinds of mistakes....

In spite of himself, John felt the old insecurities coming back, the ones he used to keep at bay with drugs and alcohol. He was here at this scene because he was useful due to circumstance—he could identify a face—not because he was good. Any layman witness could do what he was going to do. Rogers was going to use him and then call in the real pros, tossing John aside. He had never considered John a peer. Perhaps Rogers would make another deal, one that would result in John's name being stricken from any kind of record. Hardinger would be angry with him for not informing the department as soon as he knew of the possibility of a corpse being delivered, and Rogers would be furious if he broke silence now.

He was letting himself get kicked around in this situation, and he was bound to lose.

He wondered what he could do about it for a few moments as he watched the police officers unlock their trunks and pull out shovels and picks.

As they tramped off into the woods, Lewis with his bald and scarred head leading the way, he realized there wasn't anything he *could* do. He was to be the forgotten man in this case, and that was just the way it was going to be.

LEWIS LOOKED AROUND the small clearing in every direction, regaining his bearings. "It was dark when I was here last," he said. "I didn't get a chance to come here in daylight, like I did the other place."

"Should we dig here?" Rogers asked.

"I don't know..." He paced some, studying the ground, finally stopping at a mound of leaves and branches. "Here," he said. "Right here."

Rogers took a shovel from one of the men and cleared away the forest debris, studying the ground below. It contrasted with the surrounding dirt, different in texture and hue. Someone had been here before. He signaled to Sergeant Griffin. "Let's get to work," he said.

As Griffin instructed two patrolmen to start digging, John watched Lewis. The man stood by, casually observing the scene. If he had any apprehension about what they were going to find, it didn't show.

It was only fifteen minutes until they struck wood. The sky around them was beginning to darken. Griffin switched the men on detail, sending the first digging team back to their patrol cars for flashlights. "I want this done by nightfall," he ordered.

The fresh pairs of uniformed officers set to work, digging around the coffin until they had enough space for the four of them to get a hold, each wedging the blade of a shovel underneath the box. With a cracking sound, the coffin was pried free of its resting place, and the men moved in quickly to get their hands underneath it, their shovels falling into the ditch. They eased the coffin over solid ground and laid it to rest.

"How does it feel?" Rogers asked one of them.

"Heavy. There's someone or something in there."

Rogers nodded and looked at John. "Doctor," he said by way of instruction, "I believe it's your turn."

John stepped forward, letting his sense of professionalism take the place of pride. He took a hammer from one of the men and began to pry up the nails one by one, holding them in his hand. When he was done he took the claw end of the hammer and pried up the lid. It came easily.

He and Rogers lifted the lid off, leaning it against one side of the coffin.

In the darkness, all John could see was a tangle of hair. He could smell quite clearly, though, and the body inside was already in the early stages of decomposition.

He looked around him and asked for a flashlight.

"Is that her?" Rogers asked as John moved the beam from one end of the box to the other.

"Yes," John said. "It is."

"Take Lewis back to the station in the van," Rogers said softly to Griffin. "Get a backup team and I'll meet up with you there."

Griffin turned away and walked over to his charge, guiding Lewis by the elbow. He called out to Halloway, and the two other men who had been on the Tres Rocas dig, Tibbets and Sorrento.

John had not moved from his position crouched next to the open coffin, looking down at Mary Sullivan's body, gathered inside the box like a crushed bird. He felt the impulse to reach out, brush back her hair from her face, to do something for her. To say he was sorry. To let her know that he was too late.

"Stratton?" Rogers said. "John?"

"Yeah,"

"Come on. I need you out of the way. We're going to take some pictures."

I need you out of the way....

"All right," John said, standing. "You need me for anything else?"

"Yeah. I'd like for you to stick around a little bit. You mind?"

"No," John said. "I don't mind."

GRIFFIN LED THE PARTY through the woods. He and Halloway escorted the prisoner, while Tibbets and Sorrento hung back, each carrying digging tools. Griffin was the senior officer present, and that gave him authority over Halloway, even over Tibbets and Sorrento, although they might not act like it. He heard the two men talking to each other behind him. If he heard laughter, he'd tell them to shut up. This situation was too serious to tolerate that kind of bullshit.

Griffin himself would have preferred that he not get the singular responsibility of escorting Lewis back to the station. He thought it would have been a better idea for them all to go back together. But that was Captain Rogers for you. Once he got what he wanted, everyone else could go to hell. The man had his sights set on elected political office.

They reached the pavement, and Griffin turned to the other men to speak. "We're going to stop at the van first."

"What for?" Tibbets asked.

"Because I want to get something," Griffin said tightly. He didn't like having his most casual orders questioned. It was just the sort of thing he was afraid Tibbets would do. If he'd asked Tibbets for the time of day the man would have immediately responded, "Why?" or "How come?"

They stopped at the van, on the far side, hidden from the road, nothing separating them from the night but trees and grass. Griffin positioned the prisoner against Halloway. He had guarded some bruisers before, but this guy took the steroids. And it wasn't just his size, either. There was something about his look....

He waited until Tibbets and Sorrento had caught up before fishing into his pocket for the keys to the van. He unlocked the back door and reached inside, drawing out ankle chains.

He walked around the van with the chains and manacles dangling from one hand, holding them up for the prisoner to see. "Time to put these on."

The prisoner nodded.

"Sorrento, radio base and tell them we're coming back in."

"How come?" Tibbets asked.

"So they will know to expect us, and I wasn't talking to you anyway, Tibbets." Griffin bent down, kneeling in front of the prisoner, sorting out the tangle of chains and cuffs. Tibbets snorted. Sorrento handed his partner the shovel he was carrying and unclipped his radio and relayed the information. He kept the radio out and turned up loud so Griffin could hear the reply.

Base confirmed, and Griffin clicked the first ankle cuff into place. He looked up at the prisoner. "That hurt?"

"No."

Griffin nodded, and that was when the man kicked him in the face.

JOHN HAD STOOD and watched the camera flash again and again, the sudden lighting effect making Mary Sullivan's body leap out in bas-relief every time, leaving ghastly imprints on John's retinas.

By now it was almost completely dark. Rogers radioed for an ambulance, and got word that the detachment he'd sent back to the station had already checked in. Griffin was a very careful officer.

"Let's get this back together," Rogers said to John, not meaning the two of them at all. True to John's intuition, Rogers was called away within two minutes on some other matter of urgency, and John was left fitting the lid back on the coffin like the flunky he felt he was. His professional knowledge hadn't been required here at all. He would have come along if all that Rogers needed him for was to identify the body, but that wasn't what the man had told him. *I need you there, I want you to have first crack.*

Yeah. Sure.

He glanced over and could see Rogers's shaded outline: the man was obviously conferring with the uniformed cops. John hadn't seen at first what a career climber the police captain was. Rogers was a Fuchs in cop's clothing.

He picked up the flashlight to find the holes that the nails had made in the lip of the box. If he just stuck them in there loosely, they ought to keep it in place. He let the light spill over inside the coffin, illuminating Mary Sullivan's hair, part of her pinched and withered face and her two hands, clutched to the side as if in desperate prayer.

That was when he saw the scratches on the side of the coffin, so faint as to almost be indistinct. John shifted the beam of the flashlight and peered closer. There were scratches all right, right there in the wood, and fairly fresh. He bent over further and looked at Mary Sullivan's hands, to see if her fingernails were torn or bloody from having etched some final message into the wood.

Her hands were not bloody at all. Between her fingers, held fast in the vise of rigor, was the sharp end of a nail.

She had known that Gretchen Seale had been found, and she had figured on her own eventual discovery. Smart woman, John thought to himself. Smart, smart woman.

He angled his head next to hers, shining the flashlight intently on the wood, trying to read what she had written.

There were five letters, each a set of overlapping lines that would take a little time to figure out. He saw that the second letter was an *E*, the last one a *Y*—were the third and fourth meant to be *T*s? he wondered. No, they were *L*s. The first one, though, the first one was a tricky one. It looked like it could be another *Y* or an *I* or maybe just a false start, a mistake that she had tried to etch out....

He ran them all together in his mind, the letters whirling into place like wheels in a slot machine, searching for possible combinations, and as they locked into place one by one, he felt the same thrilling sensation that came with hitting the jackpot. He had found the key to this whole awful mystery.

He knew what member of the Larkin family Lewis was, how he had known about Mary Sullivan, why he had saved her for last and how he had managed to slip around his own country unnoticed and into this one without any problems.

He suddenly knew why the man's fingerprints drew a blank, why he had never turned up in any immigration records. It was the answer to what had been bothering John back at the station when he looked at the list of members of the Larkin family, numbering all of those who had been killed or were dead. What he hadn't been able to bring into words was the knowledge that he knew of one Larkin who was supposed to be dead but who hadn't shown up on the list: one that he had heard about from Mary Sullivan herself. When she had finally seen him face-to-face, in the last few minutes of her life, she had been so horrified that she had forced herself to figure out a way to strike back from the grave and reveal his identity.

K-E-L-L-Y.

The son who she thought had died when he was only ten years old.

She had said her husband, Roy Sullivan, had found Kelly's body the night she saw the banshee—had buried him the next day.

But he hadn't been dead. He had only appeared to be. No medical examination had been performed, no death certificate signed. When the child woke up the experience must have terrified him, psychologically scarred him for life because he had been accidentally *buried alive*.

It was little Kelly Larkin Sullivan, very much alive and all grown up, who was doing this, carrying out the banshee's will on earth.

Mary Sullivan had been killed by her own son.

And Gretchen Seale murdered by her own half brother.

GRIFFIN FLEW BACK, his face already streaming with blood from his shattered nose, but Frank B. Lewis—Kelly Larkin Sullivan—didn't have time to watch the man hit the ground. He wheeled and caught Halloway on the side of the head with an elbow, hearing him slam against the side of the van and slump to the ground.

He charged the other two without thinking. Tibbets had a shovel in each hand, dropping them and fumbling for his gun rather than using one of the spades as a weapon. It was a mistake that cost him his life.

Sorrento had his gun out of his holster but not yet aimed when Lewis hit them both at full speed. He brought them both to the ground, whipping an arm around Tibbets's neck while crushing his weight on Sorrento's gun hand until he heard bones crack.

Sorrento cried out and used his other arm to reach for his radio. If he could so much as depress the transmitting button...

Lewis saw that Sorrento was going to need all of his attention in a very short period of time. He brought his arm up tight around Tibbets, hearing the man choke and gasp. He didn't snap his neck, but when he had done enough damage to incapacitate him for a while he rolled over on top of Sorrento, leaving Tibbets gasping for breath.

Lewis reached down to Sorrento's belt and drew out the officer's baton, bringing it up to club Sorrento in the face until the man stopped moving. Lewis felt his body slacken and fall away from him as he rose to deal with Tibbets, who was still very much alive.

Tibbets was coughing and whooping wildly, down on his knees, one hand to his throat, the other still reaching for his gun. Baton still in hand, Lewis jammed it into the man's abdomen, sending him over backward. The baton rose and fell three times, quickly. The end came up damp and red.

He turned around, victory within his grasp, to see that Griffin was not down for the count yet. The man was lying on his side, barely able to see through the damage done to his face, but strong enough to raise a gun, the barrel trembling between his weakening hands.

Lewis hurled the baton with deadly accuracy, striking Griffin across one bloodied cheek. The gun fell from the policeman's hands and Lewis ran to him, kneeling behind him, gathering up a length of the chain that still rattled at his ankle, curling it around Griffin's neck. He tightened it, slowly.

"You chained me," Lewis whispered into the dying man's ear as his hands beat helplessly at the links biting into his throat. "You bound me like an animal."

He could have done it quickly—should have dispatched the policeman with one quick jerk—but he didn't. He tightened his grip slowly, feeling the man's life leak out of him and into the dry night air, savoring the aroma like a delicacy favored only by a chosen few.

"WHAT IS IT, John?"

John had called Rogers over, had insisted on not being put off any longer. Rogers's tone was quick, abrupt. He had more important things to attend to.

But as John explained what he had found, showed it to him by the light of a flashlight beam, he saw understanding replace impatience in the policeman's face.

"That's amazing," Rogers said. He shook his head. "You've really come through."

"I wish you'd remember that."

Rogers looked puzzled. Trying to explain what he meant would be a waste of time, John decided. Most people were blind to their worst faults.

"I want to confront him with it and see what he says as soon as we get back to the station. Then maybe a few calls back to Ireland . . . God, this is fascinating."

John smiled in spite of himself. For all his shortcomings, Rogers was addicted to excitement. A passion shared, like rock and roll or Chevrolets.

Rogers took his walkie-talkie from his belt. "I'll tell Griffin that we're going to want to question Lewis some more." He depressed the button and spoke into it, muttering call letters that John couldn't hear. After a few tries, he gave up. "Wonder what the matter is," he said to himself as much as to John. He tried again, this time trying to raise the backup vehicle. No success with that, either. "Going to try the station." The dispatcher had not heard from them since they had checked in, but that was not out of the ordinary. They had not arrived yet, and there was nothing unusual about that, either.

"Maybe they're out of contact."

"Yeah..." Rogers said. "That sometimes happens. They're probably down in the canyon and we're up here...that's probably it. I'll try again in a few minutes." He tapped the side of his walkie-talkie absently for a few moments, then clipped it back onto his belt. "Listen," he said, turning to John, "you don't have to stick around here any longer if you don't want to. You're free to go."

"Don't need me to hang out until the ambulance arrives?"

"No. We're going to need to take that box back with us. Time to call the coroner."

"I'd suggest it."

"You can meet me back at the station if you like...."

"How about I call first? I'm going to check on Annette and see how she's doing."

"You left her at your house?"

"Yes."

"She seemed a little jumpy after what that freak said to her. Probably be a good idea."

"See you later, then."

"All right, John. Thanks for all your help. I'll be sure to mention it to Dr. Hardinger."

"For what it's worth," John said. "But thanks, anyway."

He raised a hand in farewell, but no one was looking his way, so he dropped it and started trudging back toward his car.

LEWIS LET GRIFFIN'S BODY slide to the ground. He had exacted his revenge. Now it was time to turn his attention to more serious matters.

He felt around in Griffin's pockets for the keys to the handcuffs and the ankle chain that was still locked around one leg. He found it, along with a set of keys—probably to Griffin's patrol car—and a pocket knife. He lifted Griffin's walkie-talkie off his hip. He quickly unlocked the handcuffs and ankle bracelet, hurling them into the bush.

He had to get out of there, and quickly. For that he needed a vehicle. A squad car would be too conspicuous, too easy to trace. He needed something that would buy him time as well as invisibility. Something fast.

He picked up the shovel that Tibbets had dropped, and then retrieved Tibbets's gun, checking to make sure it was loaded. It was, but Tibbets had used an old cop trick that Lewis had learned in the security business; the first chamber was empty, meant to give an officer the edge in case a suspect ever turned his own gun against him. If he pulled the trigger, all anyone would hear was a dry click. Lewis turned the chamber ahead to the first round and slid it back into place.

He trotted down the road in the dark, glancing back over his shoulder quickly to make sure that no one had emerged from the trees. They would find his handiwork soon enough.

He saw something red and gleaming in the dark: the hull of the doctor's sports car. Lewis rounded it, seeing that the T-tops were off, and that the keys were missing from the ignition. No matter. That was a slight difficulty that would soon be rectified.

He opened the door and threw the shovel in the back, placing the police revolver on the passenger seat beside him. He reached under the ignition and tore out the wires, stripping them with the blade of the pocket knife. He touched them together and the Camaro roared to life.

He threw the car into reverse and gently drove backward until he reached a residential driveway. There he turned around and headed out to Miramar Avenue, and down the hill.

At the stop sign, he turned on the dome light and fumbled in the glove compartment. He pulled out the car's registration slip and insurance documents. John Stratton, M.D. 1374 Arrowhead Drive, Jicarita.

Lewis put on the left turn blinker, waiting for the light traffic to clear. If there was anyone at John Stratton's house waiting for the doctor to come home, Lewis knew exactly who it would be.

JOHN EMERGED from the trees and ventured on to the paved road, picking his way carefully in the dark.

Rogers was right; Annette was probably wondering where he was and what was going on. He would drive home and see her, let her know it was over and then, depending on how he felt, either drive back to the station or phone in. He doubted he would be of much further help to Rogers. Once the coroner's office had been called, he would only be in the way. If Fuchs or Hardinger were there, he would feel uncomfortable.

It might not be done yet for the police, or for the legal system, he knew, but it was done for him. His part in the affair had come to an end. He wondered what lay ahead for him now. He might take Annette back to her place tonight, or make up the bed in the living room again. Either way, they were bound to part company soon. The next few days he'd rest up a bit, and then start looking for another job, maybe outside of Southern California. The circumstances of his dismissal might be more easily explained in a more distant clime, say San Francisco or even Seattle. Maybe Oregon. He might as well move away, he'd made such a botch of things on his home turf. Maybe time for a fresh start. A whole new life.

Things weren't as bad as they seemed. He only had to look at them the right way.

Oh, who was he kidding? His life stank.

He walked past the parked van, past the squad cars and down the road toward his car. He took the keys out of his pocket and began to jangle them thoughtfully in his right hand.

Didn't I park here? he wondered as he stopped and looked around. I thought it was here. Maybe just a little farther down.

He kept walking. God, my memory must be going. Too many drugs in my reckless and wayward youth have cost me my precious short-term memory.

His car was not on the road. He had definitely parked it somewhere along in here, but now it was missing.

John retraced his steps, backing up, passing the squad cars once again, standing to the side of the van.

If Griffin and the backup had already left . . .

There were too many cars here.

He counted quickly. He had watched the whole caravan take off, driving out of the parking lot of the police station just a few hours ago. There had been the van and three squad cars then, a van and three squad cars at the top of Miramar Avenue, and a van and three squad cars had parked here before they ventured into the woods.

None of them had moved.

All that should be here now was the van and one squad car. Griffin and the other men should have taken at least two when they took their prisoner back to the police station. And his own car should still be here.

Something was wrong.

John turned on his flashlight, quickly shining it around in the dark. The squad cars were untouched. He touched the hood of the one closest to him. Cool. He turned to the van, circling it, the flashlight trained steadily ahead of him.

He found a nightstick, dropped in the grass as if flung from a short distance. There was blood on the end of it.

He looked further, the small circle of light skirting bushes, grass and tree stumps. He saw the bodies of the two backup officers, lying splayed on the ground.

John felt a rushing in his head, his heart pounding in his chest and temples. Lewis had only pretended to cooperate.

He had been going along with them, just waiting for the right opportunity. Once he found his chance... The scene was one of destruction comparable to the one wreaked at the airport.

He flashed the yellow light around and found the bodies of Halloway and Griffin. Griffin's eyes were open and staring, his tongue distended from his puffed and bluish face. Death by strangulation. John put two fingers to Halloway's neck, then to Halloway's lips. Pulse. Respiration. The man was still alive.

He reached down for Halloway's walkie-talkie, fiddling with the controls until he heard a squawk of static. He had to tell Rogers what had happened. He depressed the button on the side and spoke.

"Hello. Hello. Can anyone hear me? This is John Stratton calling Captain Carl Rogers of the Jicarita Police Department."

He let up on the button and listened. There was a confused jumble of voices as they all tried to sort out what they had just heard. Rogers finally broke through. "Yes, John, this is Carl. Where are you calling from?"

"I'm calling from the van, parked where you left it. Griffin, Halloway and the two other men are down. The prisoner has escaped."

"Escaped?" Rogers yelled in alarm. "How?"

"I think he took my car."

"Your—stay right there, John. Don't move. I'm coming out immediately."

"All right," John said, and turned up the walkie-talkie, listening to Rogers's voice as he barked orders out to the dispatcher, running as he talked.

A single thought came to him, one that frightened him more than anything he had seen so far. If Lewis had taken his car, then he would know where he lived, and then he would be able to find...

Annette.

LEWIS REVVED THE CAMARO up to sixty miles an hour, the walkie-talkie on the seat next to him turned up loud so he could monitor police band transmissions. Stratton had found his car missing and radioed Captain Rogers. It would take them a few minutes to sort out what had happened, but Stratton would soon be relaying his vehicle's description and license number, and he had better be off the road by then.

He took the curves and runs as quickly as he could, increasing his speed from sixty to eighty miles an hour, edging the speedometer to an even hundred miles per hour. One thing he couldn't fault the doctor for was his taste in cars. The Camaro held the road as if it was riding on a rail.

He saw the street sign for Arrowhead Drive go whipping by, and pulled a screeching U-turn, shooting up the side road, slowing only to read street addresses. He found the mailbox that read 1374, next to a driveway that wound up and out of sight.

He eased up the private road, not wanting to arouse suspicion. As soon as Stratton gave them the information, this would be the first place that the police would look. If there were private security patrols in the area, he would have to deal with them as well. What he wanted to know first was if there was anyone inside the house or not.

He saw lights were on inside. Was someone moving in there? The drapes were closed. As he sat and idled, a hand parted one of the drapes and an eye peeked out, framed by a wisp of red hair. The hand gave a little wave, and then vanished.

It had been a woman's hand.

She was in there. She had looked out and seen the idling Camaro and thought it was her friend, the doctor, come home from the fray.

He had to get inside now. The garage door was closed. If he opened the car door and stepped out, she would be able to see him. She could lock doors, get a gun, call the police. She might have company already. Things could get out of control. He needed the advantage of surprise, even by a few seconds.

There had to be some other way, some means for him to slip inside before she knew it.

He saw her peek again, but this time she did not wave. If he sat there much longer she would get suspicious. If she glimpsed his face...

Even though she probably could not see clearly against the glare of the headlights, he pulled the visor down to shade his features and in doing so his hand found something square and plastic, clipped to the visor. He worked it off and turned it over in his hand, examining it in the green glow of the dashboard.

It was a remote control.

WHAT JOHN DID NEXT he did without thinking.

He reached down into Halloway's pockets, feeling among the loose change and the folds of the uniform trousers for something metal and plastic. He found it.

He pulled the squad car keys from Halloway's pocket and stood, the walkie-talkie still in one hand.

"John?" Rogers's voice rasped, followed by a burst of static. "John, this is Carl. I'll be rendezvousing with you in just a few minutes, so hang tight."

John didn't have a few minutes. He ran around the side of the van and toward the first squad car.

"John?"

There were two keys on the plastic tab, one with a square head, one with a round head. He tried the square key in the front door lock. It didn't work. Neither did the square one. Damn.

"John, can you hear me?" There was a rising tone of panic in Rogers's voice.

John brought the walkie-talkie up to his mouth as he ran to the next squad car. "I can hear you."

"Good. I said I should be there in a few minutes."

The keys didn't work in the second squad car, either. He had to hurry or Rogers would catch up with him and there would be questions and orders and talk and delays and Annette would be killed because he hadn't tried hard enough to save her.

"I can't wait that long, Carl."

"Stay right there."

"I've got Halloway's car keys. I'm going to go after him."

Rogers's voice was tight with anger. "John, don't you dare move. You lay one hand on one police car and I'll have you—"

John turned the volume down. The noise was distracting him. He ran to the third and last squad car, parked behind where his Camaro used to be.

The square key didn't fit in the passenger door. The round one did.

He jerked the door open and slid behind the wheel.

He had never driven a police squad car in his life, but he had ridden in a few. He fit the square key into the ignition and turned it. The engine caught and started. He revved the accelerator, turned the headlights on and threw the car into gear.

He turned the wheel all the way to the left and managed to make a U-turn, bushes and long grass scraping against the car's bumper.

He turned the walkie-talkie back up. Rogers was still violently threatening him. He pressed down the transmitting button and spoke. "Carl, it's John. I'm heading for my house. I need you and your men to either meet me there or stay the hell out of my way."

"John, goddammit—"

"I mean it, Carl. I think Annette is in real trouble. The first thing Lewis will do is try to find her."

"I refuse to cooperate with—"

"Then just don't try to stop me," John said, and turned the volume back down again.

He sped down Evergreen, slowing for the stop sign past the intersection with Miramar, then winding down Miramar at twice the speed he would normally consider, both hands on the wheel, the tires squealing over pavement, rumbling when they met dirt and gravel.

He slowed again before turning onto the main road, heading west and south in the direction of his house.

The car radio had come on automatically when he turned on the car's engine. He could hear the voice of the dispatcher, talking to the various units on patrol. Below the scanner was a twelve-button numbered keypad, like the ones found on touch-tone phones. He picked up the microphone and keyed it. "Hello?" he said. "Hello?"

The dispatcher's voice came on. "Please clear this channel."

"No. I can't clear this channel. Operator, I need to make a phone call."

"This is not the operator."

"Well, dispatcher or whoever the hell you are, I'm in a squad car and I need to make a phone call to save somebody's life and I need you to help me. This is official police business. You don't believe me, ask Captain Carl Rogers. You know who he is?"

"Please identify yourself and your location."

"I'm John Stratton and I'm heading south on Jicarita Boulevard, and cut the bullshit and let's just do it, okay? Somebody is going to die if you don't help me." He had not lost his composure. Not yet.

A car pulled out from a restaurant and edged in front of him, oblivious to his presence. John dropped the microphone, hit the horn and whipped around him, narrowly missing another car coming in the opposite direction.

He picked up the microphone again. "I'm sorry, I lost contact."

"What is the number you wish to call?"

"Does it matter?"

"If you tell me, I can dial it for you and patch you through."

"Oh good. Thank you. It's my home number—555-6275."

He was not even halfway there yet. If Kelly Sullivan or Frank B. Lewis or whoever the hell this son of a bitch was, had beat him home he would stand almost no chance of saving her.

He heard a dial tone, then a number being dialed. The phone began to ring on the other line.

Please pick it up, Annette, he thought. Please still be there.

ANNETTE HEARD the phone ring as she was about to unlock the door in the kitchen that led to the garage. She had heard the Camaro pull up in the driveway, and become so excited in her relief that she had peeked out the window and waved at John. He must have had some kind of trouble with the garage door opener, as he just sat there in the driveway for a few moments, not moving. She had peeked out again, wondering if she should come out and see if anything was wrong, but then just as she was heading for the front door she heard the motor that raised and lowered the door—like the cave opening in that old Popeye cartoon about the caves of Ali Baba, she thought. The Camaro edged inside and the motor ran higher as the car was put into park. She went to the door, ready to open it and welcome him home, but right then the phone started to ring.

She had been sitting in the house for hours with nothing to do, trying to read some of John's books—mostly paperback bestsellers, but no Joan Didion or Margaret Atwood—absently flicking through the channels on the television set, even building another fire, but nothing seemed to help. She half wished she had gone along for the ride, if for nothing else than to be with him.

She was glad he was home. She wanted to hear what he had to say. She wondered who would be calling? Maybe it was Captain Rogers, asking him to turn around and come back. If he had to go back to the police station, she would go with him. She felt a lot safer with him around than when she was here alone.

She picked up the phone. "Hello?"

There was a scratchy sound on the other end of the line, as if she was receiving a transatlantic call, or the person was calling from a cellular telephone.

"Annette?" The voice was not instantly familiar, but not totally foreign, either.

She heard the Camaro's engine race and shut off, the engine clicking in the cool of the garage.

"Yes?"

"Annette, it's John."

"John?"

The Camaro's door swung open and shut. Someone was getting out.

"John, I thought..."

"You thought what?"

"That...the car...you just pulled up..."

Footsteps on cement. Someone trying the doorknob, rattling it. Whoever they were, they didn't have a key.

"Annette, listen to me. You have to get out of there now. Lewis escaped. He stole my car. He could find out where I live. If someone's shown up in the Camaro it's not me."

Annette listened, feeling the world drop away.

"Annette, *get out of there now. Drop the phone and run.*"

"Where?"

"Out the back. Through the sliding glass doors. Down to the creek. Go!"

Suddenly she heard the sound of splintering wood. If John cut his own firewood, then he would have to keep an ax in the garage...

He was coming to get her.

She dropped the phone, edging away from it, realization sinking in.

The frame of the house shuddered with the force of the second blow against the door to the garage. Three. Four. Five. The wood was giving away. All he needed was a hole big enough to stick his hand through and unlock the door. He didn't have to take the time to knock the whole thing down.

She dropped the phone and ran to the sliding glass doors. She had pulled the curtains over them after sunset, and now she fumbled with the fabric, trying to find the break in the drapes where she could reach the latch on the doors and get outside. Maybe run down to the dry creekbed....

The chopping stopped.

She couldn't find it. She was getting tangled in the drapes.

He was going to get her.

She heard a scraping sound, like the sleeve of a garment working its way through an opening in the wood paneling of the garage door. She knew the hand would be feeling for something to twist.

Suddenly she found the parting. She threw the drapes back and fumbled at the latch. As soon as John had left she had made sure the sliding glass doors were closed and locked.

She heard the door from the garage to the kitchen opening behind her.

Goddamn latch, she thought, goddamn latch—will you—Open!

The door to the kitchen banged open against the kitchen wall.

Annette threw the glass door back with a mighty heave.

He was lumbering through the house, looking for her.

She ran out into the darkness, trying to escape.

He's not going to get me, she thought. Not without a fight.

As she reached the edge of the yard she could hear him, fumbling with the curtains, tearing them from their runners, hurling them aside as if they were nothing.

She stumbled at the edge of John's property, the place where the ground fell away into a steep incline that led down to the creek. If she could get to the creek, perhaps the dry creekbed would give her a course to follow, lead her to other houses.

He was roaring behind her, bellowing like a water buffalo on the charge.

After a few steps down into the ravine she realized that there was no way she was going to make it. She couldn't see and the steep slope would have proved difficult even in the full light of day. Her foot slipped and she slid, banging her knee against a tree trunk. She held it for a second, looking up to where she had just come from, to see an immense shadow fill her vision.

He had the ax in one hand, hefting it as if it were as light as a golf club. He saw her and he reached for his gun, which he cocked and aimed at her head.

She screamed and dived forward, making a mad tumble downward, hoping through some wild turn of luck she would be able to roll to safety, that he would be as lost in the dark as she had been.

She got about a dozen feet when her head cracked against a rotting stump, sparking red streaks behind her eyes and robbing her of strength. Dimly, she heard dry branches snap and crisp leaves crush as her pursuer lumbered down the hillside with far greater ease than she had been able to manage.

Awareness returned as she felt her head being lifted up by her hair, the gun muzzle pressed into the side of her neck, and heard the hideous voice that whispered, "I've got you now, little sister. We're going to be a family again."

CHAPTER TWELVE

As HE SWUNG the stolen squad car onto Arrowhead Drive, John found himself praying fervently for the first time since he was a child. Please God, let her be all right. Please.

He bounced over the rise and screeched into his private driveway, the headlights picking out his empty garage, the door raised at an odd angle.

He had listened to the sounds that came after Annette had dropped the phone, sounds that had filtered over the police radio. From their fragmented conversation it wasn't hard to guess what had happened. Lewis had arrived at John's home, using the Camaro as a moving disguise. She had tried to run, he had pursued her, and then there was silence. For a moment, John thought she might have escaped, but there were new sounds as the killer came back into the house, dragging someone who was screaming out words John could barely distinguish: *please ... no ... help ...*

Hearing that had almost driven John crazy. He had floored the accelerator, the converted Ford's transmission feeling sluggish in comparison to what he was used to driving.

Now he was here. Through the open overhead garage door, John could see that the door leading from the garage into the house was open, a gaping hole in the wood attesting to a recent hostile presence. The lights were still on inside. John shut off the engine of the squad car, pocketing the keys as he stepped out, taking the shotgun off the rack, carefully lifting off the safety and locking the door.

He entered the empty garage, still able to smell the residue of the Camaro's exhaust. The kitchen door had been chopped at, bludgeoned with some type of weapon. He looked in the corner of the garage next to the woodpile. His ax was missing. The hole was small, but big enough for a man to work his arm through.

John nudged the kitchen door slightly with his foot and watched it swing back inch by inch, slowly and silently. He lowered the shotgun through the doorway, and then quickly stepped through, looking before he pointed the gun—first into the kitchen, then toward the living room.

No one. The house was empty.

Dishes and knickknacks had been smashed on the floor. The pieces crunched beneath his feet as he stepped over tile and onto carpet.

The sliding glass doors were open, the warm night air wafting into the house. The drapes and the track mechanism that had held them up had been torn off the wall and lay in a heap on the floor. John flicked on the outside lights and stepped out through the open doors.

He could see indentations in the grass, small divots dug up in the dirt. He walked to the edge of his yard, looking into the ravine that led to the creek. There was something metallic down there, something that definitely did not belong.

He stepped over the edge and carefully made his way down the slope, as he slipped back the safety on the shotgun. He couldn't help but hope that Annette was still hiding out there somewhere and would come stumbling out of the dark and dirt, blood seeping from a minor getaway wound....

He looked for the object he had seen from above and found it, lying next to a tree trunk. He picked it up, turning it carefully in the dim light.

It was his ax, the one taken from his garage. John inspected the blade in the feeble light. No blood, just dry splinters.

The trail of broken branches and crushed leaves stopped there.

"Annette?" John called out into the darkness. "Annette, it's John."

There was no answer.

John hurried back up the hill. He knew there was no time to waste.

ANNETTE HUDDLED against the passenger door of the Camaro in sheer terror, wind from the open roof of the car whipping her hair about. Her face was pressed against the window. She balefully looked out at the scenery rushing by, thinking how she had been in this same car with a much different man only a few hours ago. At that time she had never thought that anything like this was going to happen. Not really. Not deep down in her darkest fears.

Her throbbing head and aching scalp were harsh reminders of what had transpired, not to mention the pressure of the revolver in her side and the hideous features of the man behind the wheel, glowing green in the dashboard light. The stitched wounds that crisscrossed his scalp gave him the look of a human monster, as if he had not been born but somehow made, like Frankenstein's creation. An artificial man.

He had dragged her back up the hill and she had begun screaming, scrambling to her feet, showing him that he didn't have to hurt her, that she would come along. But then the even harder truth had sunk in that he *wanted* to hurt her, wanted to cause her pain. It served some dark and demonic purpose for him—a preview of what he was going to do to her later.

And he had said she was his sister.

He had pulled her through the house and thrown her into the car, keeping his gun trained on her as he reached under the dashboard and fiddled with bare wires until the car started. They had driven off wildly, his carelessness at the wheel terrifying her. Perhaps they might both die, pinned under the weight of the car and consumed by flames, before anyone had a chance to find them.

She did not know the canyon well at all, and so had no idea where they were heading. She only knew that there were two chances for her to survive the night. One was that this man beside her would make some horrible mistake, giving her a wide-open opportunity to escape.

The only other possibility was that the police would figure out what had happened and by some miracle track down the two of them. But if they had allowed him to escape already...

Two chances: slim and none. There had to be another hope or he was going to kill her.

She did not pray, for she did not believe in miracles. But there was someone she had accumulated a great deal of faith in ever since she had first met him. He was a person of strength and honor as well as intuition, and if anyone was going to rescue her it was going to be him.

JOHN CHURNED the ignition of the squad car until the engine caught, maneuvered the automobile around in his driveway and headed back out toward Arrowhead Drive.

He had to think, and think fast. He had to remember whom he was trying to second-guess. He had to try to think like the man he was hoping to catch.

Lewis didn't have any digging tools. He had found the ax, but left it—wait. There were shovels and picks at the site, some carried back by the police officers he had subsequently killed. He could have taken a shovel, maybe a pick as well. But to dig a new grave would take hours. A helicopter or search party could find them and Annette by then. He didn't have the materials to build a box....

John slowed the car to a stop, the logical connection thudding in his head.

The grave the police had dug at Tres Rocas. Rogers and his men hadn't had time to fill it in. The earth was open and ready.

John took his foot off the brake and planted it on the accelerator. He picked up the radio microphone again, driving rapidly with one hand on the wheel. He took a right on the main road, toward the ocean and the old canyon road, picking up speed.

"Hello? Dispatcher? This is John Stratton again."

There was only silence, and then Rogers's voice came on, angry even through the radio transmission. "John! What the hell do you think you're doing? You've stolen police property! Tell me your location and pull over at once!"

"I haven't got time for that, Carl. I need you to shut up and listen. We have one chance to pull this off right, and I'm going to need your help."

LEWIS DROVE the Camaro down the old canyon road, watching for the rusty gate to appear out of the darkness. There it was, on the left, still open. Good. The police must have left it that way when they drove off in disgust at not finding a body at the top of the ridge. He would try not to be such a disappointment to them this time.

He turned the car off the road and headed through the gate, stopping just on the other side, putting the transmission in park.

"I want you to get out of the car with me," he said to Annette, pulling back the gun so she could see it.

When she didn't move immediately, he jabbed at her a few times with the revolver's muzzle, the gun sight scraping the flesh along her forearm until it drew blood.

He got out at the same time she did. "Stand over here," he said, motioning to a clump of bushes.

Her obvious panic subsided when she saw that he was not about to end her life—at least not at that point. He swung the gate closed, and then hauled a few branches in front of it, bracing them against rocks already buried in the dirt. Then he shot one of the rusting hinges. He tried to open the gate again. It wouldn't budge. He seemed satisfied.

"Get back in the car," he said.

She did as she was told. He was going to let her live a little while longer.

Lewis put the Camaro into gear and the car bounced and rocked over the narrow and winding road, the woman beside him—his kinswoman, his *sister*—giving suppressed yelps of fear as they skidded perilously close to the edge.

He had been up here many times before, had considered this a potential burial site, but dismissed it as too slow and hazardous a climb. His Acton patrol car had barely made it up in half an hour. He thought this car, however, might do considerably better.

They climbed higher and higher, his left arm steering tirelessly while his right arm pressed the police revolver into her side. He was deliberately driving recklessly, keeping her constantly off balance, breaking her will so she would prove to be no problem once they reached the top.

The road leveled and widened into the clearing that held the Tres Rocas cemetery. On his previous visits, he had parked before reaching the first grave and walked on, out of reverence for those resting there. This time he bored on through, flattening wooden markers and running over granite tombstones. The tires dug down into the dirt and grass, and if those below resented the intrusion, they made no sign of it.

ANNETTE GRIPPED the dashboard in front of her, barely able to believe what she was seeing. Wooden crosses and headstones sprouted out of the grass at odd angles before disappearing underneath the car's bumper and pounding angrily on its underbelly. She knew that they were in the lost graveyard, the one John had mentioned to her just before she told him to shut up. Why did she have to lose her temper right then? she wondered. That was the most precious information he could have given her, and now...

Just as suddenly they were out and skidding across open dirt, the headlights focusing on a speckled gray wall only yards away. She could tell that the car was going into a skid because she felt the gun muzzle leave her side. He dropped the police revolver in his lap and grabbed the wheel with both hands, braking too hard and angling the vehicle so that Annette's side of the car would hit the wall first.

There was a brief instant when she thought that there was a chance he would regain control of the car and somehow prevent them from slamming into the wall, but that hope was extinguished as soon as it was ignited. The Camaro careened roughly over the ground, and she screamed and hid her face in her hands.

The impact was jarring, wrenching her neck painfully and blurring her vision for several seconds. A few stones, jarred loose from above, bounced down the side of the wall and cracked against the windshield. The engine sputtered and died, but the headlights stayed on.

She looked over at Lewis and saw that he was worse off than she was. His head had snapped forward and hit the steering wheel; he was forcing himself to stay conscious, not bothering to look at her.

It occurred to Annette that this might be her chance to escape.

She looked at Lewis's lap. The gun was gone, knocked to the floor in the crash. She didn't dare try to make a grab for it.

She glanced out through her side window. Her door was jammed right up against the rocks. There was no way it would open.

Then she looked up. The T-tops of the Camaro were off. An escape hatch was ready and waiting.

She reached up with both her hands, finding the central strut and the top of the windshield, coiling her legs beneath her. Using all her strength she pulled herself up as she thrust down with her legs, bringing herself halfway up and out of the car.

She had to be quick now. He would almost immediately see what she was doing and try to stop her. His reprimand might cripple her so badly that she would never be able to try anything like this again.

She locked her arms and lifted her legs out and over the top of the car, like a gymnast on the parallel bars, her arms trembling with the strain.

I'm out, she thought wildly. I'm free.

She was easing her legs over the top of the windshield, about to let herself down onto the hood when a hand suddenly reached up out of the car and grabbed hers in a crushing grip.

She screamed, looking down through the open roof and into Lewis's hard and hateful eyes. He was fully recovered, the injury that had nearly knocked him out had only left a red smudge on his forehead.

She kicked her legs out in front of her and threw her body over the front of the car, her heels banging against the hood. She felt herself sliding down the windshield, Lewis's hold on her left hand and wrist not weakening. Her legs pistoned against the slick surface of the Camaro, her tennis shoes squeaked on the hood's red paint. Her face pressed against the windshield, mere inches from his, separated only by the thickness of the safety glass.

He was looking right at her, his thick ugly features set in a cruel and deadly expression. She could see that while he was holding on to her with one hand, he was reaching down to the floor of the car with the other, feeling around for something he had dropped there.

He was trying to find the gun.

She imagined it all in her mind, playing it out in a kind of mental fast-forward: he would find the gun, hold her in place, slowly bring the muzzle up to the windshield, pull the trigger. The bullet would explode through the glass and burrow through her skull at several hundred miles an hour, the lead slug tumbling end over end, emerging from the back of her head in a somewhat untidy fashion—

He couldn't reach it.

She could see it in his face. He could feel the gun but he couldn't pick it up. Not yet. To make the stretch he was going to have to weaken his grasp on her hand.

She could feel his grip slacken as he dipped down to the floor of the car. If she did not act now she was lost.

One of the rocks that had cracked against the windshield lay next to her on the hood. She had ignored it until now, but suddenly it assumed significant proportions.

She reached out with her free right hand and grasped it, working her fingers around it in a firm hold before bringing it up and over the top of the car and down on the hand that held hers so tightly.

He grunted with pain, losing his partial grip on the gun, and started to reach up with that hand to lend assistance to the other. His fingers slipped on hers, but still held fast.

She smashed the rock down again, this time with double the strength, and kept hitting and hitting until she struck her own flesh instead of his. She dropped the rock in surprise, and through the windshield she could see it strike him above his left ear before she rolled away, free at last, onto the hood of the car and away from her captor.

She came face-to-face with the rock levee, and immediately sprang to her feet. Where she stood on the car hood, the top of the wall rose to chest level. Over it, she could see open space beyond, and at the moment that was exactly what she needed.

She leaned out, digging her right shoe into a substantial hole in the wall while using her hands to steady herself, then sprang off with her left foot. She swung up and over the wall as if she was mounting a horse, although instead of easily straddling the top she went tumbling over the side, the sharp stone edges in the rocks leaving cuts and bruises on her face and hands. She hit the dirt with her feet and set off running. Already she could hear the driver's door of the Camaro being forced open. She didn't have much of a lead. She knew that she didn't have much of a chance, either.

But it was something.

JOHN WAS SPEEDING down the old Jicarita Canyon Boulevard, often having to drop the radio microphone in order to grab the wheel with both hands and physically pull the car around a tight curve. He ignored the posted warning signs that advised safe speeds. He was trying to tell Rogers to get the helicopter back up in the air and over the canyon again.

"John, there's a maintenance problem with the helicopter."

"What? What kind of problem?"

"Something with a fuel line..."

"Then tell the pilot to get another chopper in the air!"

"I'm afraid it's not that simple, John."

"It is to me! Either we send up a helicopter over the canyon or we risk losing Annette's life!"

"We're trying, John, but—"

"No buts, Carl. Get it up there or get another one. Put it on my American Express card if you have to."

He didn't hear Rogers's reply, because right then he realized the metal gate had just gone whipping by on the left. He leaned on the brakes and jerked the wheel as far to the left as it would go, tires screeching as the Ford turned around. He stopped and idled in front of the gate. It had been open when he and Rogers had driven away from there earlier. Now it was closed.

Someone had been back.

John got out of the car, the radio squawking for his attention, and tried to open the gate. It was stuck.

He leaned over and looked at the road beyond. Branches were stuck in the ground, jammed up against the gate to prevent it from opening. He crawled over the fence and cleared them away, then tried pulling the gate open from the other side. It wouldn't move.

"Come on, goddammit," he growled, studying the fence for any signs of damage. He saw fresh scoring along the rusted metal around one of the hinges, and in the light from the patrol car's headlights he could see that it had been shot at and was now frozen into place.

He slammed his hand in frustration against the fence post. He looked at the dirt road that wound up beyond the gate. He couldn't make it on foot, not in time. He had to get through there with the squad car. Now.

He hopped back over the fence and climbed inside the vehicle. What the hell, he thought as he slipped it into reverse. It isn't mine.

"John?" Carl's voice came crackling over the airwaves. "John, do you read me?"

He backed all the way across the road, keeping the headlights on the gate. He guessed that its weakest spot was right in the middle. If metal gates had weak spots.

He eased the transmission into drive and clamped his foot down on the brake. He revved the engine, feeling the wheels tug at the road, ready to go.

"John?"

As the engine whined into second gear, John took his foot off the brake and floored the accelerator. There was an ear-piercing squeal of tires and the car shot forward, the gate leaping up in front of the windshield.

John closed his eyes and held on to the steering wheel.

"*Joh—*"

With a shattering crash, the squad car plowed into the middle of the gate, ripping it off its hinges and flattening it into the dirt.

He was through.

SHE WAS RUNNING.

She had not dared to look back, to think, to do anything other than put one foot in front of the other as fast as she could. She knew she could not keep up this speed for very long. The gym ID card gathering dust in the back of her desk drawer at home was proof that some New Year's resolutions never got off the ground.

She wished she had that extra edge right now. She did not know how far behind her pursuer was, but she knew how big he was and what kind of physical condition he was in. Mathematics alone weighed heavily against her. She heard what happened out at the airport. He was six foot six to her even five-five.

There was a noise behind her, a flat crack, its echoes lost in the heavy wind. She saw a puff of dust rise from the ground about four feet away at three o'clock.

He's shooting at me, she thought.

This time she did look—but over her shoulder while she kept running, albeit at a reduced speed. She saw Lewis, straddling the rock wall, maybe sixty feet behind her. The recoil of the gun had caused him to lose his balance, and he bent to steady himself with his free hand. Below him, lying at the foot of the wall, was—was that a *shovel*? As she watched, he straightened and took aim again.

She whipped her eyes up front and redoubled her efforts. Got to move, got to bob and weave.

Another crack, another puff of dust, this one only two feet away and directly to the side.

She risked another look, and what she saw made her heart leap.

The recoil from the second shot had sent Lewis reeling backward, and as he leaned forward to overcompensate, arms pinwheeling, he toppled over the wall, falling clear of the rocks until he struck the ground, missing the shovel by mere inches.

Annette could not believe her good fortune. She stood a chance of making it over the top of this hill and—she hoped—into the countryside waiting on the other side. Once she was among trees and bushes again, her size could prove an advantage. If she could hide out long enough, she might be able to lose him.

Lewis lay still for a few seconds, then stirred and raised himself. His movements were stiff, mechanical, as if he were being operated by remote control. Even at a distance of almost seventy-five feet, Annette could see that some of the stitches in his scalp had popped, the cuts opening, and fresh blood trickled out where the old had been wiped away. One hand still held the gun. The other one was curling around the handle of the shovel.

He was coming after her.

She faced ahead once more. Her lungs were already aching. She could feel a cramp in her side beginning to form. Her feet hurt, and her thigh muscles felt sore. She was tiring.

She kept running anyway.

THE SQUAD CAR had not emerged unscathed from its encounter with the metal gate. It had lost its right headlight. The engine had a funny whine to it. And, unless John was greatly mistaken, the left rear tire was losing air at an alarming rate. He was finding it increasingly hard to steer. The radio was out completely; the antenna had been shorn off at the base. All he got was static.

He was on his own.

The car limped up the hillside, John taking the turns slowly and carefully. Steam began to wisp out from underneath the crumpled front of the hood, and John could smell leaking coolant. He glanced at the temperature gauge. The engine was getting hot.

The branches of the trees by the side of the road were bending and swaying in the face of a rising wind, one that had not been blowing as strong when he was at the bottom of the canyon.

He hoped that Rogers was doing something about getting that damn helicopter in the air. He didn't know if he was going to make it all the way to the top or not.

SHE SAW THE ROCKS rise up before her—obsidian obelisks in the dark. In the moonlight they looked as though they were not part of the landscape, but a separate entity, floating, detached. Each of the boulders was at least twelve feet high, and their shapes had been strangely formed, giving them an eerie presence.

She had been running, but she slowed as she drew close, passing through the shadows of the stones. They looked even more unreal against the background of a cloudless starry sky, as if they had been superimposed by some special-effects process—a matte painting.

When she looked down at the ground at the base of the three rocks she stopped.

A hole had been dug beneath the stones, a large open pit at least four feet deep, three feet wide and six feet long.

An open grave.

A chill worked down her spine and lodged in her stomach. This was why he had brought her here. This was the reason for the shovel.

Chips flew off the nearest boulder, only inches from her head, and struck her in the face.

She cried out and bent over, putting a hand to her cheek. When her fingers came away bloody she realized that he was shooting at her again. She hadn't heard the pistol crack in the roar of the wind.

That shot was close. He must be very near.

If she ran around the boulders she could use them as a shield against any further gunshots—maybe long enough to find some camouflage. She turned and sprinted.

This time she did hear the bullet.

She went down, unaware of what had knocked her to the dirt. She tried to get back up, and when her right leg refused to function she felt pain bloom inside her upper thigh. The slug had tumbled around in the muscle and tissue, lodging somewhere against the bone. She could feel it in there, burning its way from the inside out.

Oh God, I've been shot, I've been shot, she screamed inwardly.

She made a few more pathetic attempts to get to her feet, but stopped when she saw a long shadow fall over her. She looked up to see Lewis looming above her, gun in one hand, shovel in the other.

He had caught her.

"Get up," he said, his voice rough and loud over the wind.

"I...I can't..." she said, clutching her leg. She could feel blood seeping out through her jeans. Oh God, it hurt so bad.

He took a step back and calmly planted a kick in her side. "I said get *up*."

She screamed and fell over, her hands flying from her leg to her face, protecting her mouth and eyes. She rolled away from him, trying to avoid the next blow.

It came from another direction. He took a few steps around and drove the toe of his shoe into the muscles of her upper back. They spasmed painfully, making any movement agonizing. She tried to crawl away from him again.

He kicked her once more, this time in the small of the back, above the kidneys. Her hands flew out from under her and she landed facedown, her head hanging over the lip of the open grave, the rest of her body lying flat in the dirt.

This was where he wanted me to go, she thought. This was where he was...kicking me to.

This time he hit her with the flat of the shovel, swinging it the way a baseball player might hit one out of the lower edge of the strike zone and out of the park. She went over the edge, tumbling down the side of the ditch, rolling to rest at the bottom.

She wanted to call out to him, not to ask for mercy, but to make a final proud stand. I won't beg for my life, she wanted to say. I won't go out without a struggle, like the others.

But then she realized she didn't know how the others had gone out, and it didn't really matter now because her struggling time was over. Even if he hadn't made her beg he had made her crawl.

Above her, Lewis stuck the gun in his belt and hefted the shovel in both hands. He jammed the blade into the mound of dirt beside the grave, lifted a spadeful and began to gently scatter it over her.

Annette felt the dirt sprinkle over her body. She made a weak attempt to twist away from it, but her body wasn't responding. It seemed as though what was happening to her had taken on a different hue. She felt detached, uninvolved. And tired, oh so tired. She could feel blood bubbling out of her, warm and full of life, soaking into the cold earth she was lying on.

I'm passing out, she thought.

Another shovelful of dirt hit her. Then another. Another.

JOHN FELT THE ENGINE in the squad car hitch. He glanced at the temperature gauge. The needle was all the way to the right. He saw and heard steam gush out from underneath the hood as the radiator hose blew. His left rear tire was completely flat, and he had been driving on the rim for the past two minutes. The right front was leaking badly as well. It made for slow going.

"C'mon, c'mon..." he said through gritted teeth, working the accelerator to get just a little farther in the damaged car. He wasn't far from the cemetery—a quarter of a mile at the most.

The extra distance was not to be had. The engine overheated and seized, pistons locking. The power steering cut out and the wheel suddenly went stiff in his hands. John found himself heading straight for the side of the hill. One sputtering headlight showed the drop-off ten yards away.

He had to leap out of the car before it rolled off the road. He reached over to his door handle and tried to work it open, but the mechanism had been jammed when he crashed through the gate. The door wouldn't open. He slammed on the brakes, his arms rigid as he braced himself for the impact. If he went over the side in the car, it might roll twenty to thirty feet before stopping. It was only going twenty miles an hour, but still it would be one hell of a fall.

In one last desperate effort, he wrenched the wheel to the right, still braking. The car responded, but just barely.

He saw the edge of the road swerve up, nudging underneath his side window.

Here it comes, he thought, and steeled himself.

The left rear tire, the tread flapping, the rim scraping, lurched over the side and spun in the air. The car stopped, parallel to the road. Any second John expected it to go careering down the hill.

It didn't. The wheels crunched to a stop in the dirt and brush. The car had three wheels on land, one in the air, but it had stopped moving.

John sat and waited, not daring to breathe. He was safe, if only for the moment. If another car came from ahead or behind, he was done for. The curve was too sharp for anyone driving down the hill to see very far around it.

He had to get out of the car through the passenger door, so he eased his weight from behind the wheel and across the front seat. The shotgun was in the back. He didn't dare try to take it with him. The shift in his weight might send the car over the side before he got one foot on the ground.

He tried the passenger door: it opened easily, swinging outward with only a slight groan. He worked his legs out and set them on solid ground, breathing a sigh of relief.

He rose slowly, standing free of the car at last, his clothes flapping in the wind. He didn't close the open passenger door. With his weight gone from behind the wheel, the vehicle was precariously balanced. He didn't want to send it tumbling down below to explode and set the entire canyon on fire. One headlight and both taillights were still on, and John hoped they would serve to warn anyone who drove up from behind, or as a landmark in case Rogers got a helicopter up in the air.

He looked up the hill toward the top. He had estimated the remaining distance at a quarter of a mile, but that had been when he thought he was going to be able to drive the rest of the way. A quarter of a mile on foot up a hillside dirt road was a different matter, and that was just to the cemetery. Beyond that was the rock levee, and then the hundred yards or so to the three rocks.

He caught himself. He was concentrating on the negative, adding up all the minuses without counting the pluses. He could jinx himself that way.

He set his feet to the road. There was one thing in his favor. He knew that if push came to shove, he could at least outrun the bastard.

LEWIS STOPPED, patting the last of the dirt down hard—bringing the shovel up over his head and slamming it against the packed soil. He wanted this one to stay put.

He turned and put his face into the screaming wind. The wind had never been this powerful before. This was the way he'd thought it should be the night he buried Mary Sullivan. He had not known then that she was not the last one to be taken, but fate had fortunately intervened so he could learn of his oversight and be given the chance to correct it. He had fulfilled his mission at last.

He scanned the horizon, green hilltops in the distance, looking for something he knew must be near. He wondered where she would come from tonight.

He looked back down at the site of his most recent victory. His work was done here. Now it was the hour of the *bain seth*, and perhaps this one last time he was not meant to witness her unearthly doings. She would be a grand sight tonight, though, glorious at the end of her quest. The power she received from Annette would transform her, perhaps into what he had glimpsed that first time, the thing-she-had-been. It would be magnificent to behold, even from a distance.

He brought himself up sharply. It was still not too late for mortal men to arrive in cars or helicopters and try to interfere with things again, to try to make history the way they thought it should be as opposed to the way it was meant to be.

If they came from the sky, he would see them first. If they came up from below . . .

He would have to meet them, fend them off as best he could.

He turned and headed back to the car.

JOHN HAD MADE the run up to Tres Rocas cemetery in less than five minutes. He was breathing deeply, but was not entirely winded. He slowed to a trot as he saw the swath Lewis had cut through the abandoned graveyard: tombstones overturned, markers uprooted. John couldn't help but feel a lingering sense of desecration hanging in the air. What had he told Rogers? That the levee had been constructed to divert rainwater that could wash off the topsoil and send the plots and their occupants drifting down the hillside—a genuine flood of the dead.

He trod lightly over the hallowed ground, following in the ruts left by the Camaro's tires. He couldn't get across the cemetery soon enough for his taste. It made him uneasy to be here alone.

Suddenly his foot disappeared into the grass and he felt it sink through the earth, coming to rest against something solid. He bent and slowly pulled out his leg and foot. He had stepped on a patch of ground disturbed by Lewis's passing and had nearly fallen in up to his knee. He couldn't help but look down in the hole to see if he had planted his foot inside a casket, violating the remains of whatever rested there. A green and bloated face might suddenly dart into view, a bony hand clutching at John's pant leg, whispering through parched lips: *don't . . . wait . . .*

He saw nothing of the kind. Perhaps it was a trick of his eyes, but he thought he did see moonlight reflecting dully off aged black wood.

He ran the rest of the way out of the graveyard.

John kept running until he saw the ghostly outline of the rock dam. There was a dark black shadow in front of it, and only when he was nearly upon it did John see that it was his car.

Judging by the deep gouges the tires had left in the dirt, Lewis must have lost control of the Camaro and gone into a skid, slamming sideways into the rocks. He had left the car there; neither Lewis nor Annette were inside. It was banged up a bit but still in one piece.

He felt in his pocket for the keys, then ran to the back of the car and opened the trunk. The interior light didn't work. No matter. He could see well enough by moonlight.

He felt around down in the spare tire well for a bumper jack, a tire iron, anything that he could use as a weapon. His hand closed around the crowbar that doubled as the jack handle. He pulled it out and it shone in the dim light. He had never used it. He swung it once, its weight pulling on his shoulder. It would do.

He set the crowbar on the ground and lowered the trunk with both hands until it caught, unable to hear the click over the roaring of the wind. A rock bounced down off the levee and banged against the side of the car closest to it. John flinched.

Another rock followed. Then a third.

He looked up slowly, realizing in horror that such a disturbance could mean only one thing. He had been making enough noise to be heard on the other side of the wall, so that anyone climbing over it would have been sure that his presence was not detected until he had the element of surprise securely in his grasp.

Lewis was standing on top of the rock dam, one foot on each side. He had a gun in one hand, and a shovel caked with dirt in the other. As John looked up at him, another rock slid down and bounced off the Camaro, hitting John in the shins. He winced at the pain, not daring to move.

"Dr. Stratton," Lewis said, his voice carrying even over the noise of the wind. There was blood drying on his face and skull. "You're too late."

ANNETTE MANDELL WAS barely alive.

She was suspended somewhere between consciousness and delirium, the gunshot wound radiating pain to the other injured parts of her body, all of them linking together to make full awareness an impossibility. Her loss of blood had begun to affect her thinking processes, and she felt herself slipping out of this world and into another.

It seemed to her as though she were sinking deeper and deeper into the ground, as if the earth in which she lay was swallowing her up, forcing itself into her eyes and mouth and nostrils, making it difficult to see or speak or breathe.

She heard a sound rushing out of the darkness, a vibration that seemed to come from within her mind as well as without. It rose from a low howl to a fierce keening: the cry of a creature gone mad with grief.

Only members of the family can see it, her mother had told her. She said she had seen it herself, hovering in the rafters of her barn. Now her mother was gone, buried alive just the way she was now....

No, Annette thought back. I'm going to be rescued, I'm going to be safe.

In the blackness somewhere behind her eyes a form began to take shape, one that at first was nothing but a glowing spark of gray light. As it drew nearer, she saw details: pale skin wrinkled by more than a hundred years of age, eyes gone black and hollow as open pits and long hair tangled with the dirt and mud of ancient burial.

It can't be, Annette thought in the last rational corner of her mind. It can't be that.

But fear and darkness overtook her in her grave, and the *bain seth* came soaring out of the night sky to take her to a life beyond the one she knew.

JOHN WAS AWARE of the jack handle at his feet. If he could just reach down and snatch it up, duck behind the body of the car, perhaps he could dodge the first bullet, gain the advantage.

It was as if Lewis could read his thoughts. "Step back," he ordered. "Away from the car."

John did as he was told, effectively eliminating his chances of escape or survival. Lewis held the gun level as he leaped down from his perch on the rocks and landed squarely on the ground, his knees absorbing the impact of his massive frame. He walked toward John. John instinctively stepped backward again.

"Stay where you are," Lewis ordered.

John stood still as Lewis walked forward, stopping just out of John's reach.

"What have you done with Annette?" John asked.

"You'd like to know, would you?"

"Yes."

"You're not the least bit concerned about your own safety?"

John said nothing.

"You're going to die within the next sixty seconds, Dr. Stratton. If I were you, I'd be very concerned."

John swallowed.

Lewis pulled back the hammer on the police revolver. John was so close to the gun he heard it click. A gunshot from a .38. Straight to the head. He had examined how many of those?

"On your knees, Doctor," Lewis said.

"Why?"

"I said on your *knees*." Lewis swung the shovel with his other hand. The blade caught John on the outside of his left knee, and pain went shooting through the joint, causing John to fall to the ground.

"You thought I might forget our little meeting out at the airport. If it weren't for you I would have gone free. Now it's time for me to return the favor."

He swung the shovel again, catching John on the right shoulder, pitching him over on his side to get an ear full of dirt. Pink spots swirled in front of John's eyes.

"They put me in a jail. They chained me like a mad dog. I had to endure humiliation—you sitting so safely on the other side of the bars asking me questions."

He moved closer to John as his anger grew at those memories, until finally he vented it by kicking Stratton in the side. John doubled up in pain, gasping for breath. He was barely able to move. He wouldn't be able to hurt Lewis if the man dropped the shovel and the gun and held his hands up and surrendered.

"I buried her, Doctor. I beat her just the way I'm beating you, and then I put her in her grave."

The blade of the shovel came right down in front of John's nose to chink in the dirt. Then it drew back, the way a golfer started his swing just before smashing the little white dimpled ball two hundred yards down the fairway.

He's going to hit me right in the face with that thing, John thought. He looked up to see Lewis turning the handle in his hand to make sure that it was not the flat of the blade that would catch John in the head but the edge, shattering bones and teeth and permanently disfiguring his features. John was dealing with an expert, someone who was practiced in human suffering, someone who could keep him alive for minutes that would seem like hours, torturing him until he could no longer be revived with whatever instruments were handy, and then ending the sport with a bullet to the base of the skull.

John had to do something, but he couldn't move. His only choice was to try to talk his way out—get Lewis off balance, force him to hurry and make a mistake.

He drew in a breath, wincing at the pain. It hurt even to talk.

"I know who you really are," he rasped, not sure he could be heard over the wind.

The shovel blade stopped in midswing. He heard Lewis's voice, harsh, loud. "What? What did you say?"

"Your name isn't Frank B. Lewis," John said, forcing the words out. "It's Kelly...Larkin...Sullivan."

The shovel dropped in the dirt, just inches from John's head. Lewis bent down, rolling John over so they were face-to-face. "Who said that? Who told you?"

"Your...mother. Mary Larkin...Sullivan."

"She's dead. I buried her. Right where I showed you."

John shook his head. "You should have stuck around to watch when we dug her up." He looked up into Lewis's thick and ugly face. The stitched wounds that crisscrossed his head were beginning to sprout little red hairs through the crusted blood, like bristles on a pig. "She's still alive."

"You lie. You're lying to me." Lewis jammed the muzzle of the gun under John's chin, making his teeth click together.

"Then how else would I know?"

He could see it in Lewis's face. Hesitation. Fear. Uncertainty. How could this happen?

Then decision. Lewis stood up, the gun leaving a scratch mark on John's throat. "The only way to know for sure is to go and find out for myself."

"It is true. She is still—"

"So our time together has been tragically cut short. If Mary Sullivan is in police custody, then I must find them before they find me. You can be assured, Doctor, that both the mother and the daughter will be dead by tomorrow morning. You, however, won't have to wait that long."

He extended his gun arm, and John realized that his improvised plan had backfired; Lewis was going to kill him on the spot. He wanted to shout out, *No!*—to buy a few seconds and tell Lewis that he was lying, that Mary Sullivan was already dead. But before he could harness the wherewithal to speak he saw Lewis's trigger finger tighten and the hammer on the revolver snap forward.

The gun did not fire.

The hammer struck on an empty chamber.

In an instant, John knew what must have happened.

On his first trip to the police firing range when he was working for the county, the gun he had been issued had jammed and the officer who was John's instructor handed over the one he carried in his shoulder holster. John aimed the gun at the target, squeezing his eyes almost shut at the expected report, and pulled the trigger. Nothing happened. Smiling, the officer explained to John that most cops keep the first chamber empty, and told him why. That was why an officer always checked out a gun, checking to see if it was loaded, and how it was loaded.

All of this flashed through John's mind at once. Lewis had stolen the gun from one of the officers he had murdered, advancing the empty chamber forward either on purpose or by mistake, and then had forgotten all about it. It meant that not only was Lewis one bullet short, he was out of ammo, period. Surprise.

One chance.

John's bodily pains had subsided, allowing him enough mobility to reach out with his left hand while still looking Lewis right in the eyes, holding the other man's expression of total bewilderment.

He felt his open palm strike the wooden handle of the shovel where it joined the blade. Good. The long end was lighter and easier to maneuver. Balance was in his favor.

With one quick motion, he rose from the ground, using his right arm for support, while whipping the hard round end of the handle up at Lewis's hand and cracking it right across the knuckles.

Lewis flinched and dropped the gun.

John scooted back and sprang to his feet, ignoring the broken glass that had ground into his left knee just underneath the patella. He lashed out again, catching Lewis on the right side of the head, then instantly reversed his grip on the shovel and swung with all his might to connect squarely on Lewis's left elbow with the edge of the blade.

The same with the left knee, and then the right. Lewis tried to grab the shovel with his one good arm but John was too quick for him. John jabbed Lewis sharply in the solar plexus and heard the man voice his pain as he doubled over.

Then John stepped in, still holding on to the shovel with his left hand, and brought his bare right fist up and into Lewis's face. Once. Twice. The third time, Lewis staggered backward and fell down. He lay there, not moving.

John knew he only had the advantage of the moment. When—not if—Lewis recovered, he would kill John, not wasting any time with proclamations of revenge as he had before. And there was still Annette to look out for.

John bent and picked up the gun, hurling it out into the tall grass of the graveyard where it would be impossible to find. If Lewis had any more bullets he would just have to bite them.

With one last look at the unconscious Lewis, John hurled the shovel over the rock wall. He heard it clang to the ground on the other side, and then scrambled up after it.

He dropped to the ground, his injured knees and back making him almost cry out with pain. He shook it off, picking up the shovel and running up the hill.

He hoped, in spite of what Lewis had said, that he was not too late.

UNCONSCIOUSNESS LASTED only a minute.

Then he became aware that he was lying facedown in the dirt, his body racked with hurt. As conscious thought returned, he remembered what had happened with the doctor, how he had foolishly forgotten that he had only five bullets, not six, and had paid so severely for that mistake.

He was amazed that he was alive. If he had been Stratton, he would have brought the dull edge of the shovel down on the back of his enemy's neck until his head rolled free from his shoulders. He supposed doctors had a thing about taking human lives. Something in the Hippocratic oath.

He lay still, waiting for the pain in his face, knees and arms to settle into a dull throbbing. His elbow hurt so badly he thought it might be broken.

Why had it happened? He had given in to pride this one last time and played with the doctor the way a cat worried a captured mouse. It had cost him dearly. This mouse had struck back. If Stratton was still around...

Still not moving, he listened carefully, trying to distinguish sounds over the whipping wind. He slowly rolled over and saw only clear starry sky above. Stratton was gone.

Lewis lifted himself up on his one good elbow and looked around. Stratton was out of sight, and so was the shovel, presumably taken in an effort to save Annette, to see if what had been done could somehow be undone. Lewis doubted it. The woman had been half-dead when he threw dirt over her as it was. Even if Stratton managed to exhume her, he wouldn't be able to get her to any sort of medical facility in time. The only available means of transportation was the car.

Lewis sat up, grimacing at the flaring agony in his joints. He had a new rule: never, ever duke it out with an M.D. They knew all the right spots to hit you. He turned himself around, slowly, to see if he had an ace left, one escape hatch still open.

The Camaro was still sitting there, unmoved from when he had skidded out of control in the dark and slammed sideways into the rock wall.

His foot nudged something hard and steely in the dirt. He reached for it and held it up in the moonlight. A jack handle that doubled as a crowbar. A weapon. If he saw John Stratton again tonight, he would use it well.

He eased forward on his hands and knees, crawling toward the driver's side of the car. If he could just get inside, he could get it started. If he could get inside.

Stratton had said that Mary Sullivan was still alive, that the police had her, that she had told them that it was her son, Kelly, who had attempted to murder her. If they had that information, it would be doubly hard for him to hide, to return and strike again, to ever accomplish his mission once and for all.

His life was becoming undone.

There was, of course, the possibility that John Stratton had been lying, that he had just been trying to buy time. Lewis didn't know whether to discount the man's story or not. What he did know was that he was not in any shape to handle more confrontations tonight. He needed to get away, to hide while he recovered, perhaps disappear for a while down in Mexico, only to return one day when his enemies had given him up for dead.

Even if Mary Sullivan died on the way to the hospital, even if Annette was beyond hope, he would still return and exact his revenge on John Stratton, and it would be a retribution that would be whispered of even in the corners of hell.

He had reached the car, swinging the driver's door open with his good right hand, pulling himself to his feet, falling over into the seat, having to lift one leg inside, and then the other—God, he wasn't sure he could walk if he had to—reaching down underneath the dashboard for the two colored wires, and then touching them together and hearing the engine rumble to life.

He closed the door, but it caught only partway. It was the best he could do. He was getting some movement back in his left arm, but not enough to steer. With his right hand he set the automatic transmission into reverse. He eased his right foot off the brake pedal. When he had enough room, he switched to low gear and steered his way out, through the graveyard, riding the brake, not daring to touch the gas pedal yet.

He might, just might, live through this night and see the new day as a free man.

JOHN SAW THE THREE ROCKS rising up into the night sky.

In the moonlight they managed to look even more ominous than they had in the middle of the day. This was the place where Lewis had sent them digging earlier, and John prayed he was guessing right on this one.

He slowed to a walk, breathing hard, his body aching all over. Before he reached the rocks he saw loose dirt scattered about in the wind, hissing off into the brush. He walked carefully; he didn't want to step on...

He saw a dark patch just to the side of the rocks, one where the ground had been stained with something. He walked over and bent down, studying it up close. He rubbed a finger into it and it came up dark, almost black in the moonlight. Blood.

He rose and saw a mark on the rock where another bullet had struck. Lewis hadn't just buried her, he had shot her, maybe more than once.

Dr. Stratton. You're too late.

John began to understand that Annette might already be dead, and all that he would find was her body, still warm and soft.

He stood at the gap between the three elongated boulders, staring down at earth recently filled in, but packed down with the shovel he was holding in his right hand. She was in there somewhere.

He raised the shovel, then dropped it to the side. He couldn't use it for fear of injuring her; he had no idea how deeply she was buried. But if he ran into Frank B. Lewis again tonight, he would need something to defend himself with.

He had only one choice.

He sank to his knees, ignoring the messages of pain the joints frantically sent to his nervous system. Leaning forward, he formed his two hands into a scoop.

He began to dig.

FRANK B. LEWIS WAS HEADING downhill. He held the steering wheel of the Camaro in one hand, his right foot alternating between the brake and the accelerator. He had to slow to negotiate many of the turns in the dirt road, and he was afraid that this was retarding his progress considerably. If he reached the old road safely, then speed would be of the greatest importance. He would need to rely on everything the Camaro still had in order to make it out to the Pacific Coast Highway. Then he planned to cut over to Topanga Canyon Boulevard and speed through to the valley, where he would be presented with a range of choices: north to either Highway 101 and the coast or Interstate 5 to the central valley, or east to the desert. South would probably be best. Tijuana. Mexico. Baja California.

If he was going to get to those options, he had to go faster.

The pain in his left arm had eased to a pulsating ache. He was fairly certain that the elbow was not broken, but severely bruised. He slowly flexed it, working the elbow, wrist, hand and fingers. He seemed to have mobility within a limited range: an arc of forty degrees or so. He started steering with both hands.

He took his foot off the brake and let it hover over it as he picked up speed, taking the corners at ten, fifteen and twenty miles per hour. The wind whipped in and out of the open top, but carried no sounds of sirens from emergency vehicles approaching from below. There were no residents in the area. As far as he could tell, he had the road to himself.

The impact against the rock dam had done little damage, if any, to the car. It was still operating at full capacity. Lewis glanced at the fuel indicator. He had half a tank of gas left. Plenty. Radiator holding steady. Oil pressure and battery—

He looked up instinctively, suddenly aware that his eyes had been off the road for too long, just in time to see the next curve rushing up to meet him. Straight ahead the road dropped off into darkness.

He grabbed the wheel and jerked it, wincing at the pain in his left elbow, trying to brake just hard enough so the car didn't start fishtailing in the dirt. He heard the tires scraping over dirt and gravel. Just as he felt that the car was going to make it he saw a lone headlight glaring directly in front of him, not ten feet away. It had been hidden by the sharp bend of the road.

This time he exerted all the pressure he could into braking, keeping the car in a sharp left turn, gripping the steering wheel hard. There was no way he was going to avoid a collision.

In the second and a half that he had before he hit the other vehicle, he was able to see the still and shrouded overhead lights and the blue-and-white body paint that marked a Jicarita Police Department patrol car. It was balanced precariously on the edge of the road. Just prior to impact, he could see that there was no one at the wheel or in the passenger seat: a ghost vehicle, sent to bring him to his doom.

The cars hit, the twisted steel bumper of the patrol car immediately hooking underneath the front end of the Camaro. As the police unit slipped over the edge and down the hillside it took the sports car with it, its driver frantically trying to think of something to do to avoid what by now looked like an almost certain death.

Lewis watched in shock as the road vanished underneath him and—by the view afforded through the open roof—the trees and sky skewed crazily out of control, above him, below him and above him again, reappearing on a different side.

His weightless flight lasted only a moment as the police vehicle hit a treetop and held, the Camaro ripping free of it and flying sideways through the air to strike solid ground. Lewis saw a sudden burst of orange light and he thought for a moment that the police car had exploded into flame. The Camaro kept rolling downhill, slamming him up and down, back and forth, first breaking bones, then shattering them, finally grinding the various pieces together into an osseous meal, blood spurting out of a dozen compound fractures, raining over him as he felt himself die. There was a sudden flare of heat and light, and with the last of his energy he raised his head to see it better. It took him seconds to understand that his car had stopped moving. It had landed upright, but he was in no shape to crawl out or even open the door. He was conscious, however, and he could still see and feel and hear as the flames came lapping up over the sides and front and rear of the car. He would be very much alive as the fire slowly burned him to death.

It was Kelly Larkin Sullivan's welcome to hell, a preview of the justice eternity would exact from him. And, he thought, perhaps exactly what he deserved.

JOHN HAD BEEN DIGGING for several minutes when he first smelled smoke.

He stopped what he was doing and sniffed the air. Only once, it was that strong.

He did not know what had happened. Maybe the police car he had left at the side of the road had tilted over. Maybe Lewis had deliberately started the blaze.

He didn't have time to ponder. Any fire he could smell from such a distance must be out of control already, and in this wind would travel well over the speed limit.

If the Camaro was still operational . . .

He couldn't even think about leaving until he found Annette.

He renewed his efforts, leaning forward to scoop out yet another double handful of soil, hoping that he would soon see something in the dirt: a hand or a piece of clothing or—

Her hair.

John's heart raced as he carefully worked the dirt away from around her face, exposing it to the shadowed moonlight. Oh God, he thought. Please still be alive. Please, God, let her still be breathing.

He dug down to her neck and laid two fingers next to her carotid, turning his head sideways, listening through his digits.

There was a pulse. It was weak and irregular, but it was there.

He dug away with his hands, attacking the ground furiously. Annette was most likely in a severe state of shock, brought on by the gunshot wounds and accompanying blood loss. Even if he got her to a well-stocked emergency room she would have only a fifty-fifty chance of making it.

He dug her out in sections: first her torso, then her arms, and finally her legs and feet, stopping to unbutton his shirt and tie it around her right thigh in a meager attempt to stanch the bleeding from the bullet wound. Every few minutes he stopped to check her pulse again. The last time it took him a few tries to find it. She was fading fast.

He bent down beside her and worked his arms underneath her, straightening slowly, grunting with the effort, knowing that in his own battered condition he could not carry her ten yards without resting, much less back over the rock dam. Once he got her inside his car, it would be another ten minutes down.

He again thought of the patrol car he had abandoned. There would be no way around it. What would he do then?

Hell, he thought grimly, you'll be lucky to even get that far.

He turned, careful not to hit Annette's head on the sides of any of the rocks, and stepped out into the open, the wind beating at him hatefully.

He took two steps and stopped.

The horizon was glowing orange, as if the sun was threatening to rise over it. Except, John reasoned, he was looking west toward the ocean and the sun didn't rise in the west.

What was creeping toward him just out of sight was not the sun.

Fire.

It had spread even more rapidly than he had figured, burning its way up the hillside the same way he had come. Most likely it had already consumed the pioneer cemetery: markers burning, coffins crisping. Ancient and unused bones warmed one last time.

As he watched, the glow became flames, spreading not only upward but around as well, skirting the dirt hilltop on which he stood, soon to surround him in a ring of fire. He had no illusions of safety; the force of the upward draft from the blaze would vacuum all air out of the immediate vicinity and he would slowly suffocate, crumpling to the ground with Annette in his arms.

There might still be a way out. He turned and walked around the towering boulders, hoping to cross over into the brush before it caught fire, the wind at his back. Forging his way through wild terrain with Annette in his arms and a fire blowing his way at a good thirty knots...he would be lucky to get fifty feet before it surrounded him.

I'm lost, he thought, walking forward, making an effort for no other reason than to stave off hopelessness and defeat for a few more minutes. Annette was already heavy in his arms. He would have to put her down in a moment, just to rest his back.

He staggered forward, sustained only by the sheer force of his will, unwilling as yet to admit that there were no miracles, there was no justice, the Lone Ranger was dead, and his life had been nothing but a pointless exercise in random biology and purposeless fate.

He stopped, ashes swirling around him, some lighting in his hair or wafting across the skin of his bare back. He sank to his knees, clumsily letting Annette's feet strike the ground. He rose again, trying to balance her weight between his two arms.

This time he got only five feet, stumbling and losing his balance. He wanted to rest for only a minute, but as he pitched forward, dropping Annette onto the dirt, his face pillowing into her chest, he knew it was over. They would burn where they lay. He felt a final scream of rage build in his throat, a last attempt to not go gently to his death.

He lifted his head, feeling the wind double, then triple its force.

And suddenly everything around him was light. Blinding light.

ANNETTE THOUGHT she was already dead.

She felt herself being lifted up, out of her grave, borne

aloft by an unseen but turbulent force. She went up, then down, floating around in the cosmic ether between life and what lay after.

Now she was definitely heading up again.

She sensed a great and luminous presence, one that she would not have dared to look at directly even if she could. It filtered through her eyelids and pressed upon her pupils. She wondered what was next—visitations from relatives who were long since deceased? Mom? Dad? Mary Sullivan?

Perhaps she would see a slightly different version of herself, and she and her twin sister, Gretchen, would be reunited at last. It would be an interesting meeting.

Now she was lying still, in the bosom of heaven. She felt a faint pressure on her leg: God's healing touch. A pinprick on her arm. Warmth seeping in.

She breathed in, and the air was sweeter here than it had ever been on earth, coming quick and easy through her nose and mouth. Her strength returned in milligrams.

She heard a joyful noise in her ears, a thunder that could only belong to the righteous, and she assumed that this was the sound of the curtain that separated the here from the hereafter being rolled back to accept another resident. Wind rushed about her and the blinding light dimmed.

She could open her eyes now and see where she was.

It required all her strength, but her lids fluttered then rose slowly, like a curtain over a stage, but instead of angels and heavenly hosts she saw a human face hovering next to hers, worry written all over it.

She recognized the face. It was John Stratton. Had he perished, too?

His lips moved but she couldn't hear him over the noise. He must have seen it in her eyes as he bent down closely and put his mouth next to her ear to shout, "You're going to be all right," and pull back, nodding and smiling. His shirt, unbuttoned to the waist, was wrinkled and bloody, but he didn't seem to be injured.

Then she saw the bag of blood dangling from a hook in the cabin of the helicopter, the IV tube running into her arm, and understood that the noise she was hearing was the sound of the aircraft's whirling rotors. The chopper bucked and dipped in the strong wind, and she heard someone shout something about getting ready to land.

John heard and nodded, leaning over to stroke the hair from her forehead, careful not to dislodge the oxygen mask strapped to her face.

She was not in heaven at all. She was on her way home. There was a great deal of comfort in the notion. She had not lost this particular roll of the dice after all.

She closed her eyes again and slept, as all living things must do.

A chilling novel of mystery, suspense, reincarnation and a love so powerful it survives time...and even murder.

FOREVER LOVE

Margaret Chittenden

An author makes a startling discovery during a tour to promote her latest novel when she realizes that the same book was actually written by a woman who was murdered years ago.